'A compulsive, delightfully absorbing and thoroughly entertaining read. Highly recommended'

★ ★ ★ ★ ★

'Engaging from start to finish . . .
A perfect balance of suspense and sheer dry
wit, this is simply complete perfection'

★ ★ ★ ★ ★

'Absolutely adored this very clever and engrossing read,
with three usually overlooked and marginalised characters'

★ ★ ★ ★ ★

'This book is beyond excellent. It is one of the
best books I have read this year . . . I will be
thinking about this book for a long time to come
and recommending it to everyone I know'

★ ★ ★ ★ ★

'An absolutely wonderful read which I devoured in a couple
of days. It was darkly humorous with a cast of amazing
characters whom I'd really love to meet in real life'

★ ★ ★ ★ ★

'The story is compelling, brave, funny and definitely
contains all the elements of a good thriller!'

★ ★ ★ ★ ★

Rosalind Stopps lives in Margate and south-east London with various humans and dogs. Her short stories have been published in five anthologies and read at live literature events in London, Leeds, Hong Kong and New York.

Her debut novel, *The Stranger She Knew*, was shortlisted for the Paul Torday Memorial Prize 2020. *A Beginner's Guide to Murder* is her second novel.

Also by Rosalind Stopps

The Stranger She Knew

A BEGINNER'S GUIDE TO MURDER

ROSALIND STOPPS

ONE PLACE. MANY STORIES

HQ
An imprint of HarperCollins*Publishers* Ltd
1 London Bridge Street
London SE1 9GF

www.harpercollins.co.uk

HarperCollins*Publishers*
1st Floor, Watermarque Building, Ringsend Road
Dublin 4, Ireland

This edition 2021

1
First published in Great Britain by
HQ, an imprint of HarperCollins*Publishers* Ltd 2021

ISBN: 978-0-00-830265-8

MIX
Paper from
responsible sources
FSC™ C007454

This book is produced from independently certified FSC™ paper
to ensure responsible forest management.

For more information visit: www.harpercollins.co.uk/green

This book is set in 10.7/15.5 pt. Sabon by Type-it AS, Norway

Printed and bound in the UK using 100% Renewable Electricity at
CPI Group (UK) Ltd, Croydon, CR0 4YY

For my beloved Dom

CHAPTER ONE

Meg

Wednesday, 27 February

We had known him for two days when we decided to kill him.
I say we, because I was there too, I was part of it, but I didn't
believe it. Not then. I didn't think it would happen, but I couldn't
think of a better idea. I didn't truly believe we would do it. I was
so scared. So terrified. I didn't feel safe and worse, I knew she
wasn't safe. That poor girl. I had to do something to help her, so
I went along with it. I was still shaking, and I don't think I knew
which way was up. In some ways it didn't seem real, although
I wanted something terrible to happen to him, that's for sure.

We knew what he was like. Two days was long enough
to know that. Two minutes would have been long enough if
we had trusted our instincts, but we weren't a group at the
beginning. No hive mind. No consensus. No we. Just a bunch
of tired old women in a coffee shop after trying to do Pilates
so that we could stay alive a little longer. Trying to cheat death,
that's how Grace put it. There's such a clarity when Grace
speaks. What *she* says, I often want to say; I think the same as
her. She puts things much better than I do.

Grace was the first one to pull herself together and say it out loud. She was probably the first one even to think it, I'm not sure about that but I wouldn't be surprised. I was still fussing with my face, and reliving that damn door lock, flexing my fingers as if I could manage to lock the memory, at least. I kept thinking about Nina's face as she was pulled out of the car, and I wondered how on earth we were going to kidnap her back, get her away from him.

I've always been slow, Henry used to tell me that. You're too slow to cross the road, Meg, he'd say. If I wasn't with you to hurry you along you'd still be dithering when the green man goes to have his tea. It was supposed to be funny, I think, only I was never sure how much of it was true. I am a ditherer, that much is certain. I think I would have been stronger if I'd had someone to look after. It would have made me a better person, I'm sure it would. I used to say that back in the days when it might have made a difference. 'Honestly, Henry,' I said, 'I'm as capable as the next person.'

'Nonsense,' he said. 'What would you do with a baby? You'd probably lose it down the plughole or forget to bring it home from the shops.'

I wouldn't, I was sure of that but after a while it's easy to believe a person, and that's why I understand what happened to Nina.

We were at the end of our tether when Grace made her suggestion. I could see that Daphne wanted to cry and I knew that if she started I would too. I've always been like that with tears. I think I've got quite a lot of crying waiting inside me and most of the time I manage to keep it there but if I see someone else being sad I'm undone, just like that, I literally can't stop it.

Pull yourself together, Henry used to say, and I always wanted to say, I can't, there's bits of me everywhere and they won't come together at all.

So I was patting my sore face with a wet tissue and trying not to cry. I wanted to think in a straight line about what we could do and that's when Grace said it.

'What about we hire a hitman,' she said, 'or a hitwoman if that's a thing. Has anyone got any money?'

I wasn't sure if she was making a joke. I mean, I didn't really think she would make a quip at a time like that but you get used to things being a certain way and even when they're not and the evidence is there in front of you saying, excuse me, everything you believed about the world is nonsense, even then you think, really? Really? Are you sure?

'I've got some money,' Daphne said.

She blushed when she said it as if it was something to be ashamed of and maybe it was, but I wasn't going to leave her to say it on her own.

'I've got some too,' I said. 'How much does it cost?'

I felt as though I was in a play.

We looked at each other in a baffled way and I wondered for a moment about the internet. The only thing was, anything on the internet can be traced back and presumably we didn't want to be found out. That was almost the first time I thought like a criminal and I was quite proud. It wasn't the last.

'We can't do any research in case it's traced back to us,' I said, happy to have something helpful to contribute. They both looked at me as if I was surprisingly stupid and for a moment Henry was still alive and nodding along with them.

'I guess we'd better be careful about all that sort of stuff,' Grace said. I think she was being kind.

'Apparently it was about $30,000 in 1983,' Daphne said.

I was wondering how on earth she would know that when Grace said, 'Way to go, girl, aren't you clever?'

'I think that's equivalent to about $75,000 today,' Daphne said, 'or 56,500 in pounds sterling.'

There was a little pause and then she added, 'I used to work in finance,' as if that explained everything.

Grace and I stayed quiet. It was clear Daphne had something more to say.

'The thing is,' she said, 'it's a supply and demand thing. The price won't necessarily have gone up in line with inflation, not unless demand has gone up too. It's difficult to guess that.'

'With anything else I guess we'd start low,' Grace said, 'but this is a job that needs to be done. How much can we afford?'

Fifty-six thousand pounds, I was thinking, that seems like an awful lot. I knew about money. I had always been in charge of household expenses. Sometimes you have to spend money, nothing else for it.

'I guess there's nothing else,' I said.

I was frightened, terrified even. I have always hated violence. I did not want the police involved for lots of reasons but I wondered if we ought to consider it one more time.

'Maybe we could tell the police,' I said, 'or make a citizen's arrest or...'

I couldn't think of anything else and my words sounded very old ladyish as soon as I had said them.

'It's just that... violence,' I said, 'I hate violence.'

Daphne spoke up then. Her and Grace, they always know what to do.

'They'll blame her, and he will get off and do it to some other girl while she goes to prison for it,' she said, 'and that's the best case scenario. He'll run, take her with him and hurt her, that's the worst.'

'We need to do this ourselves,' said Grace.

I wasn't sure – but I'm used to that. I haven't been sure about anything for a long time. I decided to concentrate on the practical side, think things through and note everything as if I was in a meeting at work. I'm not sure what kind of work would have meetings like this, but it helped, nonetheless.

'It doesn't matter how much it costs, then,' I said. 'Well, it does, of course it does to a certain extent but what else can we do? He's nasty, that man. Nasty and rough. What are the alternatives? Things become beyond price if they are life changing.'

I think my voice broke on the last few words. It's embarrassing when that happens, but I was thinking of how different my life could have been if I'd acted earlier, I guess. The things I could have done, if I'd been sure of myself.

'I can chip in twenty grand,' I said, trying to get things back on a businesslike footing. I trusted them, and I didn't want them to think I wasn't joining in. Plus Henry had been well insured.

'That's fine,' Daphne said. 'I've got the rest, no problem. What about if we start at forty-five, see if we get any takers there?'

And just like that, it was decided.

I listened hard.

What you need to listen for, my mum used to say, is a note

out of tune, a beat out of rhythm. We're funny animals, us humans, and we like to leave clues when things aren't going well.

I didn't understand that when I was a child but I do now. She was a musician, my mother, and she described everything in musical terms. Voice like a bell ringing in the mountains, she said about a new teacher, you'll love her. The strange thing was, she was usually right. My mother played the violin, and during the war she used to play in the Underground, entertaining the people who were sheltering from the bombs. If my violin hit a bad note, she said, we would know to get out of the shelter, there'd be no safety there that night. It was a shame she never met Henry.

So I listened, as we talked, to see if I could hear a wrong note, somebody saying something they shouldn't, anything off-key. I didn't hear it. All three of us agreed, that was the happy thing. My wobbles were small and not worth mentioning. As far as I knew we were all law-abiding people, all over seventy but still good citizens, recycling everything and standing up for pregnant women on the bus. I hadn't seen Grace and Daphne's tax returns but I would have been happy to bet quite a large sum of money that they were all in order. I knew they would have voted to remain in the EU, I didn't even need to ask. We were in tune. Together. Eat your heart out, Henry.

'The thing is,' Grace said, in a more quiet voice now as if we had crossed some kind of line, which I suppose we had. 'The thing is, we have to remember that we are the last people anyone would suspect of anything, any kind of crime. Have either of you noticed that?'

'Well,' said Daphne, 'I have sometimes been able to liberate items on a self-check till; not for myself, obviously, I donate them to food banks or take them to the lovely Extinction Rebellion protesters.'

Wow, I thought. I forgot my bashed-up face for a moment. Honestly, you could have knocked me over with a feather. I would not have thought it of her. I would not have thought it possible, even. I wished I had thought of it.

It's only fair, she was saying. Those big multinational shops pay very low wages and they have many unethical practices.

'Way to go,' Grace said. 'I'd high five you like the kids do if I didn't think we'd look absolutely ridiculous. You're an inspiration, girl. Only, I hope you both get this, there's a big difference between nicking a pack of long-life milk or lying down on Westminster Bridge with a lot of other people and actually...'

Grace drew her finger across her throat to make her point and we all went quiet.

'Cutting his throat,' I said when I'd recovered, 'is that really necessary?'

I was thinking of the mess. I couldn't imagine the rest of it, but I knew how much mess blood makes. I didn't think I'd said anything funny but I've noticed that in extreme situations humour changes tone slightly and the most serious things can seem hilarious. So I was a little embarrassed, but not surprised, when I saw that both of them were laughing so much they could hardly get their breath. Laughing in that way that's almost crying. I thought about how ridiculous the whole thing was and before I had thought it through I'd joined in. It took a few minutes before we could all stop and then Grace said, 'Seriously, though, how do you think they'll do it?'

We both looked at Daphne, I guess because she had known about the money side of things. She looked terribly uncomfortable, and I realised we should never have put her on the spot.

'Could be all sorts of ways,' I said, so that Daphne didn't feel singled out. 'I've read a lot of crime books. Poison is popular.'

'Guns are more American than British,' Grace said, 'but some people still manage to get hold of them here.'

'Knives,' said Daphne. 'A well-sharpened kitchen knife can be effective, I've heard.'

'Pushing someone under an oncoming train is very unfair on the train driver,' I said. I was trying to join in, be as knowledgeable as the other two, but for some reason it set them off laughing again and then I joined in with that too.

Daphne had a small laugh, a laugh that wouldn't attract any attention which is odd given that her clothes are so strange. People do stare sometimes. The day of the decision she was wearing purple leggings and a green flowered dress topped with a pink cardigan. All perfectly acceptable items of clothing on their own, I suppose, but lethal together. I couldn't help being a little envious. I didn't want to look exactly like her, it wasn't that, I just wondered what it would be like to get dressed with such gay abandon instead of sticking to the same three or four outfits in rotation hoping that I wouldn't be noticed.

Grace had a full, booming laugh. The kind of laugh that announced to the room that she was there; a confident laugh. She dressed in long things, long skirts, long, full linen trousers and long tunics over the top. The kind of clothes only a tall woman could wear. She wore her Extinction Rebellion patch like a badge of honour, and I was envious of that too. I couldn't believe that they wanted to be my friend, these two amazing women. That we were a little gang, and my opinions were worth as much as the next woman's. Even if I'd never been punched like that before and I was terrified of everything. Especially what might happen to that darling girl.

'I guess we don't need to know the actual nuts and bolts of it,' I said, 'as long as it's done, that's the main thing.'

I couldn't tell them how scared I was. Not when I didn't have another plan to offer.

'You're right,' Daphne said, 'there's no need for us to get too involved. We put up the money, and we can help Nina afterwards. Or make sure the right authority gets involved. That's our job.'

'We're old women,' Grace said, 'what does anyone expect? We've got to do what we can, what's right, do what we can to make the world a better place. Anyone would agree with us, I don't think there'd be any argument. That poor girl.'

'That poor girl,' I said in agreement.

That part I was sure about. Nina and I had bonded right from the first moment we met. She reminded me of everything I'd lost. Daphne was nodding away too.

'Could we…' Daphne said, 'I mean, I know it's… but I was thinking… would it be a good idea… do you think we could possibly… make a pact?'

Grace and I didn't say anything. Daphne shuffled and coughed and blushed until I had to put her out of her misery.

'A pact. I think that's a good idea.'

I didn't, not really, it sounded like something that a bunch of schoolgirls would come up with, not a group of three senior citizens with a girl to rescue. I just couldn't bear to see her looking so out on a limb. I had to speak. It was the fact that she was clearly used to being the odd one out, that was what I noticed. I had often felt the same in my marriage, even though there was only Henry and me. I would hate anyone to feel like that. The three of us were going to have to stick together if we wanted to get this done and bring Nina back. I thought that we had better start working on it now.

'I suppose,' said Grace. She looked vaguely around the late-night coffee shop, as if there might be instructions on the wall with the sandwich menu. 'I'm not sure how that works, though.'

'I think we're supposed to cut ourselves or something like that,' I said, 'mingle our blood and swear an oath. Isn't that how they do it?' I hoped they would say no. I didn't need to be any more battered.

'Well, I beg everyone's pardon,' Grace said, 'but I need every drop of my blood for myself. I'm seventy-five years old and I'm not taking any chances. But I'm happy to take an oath on something I hold dear. Any ideas?'

We looked at each other, then at the table. No one knew what they were looking for but I had an idea. I rummaged in my bag. I didn't want to be the first one to say anything in case my idea was stupid but I couldn't bear the silence so I jumped in. I could hear Henry's voice in my head saying, That's our Meg, jumps in with both feet and lands in the shit, but I did it anyway.

'I've got a picture,' I said, 'of a dog I used to have. A photo. He was a lovely dog.'

I got it out and put it on the table. Let them laugh, I thought, let them mock, I don't care, I'm trying my hardest. I didn't look at Bingley as I put him on the table, I didn't trust myself to. Bugger Henry, I thought, Bingley was a good, good dog.

'OK,' Grace said, 'I haven't got a picture but I've got this.'

She scrabbled in her bag and brought out a tiny, dirty old bear. It looked as though it would fall apart if it went near soap and water, but my hands itched to scrub it anyway. She put it on the table and I noticed that she seemed to find it as difficult to look at as I did the photo of dear old Bingley.

Daphne was still scrabbling in her bag and I suddenly thought, what if she hasn't got anything? That would be so awful for her. I looked at Grace and I could see she was thinking the same thing.

'Here we go,' Daphne said. 'I knew there was something.'

She pulled out a tattered green and white cardboard ticket, half the size of a postcard, and put it on the table with Bingley and the bear. I noticed the word 'Sydney' on it.

'Do we need to explain?' she said.

'Oh no, I don't think there's any need for that,' Grace said. 'I think we can trust each other.'

'Maybe when we know each other better,' I said. I would have liked to talk about Bingley.

Grace pushed the three things into the middle of the coffee table.

'We promise that we will act in good faith,' she said.

'We strive to do no harm,' said Daphne.

That's slightly ironic, I thought, given that we are contemplating harm indeed, although I knew what she meant. I sat still, thinking, and then I realised that they were both looking at me.

'Your turn,' Grace said.

'The greatest good for the greatest number,' I said, dredging up something I remembered from school. I held my hands out, hoping that no one was looking, and that neither of them minded. The café was quiet. The man behind the till was cashing up and he seemed totally uninterested in us anyway. It was the most anonymous place I could remember being in, no one knew us and no one was looking at three strange old women. We were almost invisible. Grace and Daphne took one hand each in theirs and joined us into a little circle. A circle of hands in varying shades like a Benetton advert.

'That's the one,' Grace said. 'Meg's oath. Greatest good for the greatest number and let's save Nina.'

'To Nina,' Daphne and I said, as if it was a toast.

CHAPTER TWO

Meg

Monday, 25 February – two days earlier

I was not in a good place when it all started. When I first met Nina. I'm amazed that I even managed to go to Pilates that day, I hardly went anywhere any more. Since Henry died, I had often spent fifteen minutes standing looking at the door before I left the house, and sometimes I sat down again instead, made do without whatever essential item I'd been going out for. I know there are no such things as nervous breakdowns any more, but mine was one, I'm sure of that.

I still don't know what made me go to the class that day, or to coffee afterwards – fate or something – but I knew as soon as I saw Nina that we were going to be connected in some way. There was a thread between us and I wondered if she might be a relative, someone I had known before, or even a child I had long ago given up for adoption. I had to stop and think, do I have a small dark-haired teenaged child out there in the world somewhere, one who might run into a café in south-east London dressed in a skimpy little skirt, flip-flops and a T-shirt, with no jacket, just a towel round her shoulders?

No, was the answer, no, Meg, you are far too old. This tiny, scared little bird of a girl cannot be your child. The connection must be something else. I listened as my mother had taught me, and I could just about hear it. A violin, playing off-key.

She came straight to me. All three of us were at the table, me, Grace and Daphne, but she came straight to me as if we had a prior agreement.

'Please,' she said, 'please help me.'

She was shaking, I could see that, and I did what anyone would do, I reached out from my chair, pulled her nearer and put my arm around her waist.

'It's OK,' I said, 'I'm here, we're here, are you OK?'

Nonsense, I know, not the right thing to say to a girl as upset as she was but I had to say something. The others were saying things as well, a chorus of three old ladies clucking and reaching and trying. It was heartbreaking, how much we wanted to help and how unsure we all were about how to.

Grace was the first one to say something sensible. She is the kind of person who knows what to say – the opposite of me. She is tall and elegant and although I didn't know her well I had been grateful that she wanted to have coffee with me that morning.

'Girl,' she said, 'are you in danger?'

It was such an obvious question to ask. I felt stupid that I had clucked and stared and listened and wondered, while Grace got to the heart of it straight away. Of course it was the right thing to check. If I wasn't so busy thinking about myself, I thought, I might be able to be incisive too.

The girl nodded, and looked at the door of the café as if a horde of soldiers wielding machine guns might burst in at any moment. Grace looked at the door in the same way and I realised that I didn't know anything about her past. We had talked about the class and how stiff it made us, what we were going to cook for dinner and jobs we used to do or not do, but nothing personal. It was unusual for women, our silence, but I sensed then and know now that there is too much pain in sharing for women like us. Too many pitfalls, too many traps we might fall into. I didn't know whether Grace had always lived in London, but the way she was looking at the stylish grey door of the café made me think that she might have once lived somewhere far more dangerous.

'OK,' Daphne said, 'OK, everybody, calm down. Let's see if we can work things out. I'm Daphne.'

The girl looked at us all in turn, moving her gaze from one face to the next. She seemed to be weighing something up, whether she could trust us, I suppose. We were an odd crew, and I wouldn't have blamed her if she had decided against talking to any of us. We were dressed for exercise, in a motley assortment of leggings and oversized T-shirts. Grace usually looks like an illustration of her name, but even she didn't look so wonderful in a brown T-shirt and green baggy tracksuit pants. I know now that Daphne looks a sight even in her best clothes. Her strange combinations of things make me wonder if she's giving all her clothes a turn of being worn so that they don't feel left out.

I'm hardly a style icon either. I have dumpy grandma written all over me, which is odd as I'm not actually a grandma. I'm not really anything, a widow, I suppose, although that makes me sound like I had a marriage, which I hardly did.

She looked at the three of us and she moved a step closer to me. I hope it's not because I'm white, I thought, and then cursed myself for over-thinking. Maybe she just liked the dumpy grandma vibe, maybe Grace seemed intimidating and Daphne bonkers, and it was nothing to do with colour.

I don't know how I had time for so many thoughts to go through my head while the girl moved one step closer and Grace moved between her and the door but I did. I could have counted the thoughts, that's how clear and distinct each one was, like leaves on the ground after a rainfall.

'Nina,' she said, then she looked even more scared, as if it was not something she should have told us. She took a deep breath.

'Nina,' she said again and pointed to her chest. From the way that she said it I wondered if she had arrived from a different planet, and I suppose in a way she had.

'Meg,' I said, pointing to myself and then, Daphne, Grace. Maybe we all came from different worlds, I thought, with only names in common. Like when aliens introduce themselves in films.

Nina kept looking at the back of the café, where there was a toilet cubicle.

'Good idea, girl,' said Grace. 'You go in there a moment, take your time now.'

She pointed to the toilet and Nina ran. I looked over to the counter and saw that the woman who had made our coffees was watching us. She didn't say anything but I thought that she could sense that we were bringing trouble to her nice café.

'Could we have another coffee for our friend?' Daphne called over.

She's quick, Daphne, really smart. Good at knowing what to do.

'Ladies, we have ourselves a situation,' said Grace. 'If I'm not mistaken, that girl is in one whole heap of trouble. Let's keep together now, see if we can help. You all OK with that?'

Daphne and I nodded and I wondered how things had changed so quickly. How we had gone from three acquaintances, bound only by a Pilates class for older women, to three co-conspirators, gearing up for trouble before our coffees had gone cold. We looked at each other, nodded, and before I had time to take another sip of my coffee the door to the café banged open and as it hit the wall a man came in.

I sat there, cup halfway to my mouth and thinking of something, someone other than myself for the first time in weeks. Months even. I thought of that poor little girl in the toilet and hoped that she would stay there. There had to be a connection between her fear and his anger, and when I looked at Grace and Daphne I could see that they were thinking the same thing. I put my hands to my ears to stop the jangling.

There was no one else in the coffee shop that morning. It was too early for the buggy and small dog brigade, and too late for the commuters who bought drinks on their way to the station. Just us three in there, but I was worried about the woman behind the counter. She might be our weak link, I thought. She looked tired, and she was on her own, and I wasn't convinced she would keep quiet. The man stood inside the door and it was clear that he was used to owning spaces wherever he went.

'Did a girl come in here?' he said, with an accent I recognised but couldn't immediately place. 'Only my daughter has run away and I'm looking for her.'

Daughter my foot, I thought, there's no way that sweet little thing is related to you. One, the man had no concern or panic in his voice at all. Just a kind of bored amusement. I could hear that he didn't care two hoots about her, in fact he sounded menacing. Two, he was old, not quite as old as us, probably in his mid-sixties, but too old to have a daughter that young. I know, I know it happens – look at Charlie Chaplin and Paul McCartney – but this man didn't look like a silver daddy, or whatever it is they call them these days. He looked like a toad, to be honest, like a toad that has accidentally been transformed into a man but is threatening to change back at any time. I suddenly remembered what the accent was. Poirot. He was Belgian, I was sure of it. A Belgian toad.

'Sorry?' Grace said with a question in her voice. She drawled it out in a way that made it clear that not only did she not have a clue what he was talking about, but that he was beneath her contempt anyway. I felt proud to be with her.

'Sorry also,' he said, smooth as you like. 'I may have been a tad abrupt. I was just wondering if any of you fair maidens had seen my daughter, about yay high,' he gestured with his hand, 'and terribly wilful. We had a bit of a spat, and I think she may have come in here.'

If he hadn't said 'fair maidens' things might have been different. I doubt it, but they might have. But he did, and we bristled, and I don't think there's a group of women aged seventy or thereabouts in the world who wouldn't take exception to being called fair maidens. It's condescending and it's spiteful, and it's a measure of how stupid he was that he didn't even realise that he would be putting our backs up.

'No,' said Grace.

She didn't look at the woman behind the counter as she

said it, and I admired her for that, I'm not sure I could have been so bold.

'No,' she said, 'I don't believe we have, it's just us in here.'

She made a little shrugging movement and picked up her coffee, cool as a cucumber. Daphne and I followed suit.

'You won't mind then,' he said, turning his back on us and speaking only to the woman who was serving, 'if I search the place, to put my mind at rest?'

That's done it, I thought, he'll find her now, and it'll be clear that we knew, and everything will be terrible, and that poor girl.

'I beg your pardon?' said the woman. She was older than I'd thought at first, probably nearer sixty than fifty, and out of nowhere I thought, I bet this café is her retirement thing. 'That's not going to happen. You heard the lady, and unless you come back here with police and a search warrant you're not searching anywhere. I never heard of anything like it. Do you not understand about private property? This is a café, not a free-for-all. Now, if you'd like a drink or something to eat there's a menu on the blackboard over my head, and if not I'd like you to leave, now. Thank you.'

She looked surprised when she'd finished. It was clear that those weren't the words she had been expecting to say. I wanted to smile at her in gratitude, but I kept my eyes on my coffee. Stay in the toilet, stay in the toilet, I thought, trying to send the thought through to Nina. If she came out now, I knew there would be no chance of helping her. I wanted to look over in that direction so badly but I forced myself to keep my eyes on my cup.

The man made an exaggerated bow, and doffed an imaginary cap.

'My mistake,' he said, 'I thought we were living in a free country. Good day, ladies, I'm sure we'll meet again soon. I'm looking forward to it already.'

I looked up, but Grace looked at me in a way I immediately knew meant 'stay down, as you were, wait a moment'. I stirred my coffee again and looked up in time to see him outside the window, staring in as if he might have missed something.

'He's still there,' Daphne said very quietly, 'he's still there.'

Ages went past while we sat there waiting, but it probably wasn't more than a couple of minutes. That's a thing I've found out about time as I have grown older. You can't trust it. It slips and slides like a slippery fish. We sat there, not talking, almost holding our breath.

'He's gone,' said the woman behind the counter. 'So if you can finish up and go too I'd be grateful. I don't know what's going on and I don't want to know, but I've got a café to run.'

'I'm sorry,' I started to say, 'but that was nothing to do with us.'

Grace looked at me and I stopped talking.

'It's OK,' she said to the woman. 'I'm sorry that trouble came walking in here this morning. I want you to know that you did good, you did just fine, you were great not to bring the extra coffee and to speak up to him like that. We're grateful. Aren't we?'

She looked at Daphne.

'Yes,' Daphne said, 'thank you.'

'Yes,' I said. I didn't want to be left out. 'What about...' I said, looking over towards the toilets.

I cared about her even after five minutes and that was surprising because I hadn't really cared about anything for a long time. It hurt, caring again. Like walking on a foot that's been asleep.

'OK, this is what I've been thinking,' Grace said. 'Which of us lives the nearest to the café?'

I realised that I had no idea where the others lived, and I was sure they didn't know about me either.

'I'm just round the corner,' I said, 'little cul de sac, you've probably walked past it.'

'Can you get there going round the back way, so that you're off the main road?' Grace asked.

'Yes,' I said, thinking fast. I've never been good at directions but I was sure there was a way, even if it took a little longer.

'I'm a bit further, over past the park,' Daphne said.

'Me too,' said Grace. She looked over to the woman behind the counter.

'I'm sorry to ask for your help again, but could we possibly go out of your back door? The one that leads out from the garden?'

I couldn't help thinking that this was all a bit cloak and dagger. The man was unpleasant-looking, and of course I was worried about the girl, but I couldn't believe that three old women like us needed to behave as though we were in a gangster film on Channel Four. Surely there was a good chance we would make things worse by getting involved? I knew that's what Henry would have said.

'Just go. You can go through the ceiling as far as I'm concerned, just get out,' the woman said.

I thought that was a bit harsh. I could see that she was terribly stressed, but she must have been able to see that it wasn't our fault. I was tempted to remind her that we had only been expecting a quiet cup of coffee ourselves but Grace was talking again.

'We're going to leave together,' she said. 'OK, both? I think there's some safety in numbers. We'll get to Meg's house as quickly as we can, and then we can work out what to do next.'

She sounded so serious I felt slightly unnerved.

'She can go home then, surely,' I said.

Grace gave me a look that made me feel approximately three inches high. I remembered that she had been a school teacher in another life, and I felt sorry for the children who had crossed her. Mostly, though, I was thinking about my house. Was it fit for visitors? Clean enough? It had been a long time since anyone had been to see me and I wasn't sure. Was there dust? Would they think I was strange when they saw how I lived? Or worse, would they feel sorry for me?

'Let's see, shall we?' Grace said. It was the kind of thing an adult might say to a silly child and I felt truly put in my place but everything was happening too fast for me to dwell on it.

We went down the little corridor leading to the toilets. I started to take the dirty cups over to the counter but the woman waved me away.

'Go on,' she said, 'I can clear up.'

I think she meant it kindly.

Grace knocked on the toilet door.

'It's OK, he's gone,' she said, 'you can come out. Let's get you somewhere safe.'

'Really?' said a little voice. I could hear that she had been crying.

'Yes, honestly,' I said. 'We're not going to hurt you. We're too old, apart from anything else. You could knock us over with one blow, I promise.'

There was a distinct snuffle from behind the door that sounded almost like a laugh. We heard the bolt being drawn across and she peered round the door. Honestly, she looked so forlorn that it pulled at something in my heart, something I thought had gone for ever. She connected me, that was what I felt; she connected me again to the whole damn world and all the suffering. I wasn't sure that I wanted to be connected, but I was so busy being surprised that I didn't think of that until later. It was as if the sight of her little tear-stained face had opened a door inside me, so that I could see people behind her, crying and laughing and living – a whole host of them. A clamour of people, that's what it was. I could see them, and they could see me, and I was connected to the world again. It hurt.

'OK,' said Grace, 'don't be scared, little one, we're going to help you.'

Are we? I thought. Are we really? I had a day planned, I always do. I've found that if I don't plan things, if I don't account for every minute of the day before it happens, I can easily go under. Sit in an empty room and stare at the walls, lie on the bed and stare at the ceiling. That kind of thing.

So this was my agenda for that day – I was planning on taking down the curtains in my living room and washing them, then I was going to get under the beds and clean the skirting boards, the ones that are hidden. They're awkward to get to and dust can accumulate there very easily so I thought it would take quite a while. None of it important, I knew that, but a person has to fill their day. I felt a slight panic at the idea of my day being hijacked. Calm down, I thought, none of it matters.

'No one can help me,' said the girl. I was taken aback at how old she sounded, as though a very ancient and sad person had taken over and spoken through her mouth.

'Nina,' I said, 'we'll give it a damn good try. Come on, not far to go.'

'You don't need to catch a cold on top of everything else,' Grace said. She took off the big colourful shawl she'd been wearing and wrapped it over the towel, round the girl's shoulders. It was February and bitter so Nina pulled it in tighter, snuggled into it in a way that made me want to hug her.

I wonder, I thought, and then I had a picture, as clear as anything, of wrapping a shawl round a person. I shook my head and the picture disintegrated into a thousand pieces. No time for that sort of nonsense now.

'Right,' I said, 'I'll lead the way. Onwards and upwards.' It sounded stupid when I said it out loud but no one seemed to mind. We slipped out of the garden at the back.

'Damn,' Daphne said, 'I meant to leave her a tip.'

I don't know why that seemed funny but it did, and all of us giggled. I think it was the fact that Daphne never, ever forgot her manners or the correct way to do things, even in extreme circumstances. Of course, the sight of little Nina laughing was so glorious that it made us laugh all the more. We must have looked like a merry bunch. Not a care in the world.

Once we got onto the street we stopped laughing as quickly as if a conductor had raised a baton. We needed our wits about us. Grace and Daphne flanked Nina and I walked in front.

'For goodness' sake, Meg,' Grace said, 'stop looking all around you. You couldn't look more suspicious if you tried.'

'Sorry,' I said.

I knew that she was right but really, it was difficult. I had an urge to keep peering over my shoulder, scanning the faces of everyone I could see. After all, it was my house we were going to, my safety that could be compromised if the toad man was following us, if he found out where I lived.

'Two more minutes,' I said as we turned into my close, 'it's just at the end, over there.'

'Got your keys handy?' Grace said.

I had, I'd got them in my hand, I always keep them in my pocket where I can grab them. I opened the door.

'Quick,' Grace said. 'Where's the best window for me to have a look out, onto the street, check he's not behind us?'

She seemed agitated.

Oh really, I thought, is this necessary? All this cloak and dagger stuff, not to mention going upstairs. I mean, my bedroom upstairs was the obvious choice but I have always been a private person. No one has been in my bedroom for a very long time. Henry didn't even come in there, he always said he didn't see why people had to live in each other's pockets just because they were married. I knew that was odd and not what other people did but I'd been with him for a long time and it had come to feel normal. Things do, if you live with them for long enough.

'My bedroom,' I made myself say. 'Top of the stairs and turn left.'

I hoped I'd made the bed and put away my clothes but I knew I had. I'm not one for mess, it only has to be sorted out later. Grace bounded up the stairs like someone much younger, and I took the other two through to the kitchen at the back. I offered tea, which was ridiculous as we had just had coffee but Daphne and Nina both nodded.

They sat down at my kitchen table and just like that, Nina began to cry. Big old sobs and her head in her hands on the table. She looked about eight years old. It was unbearable. All you want to do when you hear crying like that is offer a bit of comfort so we sat there, Daphne and I, on either side of her and rubbing her shoulders. We both knew better than to ask her what was the matter and it didn't seem important anyway. An upset person is an upset person so we stayed there, quiet and calm. I wondered what it would be like to be held like that, and if anyone would ever do that for me. I think Daphne was having the same thought, there was something I could see in her eyes. How odd, I thought. I might not be the only one who's lonely.

It felt strange when Grace came downstairs, knowing that she had been in my bedroom. A person in my most private place, just standing there in a room that usually only saw me. I wondered if the walls had been surprised to see her. I was so lost in my thoughts and my patting of Nina's back that I almost lost what Grace said next.

'I'm pretty sure he didn't follow us,' she said. 'There's a good view from upstairs and I could see no sign of him.'

'Thank you,' said Nina and her voice was gruff and swollen with tears. 'I can't believe that you three were there when I needed someone and you just, you're like angels.'

We all smiled. I felt about three feet taller. I don't think I've ever been called an angel before and I liked it even though I hadn't really started to understand what was happening. I was still imagining that they would all go home soon and I'd be able to get on with those curtains. Fancy being called an angel, I thought.

'He's nothing but a toad,' I said, and Nina squealed.

'He is, isn't he, that's what we call him too.'

She looked worried that she had given too much away so I patted her hand to show her that it was all OK. I must have stopped listening for a moment and I was surprised when I tuned back in to what Grace was saying.

'So is it all right if Nina stays here, until we can be sure it's safe for her to move?'

'Oh,' I said. 'What about your mum, Nina, will she not be waiting for you?'

Nina looked as though she was going to start crying all over again and Grace gave me a look that made me realise that I'd said something stupid. I'd forgotten that not every child has a mum, which is weird because I knew for sure that not every mum has a child.

'Oh no,' Nina said, 'I'm older than I look. And I've got no mum anyway, so that part's OK. But if you don't want me to stay I won't, honestly, I'll be all right. There's someone I have to help, she's ill.'

She stood up and took the shawl off.

'Thanks very much,' she said. I could hear a trembling in her voice and I felt ashamed of myself for making her feel uncomfortable.

'Stay,' I said, 'please stay.'

Nina looked towards Grace, as if she was the leader. I felt stung. It's my house, I wanted to say, but I knew that would be childish.

'Are you sure?' Grace said.

I thought of that clamour of people, the feeling of being connected that I had experienced. I remembered all the hours I'd spent cleaning and crying on my own.

'I'll make up the spare bed,' I said. 'You're welcome, Nina.'

CHAPTER THREE

Nina

November – fifteen months earlier

Nina hated birthdays. They never worked out well in her experience. The worst part was that she couldn't help feeling hopeful, as if there was a chance that the world she knew might change. Disappointment always followed. Nina had a memory of candles and a cake shaped like a little log cabin, with chocolate fingers for the roof, but she wasn't sure if it was real, or a picture she had seen in a magazine. She usually tried hard not to dwell on that kind of nonsense. The rest of the year she was good at styling it out, convincing herself and everyone around her that she couldn't care less, but on her birthday Nina changed into a little girl, a little disappointed girl, and there was nothing she could do about it. This one, her sixteenth, had been the worst so far.

Sixteen was supposed to be special. She knew it was, and not just because she had seen a programme on TV about rich girls and how they celebrated. Spoilt American girls and pink cars. Nothing like that would happen for her, Nina knew that, but still she wished that something might mark her birthday out, make it different. Maybe, and this was a ridiculous thought, Nina knew it was, but maybe her mother would remember the day and decide that she wanted to meet her daughter again, now that she was an adult. Maybe she would even ask her to go and live with her, leave the residential home. Fat chance, Nina thought.

She walked downstairs to the common room. It was a Saturday, no school, nowhere she was supposed to be.

'Surprise,' they all shouted when she walked in.

There was a cake, a home-made one, and they were all standing around, acting like they thought she would be pleased. It was an ordinary cake, a Victoria sponge, shaped like any other cake and without icing. One plain cake, two carers and three kids, all grinning and staring at her as if she was supposed to do something for them, entertain them in some way. Make it worthwhile for them by being happy, something like that. Bilbo especially, clapping his hands and staring at her with his mouth hanging open and his teeth all crooked. The sight of him, all expectant like that, made Nina want to cry. She wanted him to be happy but it was too much responsibility, sometimes there was nothing she could do.

Nina had grown to love Bilbo. His name was Billy, but Nina's name for him had stuck and now no one ever called him by his real name. She had been trying to teach him to keep his mouth shut, to stop the other kids from picking on him at school.

'Shut your mouth, Bilbo,' Nina said, 'don't dribble on my cake.'

Quick as a flash, Carol said, 'That's not nice, Nina, don't speak to Bilbo like that. And it's really everyone's cake, isn't it?'

Nina had known she would say something exactly like that. She could have written the script, Carol was that predictable.

'Well, if it's not my cake I don't know why you're all fucking standing there,' she said. Nina knew it would upset Bilbo, he hated to hear the f word, but she couldn't help it. She would make it up to him later. She might read him a story or let him listen to some music on her headphones. It was worth upsetting him for a minute or two if it meant that she riled Carol. She shouldn't be working with kids, a person like that.

Nina had been in the home for six months. She had run away from two foster placements, and the social workers didn't know where else to put her. To be honest, she didn't even know where she would put herself if she had a choice. So she was here, with Bilbo who dribbled when he talked and often said the same thing over and over again all day, Chloe who had some kind of syndrome that made her look like a tiny but sharp little bird, and Jason who never stopped trying to chat her up, ask her if she would be his girlfriend. She didn't fit in at all. Nina was planning to run again as soon as she got things sorted. She had only stayed this long because she wanted to do her GCSEs, get the kind of grades that would make everyone realise that there was more to her than just another looked-after kid. She wanted to surprise her mother, to be exact. To wake her up, remind her that she even had a kid, a clever one at that.

Bilbo looked as if he was going to cry.

'Come on, Neens, cheer up. I know birthdays can be a bit weird, but Bilbo has been practising singing 'Happy Birthday' all morning. Give him a break,' Sue said.

Nina waited for the religious part.

'We owe it to God to be happy. Look how lovely the world is,' Sue continued on cue, gesturing around her at the pale cream walls and the scuffed chairs.

31

Nina bit back a smart reply. At least Sue was kind. The kids didn't mind her too much – they called her Sumo for obvious reasons but they saved their venom for Carol. Carol clearly disliked children. They could all see it, even Bilbo, and he was her favourite. Everyone knew that Bilbo was Carol's favourite because she was always trying to hug him or make him hug her. It wasn't Bilbo's thing, hugging. It made him panic and lash out. Nina couldn't believe how stupid Carol was.

'I didn't ask to have a birthday, did I?' Nina said.

Chloe smiled and poked Nina on the arm. 'Birthday, birthday,' she said.

Bilbo smiled and jumped up and down.

'Happy, happy, what?' he said. 'Happy what, Nina Neens? Happy what?'

'Oh, for goodness' sake, happy birthday, that's what, Bilbo,' Nina said.

It was hard to resist Bilbo and anyway, if she didn't reply, Nina knew that he would go on asking until she did.

'Yes,' said Bilbo, 'yes, happy birthday, happy happy, oh yes happy birthday.'

Jason kissed his teeth and looked away. Nina knew that he only tolerated Bilbo because she did.

'Light the fucking candles, let's get it over with,' Nina said.

They all stared at her and Bilbo began to wail.

'We don't say, we don't say, Nina, what don't we say? What don't we say? Neens, what don't we say?'

'Oh, for God's sake,' Nina said. 'We don't say the f word.'

'F word, f word, we do not say the f word, we do not. No, Nina, f word is finished. F word is?'

'Finished,' said Nina, 'finished, Bilbo.'

Sue looked at her as if she was very sad and Jason began to laugh.

Just another day in the madhouse, Nina thought. She ate the cake as quickly as she could and picked up her school bag.

'Thanks and all, but I've got to do my homework,' she said. They had never had a high flyer before in the children's home. It was rare, and Nina was aware that it gave her some privileges.

'Where's Nina? Not going out, Neens, Nina is not going where?' Nina heard Bilbo as she left, sounding almost sad enough to stop her in her tracks.

'Library,' she called over her shoulder, 'maths.'

'Happy, happy, happy what, happy birthday, happy homework, happy maths,' he called.

Nina almost turned back but it really was difficult to study in the house. Often one of the young people was kicking off, or they wouldn't leave her alone. Even in her room with the door shut she could hear them all, and sometimes Bilbo cried until she let him listen to his favourite songs on her headphones. The staff had tried every way to convince him to use his own, but nothing worked. He wanted Nina's, and sometimes the staff were so desperate they asked her to let him have them. The problem was, he only wanted them in Nina's room and that meant a member of staff had to be nearby, either in the room with them or just outside the door. They had had to give Nina extra freedom to go out to the library, it was the only way she could study.

Nina had been trustworthy. She had gone to the library when she said she was going, stayed until it closed and then gone home. It's only until the exams, she told herself, then life can begin. Nina had read an article online about middle-class kids going to festivals after their exams and she giggled as she imagined what the staff would say if she asked for a ticket for a birthday present.

'Hey, what's funny?' Nina looked up, embarrassed to be caught laughing to herself in the street. People will think I'm like Bilbo, she thought.

'Nothing,' she said.

'Oh, sorry,' said the person.

She sounded genuinely sad, and Nina couldn't resist taking a quick look to see who she had offended. The girl looked about Nina's age, possibly a little older. She spoke with a slight accent that Nina could only identify as foreign. Her clothes were fashionable in a casual way, baggy jeans drawn in at the waist, a short leather jacket and purple trainers. Nina squirmed slightly. The clothing allowance for looked-after children did not run to leather jackets and smart trainers.

'I've seen you before,' the girl said, 'going to the library. You're always going to the library. You must be clever.'

Nina wasn't sure what to say. She hadn't had much experience of random friend-making and she couldn't help thinking that this girl must be after something. She shrugged her shoulders.

'I'm not that clever,' she said. 'I like it there, that's all.'

'Do you mind if I come with you?'

Nina did mind. She minded a lot, and she didn't know what the girl wanted. She hesitated.

'It's OK,' the girl said, 'I can take a hint. I'm going into town, anyway, I'm going to get some new trainers.'

Nina couldn't stop herself from looking at the trainers the girl was wearing. They were spotless. She couldn't imagine what it would be like to get a second pair of trainers when your first pair was still brand new. Stop being so materialistic, she told herself, it's not about what you've got. They had talked about that in sociology and she had realised that everyone thought too much about possessions and not enough about the important things. Charity shops and recycled fashion, that's what the climate change protesters talked about and Nina knew they were right. She just couldn't help wanting stuff, that was all. Random stuff like purple trainers and silver earrings and a little dog and a mum waiting at home, eager to hear how her school day had gone. Unattainable things.

'You can come if you like,' the girl said, 'unless you'd rather go in there.'

Nina looked at the library across the road. It wasn't a big one, it often didn't even have the books she wanted, but it was a safe place. It was the place she had said she was going to. But it was her birthday, her sixteenth. She made up her mind.

'OK,' Nina said, 'I might as well come with you.'

Nina thought the girl would be pleased, but there was something almost sad in her expression. As if she hadn't wanted Nina to come, really.

'It's OK,' she said. 'I'm not bothered whether you come or not.'

Nina thought that might be true.

'No,' said the girl, as if she was remembering something, 'no, it will be fun. I'm Shaz. What's your name?'

The girl looked older, suddenly, and Nina wished she hadn't agreed to go. And when Nina said her name, Shaz looked bored. Nina had an odd feeling that she had already known it.

'Nina,' she said, 'fancy that. Come on then.'

Nina thought that she might have made a mistake. The girl seemed indifferent now, less friendly. She picked at her fingernails in a way that made Nina feel queasy.

'Have you got a boyfriend then?' Shaz said. 'I bet you have.'

'No,' said Nina, startled into telling the truth, 'can't be bothered.'

Shaz laughed.

'I didn't know it was a bother,' she said. 'I'd better remember that.'

Nina realised that she had said something stupid. She wished she hadn't agreed to go. She had been looking forward to going to the library although she would never, ever have admitted it. She liked the order of the books, the quiet, the space. She liked studying. Nina looked at Shaz. She was tall, with short blonde hair cut so that one side was longer than the other.

'I, I, erm, like your hair,' Nina said.

Shaz glanced at Nina's hair and laughed.

'Yours would be OK,' she said, 'if you, like, put a bit of colour in it or something.'

Nina's hair was long and dark. She wished that she had taken more trouble this morning, put it up on top of her head, plaited it, done anything rather than leaving it hanging.

'Are you at school or college or something?' Nina said.

'Nah,' said Shaz. 'I wasn't much good at that kind of stuff so I stopped going.'

Nina made a mental note never to tell Shaz how much she loved reading, and learning new things.

'You'd never get away with it though,' said Shaz. 'They're stricter on that kind of thing, you know, if you're in care.'

It was true, Nina knew it. Things were much more cut

and dried for looked-after kids, much harder to skip school without anyone knowing. Not that she wanted to, school was the best thing she had, but that wasn't something she would ever admit either.

'Guess what? It's my birthday today,' Nina said.

As soon as the words were out of her mouth she regretted them. It felt childish, saying it out loud, and she didn't know why she had said it. Some acknowledgement, that was what she wanted. Nina had moved schools a lot. At least five secondary schools if you didn't count the holding placements they used sometimes while she waited for a proper place. If you counted those she wasn't even sure how many she had been to but in not one of them had she ever mentioned that it was her birthday. There was no point. She had watched the others celebrate with their friends and talk about parties and birthday outings but she had never been invited. Not to one bowling alley, garden party or cinema trip. There hadn't been a chance for her to learn how to make friends with the other girls. She didn't blame them. It wasn't worth putting the effort in for a looked-after child. They moved too often.

Nina looked over at Shaz and wondered why she had told her. Shaz wouldn't care that it was her birthday; Shaz was definitely older and they had nothing in common. She wasn't the library-going, study-partner type of girl that Nina had dreamed of meeting. She wondered if it was too late to turn around, go back towards her original destination, get herself out of this ridiculous trip.

'Oh wow,' said Shaz, 'that's amazing. Your birthday, sweet sixteen, that's so adorable. Hey, we're totally going to do this, it's going to be fun.'

Thinking back on it later, Nina would wonder whether there was a mechanical quality to Shaz's words. Whether she sounded like a talking doll with only twenty set phrases. Rehearsed, that's what it seemed to be, only at the time Nina was pleased to have the attention, pleased to feel special even if it was to someone she had only just met.

'What's your favourite thing to eat?' Shaz asked. 'McDonald's, Nando's, pizza, you name it and that's where we're going.'

'Oh,' Nina said, trying to work out what would be the right thing to say. 'Erm, I'm not sure, what do you like best?'

Shaz laughed. 'It's not my birthday,' she said, 'but if it was, let me think, yes, maybe the most fattening thing in McDonald's, maybe a massive burger and a milkshake. How about that?'

'Great,' said Nina. Her heart sank. She was a vegetarian and she had strong feelings about it. She'd seen clips online of cows crying for their babies and chickens pecking off their own legs because they were so confined. 'McDonald's it is,' she said. She decided not to tell Shaz that she didn't eat meat. Or that she hated McDonald's.

The truth was, Nina had bad memories of McDonald's. It had been the place where she went to see her mother, when she still went to see her. Whatever social worker she was with at the time would take her and then sit at a table nearby. They always pretended it was a normal thing, an ordinary girl out with her mum on a Saturday morning.

The last time had been when Nina was eleven. She had tried so hard to make her mother respond but it hadn't worked. Nina's mother was distant. Quiet and sad and often unable to think of a single thing to say, even when Nina brought her school books or a story she had written. She had her report this time, the last one from primary school. It was brilliant, and Nina was sure her mum would be pleased.

Nina had arrived at the McDonald's early with her social worker. She had brought daffodils, and she laid them out carefully next to the space where her mother would sit. Everyone liked daffodils, Nina thought. She waited for her mum to arrive. The whole place was full of families, noisy kids and happy adults. She knew that the meeting might not be as good as she had planned, but there was a tingle of anticipation in her stomach nonetheless. Nina watched the clock and waited for her mother to arrive.

She refused to give up for over two hours, convinced there had been a mistake, that her mother was lying hurt somewhere, or being kept hostage. She loved the Saturday sessions as much as Nina did, Nina was sure of it. She didn't say much, but that was OK. At the end they would both keep each other in their sights for as long as they could, walking backwards, banging into things, it was their special way of saying goodbye. She wouldn't just not turn up. Nina had to stay, to wait for her.

In the end the social worker had to call for help, and another social worker came and helped her to move Nina away, still sobbing, still clutching the daffodils. She hadn't seen her mother since and she hadn't been back to McDonald's.

Nina tried to smile. Surely it was different, going to McDonald's in a happy way, going with a friend. Even though at times talking to Shaz was like talking to her unresponsive mother.

'Veggie burgers? They're crap, they make them out of dust and shit from the floor,' Shaz said when Nina gave her choice.

Nina tried to think of what they could talk about, what they might have in common. They settled eventually on a TV show that Nina didn't really like, and some talk about trainers, but the whole thing was awkward.

What was she supposed to do on her birthday, though, she thought afterwards. Hang out with Bilbo?

It was only later, when she was back at the home and watching *Mr Bean* with the others, while Bilbo watched her anxiously and laughed whenever she did. Only then that Nina thought, did Shaz talk about her being in care before she could possibly have brought it up? Nina knew that was the case because she would never have brought it up. Wouldn't even have used those outdated words anyway. Nina would have said 'looked after'. Nina never told anyone that she lived in a residential home, but Shaz had definitely said that things were stricter for children in care.

And another thing, Nina's brain dredged up, just as she was falling asleep. Another thing, how did Shaz know it was Nina's sixteenth birthday? Was everything about her and her life written on her face, clear for everyone to see?

CHAPTER FOUR

Daphne

Monday, 25 February

Daphne was a worrier. She worried about everything, from big worries like climate change to the smaller ones like how much money she should give to a person who was begging. She always kept her pockets full of money and sometimes she gave away surprising amounts. Some days Daphne gave to every single appeal she saw online and the amount she owned still didn't go down. She had too much money, that was the difficulty.

Today, Daphne felt overwhelmed. This was different, helping someone directly rather than doling out cash. It brought back so much. She couldn't stay in Meg's house. It was too much: the girl, the man, the hiding and the being scared. Daphne was familiar with being scared but that didn't dilute it in any way. In fact, she thought, it made it worse. It meant that the echo of previous scary times was always with her. She had her own personal bogeyman who never left her wardrobe.

Daphne looked up and down the tree-lined street. She should have stayed with the others, she thought. Who the hell did she think she was, sneaking off? She felt brightly lit, easy to spot, even though the day was grey and miserable. No one else around. The man from the café was probably miles away by now. She shivered. She tried to control an impulse to look up into the trees, check that he wasn't sitting there on a branch waiting. That bruise, she thought. That bruise on the girl, it was familiar.

'Time to get off the fence, Daffers,' she said to herself. 'That girl needs you, stop thinking about yourself. Woman up.' She said it out loud but quietly, and it helped a little. Daphne had never been a team player. She wasn't sure why. She had wanted to be, that much she knew. For a moment back there, things had seemed different. For a moment, she had let herself think about how lovely it would be to be in a team, a gang, a group of women with an aim.

'Nonsense, Daff,' she said to herself in the quiet street. 'They'll manage just fine without you. That Grace, she could do anything, she'll make things OK. That amazing Grace.' Daphne smiled at the pun, and wondered if she would ever be able to tell her. People probably said it to her all the time, Daphne thought, everyone must surely notice how amazing she was.

Daphne thought again about the man who had chased the girl into the café. Chased, that was the word for it, even though he had pretended to be casual, pretended to be looking in there on the off chance. She wasn't sure if the others had noticed his eyes. Maybe they had, maybe it was obvious that his eyes were dead. Cold and fishy, that's how they had looked, as if he had swapped his human eyes for the eyes of a giant dead fish. Daphne shuddered at the thought that somewhere in the world there might be a large fish wearing the man's human eyes.

It was less than a ten-minute walk between the two houses, but Daphne had never been to Meg's house before. She had sometimes wondered where they lived, Meg and Grace, what sort of places they had and whether they lived alone like her. She thought about it in the Pilates class when she was supposed to be strengthening her core. She had imagined Meg living in a house with tasteful souvenirs from other countries on the wall, and little framed embroidered phrases that other people had given her. Embroidered phrases such as:

Why raise a princess when you can raise a warrior?

Go singing to the fashioning of a new world.

Your kids' mental health is more important than their grades.

That was the sort of thing she had imagined, but it hadn't been like that at all, Daphne thought. In fact, what she had seen of Meg's house had been plain, almost like a hotel or a tableau from a dull furniture shop. Nothing on the walls. And small, it was a little house, and that had been surprising to Daphne. She always forgot that her own house was so large. So pointlessly large, although when she was in it it seemed fairly normal. It was embarrassing, and Daphne had long ago stopped inviting people round. Good luck can be as alienating as bad, this had been clear to Daphne for a long time.

The last real visitor to Daphne's house had been a woman from work, probably fifteen years ago now and on the way back from a conference. She had popped in to use the toilet after giving Daphne a lift back from Derby. Daphne tried to think now what her name had been – Ann, maybe, or Caroline. She had stood still in the living room, Ann or Caroline, toilet needs forgotten and staring round open-mouthed at the high ceilings and the paintings on the walls as if she was in a stately home. As if she had paid several pounds for a ticket and was determined to get her money's worth. Daphne hated thinking about that. Her safe place at her beloved work had never been the same afterwards. She had never been sure whether people knew, whether it made them hate her, whether they were talking about her behind her back.

She'd moved on as soon as she could, taken another promotion with a different council and kept herself even more separate from her co-workers. It was a shame, she had always known it was a shame, always lived another life in her head. A coward, Daphne thought, that's what she was. A big fat coward, running away from her own shadow. Those women need you, she thought now; that poor girl, so small and helpless. It's not about you, or what happened, none of that matters.

Daphne stood still in the middle of the pavement. It had become sunny in the way that late February could, backlighting her decision. Both choices seemed impossible. She could go home, lock the door, keep safe, stay out of trouble. That made the most sense. Daphne was a woman who knew what trouble was, what it looked like, what it did to a person. Or she could go back to Meg's, she thought, ring the bell and say, hi, sorry I disappeared, but I'm back and I want to help. After all, it wasn't Grace and Meg's responsibility to sort things out any more than it was hers. The girl, Nina, had approached all of them. In fact, Daphne thought that Nina might have looked directly at her. She might have recognised that Daphne knew more than the others about what she had been through.

Daphne looked once in the direction of her safe, secure house and then turned, determined to go back, face up to things and try to help. She could hear her own footsteps in the quiet street and she wondered why everything was so silent. It made her decision seem more loaded than it was, like a film where something unpleasant is about to happen. She stepped out on to the road to cross towards Meg's and a black Range Rover appeared, speeding towards her out of nowhere. She hadn't seen it or heard it until it was right there. Daphne had time only to jump back, tripping on the kerb as she went. There was a shouting and a blaring of horns and Daphne sat down hard on the pavement. She stayed down for a moment, gathering her wits and her strength to stand up. Something about the car, she thought, something not quite right about the car.

The world looked different from the ground. The trees seemed taller and darker against the sky and it was colder. Daphne tried to remember what the man in the Range Rover had shouted but she wasn't sure. He had sounded angry, and there were expletives in the sentence, but Daphne couldn't catch what he said. One thing she knew though, she absolutely did not want to be on her own. To open the door to her big lovely house and call hello, pretending that someone was there. To check the doors and windows were locked and look under the bed, and yes, she still checked everywhere, in every cupboard, every day.

Daphne stood up. She felt shaky but going back was the right decision, she knew it was. They might be glad to see her, they might need her. And so much better than going home alone and thinking again about... about the bruise. There had been a bruise on Nina's arm; Daphne wasn't sure if anyone else had seen it but it was there. It looked angry, and dark, a storm cloud of a bruise. It was possible, just possible, that Nina had knocked into a piece of furniture in the dark or crashed into a tree when she was out for a run but Daphne had seen a bruise like that before and she knew what it was. Her own shoulder ached in sympathy. If Daphne had looked closer she knew she would have seen finger marks, darker circles against the grey.

Daphne thought about the bruise and she was right back there, eighteen again, and in her first term at York University. All the other students were white, and although that had been OK at school, somehow it wasn't OK here. Every room she entered, every lecture she went to, everywhere she was, she felt awkward. People smiled but they were distant, too busy consolidating their own positions to make friends with the brown girl. Nowadays, Daphne thought, students would probably be vying to make friends with the student from the ethnic minority to improve their street cred, but in 1968 life was different. People in York shops spoke to her slowly and carefully in case she didn't understand and at freshers' events Daphne sat at the side.

There was the odd question, mostly people trying to show an interest by asking where she came from. 'Hull,' she always said, but she could see that was not what they wanted to hear, that she had disappointed them. If anyone had asked further, she could have explained that her mum was from Ceylon but all she knew about her dad was that he was white and rich, but no one ever asked more than that first question. Perhaps they all ask each other where they're from, Daphne thought. Perhaps she was being oversensitive.

She had been there for three weeks when she met Andrew. She had noticed him, it would have been hard not to, but she couldn't believe that he actually spoke to her, and not to ask

46

her where she came from either. Daphne had developed a way of walking by then, head down and moving fast, no meandering, no looking around. She wore plain clothes, dark colours and nothing to draw attention. Andrew, on the other hand, wore a military jacket and striped flares and seemed to be lounging around whenever Daphne caught a glimpse of him, propping up walls or drinking pints. She had never seen him with a book. He was a handsome boy, very handsome, and Daphne had watched other girls openly admiring him.

'Hey Jude,' Daphne sang to herself now in the quiet street.

She hadn't thought about it for ages, but that was the song she had loved when she first met Andrew, she was sure of it. Andrew. The heart-throb of the university, and he had chosen her. Marked her out. Daphne still wondered why, what she had done, how she had stood, what would have made him think she was the right one. She tried to remember exactly how they had met. She'd been late for a lecture, that was it, the trunk with her clothes in hadn't arrived and Daphne had spent ages trying to make herself look OK in the same outfit she had been wearing every day since term began. She could have brought more clothes with her, but her mum had read somewhere that everyone sent a trunk on when they went to university. Hers was the only one that hadn't arrived, so she had sponged down her skirt and scrubbed the underarms of her blouse with a toothbrush and hand soap. It had taken ages to get rid of the soap marks and she was late, standing outside the lecture theatre with her arms clamped to her sides to hide the wet armpits. She was frightened to go in and frightened to stay out.

Thinking about it made Daphne shiver even now, standing in the street almost outside Meg's house. It was a long time ago, she reminded herself, he's probably dead now. If there's any justice in the world he's dead and if not, perhaps he is terribly unhappy or tormented by dementia. Yes, that would be good, that was a cheering thought, holes in his brain like a colander and unable to remember his own name. In fact, Daphne thought, in fact if that was the case, she wished she could go and visit him. Call in with the sort of chocolate he had always hated, the dark stuff with hard little nuts for punishment.

Meanwhile, she realised, she was standing outside Meg's house exactly as she had stood outside the lecture theatre that day. Stuck, unable to move and dithering over what to say. Fifty years, more or less, fifty years and a moderately successful career, but no change. She was still poor Daphne, Paki Daff, Daffy Pak. On the outside, like she always had been, watching other people. You have nothing to fear except fear itself, she thought. Daphne knew this wasn't true. Whoever had first coined that phrase, Shakespeare or Kennedy or Roosevelt or whoever it was, they had obviously had a nice life. Nothing scary, just the odd confidence issue. Daphne wondered what her life might have been like if she had never had anything concrete to be scared of. She took a deep breath and rang Meg's bell. She hoped that Grace was still there. It's not about you, she said to herself, it's about that poor little girl. The bruise, she thought, think of the bruise.

Grace opened the door.

'I'm sorry,' Daphne said. 'I was thinking maybe I could help. I mean, maybe I have ideas which might be, you know.' Her voice tailed off and she stared at the ground.

'Well, if you've got even one idea that's one more than me,' Grace said, 'so you're welcome here even though it's not my house. I'm glad to see you back. Did you bring the milk?'

48

Daphne remembered that getting milk had been some kind of excuse, that she had left offering to shop and intending to flee.

'Erm, no,' she said, turning her hands from front to back and then again, as if they might have produced some milk out of thin air.

Grace looked at her as if she understood and Daphne blushed. What a wonderful woman, she thought.

The scene inside was pretty much the same as it had been when she had left. Daphne wondered how long she had been gone, whether it was a moment or an hour. It was impossible to tell. Nina was sitting in an armchair, her feet tucked up under her, hugging herself. Daphne wanted to put her arms round her.

'OK,' said Meg, 'good that you're back, I think we need a plan.'

Daphne nodded and she could see Grace nodding too. Only Nina stayed still, staring at her knees.

There was silence.

'Oh,' said Meg, 'I didn't think, I mean, I wasn't sure, shall I speak?'

Daphne realised that Meg might be shy too, and it made her feel less alone.

'Yes, fire away,' Grace said.

'A short-term plan and a long-term one,' Meg said. 'Is that OK? Erm, first, I think Nina should stay here. Whatever is going on, I'm not convinced that she's safe. Nina, is that OK with you?'

Nina shrugged her shoulders and Daphne thought that she might be holding back tears.

'I don't want to get you guys into any, you know, maybe

it's best if I just go back,' Nina said. 'I'm worried about my friend, she's sick.'

Daphne could tell that she didn't want to leave, and her heart went out to the girl for being brave enough to pretend. She thought of the black car, and how menacing it had seemed.

'Nina,' Daphne said, 'just in case, so that we can keep an eye out, that man, the one who's looking for you – what kind of car does he drive?'

Nina shrank even further back into the chair.

'It depends,' she said. 'He's got loads, but the one he usually uses is a big black thing, high up off the road, I don't know what they call it.'

Nina looked as if someone had told her she had failed something important.

'I should, shouldn't I?' she said. 'I should know the number plate and everything, I never thought. I'm so stupid.'

All three women jumped to reassure her but Grace spoke first.

'Girl, if we all did everything like we were in some kind of film, or a story book, the world would be a different place. Everyone's got to do a little bit of what they can, and a little bit more than they can if they can, and then live with themselves afterwards.'

Daphne decided to remember that. A little bit of what I can, she thought. Bring it on.

CHAPTER FIVE

Grace

Monday, 25 February

I am so pleased to see Daphne when I open the door. I want to hug her and tell her she's been missed but I know a thing or two about people and I do not think she would be comfortable with that. I'll tell her that one day, I think, and I can't believe I feel a little smile of pleasure inside, like I'm not the hard frozen bitch everyone thinks I am. She reminds me of someone from back home, from Jamaica, and I don't know why. There's a light around her, that's what, and I know that sounds fanciful.

I always remember Eleanor with a light around her. There's something about Daphne that makes me think of a morning on the beach with Eleanor. She's standing there on the doorstep looking sad and I can practically see the waves lapping round her feet. I ask her about the milk she said she was going to get, then I think what a fool that makes me look. It was obvious there was never going to be any milk. She must think I'm having a go at her, pointing out something she's embarrassed about. She takes a deep breath, though, and I notice how brave she is.

'Is she OK, the girl?' she asks me.

'She's not fine,' I say. I want to tell her how worried I am, how scared the whole thing makes me but I look at her and I think, she's holding it together but it's worse for her. I don't know why I know that but I do, and I want to protect her almost as much as I want her to protect me.

'On the other hand,' I say, 'she's got us, and we can try to keep her safe.'

'Yes,' she says, 'I can help.'

She seems to be shaking. Messed up, that's how she looks. She starts to take a step and she winces, so I look and see there's a hole in her jogging pants and her hands are a bit bloody. She sees me looking and she blushes, for goodness' sake.

'It's nothing,' she says. 'I fell.'

I can tell there's something more than that, something she doesn't want to tell me. She's got a closed look. I have seen that look before.

'Anything we need to know?' I say and she looks so damn miserable.

'I might have seen the car. The car he drives. The man who is after…' She gestures indoors.

'Whoa,' I say. I know it sounds as if I don't believe her and I hate that, that's not what I meant at all. A memory flashes into my head and it's Eleanor on the telephone, telling me that she's fine. I haven't thought about that phone call for years. I knew later that she hadn't been fine, and I swore never to miss a clue again but I did, I missed another one and two is enough.

'I don't know though,' she says. 'I mean, I'm not sure enough to raise an alarm or anything. Big black cars, I don't know, there are a lot of them.'

'There are,' I say.

I'm aware I sound like I'm not at all interested but I am trying to think this through. No more mistakes, Grace, I tell myself. The truth is that this whole situation has got to me. Daphne looks at me and smiles and it's such a lovely smile.

'Can I help with your knee?' I say.

'It helps that you're here,' she says.

Such a remarkable thing to say. Neither of us knows what to do next. I move my hands, open them and close them, and she shuffles forward a little, then back. The sun decides it's been around long enough and the street darkens. We both look up and then at each other and then we smile. Something weird is going on, and I can tell that she knows it too.

'We should go inside,' I say and then I can't help laughing because of course we should go inside, it's mad standing on the doorstep and it's me that's blocking the way.

'Thank you,' we both say at the same time.

I wish that I could hug her.

CHAPTER SIX

Meg

Monday, 25 February

I'm not particularly perceptive, but I could see why Daphne took off. I knew it wasn't about the milk. A person didn't need to be deep or psychic or anything to get that she was scared. There's nothing to be ashamed of in that, I would have liked to tell her. I would have gone myself if it wasn't my house, and I thought about it even though it was. I was glad when she came back. I trusted them, both of the women. You're too trusting, Henry used to say. He had a nerve, because he was one of the people I trusted that I shouldn't have, when all is said and done. I hope he understood that in the end.

Maybe this time things will be different, I thought. More straightforward. I think I can trust these women. So I thought and I hoped that Daphne would be back and she was, and there we all were, sitting round the table, looking at each other like someone was supposed to take the lead, come up with a plan.

'Maybe we're overreacting,' I said. 'Has anyone thought of that? Is it really as bad as we think?'

I don't know why I said it. I think I was hoping everything

would be OK, that nothing bad would happen. I suppose I'd had enough difficulty recently, what with Henry passing and all that entailed, but still, it was a stupid thing to say. I knew as soon as I said it that it was the wrong thing.

Nina looked at me as though I had slapped her and I was sorry I'd spoken. Henry used to say that I opened my mouth and put my foot in it, which he thought was very funny. I've got to hand it to him, he was right in a way. I do say the wrong things at the wrong time.

'I don't think Meg means that she doesn't believe you,' Grace said.

I nodded like mad. 'Oh I do,' I said, 'I do believe you, sorry, I didn't mean...'

I tailed off. I was glad when Grace spoke again.

'I think we need to know,' she said. 'I mean, just a rough outline, we don't need chapter and verse, but it would be helpful to know what we're dealing with.'

Daphne nodded and I felt even worse that they were so sensible when all I could do was nod and say stupid things. Of course we needed to know what we were dealing with. I felt left out.

'Yes,' I said, as if I had been thinking the same as them all along.

'Oh,' Nina said, 'oh, it's difficult.'

'He's a bad man,' Daphne said. 'I think we can all see that.'

We all nodded like those dogs they used to put in the back windows of cars in the sixties.

'You don't have to tell us anything you don't want to,' Grace said, 'but how can a woman know how to fight if she doesn't know who she's fighting?'

The way she said it made it sound like an old proverb, and I told myself to remember it. Think about it later. Think about all of it later, especially what it was like to be in my house with three other people, all looking to me to say something.

'Why was he after you?' I said.

Grace and Daphne both looked surprised. I suppose they thought that I should have asked the question in a more roundabout way, but I was thinking back to when Henry used to ask me things. He'd ask me where I had been, what I had been doing, that sort of thing, but he never did it directly. Have you had a lovely afternoon, he might say, and more often than not I'd be caught out, and I'd say yes, thank you it was good, and it wasn't really what he meant at all so it was the wrong answer. So I prefer to ask direct questions when I can.

Nina bit her thumbnail. It was so bitten already that I couldn't see how she could get any purchase on it but she did, with a gnawing sound that turned my stomach.

'It's difficult to explain,' she said. 'He thinks I owe him something.'

We all waited. I don't know if the others were thinking it would be better for her to say it in her own time but I thought we ought to keep going so I jumped in again.

'Do you mean money?' I said. 'Is it money you owe him?'

I thought for a moment.

'Sorry if that's a stupid question,' I said.

'Hey,' Grace said, 'there's no such thing as a stupid question.'

You should have met Henry, I thought, then you might think differently. Daphne looked as though she was thinking something similar. Perhaps she had a Henry in her past too.

'Not just money,' Nina said, 'more like my soul, really. You know, the me of me.'

That shut me up. The me of me. I'd never thought of it like that but of course, it was exactly what Henry had wanted from me. The thing inside me that made me who I was.

'Nothing changes,' I said.

Nina looked confused at that but Daphne nodded and said, 'True.'

'I'm guessing he's not your boyfriend,' Grace said.

Nina looked like those people do on that TV show when they're asked to eat something disgusting, a slug or the toenail of a sloth.

'Ew, no,' she said, 'he's like, really old.' She blushed then and it was clear that she had realised that old might not be the correct term of abuse when confronted with three senior citizens.

'I didn't mean...' she said, 'I was only saying...'

She stumbled to a halt and we all started laughing. The relief from tension was so clear you could have cut it out and framed it.

'It's OK,' Daphne said, 'we think he's disgusting too. And we're old, much older than him. We have dignity on our side, though, don't we, ladies?'

'Dignity,' said Nina as if it was a new concept. 'I like that. That's what I want to be like. My friend, the one who's ill, she's dignified.'

'Speaking for me,' Grace said, 'I think you've got one hell of a lot of dignity, and you did great to get away. Good job. So tell us a bit more if you want to, and if not, leave it for another time. I think that's right, don't you, ladies?'

Daphne and I nodded. I wanted to know, of course I did, I wanted to know what I'd got myself into, but I could see that Nina had almost had enough.

'Would you like a rest?' I asked.

Nina looked scared, as if I'd said something menacing.

'Hey,' Daphne said, 'I think we've got a few ground rules to sort out first. Number one, you're safe with us. We will make sure of that. Number two, no one is going to ask you to do anything you don't want to do. Any ideas for number three?'

I'm not usually good at coming up with ideas but something popped into my head. I think it might have been from a film I saw.

'What happens between us stays between us,' I said.

I could see that all three of them were surprised that I had come up with that.

'That's a good rule,' Grace said. 'I think we're going to be glad that we said that. What happens in Meg's kitchen stays in Meg's kitchen. Or wherever we might be.'

'OK, it's about money,' Nina said. 'I mean, there's money in the mix. He says I owe him money, but it's more than that. He thinks he's all I've got, and he is, I mean he's not wrong on that one, but it's all messed up.'

I could see that she was going to cry in a minute so I looked at the other two to see what they thought we should do. I had the most overwhelming urge to put Nina to bed, make hot chocolate for her and tell her a bedtime story with nothing scary in it.

I've learnt not to act on my impulses over the years. Meg, Henry would say, Meg, if we all acted on the first thought that came into our heads, the world would be in utter chaos. He used to tap the side of his head. Use this, that's what we have to do, Meg, use the old noggin. I didn't say anything when he said stuff like that. Henry wasn't the kind of man who welcomed a discussion about things.

'Would anyone like some tea?' I said.

I hoped that I had enough tea bags.

'Thanks, Meg,' said Nina.

I looked at the others. I think we all realised that it would be better not to push Nina any more. She'd had enough for one day. I was worried though. It was getting dark, and there was a man around who was bad, if not more than bad, and we had to decide what we were going to do about Nina. It was almost more than I could cope with.

'So I'm going to go out,' Grace said, 'and get some good old junk food for us. Fish and chips, I'm thinking, halloumi burgers for the non fish. OK?'

Nina didn't look thrilled. Of course, I thought, young people don't necessarily feel excited by food in the same way that us old ones do.

When Henry and I were first married, he'd drawn up a nutrition chart for both of us. How many calories we were allowed to have, what food groups they should come from, that kind of thing. I remember the milk – it was in the days before skimmed milk was widely available and so we used powdered for me, half a pint made up every day. I hated that milk. I used to pinch a bit from Henry's allowance for my cup of tea whenever he wasn't looking, because he had the regular milk. Perhaps someone has drawn up a nutrition chart or something like that for Nina, I thought, maybe that's why she's worried about eating.

'If you're not hungry, that's fine,' I said.

Daphne and Grace sent me questioning looks. I knew they wanted to feed her, give her some strength, but you have to make a choice sometimes, I thought. Mental health or physical, they're both tied in to each other.

'Maybe just some chocolate,' I said.

Nina laughed, and the tension that had been building up seemed to drain away.

'Meg,' she said, 'you're so bad, that is such bad advice. But thank you, thank you all of you. I know you didn't plan for me, and I can't tell you how lucky I feel that you've all been so lovely. Of course I'll eat your fish and chips, Grace, only just the chips if that's OK.'

We talked about all sorts of things that evening. TV programmes, films, books, mostly just the three of us old codgers chatting, and Nina listening sometimes and falling asleep sometimes. It was cosy in parts, comfortable. We were kind to each other. I kept stretching out my legs and wiggling my toes, that's how relaxed I felt.

Finally, when it was clear that Nina was properly asleep, Grace said, 'We have got ourselves a situation here, my friends.'

I loved the way she talked. I loved it that she said 'my friends'. I wished I had made friends earlier in my life.

'I know,' Daphne said. 'I've got so many questions that my head is bursting.'

'Oh, me too,' I said, although it absolutely wasn't true. I'd been so busy enjoying the company, and watching Nina uncoil herself like a snake in the sun, that I'd kind of lost sight of the bigger picture, although I didn't want them to know that. I felt embarrassed that I had been so easily distracted.

'I've got two spare bedrooms,' I said. 'You can all stay if

you like. There's two beds in one of the rooms, and there's the sofa in here as well.'

I had had no idea that I was going to say that until I heard myself speak the words. I felt anxious. Of course they wouldn't want to stay in my house. It wasn't very welcoming. No pictures on the walls, everything painted grey, or other colours that had been there for so long they looked like grey anyway.

'I'm only round the corner,' Daphne said, 'but I'll definitely stay if you want me to. I'm not sure – what do you think, Grace?'

'I don't know,' said Grace. 'Meg, what do you think? Would you like one or both of us to stay? Would you feel safer?'

I don't know, I thought. Or rather, I did know, and I did wish that one of them would stay, but there were a couple of problems. One, I wasn't sure whether they meant it, whether they really wanted to stay, or whether they were just saying it because they thought I was so hopeless that I couldn't manage. And two, if they did mean it, was that because they thought I was so hopeless? And, on top of both of those, were my spare bedrooms clean enough? Would they be disgusted by the state of them? Or would they feel sorry for me for having such a dingy house?

'Thanks,' I said, 'I'm fine.'

Pull yourself together, I thought. At least I'd get some more time alone with that dear girl, even if it was only when she was sleeping. I'd be in charge for once.

'If you're sure,' Grace said, 'and don't forget, you can always call us back. I'm thinking we should just check that all the doors and windows are locked, you know, while we're still here. I'm probably being stupid but it's good to be sure when you're messing with people like that.'

People like what? I thought. We don't even know anything about him yet. Except I did know. I did know something – I knew that he was out of tune, out of step. I knew that he was the one to watch out for. I'd heard the violin screeching behind him.

'It's all locked,' I said. 'I live on my own so that's one thing I'm very sure of. My late husband talked a lot about security, you don't need to worry at all.'

He did, I thought, but he didn't always act on things he thought. He was really rather trusting.

They fiddled with their bags, the two of them, getting ready to go and putting on coats and all done with such quiet intent, looking at the sleeping Nina as if she was a precious baby that we had all given birth to together. That's what I thought, anyway. They may have thought something else entirely. They were nearly ready when Nina started crying. It was weird, she was crying in her sleep and pushing at something only she could see.

'Get off,' she said, 'get off, no,' and she pulled her knees up towards her chest as if she was trying to get into a foetal position.

I went to her straight away, and smoothed the hair back from her head.

'It's OK,' I said in the kind of voice I might have used to a baby, 'it's OK.'

She sat up, bolt upright but still asleep, I think, and she gave me a push that knocked me into the other two and somehow we all half fell backwards and Grace lost her footing altogether and sat down hard in the chair she had recently vacated and we were all huffing and puffing and trying to do everything

62

quietly in case Nina hadn't woken. She had. She rubbed her eyes like a child in a cartoon.

'Sorry,' she said. 'Did I? Was I? Are you OK?'

'What were you dreaming?' Grace said. 'Is there more you can tell us now, so that we can help you?'

I suddenly remembered a dream I had had when I was first married. I don't dream often, so I remember the ones I have. And this one was a corker, a real X-certificate movie of a dream complete with howling monsters and tasks that were impossible to complete. Couldn't bring all of it to mind and I didn't want to, but I remembered this – Henry asking me if I was OK and telling me I was safe there with him and all that stuff, the same kind of things that we were saying to Nina now. I had pushed him away, still in the grip of my dream reality. Pushed him away and shouted, 'It's you, it's you, you're the monster,' or something like that. I could hear the out-of-tune violin then and I heard it when Nina was dreaming too. I heard it even through all the fussing and apologising and brushing down of coats and checking of pockets. All the things that people do when they're not sure what to do.

'Are you staying with me?' Nina said to me.

She was looking straight at me as if it was the most important thing in the world. I didn't think anyone had ever looked at me like that. I nodded.

'We can stay too if that would make either of you feel better,' Grace said.

'Oh yes,' Daphne said, 'it's no trouble.'

Nina gave me a little smile, as if we were co-conspirators in a plot of some kind.

'No it's OK, you can get off home,' I said.

I couldn't have been more proud, even though two minutes before I had been unsure, even though I could hear that damned violin. One long, drawn-out note after another, getting higher until they swept down again in a trill like a bird. An out-of-tune bird, a bird who was maybe dying or at least planning to kill another bird. I ignored it.

'We'll be OK, me and Nina. I think she needs to go up to bed, get a good night's sleep. It'll all be easier in the morning.'

It wouldn't, I was pretty sure of that, but I could see the tiredness in her eyes. She was much too young to be that tired. That kind of tired was for old women like us, or people with diseases they're fighting all the time. That's the kind of tired she was. I could see that the others found it difficult to leave, but I was sure by then that I was doing the right thing so I resisted the urge to ask them to stay.

I held her arm to steady her as we went up the stairs after the others had gone. I'd exchanged numbers with the other two and promised to check in if I needed them. I made some green tea for Nina and sat on the edge of her bed as she drank it.

'I don't know why you and your friends have been so nice,' she said. 'I'm really grateful. You don't have to help, you know, I'd be fine without you.'

'There's a bit of trouble in every life,' I said, 'and when you get older you can see that, and see the trouble that other people are having, and it makes you want to help. I think that's it.'

She looked disbelieving.

'Whatever,' she said.

I'm sure she thought that old people must have somehow always been old, it's a thing most young people think. We won't be like that, they think, we'll be different, we'll stay slim and

64

healthy and we'll still be interested in the same things. No you won't, us old people could say; no you won't, everything will change. What would be the point in that? They never believe us. It's like keeping the faith about Father Christmas, we let them think they're different because it reminds us of when we thought we were different.

'Go to sleep,' I said, 'we can talk more in the morning. You're welcome here.'

CHAPTER SEVEN

Nina

March – eleven months earlier

Nina had seen Shaz a couple of times since her birthday. She still had niggling doubts, still wondered why Shaz would want to hang out with her, why someone like Shaz would choose a girl from a children's home who liked going to the library as a friend. Nina was flattered, though, and that was a feeling she wasn't used to. She was pleased, in a way, to have been chosen. Nina knew that it might not last but it made everything better to know that someone thought she was worth something.

'I don't know why you're so jolly,' Sue said. 'You're like a different Nina these days.'

'Not different,' Bilbo said, immediately anxious. 'Not different, no something different. Nina is, Nina is what? What is Nina?'

'I'm the same, Bilbo, I'm still me, don't worry.'

'Yes, Nina, same Nina, Nina is, Nina is what?'

Bilbo patted Nina's head to reassure himself, muttering, 'Same, same, same,' with every pat.

'Nina is the same,' said Sue. 'That's taught me a lesson,

Nina, don't worry, I'll never say you're different again in front of this young man.'

Nina and Sue laughed together and Nina thought that the home wasn't so bad after all. It was so much better when there was other stuff to look forward to. Friends to meet, places to go to. She might even be able to persuade Shaz to go on the protest march against the immigration laws, she thought. It would be good to go with someone else.

She met Shaz in front of the library after dinner.

'Here,' Shaz said, 'I've got some clothes for you.'

She held out a carrier bag and Nina took it and looked inside.

'What the actual fuck?' she said. 'I mean, there's some really good stuff in here and,' she pulled out a sparkly top, 'some of them still have the price tags, they're new.'

Shaz shrugged her shoulders.

'It's just stuff,' she said. 'Thought you might like it. We can't keep going out with you dressed like a nerd, it's going to ruin my street cred.'

Nina laughed.

'Thank you, thank you,' she said, 'it's all lovely, but I've got to say, I don't look too bad, do I? I mean, jeans and a jumper with an XR patch, what's not to like?'

Nina paraded up and down the street briefly, like a catwalk model. Shaz didn't smile.

'What's the matter?' Nina said. 'You look as miserable as hell. I was just messing around. Here, you keep it. But thanks, it was a really lovely thought.'

She held out the carrier bag.

'Oh for fuck's sake,' Shaz said, 'stop going on about it. It's just stuff, that's all. I nicked it if you must know, no skin off my nose or anywhere else. It's just like, do you have to be so pleased?'

Nina was stung. She felt really stupid. Typical kids' home kid, she thought, going overboard about a bag of cheap clothes.

'OK, OK,' she said, trying to use the same sort of nonchalant tone as Shaz. 'I was just saying, that's all.'

'Hey,' said Shaz, 'let's get you dressed up.'

She sounded enthusiastic again, excited even. Nina wondered how on earth she was supposed to know the right tone to use. One minute Shaz was up, dancing around and full of excitement, and the next she carried Nina along on a wave of misery. It was hard to follow.

'In here,' Shaz said, pointing to the McDonald's they were passing. 'Go on, you go in the toilets and get changed, and then I can take a picture of you.'

Nina McDonald had never managed to tell Shaz how miserable McDonald's made her feel.

'A picture?' Nina said. 'Shaz, why would you want a picture of me?'

Nina wished that she knew what normal friendship behaviour was. Perhaps this was the kind of thing people did all the time, give each other bags of clothes and then take pictures. It was probably just her, the odd one out again, the one who didn't know how to behave. She locked the door of the tiny, smelly toilet and looked inside the bag.

There had to be some kind of mistake. She couldn't put these clothes on. The sparkly top, yes. It was shimmery and lovely, tight fitting with elbow-length sleeves. The shorts though. The shorts made Nina laugh out loud. They were denim cut-offs but cut so high that more than her legs would be on show. They were ridiculous, and there was no way she could wear them, no way she could walk around with her bottom hanging out. Nina thought that she would explain, say it in a kind way so that Shaz didn't feel stupid. She put the top on anyway, amazed at how it clung to her like a second skin. The tiny thong-style knickers at the bottom of the bag were funny too. Imagine the staff at the home finding them in the wash, she thought, giggling. The bra was unlike any bra Nina had ever seen, let alone worn. She didn't think it would fit at all.

The last thing in the bag was the shoes. Nina held one in her hand and looked at it. It was like a shoe from a film, a shoe from a world where a taxi might be waiting outside to take a person to the next exciting place. This was a shoe Nina couldn't help wanting. A red shoe, a shoe with a high, slender heel and a little ankle strap. She slipped it on, amazed to find that it was exactly the right size.

That will have to be it, she thought. Shaz will have to be content that I'm wearing two of the things. She stuck her grubby trainers into the bag with her shirt and jumper and walked out of the toilets. She had to walk slowly because the heels were nearly impossible to walk in. It was like wearing stilts, and she resisted an urge to hold her arms out to both sides like a tightrope walker. She looked over to where Shaz was waiting at a table, hoping to catch her eye and smile, but Shaz was deep in conversation with an odd-looking man. He had a big head and hardly any neck, so from where Nina was he looked exactly like a toad. Shaz seemed to be holding herself stiffly, bending the top half of her body as far back as she could without taking a step. Nina's first thought was that he was dangerous, and that she should help Shaz, but something held her back. Shaz looked scared, that was what held Nina back. If Nina jumped in to help, she could make things worse. Plus, and she knew this was a terrible, cowardly thought, if Shaz was scared then the man must be terrifying. Shaz didn't care about anything, Nina knew she wouldn't be easily frightened. They appeared to be arguing about something, Nina could see Shaz gesticulating and at one point the toad man wagged his finger in Shaz's face. In a minute, Nina thought, in a minute I'll go over. Or, she looked round the restaurant, or maybe tell someone, get some help.

Nina hung back, looking at advertisements on a noticeboard. She looked over at Shaz and the man as often as she could without being spotted. Would Shaz welcome an interruption? Would a friend do that? Nina wished that she wasn't wearing the stupid shoes. Every time she looked, Nina became more and more aware that there was something about the man she really did not like the look of. He made her feel shivery, and she remembered the signs of foreboding they had talked about in her Shakespeare class. Clouds, falling leaves, climate change, the setting sun – none of them were present in McDonald's on a noisy evening in early spring. Instead, Nina could see squabbling children, tired mums and the odd courting couple. The feeling she got was foreboding, though; foreboding in great big bucket loads.

She was half reading an advertisement for a room in a shared house when Shaz tapped her on the shoulder. There was no sign of the man.

'What the fuck?' Shaz said. 'I thought you were going to

come back wearing the clothes? You've been ages, I didn't know where you were.'

Nina had never heard Shaz speak so angrily before. Anger and something else – fear, Nina thought. Yes, Shaz was still scared.

'I'm sorry,' Nina said. 'Are you OK? I was going to come over, when you were speaking to that guy, but I wasn't sure—'

'Keep your fucking nose out,' Shaz said. 'Nothing to fucking do with you. And you're not even wearing the stuff I gave you. Look at you. You've kept your jeans on and the shoes look like you're playing at dressing up with your mum's clothes.'

Shaz stared at Nina as if she hated her. Nina was confused. She didn't understand how things had escalated so quickly.

'I'm sorry,' Nina said, 'I kept thinking I should come and help you, with that man, whoever he was, and I should have only I didn't know if—'

'For fuck's sake, what man? THERE WAS NO MAN, YOU STUPID BITCH.'

Nina recoiled. What was she doing here? she thought. With this angry, frightened, furious girl? Shaz bit her lip until Nina could see blood.

'That is so not fair,' she said. 'I'm sorry I didn't help. And I'm grateful, honestly I am, but the shorts, they're too, you know, you'd be able to see my bum and everything. And the bra, it's not the right size. And those knickers,' Nina lowered her voice, 'Shaz, they're ridiculous. They look really uncomfortable too, and I'd never get away with wearing them at the home. But thanks anyway, it was a lovely present and I'm sorry to be an ungrateful bitch.'

Shaz took a couple of deep breaths in an exaggerated way.

She stepped back and sat on one of the brightly coloured chairs. Nina could see that she was trying to calm down.

'Are you for real? I literally do not know what to do with you. Are you actually from this planet? Did you just talk about putting a thong like that in the wash in a children's home? Oh please.' Shaz put her head on the table and groaned.

'Shaz,' Nina said, 'what, I mean, be careful, there's some sauce on that table. You don't want to get that on your top, it'll never come out.'

'Sit down,' Shaz said, patting the chair next to her.

Nina sat. The chairs were bolted to the floor at a short distance from the table, and Nina found it tricky in her high heels.

'You really don't know anything, do you?'

Shaz looked miserable in a way Nina hadn't seen before. She had seen irritated, angry, scared, grouchy and minimally happy, that was all. This kind of miserable made Nina feel unhappy. It reminded her of her mum.

'I mean, I could maybe try them on again, I honestly didn't mean to upset you,' Nina said.

She reached out to pat Shaz's arm but Shaz pulled away quickly.

'Sorry,' Nina said. She wondered what on earth she was supposed to do now. She tried to think of friendship rifts she had observed in the classroom but they seemed different when they belonged to other people. Smaller, although she knew how quickly they could escalate. Nina had watched several small arguments grow into huge ones, ones where people cried and screamed and stopped speaking to each other. The time that Ella, the red-haired girl in the school in Coventry, had thought that one of the other girls had taken her phone charger. Everyone knew she hadn't, and the phone charger was found eventually, but by then both girls had been so angry and upset that when Nina left the school five months later they still couldn't pass each other in the corridor without a shove. She didn't want that to happen to her and Shaz. Nina could see how vulnerable and volatile Shaz was.

'I truly didn't mean to upset you,' she said. 'I hope we can still be friends. Look, give me the bag again, I'll go and try them on properly.'

Shaz held the bag of clothes in a firm grip.

'Do you want to know what you should do?' Shaz said. 'You should go home, go home now. If you trust me at all, that's what you should do. Here,' she gave Nina her jumper and her trainers, 'here put these back on and give me the shoes. Keep the top if you like. Go back to the fucking library. I don't need you, honest, and you don't need me either.'

All the times that Nina had sat in a classroom, watching other people have friends while she was ignored, all the lonely evenings in her room with Bilbo listening to music, all the Saturdays when she had gone to markets, round art galleries, anything to stave off the loneliness, all of it flashed through Nina's head. She tried to tell herself that it didn't matter, that Shaz was an odd one anyway and that they didn't have anything in common. That the anticipation was better than the actual meetings, that she should really be studying for her exams, that she didn't need friends, but none of it worked. Nina had loved having someone to meet, somewhere to go to apart from the library. She couldn't bear the idea of it coming to an end, of being on her own again.

'I'm sorry, Shaz,' she said. 'I've been a rubbish friend, I should have helped, I should have worn the clothes, I didn't realise you'd be so upset. Honestly, I really am, I'm sorry, you've been good to me.'

Nina knew that what she should do to please Shaz was to wrestle the bag from her, take the stupid clothes to the toilet and put them on, but she couldn't bring herself to, even now.

'Aw, Nina,' Shaz said, 'you're an odd one. Just go, can't you? Take my word for it, you'd be better off without me.'

Nina wasn't sure, but she thought she heard a break in Shaz's voice. She wished that she knew what to do. Shaz stood up and turned towards the door, and Nina couldn't believe that their friendship was over. Not over a bag of clothes, she thought, it must be something more than that. It must have something to do with the man, the man who really had been there, despite what Shaz had said.

'Shaz,' she said. She knew that what she said next would be important, and that she could easily make things worse.

'Shaz, don't be like that. Come on, we're here now, aren't you hungry? You told me you were always hungry, I don't believe you're not. Let's just have a veggie burger and a cheeseburger like we usually do. Stop getting all stupid and emotional and stuff.'

'Ha,' said Shaz, 'I'm not emotional, thank you very much. I was trying to offer you some advice, like go home now or you're going to regret it. Does that make it clearer?'

It didn't. Nothing was clear to Nina and she was torn. On the one hand, she would like nothing more than to go home. That man had looked scary and things were getting too weird here. On the other hand, she felt like a complete failure.

Something had clearly happened to frighten and upset Shaz, and Nina had been a rubbish friend. Friendships seemed to be so easy for other people, everyone had them. Even Bilbo had a best friend at the special school he went to. His name was Craig but Bilbo called him Best, and he talked about him all the time. Nina couldn't understand why there was no Best for her, why there had never been a Best.

'I'd rather stay with you,' she said. 'It's boring at home.'

Shaz looked at Nina with a very serious face. She looked different, Nina thought. No longer the gum-chewing, slightly bored face she usually wore.

'This isn't something I usually do,' Shaz said, 'and I don't really know why I'm doing it now. Fuck off, Nina, fuck off back to the residential care home. I'm saying it for your own good. There's nothing for you here, nothing for you in this kind of place.' Shaz gestured around the McDonald's. 'You're a nice girl, but we're never going to be friends. You've been had, mate, had good and proper, and if you listen to me, really listen, you'll know that I mean it. I'm not kidding. Just go.'

Nina felt as if she was on a ride at a theme park, one of the ones that hurled a person into the air and then swooped them down, churning their stomach. She stood still, clutching her jumper and trainers and trying to think what to say. There really wasn't anything. She reached down and pulled off the red shoes.

'Here,' she said, holding them out to Shaz, 'take them, I can't walk in them anyway. I'll go and take off the top. Can't do it here, I might get arrested.'

Nina managed to smile as if nothing mattered, as if she couldn't care less. Her hands were shaking in the toilet cubicle as she removed the sparkly top and shrugged back into her old jumper. It felt familiar and comforting. Nina wished she could say hello to it like Bilbo did with his clothes sometimes when he was getting dressed. I'm a bona fide nutcase, she thought, and I'm rubbish at being friends. I'll make my own way.

She hardly looked at Shaz as she gave her the top but even so she could tell that Shaz looked tearful. Serves you bloody right, she thought. Karma. What goes around comes around, and I hope someone is mean to you some time so you know what it feels like. The trouble was, Nina didn't really mean it and Shaz looked as if she did know what it felt like anyway.

Nina thought about that when she was back in her own room. Shaz had looked so sad as Nina had left, as if something more had happened than two young people falling out. Nina thought about the friendship break-ups she had viewed from her desk in various places. It didn't fit. Girls had looked angry or relieved or hysterical, but never, that she could remember, had they looked as tearful as Shaz had. Plain sad. It's not my concern, she thought, she's made that clear.

Bilbo knocked at her door.

'Bilbo is not, Bilbo is not, what is Bilbo not?' he asked from the other side of the door.

Nina opened it and he leapt in. He held out a picture he had made at school.

'Bilbo is not barging,' he answered himself. 'Not barging, Bilbo is not barging in. Bilbo is,' he ran outside and knocked again, 'Bilbo is knocking. Knocking. Well done, Bilbo. Good boy.'

Nina laughed even though she didn't want to.

'Bilbo, you're a star,' she said without thinking. She then

spent twenty minutes reassuring Bilbo that he wasn't a star, he wasn't in the sky, and repeating, no twinkle-twinkle.

Nina didn't get a chance to think about what had happened until she was in bed. She usually read before she went to sleep, but tonight *To Kill a Mockingbird* didn't work its usual magic. The words seemed to blur into each other as Nina remembered Shaz's face, and how miserable she had looked. There was something else too, something Nina couldn't quite put her finger on, something worrying. Something wrong. Nina was almost asleep before she thought of what it was. The man. The man with the toad neck. The man who had been speaking to Shaz earlier, while Nina was in the toilet. He was there, outside McDonald's when Nina left in a blur of sadness. He was outside and he had looked as mad as hell.

CHAPTER EIGHT

Grace

Monday, 25 February

I'm not sure whether I should have left them, that poor girl and the white woman. I knew the girl was in trouble as soon as she came in the door. I can smell trouble, even after all these years. There's a tang to it, something like seaweed after high tide, mixed with pain. I was always called fanciful when I was a girl in Jamaica and even though that girl is far away now, people don't change. Not the inside of them, not the important part. The me of me, Nina called it. The soul of a person, that's what some folk name it but I don't know, that sounds too much like there's a higher power involved. All that God stuff, all the stuff I used to believe in before I came here. Before these kind people explained to me about God being just another white man.

I could always smell trouble. At first I thought it was something I'd left behind, and that maybe trouble smelled different in this cold country. For twenty-five years I thought that. Even when my daughter died and it seemed like the whole world around me was collapsing like a black hole.

Whatever trouble came to my door I couldn't smell it so I thought it was gone, my special power. Twelfth of January 1989, I knew better. I could smell it when I woke up that morning. I sniffed my clothes before I put them on, that's how strong the smell was. I was like a tracker dog that day, hunting through the classrooms with my nose until I found him. In a class I was teaching. Dean Smith, a boy who sat at the back of my year eleven English Lit class and didn't cause any trouble. I'm not saying he was a good student, he wasn't, but there weren't many who were in that class. A couple of girls who tried hard and about half the class were on course to get their GCSEs with a pass grade but Dean wasn't one of them. I looked at his records afterwards, they all did, and he had given in a few pieces of homework in the autumn term, not particularly good grades but better than some of the kids in that class.

There was one piece of homework he did on *To Kill A Mockingbird*, a newspaper report. The kids in his class had to pretend to be reporters, and write for the local paper about the trial. Present the facts clearly, that sort of thing. He did well in that, something sparked his imagination and he got a good mark. That often happens with the boys, they can do what they think of as proper writing, newspaper reports and so on, but they're not so good at what they see as the girlie stuff. Stories, creative writing, poetry. Anything with emotion in it.

So I looked at him that morning and there was something I didn't like, something I couldn't make sense of. He kept blinking. I could see that he was trying not to cry. I hate to see anyone try not to cry. It takes me straight back to Eleanor. My darling Eleanor rubbing her knuckles into her eyes and then wiping them on her dress. So I looked at Dean that morning, my heart already heavy with the familiar thought of my girl, and he suddenly looked more like six than sixteen.

'Is everything OK?' I said to him.

You have to be careful with the lads in that age group. They're like half-grown puppies, they can turn bad on you if they think they're cornered. So I didn't ask him until most of the others had left the room, and he was packing his big shoulder bag up. It looked full enough for a three-week mountain trek.

'What?' he said.

He looked at me as if he hated me, as if I was the most loathsome thing he had ever seen crawling on the floor. It was a look that made me flinch. Black people get used to those kind of looks. They get used to them but for me, at least, I think it's fair to say that I never expect them. Not now and not then. Who could expect a look like that? I always get taken by surprise. OK, I thought then, OK, Dean, we'll play it your way, suit yourself. I went over to my desk to pick up my books and the register. I was trying to stop worrying about him, I remember that clearly. It had annoyed me, it had hurt my feelings to see him look at me like that so I tried to switch off any concern I felt. I tried to think about the cup of tea I was going to make in the staffroom with the other teachers, and what I was going to watch on the TV that night. I didn't realise for a moment or two that everyone else had gone, and that there was just Dean and me in the room.

'Come on,' I said, 'what's your next lesson? You'll be late.'

I looked at him again. I didn't want to because there was such a high chance of another upsetting look from him, but all the emotion seemed to have been wiped off.

'I can't,' he said.

I didn't even ask him what it was he couldn't do.

'Of course you can,' I said.

I'm sure I didn't use an unkind voice. Maybe a little abrupt but nothing unpleasant, I'm sure of that.

'Come along now.'

That stock teacher phrase.

He pushed the desk away and stood up. There were tears in his eyes, I was sure of it. Real tears. He ran out of the room before I could think of what to say next. Here's the strange thing, though, that smell of trouble, that seaweed and steam or whatever it was, that smell got stronger for a moment. As if my nose was the only part of me that was working properly, the only organ that knew what trouble was.

I've smelled it since, never quite so strongly, but I smell it sometimes and when I do I stay indoors. Feels like a warning to me or to someone else that there's trouble on its way and I'm old enough to want to keep out of the way of any trouble. I've seen enough of it. But there was something about Nina this morning. I'm not saying she looked like Dean Smith because she didn't, but she had a look that worried me. She had a look that said, I can't, and I could see she was at the end of her tether, the very end. And I wanted to get involved, I wanted to jump right in there and get my hands dirty so I did, and nobody made me. I made myself. So I can't blame the other women, that lovely frightened Daphne with the clothes that make her look like she lives on the street, or the dizzy one who's frightened of her own shadow and everyone else's. I got my own self involved and I'm going to see it through. There's something bad, and that usually means someone is behind it, and I think that someone must be toad man. The man who came into the café, for all the world like a no-neck toad up to no good.

I'm thinking about him tonight and I'm thinking about Dean too, and what I should have done then that I didn't and what it means to have a second chance.

'What would you do,' a friend said to me once, 'if you had a time machine, and you could go back and change history? Where would you go?'

It was hard to know where to start. Hitler, that's the easy one, that's the one everyone thinks of and I'm not saying he wouldn't be a good choice. But it's so much more complicated than that. Maybe that guy who thought he was discovering America when it already belonged to a whole other group of folks. Maybe the first person who decided that they could own another person and make them do the work they didn't want to do, just because their skin was a different colour. History is full of stupid men who should have stayed home and read a book, kept themselves from troubling anyone else. Hundreds, thousands, millions of them.

If they asked me now, though, I'd have an answer. I'd say the day I left my daughter in Jamaica. I'd bring her with me to England and even if it made no difference, if she still died of some stupid childhood disease, at least she would be with me when it happened. And if I could have two turns, I'd say 12 January 1989, as well. I've been thinking about that a lot. I wouldn't kill Dean Smith, not straight away. No, I'd sit down with him and talk to him. I'd ask him why he wanted to do what he did, what it was that had made him that way. I'd ask him and then if the answers weren't right, if he didn't explain to my complete satisfaction what he was thinking and why, if he wouldn't listen when I explained why he couldn't, then I'd wring his scrawny neck. It might not make the world a better place for everyone, but it would certainly improve things for at least three families.

Toad man, though, no sitting down and talking for him. No point. He is surely a level of bad I haven't seen in some time, and I do not want to sit down and talk to him, try to help him through his troubles. No thank you. If that needs to be done then I am not the woman for it.

Toad man. He's out there somewhere, doing what he does, hurting who he can. I can't help looking around my flat as if he might come knocking on the door any time. What would I defend myself with? One of the hundreds of books I should have got rid of by now? There isn't much else in the living room. Just floor-to-ceiling books, and more piled up on the coffee table and in the corners. I can't believe how many books there are. It's a long time since I looked around me. It's not much of a place for a person who has lived for seventy-five years, not much to show for a life except reading. No photographs, no ornaments. I reckon all the pictures I need are in my head. I chose a quiet life. An empty life, some might say.

I walk up and down a bit, picking things up and putting them down, opening a book here and there, looking for a clue. I'm not sure that I should have left them, that's the rub. Meg and Nina. I'm not sure I should have left her to look after that little girl. I check my phone again, to see if they've called me. Don't be stupid, I think, don't suppose that the world revolves around you. Even while I'm thinking it, I'm putting on my boots, tying my scarf around my neck and zipping up my padded coat. I'm not sure if they need any help, I'm not even sure if they're still awake, but I have to go. They might have gone to bed by now. I need to check, that's all. I need to check that everything is OK. I had a chance before to change things, make things better. Twice. Twice I could have altered history, twice I took the easy option. That's not going to happen any more.

The lift isn't working so I walk down the stairs and it's funny, I can hear Eleanor all the way down. Go on, she says, go on, check it out. She sounds more grown up than I remember her, and her accent has become British. Cockney, even. Eleanor would have loved London. I used to collect things that we could do together, when I was first here. Tower of London, St Paul's, all the tourist stuff. I used to write her letters about them, with little sketches, always with her in them. *Here you are by Buckingham Palace,* I wrote. *Maybe you'll live there one day.* I wonder now, of course, if the drawings and the descriptions made her sad. If she knew, in some way. If that was why she was such a quiet child, such a thoughtful one.

It's only a few minutes' walk from my flat to Meg's house. Funny that we've lived close all these years and not met. Funny how old age gives you the chance to stop and look around and think, yes, that's a person I might like to be friendly with. It's a last chance to change things and if you're not looking you might miss it. We haven't missed it, me and the old girls. We haven't missed it but we might blow it if we're not careful.

I'm almost at Meg's house when I see another person

hovering nearby. I've done my women's self-defence classes but the only bit that stuck was the part about how to hold the keys, so I'm gripping them tight, trying to make sure that there's a bit of metal sticking out between each finger. The person walks away, then walks back again, and as soon as she gets near enough to the streetlight I realise it's Daphne. No one else would wear a beautiful designer overcoat with a headscarf. Yup, a headscarf, like the Queen used to wear, tied under the chin and like no one ever, ever wears any more. But it suits her.

We acknowledge each other in an awkward kind of way.

'Hi,' I whisper, because now we're almost directly outside Meg's house.

There's one light on upstairs but it's early morning and I hope they're both asleep.

'Hi,' Daphne says, and I think for a moment she's going to hold her hand out for me to shake. 'I, erm, I couldn't sleep and I just thought I'd check, you know.'

'I do know,' I say. 'Same here.'

I'd like to hug her, this nice, quiet, odd woman. Or give one of those special handshakes with different parts that I've seen on American TV series. The ones where people jump up, turn around, clap, do little dances, and all in synch. I've never thought about them before but right now a secret handshake would fit exactly. We're in a club, me and Daphne, we're bound together and I wish I could affirm it in some way.

I hold my hand out anyway, but then I think better of it and withdraw it in case it's too weird but she's noticed, and she holds her hand out just after I've put mine back in

85

my pocket. It's OK though because we both laugh and that breaks the ice.

'Do you think we should knock?' Daphne says. She's really quiet, she almost breathes the words into my ear.

I'm not sure, so I make a pantomime of shrugging my shoulders and scratching my head.

'It seems quiet enough,' Daphne whispers, 'but I'm just not sure.'

'Me neither,' I say.

I am so close to her ear that I can smell her perfume. Understated and lovely. I've no idea what it is but it smells delicious. I'll tell her later, I think.

We look at each other in an embarrassed sort of way.

'Maybe I'll just do a walk past, every now and again,' she says. 'I don't sleep so much these days anyway.'

'Me neither,' I say. 'I think maybe I did all my sleeping when I was young and I've used up my quota.'

That isn't strictly true but the strict truth has never done anyone any good in social situations.

I'm left with this feeling of wanting to do something special, something to mark the fact that we're in this, whatever it is, together so I surprise myself. I put my hand on her arm, at the elbow, and I say, 'Shall we take a turn around the block together?'

She doesn't say anything at first and I think, oh, bloody hell, I've gone too far, she'll never trust me now, but then she laughs, and it's a quiet laugh but a genuine one.

'How funny and nice,' she says. 'I feel like I'm back at school.'

'I don't know what kind of school you went to,' I whisper

as we trundle off down the road, 'but my school back home never included walks while everyone else slept, or old women keeping the world safe by wandering the streets in the dead of night.'

That makes her laugh, so I'm glad we've moved away from Meg's house. She laughs a lot.

'Is that what we're doing?' she says. 'I never thought of it that way. I just, you know, sometimes it's not right to keep quiet, is it? Sometimes things have to be said, and people need to, need to...'

Daphne tails off as if she isn't sure of what these people might need to do. I wasn't sure either, so I said, 'They most certainly do,' as if she had made a suggestion.

It's dark so I can't see her reaction but I think she's grateful. We walk around the streets as though we're walking around a beautiful park in the summer. I tell her that's what I'm thinking. I want to hear her laugh again and it works, she laughs like there's nothing bad in the world, like there's nothing unusual about what we're doing. The night is still cold, and the trees are still gaunt and forbidding but she does this whole routine that takes my breath away. She's fluent, as if it's been scripted.

'See those white flowers,' she says, pointing towards a carrier bag that's got stuck in a spiky bush, 'what do you think they're called?'

'Hmm,' I say, 'I've got a book at home, I'll look them up later.'

'Can you smell them?' she says, and she stops and sniffs the air.

We're near to a kebab shop and it's closed now, but the

spicy fat smell still lingers. I can still smell that lovely perfume on her so I nod and say, 'We have a flower just like that in Jamaica.'

It's a different side of her. She unfurls, that's the word. Like watching a bud opening on a speeded-up camera. She seemed so worried this afternoon, so careful not to say anything, not to speak up for herself if she could help it. I'm thinking about that as she chats on about flowers and bushes, still pointing to rubbish and trees that might or might not be dead, and then I realise why. Under cover of dark, that's when she feels comfortable. What happened to you? I think. What happened to you, Miss Daphne with the strange flappy clothes, what made you feel so insecure that you can only come out of your shell in the dark? I give her arm a squeeze.

'They have such colours back home,' I say to her, 'colours you would never see here.'

I don't know what makes me say it. It's not like I usually talk about Jamaica as home, I don't even think about it that often. Here's home now, for all its shortcomings. But something about the night and the tiredness and the worry I know we're both feeling makes me invoke it like a mantra.

'In Australia too,' she says. 'Animals like cartoons and flowers like picture book illustrations.'

She sighs and I can feel a part of her energy, her spark, leave her. I am sure that if I refer to it she will be embarrassed or sad, and then she might clam up and I'd hate that. So I do the only thing I can think of to do. I take over. Gently, so that she doesn't feel put out, I start pointing to things like she was doing, letting her be quiet for a moment.

'Look at that,' I say, pointing to some tinsel that has wrapped itself round a lamp-post. 'It's trying to stretch Christmas out until spring. It looks sad somehow.'

'Poor tinsel,' she says. 'Shall we put it in the bin?'

It seems like a good idea so we let go of each other's arms for a moment and pull it off. She's dignified, as if she grew up pulling tinsel off lamp-posts and she knows the right way to do it. Just thinking that makes me laugh, so I giggle a bit and then she joins in and before we know it we're doing a silent guffaw that would wake the whole street if we let it out.

'Come on,' she says, and this time she takes my arm and we walk on back towards the house where they should be sleeping, nervous Meg and that sad, hurt little girl.

It's all quiet in the street. No one loitering, no strange cars going past. The light is still on in an upstairs room, Meg's bedroom, I think, but it looks like a softer light now. As if she's changed it from an overhead lamp to a bedside one.

'Do you think we should stay a little longer?' Daphne says.

'I'm not sure,' I say. 'I mean, we want to be ready to help and old ladies don't do well on no sleep at all.'

'It feels like something big, helping that girl,' Daphne says. 'I don't know exactly what's going to happen or when, but I'm getting some energy from somewhere. I feel like I'm gearing up, getting ready. I'm not sure what for.'

Even in the dark I can see that she looks embarrassed.

'I know what you mean,' I say.

And I do, in part, it does feel like something big but I'm afraid I haven't got a rush of energy to meet it. Not yet.

'You go home,' she says. 'I think you need sleep more than I do. I'll wait here. As soon as there's a flicker of light in the sky I'll pop home for a quick nap.'

'No,' I say, before I've had a chance to think it through properly. 'Come back with me and you can get your head down on my sofa for an hour. It's comfortable and then we can set the alarm and go round early.'

I don't tell her that no one has ever slept on my sofa before. I don't tell her that I normally keep myself to myself. There doesn't seem to be any need.

CHAPTER NINE

Meg

Monday night, Tuesday morning, 26 February

I asked Nina if she'd like me to stay while she slept and she was so relieved that she cried, so I decided that my sleep was not at all important. I sat in the little chair by her bed. A nursing chair, it's called, little stumpy legs just right for a short person like me. We might as well take that old chair to the dump, Henry used to say, there won't be any nursing going on here. I loved it though, and I used to sit in it sometimes when he was out and pretend. Pretend I was holding a baby. I haven't used the chair for a while, apart from the night Henry passed away. I needed the comfort, then.

I didn't think of any of that, the first night I knew Nina. I sat still, watching her breathe. She was very restless, and a few times I had to tuck the blankets round her, pat her shoulder so that she went back to sleep. She was a quiet sleeper, no snoring, which was a relief. I had plenty of time to think and I almost didn't think about Henry at all. He seemed very far away, and I couldn't quite imagine what he would say about the situation. He wouldn't like it, that's for sure. A stranger sleeping in his bed, he'd want to throw the mattress out the next day and get the place fumigated or exorcised or something. It made me laugh, thinking of that, and I accidentally woke her.

She sat bolt upright as if someone had called her.

'What?' she said. 'I can't.'

'Sorry,' I said, 'stupid me, I made a noise but you're OK, there's nothing happening, you can go back to sleep if you want to.'

'Oh,' she said, 'sorry, I forgot where I was. This is a nice bed, thank you.'

I think of Henry's lectures on the right sort of mattress and I want to giggle again but I don't. It's bad enough that she thinks I'm as ancient as some wrinkled old woman in a fairy story, sitting by the fire and darning holes in socks or something. She doesn't need to think I'm always laughing when there's clearly nothing funny. I wouldn't be able to explain about Henry, about how funny he is, especially now he has passed on.

'I don't need to go back to sleep,' she says. 'It's getting light outside and I've had enough rest, thank you.'

We had set up a WhatsApp group the night before, so it's easy to message the others to tell them that Nina is awake.

'I thought teenagers needed loads of sleep,' I said. 'I heard it on the radio, a *Woman's Hour* special on it.'

'Some teenagers maybe,' she said, 'but I've always been good at getting by on less. Some people don't like you to sleep in. Especially if you're a looked-after child.'

She could tell that I wasn't sure what she was talking about so she said, 'That means in care to the local authority.'

What a way to put it, I thought. This child must be the

least looked-after child I've ever come across. I didn't say anything, because she was looking at me in a way that made it perfectly clear that she knew she had given me a big piece of information. It was like a thank you for the night and the sleep she'd had and the fact that I had sat with her, I think, only it made me sad that she might think she had to offer me something in exchange. I wasn't sure whether to ignore the information, pretend that she hadn't said it so that she didn't feel vulnerable, or whether I should acknowledge it and build on it. I only had a split second to decide and I chose to ask her a question about it. I remembered how awful it feels when you tell someone something, hoping they'll ask more about it, show an interest, and you're met with a stony silence.

'Have you been in care for long?' I said.

'Most of my life,' she said. 'I was in foster homes and then in a children's home but it's not my mum's fault, she's got issues.'

'Poor Mum,' I said without thinking but it seemed to be the right thing because she flashed me a most delightful smile.

'Are you still looked after?' I said. 'Is there anyone who needs to know that you're safe here?'

'Oh no,' she said. 'Oh no, there's no one, I'm almost eighteen now, thank goodness.'

Eighteen, I thought, eighteen, and don't we all think we're grown up when we get to eighteen. Just babies, we are, but you can't tell a person that. I thought I knew the lot at eighteen. Thought I could arrange my own life just fine.

'OK,' I said, 'I'm going to go and have a shower and I'll leave you to get ready. There's some clothes on the chair. Sorry the joggers and jumper are a bit old ladyish but I'm sure they'll look lovely on you anyway. Do you like porridge?'

She pulled a face at that and I remembered, of course, young people don't like porridge. It's for the oldies.

I was still chuckling away about the porridge when the doorbell rang. It was the other two, my new best friends, my gang. I wanted to clap, that's how exciting it was. Daphne and Grace, together and both looking more comfortable than they did the night before. They must have had a proper rest. I marvelled at the technology that had made this work so smoothly, although I was glad Henry and I hadn't used it much.

The sun shone on the table as we ate our breakfast even though it was still the cold middle of winter. The window faces south, north, east or west, I can't remember which, but it means it can be the sunniest room ever at the right time. The light picked out individual crumbs and a smear of butter until they looked like a painting I had seen on the wall in a gallery. If only we could stay like this, I thought. Just the four of us eating breakfast together in bright light.

Grace went over to the window several times whilst we were eating. She stood to the side so that she couldn't be seen, and peered out through the net curtains. Daphne watched her whenever she could, and I could hardly blame her. Grace is one of the most lovely women I've ever seen, and strong with it. She's like a person you would want with you on a desert island, I thought, and at that moment I could almost believe that the four of us were on the island, and that the bread had been toasted over a fire of sticks.

'I'm just checking,' Grace said, 'to be on the safe side.'

I've got to admit I wasn't sure that was necessary. In fact I was on the verge of asking her if she really needed to do that, point out that she was frightening Nina. I'm glad I didn't, because exactly when I was thinking of saying it there was a snap of the letterbox. Pizza flyers, I thought, or an offer to value my house in case I wanted to sell, but when I went to the door it was neither of those things. It was a small sheet of paper, folded in half. When I opened it, there was a picture of Nina's face staring out at me. An older-looking Nina, much older, as if it was a message from a future time when she would have her hair up and wear lots of make-up.

Have you seen this girl? Missing since 25 February. Please call this number with any information. If you see her tell her we love her and we can't wait to see her back again.

There was a phone number underneath. I stood and looked at it.

'Meg,' Grace called from the kitchen, 'is it OK if I put some coffee on? Would you like some?'

'Thanks,' I said and I stuffed the flyer into the pocket of my skirt. There was no point worrying Nina about it. I had to find a time to discuss it with the other two, see what we should do.

I didn't get a chance until after the coffee, when Nina went off to have a shower.

'Spill,' said Grace. 'What happened?'

I hadn't thought I had let it show at all, but she is perceptive, that Grace, she doesn't miss a thing. I got the flyer out and smoothed it so that they could see.

'Shit,' Grace said. 'You didn't think of telling me straight away so that I could look out of the window?'

I hadn't thought, of course, I never do. That's your trouble,

95

Henry used to say, tapping my head with his knuckles until it really hurt. You've got a brain in there somewhere, I suppose, because you certainly know how to eat and spend money, but you choose not to use it when it suits you.

'I'm sorry,' I said.

I was going to say more but Daphne jumped in.

'Come on, Grace,' she said, 'what was Meg supposed to do? Make a huge song and dance in front of Nina? I'd have done the same as her, kept it until we were on our own and we could focus on it.'

'OK, point taken, sorry, Meg,' Grace said.

I was astonished. Just like that, sorry, Meg? I wondered for a moment whether that was how most people carried on and for a mad moment I missed Henry intensely. I wanted to tell him that not everyone carries an argument on to the bitter end. I wanted him to listen to me.

'So what we need to know is,' Daphne said, 'whether every house has had a flyer like that or whether it's specific, targeted at us because someone knows something.'

'Meg,' Grace said, 'could you maybe find out from your neighbours?'

I could feel my face going hot. 'I expect they're at work,' I said.

It was the first thing I could think of.

'What, all of them?' Grace said. 'It doesn't matter which one you ask, any will do. They've either done everyone or no one.'

'OK,' I said, 'OK, give me a moment.'

I stood there trying to work out what to do. I couldn't possibly admit to them that I didn't know any neighbours, that after almost fifty years in the same house I was not even on 'hello, good morning' terms with a single one. I knew that wasn't how other people lived. I had always known, but Henry had been so very furious if I ever spoke to any of them that it had become second nature for me to ignore everybody. I'm sorry, I used to say to them in my head as I walked past, I'm sorry but it's easier this way.

'An accident of geography does not a friendship make, Meg,' Henry used to say.

Daphne came to my rescue again.

'Not everyone is as outgoing as you, Grace,' she said. 'Not everyone knows all their neighbours.'

'Sorry,' Grace said, and the two of them smiled at each other in a way that made me feel a bit lonely.

'I'll go,' Daphne said. 'I'll knock and ask a question. I'll say I've just moved in up the road, and I'll get the conversation round to it. We really do need to know.'

She wasn't gone long. What would it be like, I thought, to be able to act so decisively? Daphne didn't even seem all that confident, but when it mattered, she could obviously pull it out of the bag. I imagined all the things that would become easy, all the obstacles that would suddenly clear, if I could make myself act like that.

'Young woman at twenty-two,' she said when she came back. 'Really nice, said she's got a flyer too.'

'OK,' said Grace, 'that gives us some breathing space.'

'What do you mean, breathing space?' Nina said.

None of us had realised that she was there, she had come down the stairs so quietly. We looked at each other, us three oldies, and I knew instantly what they were thinking and that we were all in agreement. It's not fair not to tell her, we decided.

Daphne held the flyer out to Nina. Nina opened it out and read it. It was horrible to watch the colour drain from her face.

'I'll have to go,' she said, 'I can't put you lot in danger. And there's my friend. I don't know how she is.'

She started to fuss with her hair but I think it was only to stop herself from crying. Grace took hold of her hand, really gently, pulled it away from her head and held it.

'It's OK,' Grace said. 'We're not going to give up now, just because of a stupid flyer. Are we, ladies?'

Daphne and I shook our heads.

'But you're going to be brave and help us, tell us what's going on, what the hold is he's got over you, that kind of thing. So that we can help you in the best way. And your friend. So that we don't make things worse.'

I nodded along until I must have looked like a mad woman but I couldn't think what else to do. And there was the other thing too, the damned violin. It was in my ears screeching like a fox in the throes of sex. Anyone who has heard that would agree with me that it's the worst sound, and if they haven't heard it, they're lucky. It's a terrible noise and so was the damned violin. And the snoring. It was almost as bad as the night Henry passed. I didn't want to do anything dramatic, honestly I didn't, but I couldn't help sort of sinking into a chair and holding my head. The noise was so intense and I think I was groaning. This is about Nina, not you, you stupid old fool, I was thinking but it didn't make it any better. It's not always about you, Henry used to say and usually it was a very unfair thing to say but today he would have been right. It was that damn violin. It wouldn't let up.

Daphne knelt down by the chair.

'Can someone get a wet cloth?' she said.

It felt marvellous when she held the cloth against my head.

'I think you might be having a panic attack,' Daphne said.

I could hear the sound of the other two agreeing but I managed to hold my hand up, and wave it a little to show them that I was fine. It couldn't possibly be a panic attack and as soon as the violin was quiet for a moment I explained it to them.

'My mother,' I said, 'she used to play the violin in the Underground shelters in the war. To entertain the people down there. They were there for whole nights, quite often, and it was too crowded to sleep.'

'You don't have to talk if you're feeling rubbish,' Nina said.

It was sweet of her but for the first time ever I really wanted to explain.

'This one night, she was in Balham station,' I said. 'There were a few of them, someone had a trombone and another person had an accordion and they got everyone singing along. I suppose it stopped people from thinking about where they were. What was going on.'

I wanted to say so much more. I wanted to explain it properly but the noise in my head had started up again and I was grateful when Daphne helped me to the sofa. I held the cloth to my head and I must have fallen asleep, because the next thing I knew it was the afternoon. I felt so ashamed. I sat up, no violin at all now, no snoring, no fox and everything was nice and quiet.

'I'm so sorry,' I said, and they all laughed.

All three of them. I was about to feel hurt when Nina said,

'Meggie, that's exactly what we thought you'd say when you woke up. We betted on it and we were right.'

I could see that was quite funny.

It was amazing to wake up with the three of them there. Almost like a party. Daphne made me some tea and Nina came and perched on the end of the sofa while Grace filled me in.

'We're going to keep Nina with us a bit longer,' she said. 'Things are pretty bad, we'll talk to you about them later. No need to go through it all again right now.'

'No, no, later will be fine,' I said. 'I'm so sorry.'

They all burst out laughing.

'Do you realise, Meggie, how often you apologise?' Nina said. 'You should stop, you know. No one is cross with you. In fact, I think you're really cool, letting us all camp out here and everything.'

Meggie, I thought, that sounds nice. Stupid woman that I am, I had to pretend to cough so that she wouldn't see how grateful and pathetic I was. Stupid woman.

CHAPTER TEN

Nina

October – four months earlier

In the months after the incident with the clothes, Nina sometimes caught sight of Shaz in the distance as she went between the library and home. She was never completely sure. She felt tingly at the sight of her, as though her skin knew that someone was watching her, and every time, she turned away as quickly as she could. Occasionally, she would see a flash of purple or orange, bright, Shaz-style colours, dipping into a shop or turning a corner. She might have been mistaken, she knew that. Nina had done the same thing before, after her mother stopped turning up to contact meetings. She had seen her everywhere: on buses, in the cinema, even once dressed as a dinner lady serving food at Nina's school. Nina had run crying from the dining hall when she realised that the woman was nothing like her mother, with different-coloured hair and at least ten years older. You're too old to get fooled by that sort of nonsense again, she told herself.

Nina concentrated on her school work, tried to make friends with students of her own age and looked out for

Bilbo when she could. Some of the girls had realised now that she was clever and funny, and living in a home didn't seem such a big deal as she got older. In fact, some of the girls thought it was quite cool. The Tracy Beaker effect, Nina called it to herself. She pushed thoughts of Shaz and her strange behaviour to the back of her mind and concentrated on exams and fitting in.

It was autumn again before Nina spoke to Shaz, and Nina was waiting for a bus. It had been difficult getting away without causing a major meltdown for Bilbo and she was worried about him. She thought he might have followed her, he had been so desperate to come along. She pulled her coat up further around her ears and turned her head. Shaz was there, right behind her. Nina jumped.

'Shaz,' Nina said, 'when did you creep up on me? Are you OK?'

Stupid question number one, Nina thought. Shaz was obviously not OK. She had a black eye and she looked unkempt in a way that surprised Nina. Her fingernails were unpainted and crusted with dirt.

'College girl,' said Shaz in a sneering tone.

Nina wasn't sure what to say. She was becoming more confident now in her friendships and her dealings with other young women, but Shaz was different and Nina hoped the bus would come soon.

'Don't be like that,' she said. 'I'm sorry we don't hang out any more.'

Nina wasn't sorry at all, and just thinking that made her feel guilty. After all, Shaz had been there for her when she was at her lowest, and she had tried to be friendly. Nina thought of the bag of clothes and how she had laughed at them, and a feeling of shame washed over her.

'Would you like to go for a coffee now?' Nina asked.

Goddammit, girl, she thought, bang goes your quiet afternoon away from the house, away from the kids. What are you thinking of? The trouble was, Nina knew quite well why she had suggested it. There was a horrible unfinished feeling to the friendship with Shaz, and she had fretted over it often in the past year. She wasn't sure exactly what had happened, but she knew that Shaz had been hurt by her.

'I haven't got any money, college girl,' Shaz said.

Nina could hear that Shaz sounded more defeated than aggressive and she felt sad for her.

'Come on,' she said, 'I can stand you a coffee. Even a burger, if you play your cards right.'

Shaz shrugged and the two girls left the bus stop and walked down the hill towards McDonald's. Nina had taken even more trouble than usual to avoid it since the previous year, and she wasn't at all happy to be back. It was still a place where nothing good could happen, she thought. Nina would have liked to walk in the park instead, but she could imagine how ridiculous that would seem to Shaz. Just a veggie burger, Nina said to herself, an old debt sorted and then I'll go into town.

The streets seemed colder than they had when Nina first left the house. The sky was a uniform grey, pressing down on them as they walked, like the lid of a sandwich box.

'You did good, then, in your exams, college girl?' Shaz said.

Nina bristled, feeling for the first time that day like the lonely little nerd she had been the previous year.

'OK,' she said, shrugging.

'What are you doing now then?' Shaz said.

Nina thought that she could hear that Shaz was trying to be nice. She wished she was a kinder person, the kind who could give Shaz a hug, tell her it was all right, that they could be friends again.

'Just the sixth form college in Lewisham,' Nina said, 'the one up near Blackheath. It's OK.'

Nina wondered how long they would have to drag this out. It's your own fault, she told herself.

McDonald's was warm and steamy after the drab cold outside. Nina could smell the familiar smells, frying meat undercut with a tang of broken toilets.

'Have you noticed,' Nina said to Shaz, 'that McDonald's always smells exactly the same, no matter what time of day or year you come in?'

Shaz laughed and for a moment Nina could see the fun-loving girl she had been so attracted to before. She bought the food and watched as Shaz tore at the burger.

'Here,' Nina said, pushing her own food towards Shaz, 'I had lunch at home, I'm not really hungry.'

The old Shaz would have been far too proud, Nina thought, and she also used to worry about her weight. This new version of Shaz grabbed at it without a second thought. Nina watched the family on the next table so that Shaz wouldn't be embarrassed, or feel that she was being scrutinised. There were four of them, a mum, a dad, a little girl and a slightly bigger boy. The perfect set-up, Nina thought. She looked back to her table and realised that Shaz had noticed too.

'Looks perfect, doesn't it,' Shaz said, wiping a smear of tomato sauce from her mouth, 'only I bet it's not all it seems.

Never is. He probably hits her when no one is looking. Or peers under the door when the kids are getting undressed.'

'Shaz,' Nina said, 'honestly, keep your voice down. They're not like that, I'm sure they're not.'

'Ha,' said Shaz as if she'd proved an argument with a winning, unanswerable point. 'They're all like that, college girl, didn't you know? You can't believe anything anyone says, or anything anyone does. The sooner you realise that, the better.'

Nina felt adrift, unable to work out what to say to calm Shaz down.

'OK,' she said, 'I get where you're coming from. But I'm still going to have to defend them.' Nina spoke in a quiet voice, hoping that she wouldn't be overheard. 'I mean, they look really nice. Look at him helping that little girl wipe her fingers and everything, she doesn't like being messy.'

'Oh for fuck's sake,' said Shaz loudly. 'Load of fucking losers.'

She pushed the wrappers and boxes from the table on to the floor and moved towards the door. Nina bent and scooped up the rubbish before following her. She was torn between giving the family on the next table an apologetic look and keeping her head down, hoping that no one would notice her. The parents both tutted, and several other customers turned to look at them as Shaz barged out, Nina behind her.

'Shaz,' Nina said as soon as they were outside, 'what on earth is the matter? What's going on? There were kids in there, you know, what's got into you?'

Shaz didn't answer, and Nina realised that she was crying.

'Hey,' Nina said, 'it's OK, it's OK.'

She patted Shaz on the arm. I should have left the house

at any other time, she thought, any other time at all. I could have been sitting down with a coffee and a book by now, or looking at the jeans in TopShop. Shaz had been there for Nina when she had no other friends, tried to make a friendship even though they were so different. Nina didn't want her to think she was ungrateful, or a stuck-up bitch. The truth was, she would rather be anywhere than here, but she would hate Shaz to know that.

'Is there anything I can do?' Nina said. 'I hate to see you so upset.'

'Have you got any money?' Shaz said. 'Anything at all I can borrow?'

Nina thought of the clothes, and the burgers Shaz had bought her when she hadn't had any money. She hardly had any now, but she owed Shaz and she wanted to get away. Maybe if she just handed over what she had left, Shaz would leave her alone and she could get back to her day. That'll teach me to be nice to people, she thought.

'Yeah, sure,' Nina said, 'I've got a fiver, but only that. You can have it.'

'I'm sorry,' Shaz said, holding out her hand for it, 'I'm sorry for taking your last bit of money and I'm sorry for everything else. Honest.'

'There's nothing to be sorry for,' Nina said, 'nothing at all.'

CHAPTER ELEVEN

Daphne

Tuesday, 26 February

After the fuss about Meg's panic attack had died down, Daphne went to rest for a quiet ten minutes on Meg's bed. She had hardly slept at all on Grace's sofa the previous night after her self-appointed guard duties. Daphne was used to insomnia, but it had been very odd being in someone else's house and also Meg's upset had shaken her. She could feel her thoughts starting to circle in a way she didn't like. Daphne was thinking about her Big Mistakes, and she hadn't thought about her Big Mistakes for many years. That's what she told herself, but in fact it wasn't true. Daphne knew it wasn't true. In a superb act of self-deception that had taken nearly all of Daphne's available emotional energy for more than fifty years, Daphne had decided not to let herself know that the Big Mistakes were occupying every thought she had in every waking moment. There had been no time, with the thoughts she couldn't keep out; no time for relationships, no time for children, no time for anything outside of work.

Work was the best thing. They had told her that in prison, everyone had said it.

'At least you haven't got any kids,' the nice writing teacher had said, 'and you're educated. You'll still be able to get a good job, this is just a blip.'

At least I haven't got any kids, Daphne used to think as she got ready for her job in the council each morning. Think how difficult this would be if I had kids. She wasn't sure though. It didn't always feel like a blessing, especially when she heard children playing. The squeals, the happy shouts, the occasional tears. Daphne's life was so quiet.

Work, though. They had been right about the healing properties of work. Daphne had loved it, going to the same place every day, the steadiness of it and the predictability. She had even been able to open Beth's letters after the first few years, read them right through and look at pictures she had sent without crying.

Daphne had been happy to go in to the office early, stay late and take files home. Every part of the world of work had been a respite from the fear and the terrible thoughts that she could never admit that she had. Until retirement, that is. Daphne worked later than most people, stayed at her various desks doing council maths until she was sixty-five, but her age had finally caught up with her when she became unwell. Only then had she been noticed, only then had her bosses realised that she needed to be pensioned off. They waited until she was back from a skirmish with breast cancer to present her with a voucher. A voucher, Daphne thought, a voucher. Not even a personal thing, a golden gardening trowel or a designer suitcase. She had taken such care to keep hidden, to make sure that no one knew her, and she had been successful. It was only at the end, when she left, that Daphne realised she hated her success. A voucher. That would never have happened to Grace, she was sure.

Daphne thought that she would like to talk to Grace about the voucher, amongst other things. She seemed like the kind of person who would understand. They might even be able to be friends, when all this stuff was over. Daphne couldn't hope for more than that.

Daphne sat bolt upright. She realised that she had been thinking about the past again when she should have been trying to save that girl's life. The mistakes, the prison, the voucher, all of that needed to go. She shook her head and concentrated on keeping her breathing even. Think of something else, she told herself. Look around. Meg's bedroom was quiet and tastefully grey but Daphne could see nothing personal, nothing to show who Meg truly was. Nothing on the bedside table, nothing on the chest of drawers. Nothing at all like Grace's book-lined living room. Perhaps this was normal, she thought. Perhaps she was so cut off from other people that she had no idea what normal was.

She wasn't going to sleep, that was clear, so Daphne got out her notebook to try to make a plan. *One,* she wrote. *What is Nina escaping from?* As soon as she had written it she felt better. It's obvious, she thought, it's some kind of Big Mistake of her own. It doesn't matter about the specifics, that toad man had a look of Andrew about him, even without the striped flares and the military jacket.

Daphne went over to the window and lifted the net curtain a little. There was no one there. No one lounging against a lamp-post or standing consulting a map. Nothing suspicious. Still, though, she could feel menace in the air. The street looked like a film set before the action starts, waiting for something to begin. The day was closing down early and Daphne thought, something is going to happen. The light had been like this another time, she remembered, just like this so that you weren't sure, if you cleared your mind, whether it was end of the day or the beginning. Tricky light. Time to draw the curtains. Daphne shuddered.

Downstairs felt much safer. Meg was teaching Nina to knit, and Grace was chopping vegetables. All three looked up and smiled as Daphne came in.

'I've been thinking,' Daphne said, 'I don't think we're safe here. I mean, I'm not sure or anything but I've got a feeling, like your violin thing, Meg, and I don't want to frighten anyone but I'm wondering if maybe we should move on, go somewhere else.'

There, she thought, I've said it now, and whatever happens next, at least I've tried.

'Did you see him?' Grace said, wiping her hands and putting down the knife. 'Is he outside?'

Nina started to cry, and Meg put her arm round her.

'No, no, he's not outside,' Daphne said, 'and I'm really sorry to upset everyone, but I have a feeling, and I'm sure I saw him yesterday, and I was thinking that there was a time before in my life when I sat like a sitting duck, whatever that is. I sat and I waited and I thought that was best for me, least likely to cause any trouble, best for everyone. I should have acted then and I didn't but I don't want that to happen again so I'm just saying, for what it's worth, that this time I think we should act, we should move rather than sit here waiting. Sorry.'

'OK, OK,' Grace said. She moved over and put a hand

on Daphne's arm. 'I guess I'm not saying feelings aren't very important, but you might be wrong, and it might be a crazy thing, uprooting everyone and taking off for God knows where, with God knows who following. There's nothing to make us think that toad man knows Nina is here with us, in fact he could be miles away by now. And where would we go anyway? And how would we get there?'

Daphne felt better with Grace's hand on her arm.

'I've got a place,' she said. 'I've got a place at the seaside, Margate, not far. I've even got a car but it's a long time since I've driven anywhere. I'm happy if either of you wants to drive, I can assure you of that.'

'I never learned,' said Meg. 'Sorry, I'm hopeless at things like that.'

'I can drive,' said Grace. 'I can drive but I don't believe we ought to go anywhere. What have we got, really, to go on?'

Grace looked at the other women in turn and Daphne thought, she's a natural born leader. She probably knows best.

'I was just saying,' Daphne said, 'I mean, I'm not necessarily right, in fact I'm probably wrong, it was just that...' She tailed off.

'Hang on,' said Nina. 'I mean, I've told you some of it, but maybe there are more things you need to know. He really is bad, you know, unscrupulous, that's the word. And I'm grateful, really grateful, but I don't think it's fair you should all put yourselves in danger for me. But Daphne is right, he is a bad man, and he's dangerous.'

Meg looked at Nina with admiration.

'Well said,' she said quietly.

'I get what you're saying, my lovely,' said Grace, 'but I also think you're going to have to tell us a bit more about who he is, and who you are. I don't mind running, lord knows I don't, but my basic stipulation is that I want to know who I'm running from, and why.'

Meg looked worried. She twisted her hands together and looked from Nina to the others. Positively fluttering, Daphne thought, and she felt sorry for her.

'I think it's for the best, Meg,' Daphne said.

Nina looked calm but Daphne could see that she was trembling. There was no colour in her face and her long hair seemed darker in contrast.

'I do too,' Nina said. 'It's OK, honestly, I'll be OK, I don't mind telling you. I trust you. All of you. You've all been so good to me and I think you should know.'

Nina told her story while they ate vegetable stew and mashed potatoes, comforting, old-fashioned food. Daphne could see that Nina was hungry, and the women waited quietly while she ate and talked. When Nina had finished Daphne knew she had heard a story like that before. A long time ago, and maybe not the same story but a similar one, or even a part of her own story and nothing similar at all, she wasn't sure. She wasn't sure of anything as she stood up and peered round the curtains, but she heard an echo of the clanking slam of the prison doors, and she definitely saw a big black car cruise slowly past the house. Daphne knew that her original plan of taking them all somewhere safe was a good one. Grace had seen the car too, Daphne could tell that from the worried look Grace sent her. It was as if the two of them were communicating without words, Daphne thought, and even in the middle of her terror and anxiety she was glad of the connection.

Daphne didn't need to say any more. Hearing Nina's story was enough to convince Meg that they should be on the move, and Nina seemed happy to follow whatever the older women suggested.

'So I'm going to go and get the car,' Daphne said. 'Meg, can I go out the back way, through the garden? I think it would be easier. My car is parked quite near here – I don't keep it outside my house. I'll bring it closer, I'll be a couple of streets away, by the old library. It's well lit there, and I think that's better than meeting somewhere dark. Bring yourselves, you don't need anything else. I've got food in the freezer down there and coats and woolly hats and in case anyone is watching, it's better if we look as though we're just going out for a while. I'll text Grace when I'm at the car and you all come out. Is that OK?'

Daphne couldn't believe she had been so assertive. She felt as though someone else was speaking, and she hoped that none of them were offended. She looked at Grace. Grace was a natural leader, much better suited to the role than Daphne. Grace seemed so sure of herself, so aware of everyone else. Daphne looked at her and Grace grinned and put both thumbs up.

'Way to go, Daff,' Grace said. 'Sounds like a plan to me.'

Meg put her arm round Nina. 'I'll just put a few bits to eat in a carrier bag,' she said.

'You're like everyone's mum,' Nina said.

Meg blushed. They all laughed, glad for a break in the tension.

Daphne felt better once she was outside on her own. The

night had always been her time and wandering in the dark through London's secret places cleared her head. Daphne had always been unafraid, sure that nothing that happened to her could ever be as bad as events in her past. Until now. Until there were other people in the mix, other people to worry about and look out for. It's not just about you any more, she said to herself as she let herself out of the little door in the fence at the back of Meg's garden.

The door opened on to a courtyard in front of a block of flats. No one was around. It was cold and dark and Daphne felt invisible as she slipped round the side of the flats and down the quiet road where her car was parked. She was grateful that no one had asked her why she didn't park it outside her own front door. If they knew, she thought, they would never, ever get in it with her as a driver. They'd be right not to, in Daphne's opinion. She knew she was the worst driver who had ever passed a test. In fact she had no idea why she had passed, and could only assume that her examiner had not passed enough people that day and was forced to put her through regardless. The truth was that after nearly thirty years, Daphne could not reverse into a parking space. She was forced to park her car wherever she could find a big enough space to drive forward into.

Daphne used the car less and less. It had been several weeks since the last time but she crossed her fingers and it started.

'Well done,' Daphne said, 'my good and trusted friend.'

The others were waiting at the library when Daphne pulled up. They got in quickly, Grace in the front passenger seat and Nina and Meg in the back. Daphne could see straight away that something had happened by the way Grace held herself.

She looked tense and grim, her mouth set in a line. Daphne started the car and reached over to squeeze Grace's arm.

'Seat belts on, everyone?' Daphne called and Nina giggled.

'It's like going on a school outing,' she said.

Grace didn't smile and as they moved off, Daphne could see that she was constantly checking in the rear-view mirror.

'Everything OK?' she asked.

'Yes,' said Grace quietly, 'I think so, only I'm not sure if there was someone around, as we left the house. We came out through the garden, so that was OK, and we left the radio and the lights on but I think I saw someone in one of the doorways of the flats. They didn't look right, somehow. I didn't say anything because I wasn't sure, but I think there may have been someone, hanging around a couple of doors down.'

Nina leaned against Meg as if she was very tired and Meg patted Nina's arm. Daphne drove faster.

'OK,' said Grace after a few minutes, 'I think we have now managed to leave behind anyone we might have seen, unless they have a fast car. More than fast, it would have to be a very special car, the kind that James Bond or another mega spy slash double agent might use.'

'Oh,' said Daphne, 'am I going too fast?'

Meg, Nina and Grace all laughed.

'No offence meant,' Grace said, 'but jeez, have you ever won a Grand Prix?'

'I'm sorry,' Daphne said, 'I didn't want to scare anybody but I am a really bad driver.' Daphne turned to the back and the side as she spoke in order to speak directly to the passengers, and all three of them shrieked.

'Keep your eyes on the road, darling,' said Grace.

Daphne was so surprised and pleased about the 'darling' that she didn't mind about the driving comments. In fact, when Grace offered to take over, Daphne felt nothing but relief. As soon as it was possible she pulled over and got out to swap seats with Grace.

'OK,' Grace said quietly as they stepped past each other outside the car, 'FYI it definitely was him, toad man and some kind of beefy mate, and they hoofed it back to their car after they'd seen us I suspect. And they definitely did see us but I don't want to frighten the little one. OK?'

'OK,' Daphne said and gave Grace a quick kiss on the cheek.

Did I do that? Daphne thought. Did I really just kiss this woman in the middle of the night while we're changing seats and driving a getaway car? Perhaps my life isn't a done deal yet. How strange.

CHAPTER TWELVE

Meg

Tuesday, 26 February

It was lovely being in the car all together. I felt safe for a moment or two even though I was sure I'd caught a glimpse of that man's car, too. Just being together, the four of us in the car with the doors closed against whatever might be out there in the dark, made me feel for a moment as though I could relax. I didn't say it because I could hear from her voice that Grace was panicked, and Daphne was nervous about the driving on top of everything else. I was worried, of course I was, but the thing is I've spent my whole life being worried about one thing or another and it's never made a single bit of difference. The violin was not playing then, I was sure of that. And the other thing was that even though it makes me sound a bit crazy, I was starting to realise, I mean really realise, that Henry wasn't coming back. No resurrections. No snoring. I think that, up until we got into the car to go to Margate, I wouldn't have been surprised if he had popped his head around the door and said, 'Here I am, what's for tea?' He used to go away on business trips, you see, three, four days at a time. He stayed in budget hotels mostly, and he used to say the food was better than anything he got when I cooked. And the company too, although I wasn't surprised at that. I have never been very exciting company.

When we got into Daphne's car and drove off, it was like we were leaving the ordinary world behind. Including Henry, dead or alive. I could hear Grace and Daphne talking to each other quietly. I couldn't always make out the words but I could see that they had a special closeness. The way they looked at each other, the way they touched each other's arms. I wasn't jealous. Henry always said I was a jealous person but he was wrong, I liked seeing Grace and Daphne do their own thing. Maybe because of my relationship with Nina. She needed me, Nina, and she was so lovely. She called me Meggie. She was special from the word go. There's no such thing as love, Henry used to say, it's a social construct. I was never sure what that meant and the more I think about it, the more I'm sure that he didn't know either. It was probably something he'd read in a Sunday paper. I think there's such a thing as love, I always did, and I think I loved Nina from almost the first moment I saw her. She's little and skinny, with big curly hair that she's always trying to tame, but it's wild and won't lie down at all. She twists it up into a topknot and I love that. I would have loved to do that with my hair, but I have the thinnest, flattest hair you ever saw. It takes all sorts to make a world. She's got a way of talking, Nina. She looks at you really earnestly and says things with such conviction. I like listening to her.

By the time we were on the dual carriageway and heading for Margate, things were pretty dire.

'Am I driving OK?' Daphne asked Grace.

It was easy to tell that Grace had been a teacher. She was calm and encouraging, exactly the kind of teacher I would have wanted for my children. She might even have taught my daughter, I thought, that's the kind of coincidence that could happen so easily. It was a shame I didn't know what her name was, or what she had looked like.

Daphne was getting more panicky.

'I'm sure there's someone,' she said.

I decided to try not to worry but when Grace joined in I thought, hey ho, something really isn't right with the world. I didn't listen to the violin. I blame myself, I did then and I do now. I didn't listen to the violin because I couldn't hear it above the happiness. I was so happy, truly madly deeply happy, just for a moment. I remembered once before when I was happy like this, it might have been when the baby was born, before they took her, or in that summer when Henry was away, or maybe it was in the winter before I met him. Or when I had a dog. It was a slightly familiar feeling, the feeling I had that night in the car, that's all I knew.

There was a feeling of togetherness in the car. Nina snuggled in to me and every so often Grace would turn around and say, 'Everyone OK in the back?' and Nina would give a thumbs up. Of course I knew there was scary stuff outside. I hope Daphne and Grace knew that I knew that. Dogs, babies and young people though, you have to keep calm for them. I think Grace tried to give me a look to show that she was worried, to include me with the grown ups, and I was grateful for that.

'Good driving,' I called once, when Daphne overtook something.

'Thanks, Meg,' she said and it sounded as though she was pleased.

Sometimes I think they're not sure if I'm on the same page as them. I think it's the way they look surprised if I make an intelligent suggestion, but I might have been imagining that. I'm not sure. I didn't mention how cosy it was, despite the danger, how happy I was. That would have proved that I was stupid. But it was, nonetheless. Just the four of us. I wished I had some way to keep us all safe. A foolproof good luck charm.

It was good when Grace took over the driving. Much less jerky. I wondered for a moment whether I would have been a good driver. I knew exactly how to do it, I'd watched Henry often enough. He had a way of explaining things to me that was crystal clear, even though there was always a built-in clause that also made it clear that he thought I wouldn't understand at all.

'You see here, Meg,' he said one day when we were going shopping, 'I'm moving down through the gears as I approach the roundabout. A lot of people slam on the brakes at this point, I'm sure if it was you behind the wheel we'd be hopping like kangaroos, hoppity-hop.'

He threw back his head and guffawed, slapping the steering wheel at his own joke. 'Hoppity-hop, oh dear,' he said. 'That's funny, isn't it, kangaroo Meg?'

And just like that, it was as though I'd actually done it. I hated that. It was unfair, and it drove me mad. He called me kangaroo Meg for months even though I had never had the chance to drive in any way, badly or not. I think I might have become a good driver, in other circumstances.

'Do people sometimes learn to drive really late in life?' I asked the other women in the car.

'I don't see why not,' Daphne said. 'Do you, Grace?'

'I reckon,' said Grace, driving more smoothly than Henry ever did. 'I reckon that we do most things better when we're older.'

'Thanks,' said Nina and everyone laughed.

I could tell that she wasn't really offended. It broke the ice a little and Grace and Daphne started talking about when they learned to drive and how quickly they passed their tests.

'Driving is good if you have a dog,' I said. 'You can take it for walks in nice parks.'

Looking back I think I was hoping to move the conversation to dogs for safety, and that might have happened if it hadn't become clearer and clearer that the car behind was following us.

'I'm going to swing off the main road and double back,' Grace said. 'Hold on to your seats, folks.'

She was sniffing a lot, as if she had a cold or she'd been crying.

I wasn't sure if we should be turning off, it seemed safer to be on the main road.

'Isn't it better if we stay on the main drag?' I said but she had turned by then so it was pretty pointless.

'I was probably wrong,' Grace said, 'he probably wasn't following us at all.'

'Yes,' Daphne said, 'tailgating for no good reason, more like. Better safe than sorry.'

I murmured some kind of agreement but the air in the car felt tense and I know what I'm talking about when it comes to tense. I could sort and grade tension into many categories and sub categories if I needed to, having lived with it so long. This tension felt tight, as if the air was being sucked from the car. It wasn't good, and I had to remember that we were doing what we thought was best in difficult circumstances, that was the important thing.

We were going fast along a small road when it happened. The houses along the road were set back, with big gardens. They mostly seemed to have their lights out and I was going to say something about everyone being in bed when there was a kind of bumping, splintering sound.

'Shit,' Daphne said, but Grace just hunched over the steering wheel, picked up speed and carried on. I put my arm round Nina and she grabbed my hand and hung onto it so tightly I could feel my arthritic thumb joint howling.

'It's OK,' I said, 'don't worry, everything will be all right.'

I shouldn't have said that. It wasn't. It wasn't all right at all. The car swerved like crazy and I realised that the big black car, the big black car from someone's nightmare, had overtaken us and skewed to a stop right in front, so that we had no choice but to stop too. I had time to think that in a film Grace would probably have revved up, reversed and screamed round it but Daphne's car was a little old French one and no good for car-chase manoeuvres so it came to a halt.

'Lock the doors,' Daphne shouted and I realised that Nina had frozen with terror so I reached over to do it but I wasn't quick enough.

I didn't get there in time and I've relived that moment so many times since. I think I could have done it if I'd been quicker, I'm sure I could, but I had the damn violin screeching in my head so hard it slowed me down. I wondered if my mother had been slowed down by it as well. It's amazing how many thoughts can go through a person's head in a teeny-tiny amount of time.

I leaned past Nina and grabbed the door handle. I tried to keep it shut and lock the door but there was already someone out there, pulling on it and then pulling on Nina and she shouted, 'Meggie,' and reached for me and I reached for her but something slammed into my face and I let go.

I let go. I could hear her screaming and then I heard Grace and Daphne get out of the car and they were shouting and Grace thought later that she had got one punch in but it was dark and confusing and we are old. We are old enough to need a hand getting out of a car on a good day, never mind with someone thirty years younger and his nasty crew pushing and shoving and hitting and pushing.

They were in the big car and away before we could do anything to help her. Nina. With those thugs, the thought was unbearable.

'The registration number,' Daphne said, 'the registration number, did anyone get it?'

I think she knew before she said it that none of us had.

'It was covered up,' Grace said. She was crying as she spoke. 'It was covered, I couldn't see it, shall I try to follow?'

'Yes,' Daphne and I said, 'Go, go, go.'

I forgot my poor sore face and sat on the edge of my seat, as if I was watching a car chase in the cinema rather than being in one. I held on to the back of Grace's driving seat and tried not to push her forwards. I think we all knew it was pointless but that was not a thing that could be admitted. Not then, not ever. 'Go, go, go,' I muttered under my breath. Every part of me was taut, strung out and buzzing like an electric train line as we raced off down the road in the same direction but there was no doubt about it, their car was faster. It wasn't long before we had no idea which way they'd gone. No sign of which road they might have taken at the crossroads. We tried all of them, of course, getting more and more desperate with every turn, but there was nothing to see. Somewhere around Bexley we pulled into a lay-by and Grace put her head on the steering wheel and sobbed. Daphne put her arms round her and made sshh, sshh noises but Grace was as sad as a person could be.

'They'll kill her,' she said, 'they'll kill her.'

I suppose I hadn't allowed myself to think it through until then but as soon as Grace said it I realised it was true. They would be mad as hell with her and they would know that she had told us everything. They might well kill her.

'What about the police?' I said. 'Shouldn't we go and report it to the police?'

'I don't know,' Daphne said. 'I don't know, I don't know. Have things changed? Is it OK now? I want to help her so much but I'm not sure. I'm not convinced that wouldn't make things worse.'

Grace looked at Daphne, the kind of look that makes a person stop and think.

'What do you know, Daph?' Grace said quietly. 'Help us to make the right decision here.'

'OK,' said Daphne, 'OK, let me think this through. Worst case? He kills her, to shut her up. Or, he slithers away, and she ends up in prison. In prison, that sweet little girl. It happens, I mean it happened to me, oh, long ago and far away but it can happen.'

I had guessed that something terrible must have happened

to Daphne and I could see from Grace's expression that she had thought it too.

'Thank you for telling us that,' said Grace and I nodded along, wanting to show her that I had realised what a big deal it was, her sharing like that. Grace touched Daphne's face.

'Not to mention,' said Grace, 'the credibility angle. Think about it. Three old women, two of them women of colour, turn up with a story about a missing girl. She was probably reported missing by social services, but even though she's still under eighteen the police probably assumed she'd gone off with friends. They don't look for those kind of young people so hard, I'm sure they don't. So she won't be on their radar. We're not related to her, we don't know her second name, we don't know the address we want to report her missing from. We could be making things worse.'

There was silence for a moment as we all tried to take in what was happening. I wasn't sure. I still wanted to tell someone in authority, play by the rules. Someone other than us should be out looking for her, that's what I thought, although Daphne and Grace were convincing too. That's the thing with you, Meg, Henry would have said, you don't know anything, do you?

'I'm not sure,' I said.

'Me neither,' Daphne said. 'Maybe we should just cover all bases? Maybe the police have changed since my day?'

'Oh God,' Grace said. 'Oh lord, I suppose we've got to. We don't want to annoy them in any way, while they've got Nina, but someone needs to know. I'll ring the police.'

I was relieved, I'll admit it.

Grace pulled her phone out of her pocket and as if on cue, it rang.

'Shit,' she said, looking at it, 'it's her, it's the phone I gave Nina last night.'

She pressed loudspeaker and opened the call.

'No need to say anything,' he said. His horrible voice with the Belgian accent and the menace made me shudder. 'Let's face it, I'm not interested in anything you have to say. So shut up. I just want to tell you, in case any of you were getting any stupid ideas, that I have papers that prove she is my daughter. And if you report my daughter missing to the police, not only will I say that you are all demented, but also I know where you all live. I know that and I will use it and I will come for you. Do you get that? Oh, and one other thing. Before I come for you I will hurt this stupid, stupid girl. Do you understand me?'

We all sat there, in the dark car, looking at each other. None of us said anything.

'Nina,' he called, 'or Zodiac or whatever the fuck we're going to call you next, come here and tell the nice ladies that I'm serious.'

We all held our breath, wanting to hear her speak.

'I'm OK,' she said. Her voice sounded small and very scared. 'I'm OK but please, he means it, stay away.'

Nina's voice tailed off into a grunt as if she had been winded but was trying not to make a sound. The phone call ended. I felt absolutely desperate. If he had turned up at that moment, that toad man, I think I could have torn him into pieces by myself. I could see that the others felt the same.

Grace was the first one to pull herself together.

'Buckle up,' she said, 'we need to talk this through.'

I didn't bother to do up my seat belt and Grace drove fast until we got to a lighted street, and a coffee bar.

'Come on,' she said, practically leaping out of the car, 'we've got to talk. I've got an idea.'

It seemed weird, being in a coffee shop when I was usually sitting at home. I couldn't stop thinking about Nina, and whether she was OK, whether she was hurt, what was happening to her, whether she blamed me. People all around us living normal lives, on dates, on the way home from a shift, all sorts of reasons to be there but none of them as terrible as ours. I was sure of that. I wondered what they would do in our situation, whether they would have better ideas, or contacts in the police force, or a safe house they could use. I even wished for a moment that Nina was someone else's problem, in case they would handle it better.

I was desperate to hear Grace's idea but I had no idea what it might be. I was almost at my lowest ebb when Grace made her suggestion. Her suggestion, her great suggestion, her amazing suggestion about killing him, killing the toad man. It was the best idea I'd ever heard. It was great and it was brave. I wanted to clap. I didn't care about my bloody lip and my swollen face, I felt like life had a meaning, maybe for the first time ever. I felt alive.

'I feel as though I could do it myself,' Daphne said.

I couldn't speak so I just nodded.

Grace put her head in her hands for a moment, and then we did it. We talked about money and methods and everything, the whole thing. I took notes in my head to keep myself busy and we made the pact, to consolidate it all.

'It's like going back to being beginners, isn't it?' Grace said. 'I mean, I'm used to knowing what I'm doing, most of the time at least,' she blushed then as she looked at Daphne.

'I know what you mean,' I said. 'We are all beginners at this.'

Of course I wasn't actually so much of a beginner as them but that was different, and I didn't feel the need to share.

It was really late by the time we had finished. I'm old, and that's the only excuse I have, but it wasn't until I felt my phone buzzing and saw the word 'Henry' on the screen that I remembered.

'Nina has got another phone,' I said. 'I gave her Henry's old one last night.'

The other two stared at me. I couldn't believe I'd forgotten.

'I can't talk for long,' Nina said, 'but I'm OK, honestly. Don't worry. I'll be fine.'

That was it, and then she was gone. It was almost like winning the lottery, except I didn't believe her. She didn't sound OK, and I was glad we had made our plans. There was something else though. The phone call had made me remember something else. Something modern, something that made me feel I could hold my own with the other women. Something that made me feel pleased for once that Henry had been such an old bore. A control freak, I think they'd call him these days. Coercive control, that's what he specialised in.

'Henry liked to know where I was all the time,' I said.

I could see the other two wondering what on earth I was talking about.

'Henry was my husband,' I explained, 'not the right kind of husband, but nonetheless.'

'We've got to get on with things, Meg,' Grace said, 'maybe we can talk about this another time.'

'No,' I said, 'no you don't understand. Henry liked to know where I was all the time. So he had this thing, on both our phones, so that we knew where each other was. He only wanted it one way, you see, he didn't think I needed to know where he was, but he wasn't great with technology. He thought he was, but actually he wasn't very good at all. I could do more of that sort of thing than he could, but I never said. I pretended I was stupid, it wasn't difficult. I never disabled it, that's the thing, I don't know why. I think I liked knowing where he was, which was nowhere, so it was kind of ironic.'

They both looked puzzled and I remembered Henry saying, you discombobulate people with all your going round the houses to tell a simple fact. Just say it, you nincompoop. So I did.

'All the time Nina carries that phone,' I said, 'we'll know where she is. Look.'

I got my phone out and went to the app.

'She's back in Brockley,' I said. 'She's in spitting distance of my house. Look.'

They both crowded in this time, looking to see the miracle I seemed to have performed. Grace punched the air and Daphne blew me a kiss.

'Oh, well done, Meg, I'm so glad you're here. Technical skills and everything,' Daphne said.

I felt so proud. For the first time I believed in our plan, really believed in it. We were going to do it.

'Let's go home,' Grace said, sniffing as she spoke. 'We've got this, ladies. We may be beginners, but we're smart. We're going to smash it.'

CHAPTER THIRTEEN

Nina

Christmas – two months earlier

Nina occasionally saw Shaz in the distance, although she was never sure. She always turned and walked the other way. By the end of term, she had almost forgotten her. There was college now and new friends and so much to think about and the memory of their brief time together made Nina feel uncomfortable. She remembered her grandmother saying that seeing magpies and crows made her feel as if someone was walking over her grave and that was how it was for Nina with thoughts of Shaz. Something nasty, something unclean.

So she didn't miss her, and she didn't think about her, and when Shaz was waiting outside the sixth form college gates one December afternoon as Nina came out, her first thought was that she didn't want her new friends to see her. It was easier to greet Shaz and walk off down the road with her than to stay and explain and introduce. They walked quickly up on to Blackheath, where the wide open spaces and the windswept grass gave an illusion of privacy. Nina sat down on a bench and they watched together as a man tried to fly his kite.

'How have you been?' Nina asked.

There was an edge to her voice, she knew there was, because she really didn't care how Shaz had been. That old Nina who was so insecure and lonely had gone now. Nina had aced her GCSEs, all A stars except maths despite being a looked-after child. She was enjoying her A levels and her sixth form college and she felt as though she had a future. She had decided to study psychology, to try to get some kind of understanding of the people around her and her mother and to maybe try to help looked-after kids, something like that. Nina was going places.

'OK,' said Shaz.

She kept looking over her shoulder in a way that made Nina uncomfortable.

'What are you looking for?' Nina said.

Shaz stood up and sighed in an exaggerated way.

'Nothing,' she said. 'Jeez, can't a girl even look around without being picked on?'

And that, Nina thought, is why I don't want to be around you and your mysteries and your weirdness any more. She got up and started to stroll off.

'Hang on,' said Shaz, 'I didn't mean anything.'

Something about the desperation in Shaz's voice stopped Nina in her tracks. She wanted to get rid of Shaz, not to hurt her feelings.

'It's OK,' Nina said, 'it's just, you know, I've got a lot of work to do. Course work. I can't stay.'

'Don't go yet,' Shaz said, 'it can't be that urgent. I mean, you came up here, didn't you.'

Nina sighed and sat down again. She wished that Shaz would stop gnawing at her nails. They were bitten down to tiny stubs and the noise of her nibbling at them set Nina's teeth on edge. The heath felt still, and Nina thought there might be rain on the way.

'Five minutes,' she said, 'then I've really got to go.'

'They're right,' Shaz said. 'You actually do think you're better than me, don't you?'

'You don't really think that, do you?' said Nina. 'Why would you say that?'

'You'll find out,' Shaz said. 'You'll find out soon enough. Bye. And sorry.'

Shaz got up and walked away, and as she did a man and a woman came towards Nina. They looked intent, and Nina thought that they were going to ask her for directions but they didn't, they just kept on coming closer until Nina realised that she had left it too late, that she couldn't get up, that they were blocking her on both sides.

Nina looked for her friend to ask for help and then realised that Shaz was standing just a few metres away, and that whatever this was, she knew about it and was part of it. She had an envelope in her hand, a big brown one. I've been sold, she thought.

'Shaz,' she shouted, 'what's happening?'

Shaz turned away as the man and the woman took one arm each and hustled Nina towards a small van waiting at the side of the heath. Nina wasn't sure, but when she thought about it later, she could have sworn that Shaz was crying.

CHAPTER FOURTEEN

Grace

After midnight, Wednesday, 27 February

I could still smell the trouble when we got into the car but it drifted away the faster I drove. I wasn't sure whether Meg and Daphne were scared by my crazy driving but they didn't say anything. There was so much more to worry about. We're gangsters now, I thought, outside the law. Sisters doing it for themselves. Me and Meg and Daphne. I couldn't think about Daphne, not yet. I knew we were doing the right thing, mad as that sounds. I could see Eleanor, the Eleanor she never got to be, the big grown one, and she was clapping and waving. I tried to assess things in my head while I drove. I'd made a pact to kill a bad man with two almost-strangers so that we could rescue that young girl who could be our granddaughter. It had to be the right thing. And did that make me less angry? No, I'm afraid it didn't, I'm afraid I went on being angry, driving faster and faster until I thought I might explode with it. If that man had stepped out in front of the car on the way back I would have enjoyed running him down.

So I'm glad when we get back to Meg's house intact, and I'm

tired. Anger is always tiring so as soon as we get inside I want to go to sleep, pass out, get away from myself and everyone else. Maybe except for Daphne but I can't think of that now. I want to sleep and then wake up and find this is all a dream, like the stories my year seven children used to write. *And then I woke up and it was all a dream*, they used to put when they couldn't think of anything else to write. They were always so proud, as if they were the first story writers to think of such a neat way of finishing. Maybe I was hard on them, I think now; maybe that is the only kind way to end a sad story.

'Sit down,' Daphne says.

I'd like to say, no, no, we've got a job to do but it's a welcome idea and I sit on Meg's nice grey couch.

'Sorry,' I say, 'I haven't driven for a while.'

It's not the right thing to say, I know it isn't, but it's the best I can do. I don't need to say the rest. I can see in her eyes that Daphne knows it, knows the pain and the anger, and feels it too. Even Meg, even Meg is on the same page as we are even if she doesn't understand all of it. I can hear her muttering, 'Stay safe, stay safe,' under her breath like an incantation. She probably doesn't know she's doing it.

They both nod and agree and sympathise and no one mentions the actual killing, the nitty-gritty. My nose tickles with the smell of trouble and I feel desperate but it really does help to know we're in this together. It's not a cliché. Stronger together, I think, however different we are, however dire the situation, we're stronger together. Old and bold, I think, old and bold. Strange thought for a strange day. It keeps hitting me afresh, that we've made a pact to kill. It almost feels strange that I have never thought of it as a solution before – lord knows there have been people in my life who might have benefited from being bumped off.

'I'm going to make a cup of tea,' Meg says.

Daphne perches on the arm of my chair while Meg is in the kitchen. I put my hand on her arm, to comfort her or me, I'm not sure which. Both, maybe.

'It's the right thing, isn't it?' I say.

'It is,' she says. 'We have to save her, and we have to do it quickly. I've met people like him, and I know a little about that world. He wasn't bluffing, I can tell you that.'

'How on earth are we going to find someone?' Meg says. 'It's not like they advertise in the local paper.'

She puts the tray of tea down on the coffee table. It seems so incongruous with its plate of biscuits and little milk jug, so strange to balance it there in the middle of a murder plan. So English. I think we all feel that because we stare at the tea tray as if it is something peculiar.

'Let's think,' I say. 'There has to be someone somewhere.'

I don't want to tell them that I've got absolutely no idea where to find someone either. It wouldn't be good for morale. I think so hard my head hurts, but my creative powers don't seem to be functioning as well as they usually do.

'I don't know many people,' says Meg, 'and also I'm pretty bad at forward planning. I've got no common sense at all.'

Jesus, I think, that woman drives me mad when she puts herself down like that.

'Meg,' Daphne says, 'I don't know who's told you such a load of nonsense but it's not at all helpful to you just now. Or us. Or Nina. We need you. We need all of us, and we need us to be as tip-top as any group of pensioners has ever been. A lot depends on it, and I think we're up to it. But we all need to think as hard as we can to try to come up with a viable plan.'

Wow, I think, you go, lady. She could persuade anyone to do anything, I am sure of it. She could certainly persuade me. I think as hard as I can.

'I don't know many people under sixty-five,' I say, 'and I don't know anyone right now who'd do that sort of... who'd kill a person.'

As soon as I'd said it I realised I sounded very prim. It was true though. I've led a quiet life.

'I've got a friend,' Daphne says, 'who used to be in prison. He's called Des and he lives in my street. Don't get me wrong, he's not a bad man, not at all, but he might know people who could be just bad enough to help us.'

'Oh my goodness,' I say, 'Daphne, you are the real deal. That is amazing. Will he mind? Being asked?'

'Oh no,' Daphne says, 'we've got a bit of history. I've helped him a bit with job applications and he mended my tap, that sort of thing. And we both like films that make you cry.'

I make a mental note of that, decide to ask her when we've got more time. I love *The English Patient*.

'Let's get started,' I say. 'Can you ring him, Daph? We need to get her back.'

I'm not so tired any more and I stand up and give Daphne a quick hug, then one for Meg too so that she doesn't feel left out. It feels good to be doing something.

'Hang on,' Meg says, pulling back, 'is he, you know, is he safe?'

She looks around her pale front room and I look at her and

realise that Meg is frightened. That she's worried about more than her possessions, she's scared for her life. I can see it on her and I can see that she too has scary things in her past, this nice middle-class Englishwoman. I feel sad for her.

'Yes,' Daphne says, 'I'd trust him with anything. He's my friend.'

She looks surprised as she says this and I think, what made you not trust yourself, lovely Daphne?

'I understand why you are worried, Meg,' I say.

Daphne and Meg become very still. I'm aware that they are listening to me.

'Go on,' Daphne says.

'It's a worry, using another person. Getting someone else involved. Always scary to let someone else in. But look at us, we're not so young.'

I hold my hand out, complete with age spots and wrinkles.

'I reckon,' I say, 'that between the three of us, we could have sorted this out with no problem when we were thirty. Done it ourselves. But we ain't, ladies, and we're going to need a bit of help.'

'And we're going to be so careful,' Daphne says. 'We're going to find exactly the right person. I wouldn't suggest my friend if I didn't think he would be able to help us, I promise.'

'OK,' Meg says, 'I guess I trust you. We're all in it together.'

I'm surprised at how quickly Meg can appear calm. Something happened to you, I think, made you learn to keep it all under control, not let anything show. I guessed it was something to do with that husband of hers.

'I'm going to ring my friend,' Daphne says.

She leaves the room and I can hear the murmur of sounds as she speaks.

'Please,' I can make out, and, 'we really need some help.'

I hold Meg's hand.

'It's OK,' I whisper, 'she'll do the right thing.'

Meg nods but I can hear from her breathing that she's crying. She seems to be pulling at something, as if she's pulling a door shut. I try so hard to stay awake but the sofa is comfortable and I must have closed my eyes for a moment, because the next thing I know there's a person knocking on Meg's French windows, the ones that face on to the garden. I go into defence mode and pick up my handbag ready to swing it but Daphne is back and she shushes me down.

'It's OK,' she says, 'it's my friend, we thought it best to avoid the front door. Don't worry.'

Meg opens the garden door and Des steps up to the sill. I don't know who I was expecting but it certainly wasn't him. He is Asian, and tall, and his smile lights up the night. I feel like I know him from somewhere. He stands there, seemingly unable to step into the room.

'Come on in,' Daphne says.

'No disrespect to anyone, but I'm not sure about this,' he says.

Meg and I look at Daphne.

'Please come in anyway,' she says. 'We won't expect anything, but we need some help. Could we just talk?'

I'm not sure Daphne has got it right this time. This can't be our person.

'OK,' he says but he still hovers on the edge until Meg realises what's bothering him.

138

'Oh,' she says, 'your shoes. It's OK, I don't mind.'

'But,' he says, and he lifts up one foot after another as if he is executing the opening moves of a dance.

'I know,' Meg says. 'Take them off, that'll be fine.'

He looks relieved at the idea and my heart goes out to him.

'Yes,' he says, 'yes, thank you, I will do that.'

I look at Daphne to show my concern but she doesn't seem to notice. She's worried too.

He takes his shoes off and places them next to each other by the window. My heart hurts again when I see that his socks have more than one hole in them. Meg starts looking round her and I think, I bet you have a darning kit somewhere, woman. She reminds me of my grandmother in the countryside outside Kingston, even though Meg lives in this nice house in London.

'I'm really not at all sure I can help,' he says. 'I understand roughly what you need and I can't do it. I can't.'

I look at the other two and I can see that they are desperate for him to say something different. But they resound for me, those two words. *I can't.*

'OK, no worries, thank you for even considering it,' I say.

Daphne raises her hand slightly in my direction and I know that's a sign for me, a sign that we should persuade him, work on him, but I don't think that's right. Don't worry, the hand says, don't worry, he's OK.

'We're in trouble,' Meg says. 'That poor girl.' She starts crying, Meg, and Des looks horrified.

'I wish I could help,' he says.

Des examines his fingers, one by one. He looks nervous. There's no dark side to him that I can see, no smell of trouble, and what's more, his eyes crinkle slightly so they look as if they're smiling even when he's being serious. This will never work, I think. We should send him home. I'm about to say this when Daphne jumps in.

'The thing is,' she says, 'we are in a situation. There's a man, a really horrible man, we think he's a possible people-trafficker and a definite pimp, and he's got a young woman we know. She's really young. He knows we know, that's the difficult part, and we wanted to...'

Daphne trails off and Meg looks panic-stricken so I jump in.

'We want to pay someone to kill him,' I say, 'but it's OK, we'll find someone else, I can see that you're...' I'm not sure how to finish the sentence so I leave it there. Des stretches his mouth into a straight line and back again several times and everyone looks shocked. I suppose I could have put it less starkly but I don't know how. It needed saying.

Des strokes his chin as if he has recently lost a beard.

'I'm a very non-violent person,' he says. 'I am more along the Quaker lines, you know, not killing and all that. How old is she?'

'Seventeen,' Meg says.

'I had a sister,' Des says, stroking his chin again for all he's worth, 'and whilst I would never, you know, that's not me, I do know some people. These people may be able to help you out, but I'm worried.'

Des gets up and walks over to the windows and back before sitting down and standing up, twice. He keeps opening his mouth to speak and then closing it again.

'We're very worried too,' I say, 'and it's not right for you to get involved, we'll think of something else.'

I look at the other two and I can see that they agree with me.

'Sorry, Des,' Daphne says. 'Sorry to put you in a difficult position. We'll manage, don't worry, you're off the hook.'

She shrugs her shoulders and looks at Meg and me. 'I shouldn't have,' she says, 'I'm sorry.'

I'm thinking that's that, back to the drawing board, but I had reckoned without Meg.

'Are you sure?' Meg says. 'Are you really, really sure? Only this girl, she's a nice girl, a lovely girl, and the things they make her do...'

Des redoubles the scrutiny of his hands. If ever anyone had a bubble above their head saying, 'Thinking,' Des was that person.

'I think I might be able to help,' he says eventually. 'Seventeen, that's very young. Just a kid. I really do want to help. My sister, she, erm, she was very young. Scared. I did what I could. But I'm worried because these kind of people are dangerous. Could we not go to the police?'

Daphne starts to explain and he holds his hand up.

'I'm being stupid,' he says. 'I know exactly why, I hope you'll pardon my stupidity. I'm no hero but, yes, I'm at your service.'

'Heroes come in all shapes and sizes,' I say and the others nod as if I've said something wise.

'Indeed,' he says, 'and you three ladies are heroes. But even heroes need a helping hand.'

With no warning, I feel as though the room is closing in on me. I think about Nina again and I think, we can't do this. We're not up to it, not one of us. I'm about to say something about abandoning the whole thing and taking our chances with the police when he says something that makes me look up.

'They've done it before, that's the thing. Had successes, I mean.'

We all look at each other and suddenly, it's real. Suddenly, we've got a fighting chance of getting that lovely girl back, and helping her to have the life she should have been having all along.

'I'm going to call a number,' he says, 'but I'm not going to bring them here. You wouldn't want them in your house, I can assure you of that. They're friends of mine, acquaintances really, and they're good guys, solid gold, but they need the money if you know what I'm saying. They really need the money.'

I can hear alarm bells ringing straight away. I mean I'm not saying the person we use has to be doing it for job satisfaction or because it's a vocation, I'm not that crazy. It's just I've met some people in my life who are desperate for money, really desperate, and they're not always the most trustworthy. Or calm. We really need someone we can trust, but I can see that's a tall order. I think that Meg and Daphne might be thinking along those lines as well because neither of them says anything for a moment.

'Oh,' Des says, 'I can see that you're not quite happy with that. I feel like you were expecting something else. Am I right?'

The three of us look at each other, no one sure what to say so I jump in.

'We're worried, that's all, Des. We're very grateful but we are worried.'

'Would it help you to trust me if I tell you my story?' Des says. 'The brief version?'

I nod and Meg does too. I really want to know more about

this young man. A lot rests on him. I guess Daphne already knows, and that's almost enough, but still…

Des looks at his holey socks and holds on to his knees as if they might leave the room without him if he gave them a chance.

'I tried to help my sister in a time of crisis and something terrible happened,' Des says. 'I was in prison for many years. I am not a troublemaker, but my whole life has been spoiled. Daphne here, she helps me.'

'Sorry, Des,' Daphne says, 'sorry to ask for your help. I know how much you hate trouble.'

'I understand,' Des says, 'and I'd just like to say that I'm not sure that this is a course of action to which you are totally committed. I get that and perhaps I could be of help, you know, with the decision-making process. I've made some poor decisions in my time. I know the wrong decision when I see it, usually.'

That isn't what we asked for, I think; this isn't helpful at all. All we were after was a hired hand, it's easy in the movies.

'What else are we supposed to do?' I say. I didn't mean to say anything but the words kind of erupted, as if they had a mind of their own.

'You don't know,' Des says, 'by any chance whether the gentleman in question has any allergies? For example an allergy to bananas, that can be life-threatening in some instances. Or nuts, that can have tragic consequences for the sufferer.'

Oh my God, I thought, and I thought it in capitals, like the kids use when they're texting. OMG. This guy is a fruitcake. He watches too much TV, and that's clear. I mean, that might work, if it was a drama series on the TV. He might well have a fatal allergy, but this is the real world.

'I'm afraid,' I say quietly, 'we don't have access to the person's medical records. And we're serious, Des, make no mistake about that.'

The others look at me as though I've kicked a puppy and I shrug my shoulders. Someone has to think clearly, I hope the shrug says. Daphne pulls herself together first.

'There's always poisoning,' she says. 'Everyone is allergic to poison.'

'I'm more of a brute force kind of guy,' Des says. 'I mean, not personally, but by way of a belief.' He removes a couple of invisible specks from his trousers.

It's incongruous, the idea of Des and brute force, and I try not to smile. Meg looks alarmed.

'If you're sure, then I think I've got a plan which will work,' Des says.

This is not what I'm expecting.

'What we need,' Des says, 'is to get him somewhere on his own. Maybe arrange to meet him or something like that. Then we can send in the guys and hey presto, job done.'

Des looks pleased with his idea. He stretches his mouth out once and then looks up, smiling.

I am horrified. Oh really? I think, no shit, Sherlock. I can't believe the other two are nodding, but then I look at Daphne and I realise that she's trying really hard here. She wants this to work, for Nina and for Des and for all of us, and I need to join in properly if I want to help her. No matter that he's stated the obvious, no matter that we could have come up with this on our own. It still had to work. Get him on his own and drop him. That's the suggestion? Even though that's the basis for every murder plot I've ever watched or read, even though I was hoping for something a little more specific? He's a beginner too, I think, prison or no prison. I walk over to the window and lift a tiny corner of curtain. There's a thick silence in the room and I realise that the other two are waiting for me to comment before they say anything. OK, I think, steel yourself, girl, there's something in it even if it's obvious. I nod.

'That's a great idea,' Daphne says.

'Really good,' Meg says.

'How would we get him on his own?' I say. I can't shake the feeling that we're role-playing in some ghastly management training course.

'If I might offer a suggestion?' says Des, crossing one knee over the other so that I can't help seeing the underside of one of his socks, which is more or less one big hole. 'This is a man who likes money. I can tell that. Don't we all, I can hear you thinking, but some more than most, I'd say. For some people it's the reason they get up in the morning, the reason they go to bed at night. I think this guy is one of them.'

Good point, I think, keep going.

'And a man who likes money may not always use his head, if he thinks there's some more he can get hold of.'

The way he speaks reminds me of year eight pupils writing a stilted essay, but I try not to feel like his teacher.

'So what I propose is,' he continues, 'that you ladies should offer him some money in return for the release of your friend.'

'He wouldn't do it,' Daphne says. I'm glad she's thinking straight.

'Exactly,' says Des, clapping his hands. 'This is a fact we know already, he would not at all do this under any circumstances. This is where the essence of this plan lies. He turns up to take the money – I am predicting with all the powers of prediction at my disposal that he will not be able to turn down the money – and we then bish, bosh, bash and all is done.'

As he says bish, bosh, bash Des slaps his knees hard to emphasise each word. Meg looks terrified.

'What about our friend?' Daphne says. 'How will that help us to get her?'

'Aha, I haven't finished yet,' Des says. 'Part two, of course, we need to rescue the girl. This is the great part. We will ask him to bring her to the rendezvous so that we can see her before we hand the money over. He brings her with him and this is our chance to obtain her. Snatch her back from the jaws of, jaws of…' Des runs out of steam and stands waiting for us to react. I can see that he's pleased with himself.

'There's a hole in that argument I could drive a bus through, Des,' Daphne says. 'If he brings her, he'll bring someone else with her, so that she doesn't run away.'

Meg and I nod.

'No, no,' Des says. 'Oh no, we can nip that one in the bud. We have to tell him, don't bring anyone with you except the girl or we won't hand the money over.'

We all stare at him. I don't know about the others, but I'm thinking, what? Why on earth would he do what we ask him to? Can we really help that poor girl?

'You have an advantage here, ladies,' Des says, 'although I don't think that any of you have realised it yet. He's not expecting any funny business, our man, that's the thing. He'll be thinking, and pardon me for taking a liberty and stepping into his shoes, he'll be thinking, these are old women with no power. Stupid old women. I can do exactly what I like, take their money and run for the hills.'

'That's outrageous,' Meg says, 'but very familiar.'

That Henry again, I think.

Daphne looks at me with a slight shrug of her shoulders. I see what she means. It's not as if we have an alternative plan, and we have to try something, for Nina.

'OK,' I say. 'If we go with that idea, what happens next?'

I'm not sure. I could be so wrong, here. I've been wrong before when it mattered.

'Right,' Des says, 'right, OK, let's see.'

He taps his fingers on his knees and looks up to the ceiling as if there might be some kind of auto prompt there.

'I can contact the gentlemen involved and arrange a meet up,' he says. 'I use the word "gentlemen" loosely, I hope you understand. As I said, the meet up is better away from here, possibly in a park or a café.'

Another café, I think. It's good that south-east London is riddled with them these days. I name one on the Brockley Road, one we haven't used yet to make a pact or rescue a teenager.

'Ten o'clock in the morning?' Daphne says. 'Will that give you enough time? Only all the time we're talking about it, Nina is...' She tailed off.

'Plenty, plenty,' Des says, looking at his watch.

I can't help thinking that I'm not terribly hopeful but he's all we've got. All we have between us and leaving Nina to a terrible fate.

Des gets up to leave and there's an awkward moment while he stretches and then undoes the laces on his shoes. I wonder what's taking him so long and I can see that the others are too.

'The thing is…' he says.

We wait. Don't back out now, please, I think.

'The thing is, I'm in a bit of a sticky situation at the moment. I'm just wondering – no obligation, obviously, ladies – just wondering whether I might at all be able to stay here tonight, make my phone calls from here, as it were?'

We all stare at him without speaking. He seems genuine, but it's not my house so I'm glad when Meg speaks up.

'I only have three bedrooms,' she says, 'and we're all staying here, there's three of us, I'm so sorry.'

I look at Daphne and realise that Meg is right, it's probably best to stick together. We'll stay together, until something has been sorted out. Whatever that means.

'I'm not sure how to say this,' Des says, 'and I know it's the biggest cheek ever, but I can't help thinking that your sofa would be utterly adequate for me. And the other thing is, these phone calls I'm intending to make, on your behalf, they're not the kind of phone calls a person should make in the road, where anyone could hear them. Better behind closed doors, I'm thinking.'

'Des,' says Daphne, and her tone takes me right back to one of the schools I worked in, where the teacher in the next-door classroom always spoke in loud and disappointed tones, even when she was taking the register. 'Des, has there been another problem with the rent? I told you, come to me before you get turned out next time. It's much easier to help you before than after.'

Des examines his nails.

'There was a series of unfortunate coincidences,' he says, 'many of which I couldn't have predicted, I swear.'

'And none of them your fault, Des?' Daphne says, with a smile.

Des hangs his head like a year seven pupil who has forgotten his homework.

'OK, OK,' Meg says, 'I'll bring you down some blankets and a pillow. You can have a shower if you'd like, too, I'll bring a towel.'

Des looks embarrassed to the point of desperation and I wonder how the hell he's going to be able to do the tasks we've trusted him with, but later, upstairs in Meg's bedroom when the three of us get together for a quick debrief before bed, Daphne says differently.

'Don't be fooled,' she says. 'He's smart as a whip, and sweet with it. If gambling had never been invented, he'd probably be living in a mansion or running a successful business. He just can't resist, to the point where he literally has nothing. He's gambled everything away, and failed every rehab and treatment programme that's been tried. And that's not all, but he can tell you the rest another time. The thing is, I think he will know the right kind of people.'

Meg bursts out laughing and despite the oddness and desperation of our situation it's hard for Daphne and me not to join in.

'The right kind of people,' Meg says, shaking her head. 'Henry used to talk about them all the time. The right kind of people.'

CHAPTER FIFTEEN

Meg

Wednesday, 27 February

I couldn't sleep at all now that Nina was gone. I moved from one side of the bed to the other, trying not to hear the echo of Henry's snores and thinking about her, wondering where she was and how she was coping. The feelings were familiar. I had felt like that before, I knew I had, but I didn't want to think about that. I couldn't bear it, and I couldn't bear to think of what might be happening to Nina either. I thought of all the times I'd lain awake, especially recently, since Henry passed, and I realised I didn't need much sleep any more. It was strange, finding out new things about myself. I'd always thought I needed lots of sleep but it seems I was wrong about that as well as everything else.

Long ago, Henry's boss had asked us to go on an early morning walk with him and his wife. I think it was some kind of bonding exercise for the staff but I heard Henry on the phone saying, 'No, I'm sorry, Meg would be hopeless any time before twelve, she doesn't do mornings.'

The boss must have said something about how it was a good

thing we didn't have any children and Henry said, 'Yes, well, the lord moves in mysterious ways but I would have been the one who had to disrupt my day with the school run so I'm grateful for small mercies.'

I was terribly upset at the time. I would have loved to go on the walk – I think some of them were bringing dogs. I would have loved the school run even more. I would never have entrusted a child to Henry and his foul temper.

I gave up on trying to sleep at about six o'clock. I couldn't think of anything helpful I could do except make breakfast for everyone. Thinking about that took my mind off the plan and poor Nina for a moment or two but when I got downstairs they had beaten me to it. Everyone had hot drinks and empty plates and I had to listen hard while I made toast to bring myself up to speed. I didn't want to make a fool of myself by not knowing what was going on. It seemed that Des had contacted his 'friends' and we were going to meet them that morning in the park, not a coffee bar.

'Meeting in the park,' Grace said, 'are you sure? No one goes to Hilly Fields in this sort of weather. We'll stick out.'

I looked out of the window and saw that she was right. Rain and wind and winter. Even the dog walkers would probably be at home.

'No, it's best,' Des said. 'No one will see us, we'll be home and dry if you'll pardon the pun.'

I could see the sense in that. I glanced at the other two and saw that they felt the same way.

I dug out some of Henry's clothes for Des, including Henry's hiking socks. Henry had never gone hiking, and the socks were still bound together with a plastic tag. We all smiled despite the circumstances as Des sat in a chair and turned his feet this way and that with the new socks on, admiring how they looked. I found scarves and hats for all of us, and was in the middle of doling them out when Daphne said, 'Don't you think we should have a clearer plan? I mean, I know what we're aiming for, and how much we can pay, but that doesn't seem enough somehow.'

Grace and I agreed. Des had gone to the bathroom to put on Henry's jogging pants.

'We've only got a minute or two on our own,' Grace said. 'Are we confident that we know what we're doing? Let me just take us through it. OK, we're going to meet these chaps, two of them, I think. We won't have to explain from scratch because Des has already done that, but we will have to check that they know what we think they know, and fill in any gaps.'

'Will we be asking them how they're going to do it?' I said. 'Only I'm thinking maybe it's better not to know. Not because I don't want it done, I do, but...'

I couldn't really explain. It was too much, that was the beginning and the end of it. I'd seen enough. I didn't want to seem like a big coward, but I knew my limits.

'You can stay out of that bit if you're squeamish,' Grace said, 'but I think we need to know the details, so that we can check it all out. There's so much that could go wrong.'

I could see that I needed to know.

'I'm fine,' I said, 'sorry. We're in this together.'

I crossed my fingers behind my back for luck and left my toast on the plate to get cold.

There wasn't time for any more talking. We left the house by separate doors in case we were being watched. I went out of the front door with Grace. I think she thought that talking would make me feel better. It was kind of her.

'Did you ever go to one of those laser shooting party things?' Grace said.

I opened my mouth to say that I hadn't but she just went on talking.

'I did,' she said. 'We went on a team-building thing from school and it was terrible. You walk around in the dark knowing that the other team are all trying to shoot you, even though it's only with a laser. I feel a bit like that, do you?'

Bloody Nora, I thought, is Grace scared? I had thought she was practically invincible. I felt as though the odds against us were getting shorter all the time. Or longer, I wasn't sure which one was appropriate. And did she want me to say something comforting? Me? I felt a surge of pride, and something like comradeship. Like a soldier in battle.

'Do you know,' I said, 'to most people all old women look the same? It's true, honestly, they did a test with students, all young, and they asked them to memorise eight older faces. They left them for twelve hours then showed them twenty-four to choose from and nearly all of them got less than four right. They didn't even get the right nationalities, they chose mainly white when half of the women weren't white, that sort of thing. So, we're almost anonymous. We can relax.'

'Is that true?' Grace asked.

I changed the subject but I think she knew. Henry would have hammered away at me until I admitted I made it up to make myself feel better.

She smiled at me.

'We'll be OK, Meg, it'll be fine,' she said.

I could have kissed her. Daphne probably would have.

They walked more quickly than us, so we had arranged to meet them by the stone circle. I couldn't help thinking we looked suspicious, but we wouldn't be overheard. The stone circle has been in the local park since the year two thousand, and locals are as proud of it as if it had been there from prehistoric times. It's tucked away at the top of the park behind the café. I like to go there on sunny days and watch the children and the dogs playing, so I hoped that whatever was going to happen didn't spoil that for me in any way. It was odd to be there as part of a group, instead of on my own. I'm usually on my own.

Des and Daphne were already there when we got to the stones. Daphne was amazing. She and Grace were so strong. So cool, so collected, it made me feel better just to look at them. They clearly belonged together. I heard a burst of soaring, tuneful violin and I felt relaxed and ready.

'Hello, everyone,' Daphne said.

She beamed as if we had all gone to her house for a cocktail party. Grace and I couldn't help smiling.

'It's an honour to help you ladies,' Des said, still staring down at Henry's socks.

There's a cracked sundial on the ground between the standing stones, and I was looking at it when they arrived, Des's contacts, so I didn't see where they came from. It was as if they'd dropped to the ground from outer space, or been parachuted from a passing plane. One minute they weren't there, and the next they were. Two of them, a man and a woman, and nothing like I expected. Nothing at all. I wasn't expecting a woman, for a start. I didn't think it was any sort of job for a woman but the world has changed, moved on, and Henry always said I was behind the times. They were both rather small, and that was the next surprise. I mean really small, because I'm only five foot one and I almost felt like a basketball player next to the woman. The man was probably an inch or two taller than me. They were broad, stout even, and they both looked like people you wouldn't mess with, despite their height. That was good, I liked that about them.

'Erm, we all know why we're here,' Des said, 'so we don't need any introductions.' Everyone nodded and for a moment I was reminded of a church service, the bit at the beginning where the priest says something like, Dearly beloved, we are gathered here today.

The man looked to the woman. She was clearly the spokesperson for the two of them.

'We don't often do business with ladies,' she said, 'and I must say it's a pleasure. Des here has given us an outline of the problem we need to deal with and in principle, in principle only, we are happy with the terms and conditions he has set out. As I understand it, we are to turn up when told, and carry out a job for you, clearing up afterwards if possible. Any questions so far?'

We all shook our heads. I didn't think any of us were able to speak.

'These are our terms. We would like half of the money up front, today if possible, and half when the act has been completed. Should anything go wrong, there must be nothing to lead from us to you, and nothing to lead from you to us. Understand? So no emails, texts, using your phone for calls, we'll do everything the old-fashioned way.'

'I don't like computers,' the man said.

I could see Daphne trying to give him a sympathetic look but the small woman got in first and shot him a terrifying scowl. He didn't say anything else.

'How soon do you think you can arrange a meet?' the woman said.

'I'm not a hundred per cent sure,' Daphne said, 'but I think it would be best to do it as soon as possible. We should be able to tell you within the next twenty-four hours.'

I had been hoping that Daphne would tell them about the phone I had given Nina, but when I thought about it I could see that she needed to keep information to a minimum.

'Right,' the short woman said. 'For the purposes of this proposed action, you can call me Clara. It's not my real name. You take this phone, use it when you tell me the time and place. It's new and mine is the only number on the SIM card. Throw it away afterwards. You got that?'

Suddenly the whole scene stopped feeling like a game, or something on TV. It felt scary, and it felt real. Someone was going to die, because we wanted to stop him hurting any more young girls and because we needed to rescue Nina. We were going to make this happen. I had a sudden lurch in my stomach and I think the others did too. We all looked at each other and then looked away, as if we each had to find something else to focus on. Something safe. Of course it was then that I noticed the dog with the couple. With the man, to be exact. I don't know how I'd missed it before, but I had. Probably because it was so quiet. Henry used to say that small dogs were the worst, always yapping and trying to prove that they were big dogs at heart, but this little scrap was as quiet as a mouse on a lead. The male assassin saw me looking and sent me a very small smile.

'She's called Shoe,' he said.

Clara shot him a killer look and he turned to stare straight ahead.

I clamped my hands to my sides to stop myself going over to stroke Shoe. I could just imagine how soft she would feel under my fingers, and how glad she would probably be for a bit of attention. I smiled at her instead, some dogs like that, and I think she was one of them. I hoped they weren't going to take her with them when they did whatever they did.

There was a silence.

'Have you got references?' Grace said.

She looked slightly worried, which was unusual for Grace. I was glad she had asked.

'Ha,' Clara said, 'sensible question. You're thinking, have this pair of clowns ever done anything like this before, aren't you?'

'I'm sure if Des recommends you,' Grace said, 'that's good enough, but it would be useful to know.'

I marvelled at how professional she sounded. Des bit his nails and stared off into the distance.

'We operate on a need-to-know basis,' Clara said, 'but I can assure you we have glowing references, if only we could show them to you.'

'Need to know' had been one of Henry's favourite phrases. He often used it to keep me out of things, so I had a bit of resistance to it, although I understood why she would say it. Grace still looked worried.

'Maybe we could discuss that on a more intimate basis,' she said.

She motioned and the two of them walked a little way away from the rest of us. I couldn't hear what they were saying, but I could see Clara talk and gesticulate and I'm not sure if it was my imagination but I thought Grace stepped back from her. Just a small step.

We were an awkward group left kicking our heels. Me, Daphne, Des and the small killer with the dog, Shoe. I bent down and stroked her. I tried to think of things to say, but I could only come up with 'Nice dog.'

'Thanks,' the killer said, 'she's a star.'

Grace and Clara came back and Grace nodded to show us that she was satisfied with whatever Clara had said.

'One more thing,' Daphne said. 'I'd like to know, even though it might be difficult to be clear, what method you are going to use.'

Value for money, I thought, of course we need to know. Another Henry phrase. I wondered how he would get on if it was him who was here negotiating. Would he be better at it than us? And what would he have done if that lovely girl had run into the café while he was sitting there? I thought I knew.

'Other people's lives, Meg, other people's lives.'

He used to say that to me whenever I got upset about something awful that had happened, a flood or a tsunami or tiny children left with no parents. Babies at borders in cages, young women being beheaded, schoolgirls captured for slaves. It didn't matter how gruesome the story, to Henry it was just 'other people's lives'. So I can guess that's what he would have said.

For a moment I forgot where I was, that's how real Henry seemed. Thinking about those words really brought him back.

I'm different now, I wanted to shout at him, I've got friends and everything, we're doing something important. I pictured him at the end, when he was gasping for breath. Poor Henry.

I tuned back in and heard Clara say, 'The method is not important. It will be determined by the research that is done beforehand.'

Her partner bent down to fuss with the dog. It was clear that he was embarrassed by Clara's speech. I thought that given the choice, he might be the easier of the two to talk to and I resolved to mention this to the others later.

'There will be a short surveillance interval, after which you will arrange a meeting offering money,' Clara said. 'Is that understood?'

Des tried and failed to look nonchalant about the way things were going and his part in it. He stood there, resplendent in Henry's coat, jumper, socks, underpants and trousers and I moved a little closer to him. I liked that he was wearing Henry's clothes, I think, that was all.

Daphne handed over an envelope of money and the meeting was over. I felt closer to Nina already. We went home, and this time I went into the house through the French windows with Grace. It's an odd way to enter your own home but I understood it was for the best. Des came too. He wanted to stay, and I could see that he was relieved when I didn't ask him to leave.

It was awkward at my house. I think we all needed to be alone with our thoughts and our worries, but instead, there we all were, together as if it was an afternoon tea party. I kept thinking of Nina and I wanted to howl and cry but I had to keep myself together for the others, and I guess they felt the same way. Des broke the silence.

'Shall I just put the hoover round, ladies?' he said. 'No need for anyone to get up.'

I was shocked. No one has ever hoovered this house except for me, and I thought the carpets would be shocked too. They had probably never realised that men could do housework.

'No, it's fine,' I said, 'thank you for asking.'

'Oh Meg,' Grace said, 'we can't help Nina right now, not this second. And we've foisted ourselves on you, probably walked in all manner of dirt. I can see that you usually run a tight ship, why don't you let him help?'

I felt a little bit panicky. I didn't want to make too much of refusing help, but on the other hand I was terribly worried in case he discovered ancient piles of dust under chairs and thought I was a terrible housekeeper. In the end I couldn't help thinking, what does any of it matter when poor Nina is with that man?

I needn't have worried anyway. Des was of the surface school of cleaning, going carefully round objects and furniture as if they were militarised no-go areas. We didn't speak about the matter of the contract for a few minutes, and then Grace said, 'I'm not ecstatic about this. What does anyone else think?'

'Nor me,' Daphne said, 'but I think there's still a chance things could turn out OK. I mean, when we offer him the cash, if we make it tempting enough, he may just take it and run, I mean really actually hand her over. What did Clara say, when you talked to her on her own?'

I was glad that Daphne had asked. I wanted to know too.

'She thought there was a possibility that he might take the money and give us Nina,' Grace said, 'but I got the feeling she was clutching at straws. I'm not even sure that they've ever done anything like this before. I mean they talk the talk, but…'

'There's a chance, though,' I said. 'They knew quite a lot about it, and it's got to be better than nothing. We have to try. And maybe we can do it with money. Think of that!'

I didn't mention that Henry had been a believer in every person having their price. It wouldn't have helped. I hoped so much that we could avoid any more bloodshed. I don't even like killing wasps, although there was something else nagging at the back of my head, something about Henry but I wasn't sure exactly what. There was a complete silence on the violin front, which was welcome if not particularly helpful.

Grace seemed happy at the idea of avoiding the killing.

'Oh wouldn't that be great,' she said, 'just to pay him off and that would be that, no harm done.'

'Erm, I have a good insight into the criminal mind,' Des said, 'which, pardon me, I don't think you ladies have.'

'Perhaps,' Grace said, 'we haven't led quite such sheltered lives as you think we have.'

She sounded slightly snappy. I looked at Daphne and we made brief, polite, grimacing faces at each other. It would be the worst thing if Grace and Des fell out with each other. And I actually have had a sheltered life, I thought. I wished for one second that I had sold the house and moved to a seaside bungalow when Henry died. A lot of people do.

'No offence meant,' Des said, 'only his type, they're scum if you'll pardon my expression. He would sell his grandmother down the river for ten pence. I'll bet you any money you like he has no redeeming qualities at all. No amount of money will

161

be enough for him. Not to mention the fact that if he's spared, as it were, it'll be some other poor girl next time.'

'I know,' Daphne said. 'I know that really, but I just hate to think—'

'Maybe we should tackle it head on,' Grace said, 'think through the various methods so that nothing comes as a shock. Do you think that might help?'

Daphne looked doubtful.

'It's just I knew someone like him once,' she said, 'when I was at university, and he was a terrible person, I see that now, he did a lot of harm but at the time, I didn't always realise. I used to collect nice facts about him, like he always called his mum on Sundays and he once fed a stray cat, that sort of thing.'

We all stared at Daphne, wondering where this could possibly be going.

'It made me realise,' she said, 'that there are, you know, good things sometimes about people. Even bad people.'

This seemed such a surprising but true thing to say that I couldn't think how to answer. You see, Henry? I thought. You see what subtleties you miss by being so sure about everything?

'Some people may have little patches of good,' Grace said, 'and I can see how that would make a person think twice. But that man will use that little girl just to make money for himself. He'll use her and allow her to be used again and again and again until she isn't Nina any more. Remember what she said about him wanting her soul, or however it was she said it. She'll get hooked on drugs or alcohol or both and there will be absolutely no hope for her. I've seen it happen.'

The me of me, I thought, that's how she said it. The me of me.

'I know,' said Daphne, 'I have seen it too. Men have been selling women's bodies for ever, probably. I know we're doing the right thing, but still.'

'Well, I'm not sure if I've seen it before or not,' I said, 'but I know a very bad egg when I see one, without having to crack the shell open and smell it.'

They laughed at that. It lightened the atmosphere, but I meant it.

'Maybe if we talk about it, the nitty-gritty, normalise what's happening, it might help,' Des said. 'I went to this group thing in prison, where we were encouraged to talk about the things we didn't want to talk about, so that we could, erm, confront them. It didn't work too well then, but it might now.'

I think we were all so surprised at the idea that specific murder talk might be helpful that none of us spoke. We just gawped at him.

'Cars,' he said. 'That would be a favourite for me, if I had a choice. Running someone over, it doesn't look deliberate, everyone is happy. That Russian poison stuff if we could get hold of any. It's quick, it's clean and they'd think he had Russian connections. It could work.'

'I don't think,' said Grace, 'that it's available to purchase on the open market.'

I was glad that the twinkle was back in her eye.

'Bees,' Des said, undaunted. 'Bees are a friend to all but a deadly enemy to some. If he's allergic, bam, but even if not, a thousand bee stings all together can kill the average human. Depending on body weight, of course.'

'Of course,' Grace said.

'Poison in the food,' Des went on, really enjoying himself

now. 'Lots of people die of food poisoning every year and no one knows how much of it is deliberate.'

I thought of Henry, drinking his soup. Tastes vile, he'd said, have you poisoned it?

'Of course, the good old London Underground,' Des said. 'Crowded platforms, people not standing behind the yellow line, anything can happen. And it does.'

I could see that Grace had heard enough. She had managed to keep it light but she looked exhausted now, and I hoped that Des could pick up the signals. She looked at Daphne and I think a message went between them. I was relieved.

'That's probably enough,' Daphne said. 'I don't think this is helping. If we're going to get through the next few days, maybe we should talk about the matter in hand as little as possible. Unless we're trying to work out a back-up method, if we think our first plan won't work.'

Des looked disappointed.

'I haven't even finished,' he said, 'there's loads more, honestly.'

CHAPTER SIXTEEN

Nina

January – one month earlier

In just over a month Nina's world had changed. Christmas had come and gone without her even noticing. She no longer studied, or read, or even talked to anyone. She often wished that she was dead, but anything she might have been able to kill herself with was kept away from her as carefully as if she was in a locked psychiatric ward, or a prison cell. No belt for the dressing gown they'd given her, no razor for her legs unless she was supervised, and absolutely no leaving the house alone.

They took her out of London at first, to somewhere near the sea. Nina knew this because she could hear it at nights, sucking and whooshing as if everything was perfectly normal. Nina wasn't sure how she knew it was the sea but she did. She thought she might have been there before on a holiday with her mum when she was tiny, or maybe a trip with one of the schools she had been to. Or maybe she'd heard the noise in a dream or read it in a novel. Whatever way it had made itself known to her, she was grateful for it now. The noise felt like a friend and she would listen to it above all the other noises that were happening around her.

There were other girls. They weren't always the same ones, girls seemed to come and go the way they did in dreams. Some weeks they would be around for a few days and Nina would almost feel able to smile at them, and sometimes she saw them once and never again. A few of them did not speak English but an exchange of looks meant that Nina understood the shape of their sorrow, and that they were as unhappy to be there as she was.

There was a fish, a goldfish, in a small tank in the room Nina and the other girls were allowed to wait in. Nina watched it whenever she could. It swam more to her side, the side that she was sitting on, when she was there. She was sure it did. The trouble was, she thought, she had no way of telling if it swam to the other side of the tank when she wasn't there. Maybe it just liked her side more, and wasn't looking for company at all. The girls had allocated seats where they had to sit. Nina thought about sitting on the other side of the room so that she could observe the behaviour of the fish, see if it came towards her. She thought about it every day, every minute, until it became her dearest wish and her obsession.

It was a Friday when she managed it. Nina knew it was a Friday because it had been busier, and the men had been rowdier, more excitable. One of them, Paul, was a regular. He had come every Friday for four weeks, and he called Nina his Girl Friday. Paul was one of the worst, because he seemed to think he was Nina's boyfriend in some way and that he was entitled to some kind of boyfriend/girlfriend thing which made Nina's skin crawl more than anything else.

'Have you missed me?' he said. And, 'I bet you've been looking forward to this.'

Nina didn't even pretend to smile or join in. It made no difference. No difference at all. The relationship he thought he was having was in the man's head.

He'd been in early on the Friday of the fish, which meant that Nina was able to go and sit in the waiting room afterwards before the other girls came in. She was sore and desperate, but to be alone in the waiting room at last was a small relief. Her world had shrunk so much that this was important. This was something she wanted to do for herself, not because she had been told to. Friday for me too, she said in her head like a mantra.

If I can do this, maybe I can run, Nina thought as she crossed the room to sit on the chair on the other side of the tank. Maybe I can wait until the door is opened for some reason and I can run. She sat down in the other chair, the forbidden chair, the chair that had not been allocated to her, and she waited for the fish to swim towards her. It would prove that the fish liked a friendly face, the same as everyone else, she thought. And if fish could make choices, so could she.

Nina was never sure afterwards whether the fish did swim towards her. She thought it did, she hoped it did, but there were a lot of variables for her to take into account. There was the noise, for a start. It seemed that it was not OK, it was far from OK, to sit in a different seat. She hadn't realised that they were watching, but as soon as the two of them burst in, the woman with the clanking bracelets and the man with the thick neck like a toad and the accent like Poirot, Nina noticed the blinking eye of the camera attached to the light in the middle of the ceiling.

Of course, Nina thought as they dragged her off the chair, of course they have to keep an eye on the room, on their property. Call yourself an A star student? she taunted herself. A child might have guessed that, or a fish.

'We gave you a chair to sit in,' the man kept saying, as if it was an extraordinarily generous thing for him to have done. 'We gave you a chair, but you couldn't do what we asked, could you?'

I wanted to see the fish, Nina thought. I wanted to see the damn fish from the other side. She didn't say anything. There was every chance that mentioning the fish would be enough for them to empty it down the toilet, or worse.

Nina understood how Bilbo must have felt when people made him do things he didn't want to do for reasons he didn't understand. If I ever get out of here, she thought, I'm going to play that song he likes on repeat if he wants me to, and pick out all the green sweets before I give him the packet.

'Now sit in the fucking chair we told you to sit in,' the woman said, her bracelets clanking again on her skinny arm. She pulled Nina by her hair across the room and shoved her down. Nina kept her face impassive. She had been practising it ever since she got here, the trick of letting no emotion at all show on her face. Sometimes she was worried that it would stay with her, and that even after she got out of this place she would never again be able to show any emotion. Other times she thought that there would be no after this place, that the chances of getting away in one piece were too slim for her to hope for. Today, the Friday of the fish incident, there seemed to be no hope. Nina sat in her chair counting the places on her body that hurt. Her head, where she had been dragged across the room by her hair. Her wrists, her shin where she had been kicked, and, from earlier, places inside her that she didn't want to know the name of.

Think of something else, Nina told herself, think of something else and stay with it. She wasn't sure of the date, but it must be roughly the time of the mock exams she would be taking if she was still at college. The thought of all her friends sitting together in the exam hall, thinking that she had just left and run off, was a sad one. They're probably all thinking, typical children's home kid, no loyalty, no staying power. They might occasionally wonder why she hadn't even been in touch on Instagram, but that was all. They wouldn't be looking for her, they wouldn't have reported her missing like they would have if she was one of them.

Nina began to quote a speech from *Hamlet*, for comfort. She kept her voice low and concentrated on retrieving the words and saying them in order. She hadn't even noticed that one of the other girls had come in and was sitting on the far side of the room until the girl quietly said, 'That sounds like a poem.'

'Oh,' said Nina, 'I didn't realise you were there.'

'I knew it was poetry,' the girl said, as if she had scored a great victory. 'I'm sensitive like that.'

It was the longest exchange Nina had had with anyone for days. So many days that she wasn't sure how many.

'I'm Romana,' the girl said, 'only that's not my real name. It's just my working name, you know.'

'Oh,' Nina said, 'I'm Nina. I don't know what name they've given me today, it keeps changing.'

'Have you got a plan?' Romana said. 'You'll find you need a plan, to get you through this. We've all got plans here.'

Nina laughed. Her laughter felt creaky and unused.

'I'm not creative enough,' Nina said. 'I can't think of a single plan that doesn't end with me dead on the floor.'

'Hey, sssh,' Romana said, 'hang on.'

She stayed silent for a moment.

'Right,' Romana said, 'the first thing is, keep an eye on that camera.'

She nodded her head a little towards the camera attached to the central light that Nina had already noticed.

'Only talk when it's facing away from you, it turns all the time, sometimes faster than others, so you need to keep an eye out. Otherwise, we don't think the sound works too well so it might be OK if you look away while you speak or,' Romana waited for a few seconds while the camera rotated again, 'just cover your mouth with your hand as though you're coughing.'

'I didn't know,' Nina said, 'no one has spoken to me since I've been here.'

'Can't take the chance,' Romana said. 'There's rumours that sometimes they put a plant in, a stooge, someone who will tell them what's going on.'

'I'm not that,' Nina said.

'I could tell that when I heard the commotion in here just now, it sounded like they dragged you across the room,' Romana said. 'Are you OK?'

Nina shrugged. She was about as not OK as she had ever been, and the fact that Romana cared enough to ask made her want to cry. She kept quiet in case her voice gave her away. The girl seemed nice, but Nina was wary of showing weakness to anyone. A shrug would have to do.

'Stupid question, sorry,' Romana said. 'Right, I'll tell you my escape plan so you know I'm on the level. Only you can't use it, right? It's definitely mine, copyright me. I'm going to stop eating, stop drinking too if I can. I'm not ready to do it yet, but I'm gearing up to it. When I get going, I reckon I'll get ill really quickly, I've always picked up any bugs going. I'll get ill, I'm sure I will and they'll have to call a doctor, or take me to A and E. See?'

Romana smiled as if her plan was perfect and she was just waiting for Nina to acknowledge it. Nina wasn't sure what to say. There were so many things wrong with Romana's plan that it seemed cruel to point them out. Everyone needed some hope. Wasn't that exactly what had been the worst thing since she was here, she thought, the absolute, glaring lack of hope? And the lack of knowledge, the utter confusion. Maybe Romana could help her with that.

'Sounds like you have a plan,' Nina said. 'I wish I had one. I don't even know where we are. Do you?'

'I'm not sure of the name of the town,' Romana said, 'but one of the others thought it might be Hastings. Dunno though, she's a bit flaky. Coast, anyway. You can hear the seagulls.'

'Why here?' Nina said. 'Why here, why me?'

She concentrated on breathing so that she wouldn't cry.

'Ah,' said Romana. 'Are you a children's home kid or a runaway? That's mostly what we are. They pick us carefully.'

'What?' Nina said. 'What do you mean?'

She felt stupid, as if she was in the bottom set at school trying to understand a simple maths process. She just couldn't get it, her brain wasn't working.

Romana waited again while the camera did its spin.

'No one looks for us,' Romana said, 'they can do what

they like. No one expects us to do anything so they don't care if we disappear. I'm a runaway. I bet my mum didn't even notice I was gone. I'm sure she wouldn't have reported me. So I was doing a bit of begging and this and that, trying to get by, when they found me.'

Nina understood the logic immediately. Expendable girls, that's what they were.

'Hastings,' she said. 'I think I've been here before.'

'You'll probably be here again,' Romana said, 'who knows? We'll probably move tomorrow. It's what they do, rent some house short term, Airbnb or something like that, then they advertise us, take pictures and all that, put them on the internet. Set up the cameras if they can. Wait for the punters to arrive, it never takes long. The police can't find us because we keep on moving, going to new places.'

Nina's heart sank. It was worse than she had imagined. She wanted to ask Romana more questions, but the man who looked like a toad came in with two other men. They were old, and Nina could smell the alcohol on them. She looked at the floor and out of the corner of her eye she could see that Romana did, too.

'Shy girls,' said one of the men. 'Oh, I like shy girls.'

'My girls are terribly shy,' toad man said, 'but you'll find that they are very obliging. That's the special one I told you about there.' He pointed to Romana. 'You'll find her most surprising.'

'Obliging,' the smaller of the two men said. He had a slight lisp that made him sound menacing. 'I like obliging, I like the sound of that. Come here, girls.'

Romana went straight to him. She giggled and the noise was hideous to Nina. Can they not tell, she thought, that laugh sounds false and scared? Would that not stop any normal person in their tracks?

'Oh I like you, I think you've got something to show me,' he said, putting his hand on Romana's flat chest. 'Come with me.'

The taller one looked Nina up and down as though she was a horse he had been offered in a market.

'She's a spirited one,' toad man said, 'needs a bit of training, you know how they get.'

'Indeed I do,' said the taller one, 'indeed I do.'

He placed his thumb and forefinger round Nina's skinny arm and dug them in so hard Nina was sure she could feel the bones crunch.

'Come along, my dear,' he said.

'No,' Nina said.

She had no idea that she was going to say that until she said it but the conversation with Romana, another human being who wasn't trying to hurt her, had given her courage. She stamped her foot.

'I will not,' she said.

Let him kill me, she thought, let him just go ahead and do it. Nothing could be as bad as whatever will happen if I don't make a stand. Nina closed her eyes and waited for the blows.

'So basically,' toad man said, 'I'm going to find you someone else.'

Nina heard the door shut and opened her eyes to find that both men had left the room. She stood still, unable to believe that they had left her alone. She was still standing there when toad man came back.

'Sit down,' he said. 'What do you think I am, some kind of purple demon?'

No, worse, Nina thought. She stayed silent.

'Look,' he said, 'Fee, I'm sorry about Fee. She's mad, you know. Try it if you want.'

Nina looked at him. She had no idea what he was talking about.

'My girls,' he said, 'I like them to be happy. Sit in the other chair if you want. It's fine.'

Nina stayed standing.

CHAPTER SEVENTEEN

Daphne

Wednesday, 27 February

Daphne's thoughts were whirling. The feeling reminded her of being little and tipping her head back, staring up at the top of a high building. She needed to hold on to something to ground her. She wished for one moment that it could be Grace who steadied her, but settled instead for sitting heavily in one of Meg's grey armchairs, gripping the arms to keep her from flying away. So many memories flooding in from wherever it was memories go to lie in wait. All that stuff about poison, and different methods. Daphne shuddered. She remembered a conversation she had had shortly before she left university, shortly before she had walked away from her dreams of a life of study and peace. She had been talking to Margaret, the friendly girl who lived on her corridor. It was the only time, Daphne realised, that she had tried to tell anyone what was going on. For years she had imagined that everyone knew, that she had been an object of gossip, but now, looking back, Daphne wasn't so sure.

'Andrew,' she had said to Margaret, trying to find the right words, 'Andrew, he's kind of scary.'

'Gosh,' said Margaret, 'I'd be scared to go out with someone like that, too. He's so, so cool, isn't he?'

'That's not what I meant,' Daphne said, 'and honestly, he's not really that cool underneath.'

'It must be hard though, for you, trying to fit in with his world,' Margaret said. 'Honestly, I feel sorry for you, I do. You being, you know, coloured and him being so, well, you know, popular and everything.'

Daphne remembered the hated word, 'coloured', that everyone had used in the 1960s for anyone who wasn't white. How she had never objected to it for fear of being thought stroppy or worse, 'having a chip on her shoulder'. She had known what would happen if she had said anything about it. The person who had used it would immediately tell her that they didn't mean any harm by it, that she was too sensitive. Daphne had been at a party once where she had stood and listened to one of Andrew's friends hold forth on the fact that he didn't see colour, and that he didn't see why coloured people banged on about it so much. It was less than ten minutes before he asked her where she came from.

She remembered the sinking feeling she had felt at Margaret's words. The time it had taken her to build up to saying anything. The guarded excitement at the thought that someone might understand at last, that someone might be able to help her. The horrible, lurching realisation that no one was listening, that she could shout and shout but no one would hear. It would be like shouting down a well or into an extinct volcano. Shouting to hear the sound of her own voice, nothing more.

She didn't try to explain to anyone again. There had been a couple of times in the years since university when the conversation had got close, especially when Daphne was in Australia. Or if she had drunk a glass or two of wine, never more than that, with friends. And the friends then talked about an uncle, or a stepfather, or a stranger in the park. Women give each other their stories when they are safe, Daphne realised, only she was never safe. Not even when she got rich. When the small investment in a start-up online company her father made for her before he disappeared made her rich, not even then was she safe. She would never be safe. Nina deserved better than that. She always remembered what Andrew had said when she left.

'If you ever,' he said, his face so close to hers that their noses touched, 'ever tell anyone, then I will find you. I will hunt you down like a dog. Do you hear me?'

Daphne heard him. She heard him so clearly that his words rang through the years, through the career she had half-heartedly managed to have, through the friendships she had kept at arm's length. Through the time in Australia, even. Through the loneliness of keeping herself to herself, through the children she had never had, through the money she had never been able to enjoy.

'Are you OK, my lovely?' Grace said. 'We can talk if you want. You're doing so well, we all are. I don't know much about you, but I'm beginning to see how difficult this is for you. Something echoes, doesn't it – there's something especially hard for you.'

'It's not easy for any of us,' Daphne said, 'honestly, nothing special about me, I'm fine. I'm just taking a moment, that's all.'

'Say no more, ladies,' Des said. 'A good man should never intrude on a conversation between women. I'm staying as a kind of resident bodyguard, if that's cool with you all, but I'm going to go upstairs if that's OK. Call me if you need me.'

Meg bustled after him, fussing about the mess and the dust. Daphne and Grace were left alone.

'Really, Daff, this is difficult stuff, don't feel bad,' Grace said. 'I feel your pain, as the kids say. I need you, and I know you're strong. You and I, we're survivors, I recognised it in you the first time I met you. Not to mention the fact that we're sane, more or less, and sanity seems to be in short supply around here.'

Daphne smiled. She felt sustained. Grace's words were nourishing, like water on a dried-up houseplant.

'These are extraordinary times we are living through,' Grace said, 'and sometimes that brings up other extraordinary times a person has lived through, I reckon. And that's OK. That's what has happened to me too, I guess. I see her face, my daughter, my Eleanor, I see it more clearly now than I have done for years. I feel like I could reach out and touch her sometimes, especially at night. Just put my hand out and she'd be there. It's the strangest thing.'

Grace shook her head. Daphne could see that Grace was truly bewildered, and her heart went out to her. Grace settled herself on the floor at Daphne's feet.

'How old was your daughter?' Daphne said.

She wasn't sure if it was the right thing to say, but normal rules of conversation did not seem to apply any more.

Grace shook her head. 'It's the strangest thing,' she said, 'she was four when I left Jamaica, four years old. She made me a good luck card, and she waved me off. I never saw her again, but even so, when I think of her she's a teenager, like our lovely Nina, all long legs and gawky, you know how they get. It's like that's how my head remembers her, even though she never got to that stage.'

Daphne realised that she had been given a gift, a valuable present that she felt she didn't deserve. She took a deep breath.

'It must be nice, to have her to think of, I mean,' she said. 'Oh gosh, I didn't mean... I wasn't saying it's not sad. As sad as can be. It's just...'

'Hey, I get it,' Grace said, 'and you're right, it is good to have her to think of, especially on the days when I don't feel quite so sad. I'm even glad sometimes that I didn't see her when she was ill. It means I've only got good pictures in my head. She got ill with measles and died in two days, so the first I knew about it was a phone call to my landlady. I had to take the call in her living room, just after the landlady's daughter's seventh birthday party, cake and balloons everywhere. Sometimes I dream of that party, and Eleanor is always there, laughing. Gosh,' Grace shook her head, 'what did I say about extraordinary times bringing things up? I haven't talked about this for many, many years. For ever.'

'How long was that after you came here?' Daphne asked.

'Two years,' Grace said. 'Two years of saving and planning and thinking about her all the time. I got a reputation for being standoffish at college, because I never wanted to go out. It was all about money I didn't want to spend so that I could save it for her, but then it got to be a habit. I preferred to be apart from the others.'

Daphne nodded.

'I'm a loner too,' she said and the two women smiled at each other. Daphne held Grace's hand. 'It must have been terrible,' she said.

'Did you ever have children?' Grace said.

Daphne could tell that she needed to change the subject.

'You don't have to tell me,' Grace said. 'I'm assuming no, but maybe you've got some tucked away somewhere? My guess is, it's not a happy story. Am I right?'

This was the kind of question Daphne usually dreaded, the kind of question she would walk away from whenever she could. But Grace had shared something with her, and that meant she could share back. The relief was overwhelming.

'No, I couldn't have any,' Daphne said. Her voice felt scratchy, as though she hadn't used it for years and it needed oiling. 'I met a man, when I was young, a man a lot like the man we are trying to, erm, stop, right now. A man who thought it was OK to use people in a terrible...' Daphne couldn't go on.

'You know the kind of thing,' she said in a brighter, breezier tone. 'It's one of the oldest stories there is.'

'No, Daphne,' said Grace, 'no I don't know, but you don't have to tell me if you don't want to. It's not an exchange thing, mine for yours, I think we both know that wouldn't work.'

Daphne leaned forward and grabbed Grace's hand.

'I've never said,' Daphne said, 'but you know, this man, the toad man, what he's doing to that child. That's my story too.'

Daphne stopped again. Meg's front room faded and suddenly she was back there, in Andrew's bedroom. He didn't live in a hall of residence, because he wasn't a student, Daphne found out later, but at the time it had seemed so very hip to live out. To have a flat with purple walls, huge speakers and drugs in a drawer marked 'dope'. Daphne had wanted to concentrate on her studies, but Andrew had been very persuasive.

'How do I know you love me, baby, if you won't even let me make sweet love to you?' he had said, over and over again. He brought her flowers, and records, and listened when she talked.

I can't believe he's interested in little old me, Daphne had written to her friend at home the night before. *Honestly, he could have any of the girls, he looks like a pop star off the TV. Everyone looks when he goes past, I can't believe he chose me. He's so kind. He's the one, I know it. Don't worry, I'm going to be careful, and I'll tell you all about it afterwards.*

Only Daphne never did tell her friend. She never wrote to her again, hardly went home again. Her friend was a nice girl, a plain, happy girl with a nice boyfriend and a job in a bank. She wouldn't have understood about Andrew, about his flat or his drugs or the fact that he could quote Nietzsche or the fact that he brought three men round the evening Daphne decided to let him have his way, three of them, and he left Daphne with them even though she was crying. He wasn't interested in her at all, it seemed, or he was, but only so that he could sell her virginity to the highest bidder. It was an established practice with freshers at universities in those days. Daphne had read about it since but at the time she was sure she was the only one. The only one stupid enough, the only one bad enough to go along with it. The only one who didn't run screaming and tell someone, who went back again and again, thinking she was good for nothing else, that the die was cast.

'I got an infection,' Daphne said. 'He was a really evil guy. I couldn't have children, it seemed, after that. I left uni, lost my way for a few years.'

That must be the shortest version possible of what happened,

Daphne thought. No mention of the tears, the drugs, the booze, or the men, one after another because Andrew needed more money, always more money. No mention of the shame of not finishing the studies she had longed for.

'Thank you,' Grace said. 'Thank you for telling me but you know, it really, really wasn't your fault. I can tell from the way you're holding yourself that you think you did something that made this happen but you've got to stop thinking that, Daff. You don't think little Nina deserves what's happening, do you?'

'God, no,' Daphne said, 'of course not. But I…'

'You what?' Grace said. 'You asked for it? Is that what you were going to say? You cannot think that. You can't. You know what? I think you just forgot to think straight. Simple.'

Daphne couldn't believe that Grace had made her smile. And maybe, maybe there was something in what she had said. She felt a tiny spark of hope that life could be different, that she could maybe even, if they rescued Nina, be happy.

'Hey,' Grace said, 'I'm so sorry that happened to you. And I'm so honoured, so proud that you chose me to tell it to. I know it's not about me, don't get me wrong, right time and place and all that, but still I'm proud.'

Daphne blushed. Grace knelt up to look at her and her gaze was so direct that Daphne thought that perhaps she did understand, perhaps there had been an Andrew in Grace's life as well. I could kiss her, she thought.

'What happened after Eleanor died?'

Grace opened her mouth to speak, but just at that moment Meg came down the stairs, phone in hand and faster than usual.

'I got a text from Nina,' Meg said, 'on the phone they don't know she's got. She says things are OK, really, nothing too bad has happened. But they're planning something for her tomorrow, she said that.'

The three women looked at each other as they all realised what had to happen.

'Who's going to make the call?' Meg said.

Grace and Daphne both started speaking at once.

'Do you know what?' Meg said. 'Maybe I should do it. I mean, I'm not very good at those sort of things, but...'

'I'm not sure that any of us are very good at those sorts of things,' Daphne said. Grace smiled.

'I never stood up to Henry,' Meg said, 'my husband, Henry. He could be a bit of a bully, and I never really said anything. Well, not till the end. But I'd like to now, if nobody minds. I'll do it for that lovely girl.'

There was no way that Daphne could say no when Meg put it like that, and a glance at Grace told Daphne that she felt the same. The only thing that worried Daphne was the possibility of Meg saying the wrong thing, or spoiling their surprise advantage in some way. It would take planning, that was all, Daphne thought, but she needn't have worried. Meg took to it like a pro. The four of them wrote it down together, Meg's script. She was to offer the money in return for Nina, arrange the meeting but nothing else. No being drawn into conversation. Meg stuck to it like she had the lead role in the school play.

'Just one of you,' Meg said into the phone. She used her own but with the number withheld. 'No hidden extras or we'll just give up on the whole thing and keep the money. We're quite tempted to do that anyway.'

'Wow,' said Daphne afterwards, 'you really made it sound

as if you didn't care whether you got the girl back or not, that was a clever move.'

'Was it?' Meg said. 'It's a thing I learned with Henry: never show that something means a lot to you, or he would take it and smash it. Pretend you don't give a damn. It's the only way.'

CHAPTER EIGHTEEN

Meg

Wednesday, 27 February

I was the one who made the phone calls. I wanted to, but I was scared and I couldn't believe they trusted me to do it. I was sure that Daphne or Grace, probably Grace, would be better at it but they said I'd be fine and I was. I didn't completely mess up, even though I was shaking like a leaf. I gave myself a pat on the back afterwards and I tried to calm down. I wondered for a moment what else I could have done in my life, what job I might have had if things had been different. I could have been a spy, maybe, making international deals and rescuing people stuck in countries they didn't want to be in. Or head of a big multinational corporation, flying from one city to another to negotiate with other important people. I wouldn't have looked at a no-hoper like Henry, I'd have had a different sort of husband altogether. Someone supportive, a little taller and maybe with a moustache.

The second phone call was way more difficult even though I was on a roll. In the first, toad man had been positively gleeful at the thought of getting one over on us, and once he realised that we were offering money he could hardly keep the excitement out of his voice. The second one, the call to the small killers with the dog called Shoe, that was a different kettle of fish. I had to think on my feet, work hard. Start as you mean to go on, Henry used to say. Not everything he said was unhelpful.

'It's tonight,' I said.

'That's quite soon,' Clara said, sounding for all the world as though she was consulting her diary.

'I know,' I said, 'but best not to hang around. Give him time to think of—' I was going to say more but she cut me off.

'Let's not talk about anything extraneous,' she said.

She pronounced each syllable of extraneous as if she was sounding it out from a book, and it was a new word to her. I caught an edge of pride in her voice and I had a flash, just a flash of how it might be to watch a child learning to talk.

'OK,' I said.

I was trying to sound as businesslike as she was but my voice may have been shaking. Everyone can read you like an open book, Henry used to say, you wear your heart on your sleeve, and all your other organs as well.

'OK, there's a road runs up the back of Hilly Fields, leads to the café. The café near the stone circle. It closes at five so there won't be anyone there. It's called Eastern Road. It ends in a kind of car park. He's going to meet us there at midnight, and we're—'

'Over and out,' Clara said. 'I roger that completely. We'll be there.'

I ended the call and looked over at the others.

'Was that OK?' I said. 'Only it's not the kind of thing I usually do.' All of them burst out laughing.

'If you think it's the kind of thing I normally do,' Grace said, 'then you're in the wrong ball park altogether.'

I hadn't realised until the last few days how people can laugh at each other without it being unpleasant, or judgemental. That's a thing I'd like to tell Henry if he ever came back to life. It buoyed me up, the laughter, made me feel OK about the phone call with the Shoe killers, as I'd come to think of them.

'Does anyone else think that this suddenly feels rather dangerous?' Daphne said. 'And should we throw the phone away?'

We all stopped laughing.

'I think we can wait before we decide that,' Grace said, 'and I think I'd like to go and look at the place again later, once it's dark. That'll make us feel much better. Where everyone is actually placed is going to be vital. He's younger than us, fitter than us and he's also more used to this kind of thing.'

'"This kind of thing"?' Daphne said. 'What, you mean like people trying to kill him?'

I could hear the violin and it was screeching. There was snoring, too, but I knew it was in my head. I felt spooked, and I could see that the others did too. We stared at each other and I thought that I might cry if someone didn't say something to break the spell. What about Nina? I thought. What if we fail? What if he punishes her for what we've tried? What if it's even worse for her that we tried and failed, than if we had just left her alone? I was sure that the others were thinking something similar. I had a sudden urge to go to the toilet, just so that I could be alone for a moment or two.

'It's OK, ladies, calm down, calm down,' Des said. I was reassured for a moment when he spoke. It seemed like a gentle word, ladies.

'Let's go back over Meg's call with the toad,' Des said. 'Let's go over it until we know it off by heart. Right, I'll be toad and you be you, Meg. What did you say?'

'You were all here when I was speaking,' I said. 'I feel silly.'

'No,' Grace said, 'Des is right. We probably all heard something different, concentrated on a different part of it. We need to put all those parts together, so that we all know the same things. I know this from being a teacher. Sixteen per cent, I think that's all anyone retains first time around. Even if they're trying hard. It's probably less for old people.'

'Or people who are stressed,' Daphne said.

I could see the sense in what they were saying. I tried to get as near as I could to the actual words I had spoken.

'We have a plan,' I said again, 'we'd like to meet you. We are worried about the girl and we have cash we can offer if you'll hand her over to us.'

We had offered twenty thousand, because it seemed the right amount to start with. I went through all that again in the repeat pretending phone call with Des, explaining where we would meet and at what time. We'd talked about it so much before I made the phone call, I knew it off by heart. Des answered as if he was toad man. He even put on a deep, menacing voice which made me want to laugh, but he was trying his best. We all were. Trying our best in a situation that was completely out of our comfort zone. Another thing I noticed was, whatever kind of criminal Des was, or might have been, he wasn't very good at it. That much had been obvious from the beginning.

'Meg,' Daphne said, 'are you OK? Only we need you to remember exactly what he said, toad man, at the end of the call. It could be important.'

'Sorry,' I said. 'Henry always said my daydreaming would get me into trouble.'

Daphne and Grace looked at each other.

'It seems to me,' Grace said, 'that Henry said a lot of things.'

'What Grace means,' Daphne said, 'is that Henry seems to have been the kind of man who put you down a lot with his sayings. Maybe remembering them makes you put yourself down, and that's a shame. You're doing so well.'

It took me a minute or two to process what she was saying. I mean, I'm not completely stupid, and I was certainly aware that Henry quite often pointed out my shortcomings in a way that made me cringe. But there was a grain of truth in there somewhere, that's what I had always believed. If Grace and Daphne were right, that could be a burden off my shoulders, a lighter way to think about my life and how things turned out.

'OK,' I said, 'I'll think about that.'

I went back to repeating the call, but I kept thinking about Henry.

I repeated the part where we agreed that toad would arrive alone with just Nina, and that they would get out of the car together.

'I think I asked him to keep his hands in sight,' I said.

'You did,' Des said. 'I was proud of you.'

'They're going to walk towards us slowly,' I said. 'He knows all three of us will be there and he doesn't seem to mind.'

'No,' said Grace, 'he thinks we're silly old women, why would he mind? And are we agreed, if he does do exactly as we've asked we'll call off the Shoe people?'

'Yes, the Shoe people know that,' I said. 'They're waiting for one of us to give them the signal. As soon as we say "gosh", really loudly, they're going to act. If we don't say it, they're going to keep to the shadows by the café, and we will pay them anyway.'

We all agreed that it was the only way and said things like, 'It's only money, it'll be worth it.' Henry would have hated paying for nothing, but I thought it wisest not to share any more of Henry's wisdom for a while.

It was difficult to know how to spend the rest of the day. In one way it felt exciting, as though we were waiting to catch a train or a plane and go somewhere special, but in another way there was more than a touch of dentist's waiting room or death row about it. At first we didn't feel that it was safe to leave the house. Des decided to cook, and he spent some time in the kitchen going through my cupboards. He seemed personally outraged that I had so many tins and packets past their sell-by dates and called through to the living room, where we were sitting, every time he found one. I thought a little of Henry, and how he would have loved that kind of activity, but I didn't say anything.

Daphne slipped out mid-afternoon to get more cash after making lots of quiet phone calls and doing calculations on a piece of paper. She said I didn't need to cough up for a while, she trusted me to get hold of money later if we needed more. I got the feeling that money wasn't a problem for her at all, despite her odd clothes.

She'd changed her outfit when she got back with the money, so she must have been back to her house. I think it was her attempt at camouflage clothing, because she was dressed more drably than usual, although the combinations were still odd. Brown trousers with an orange check, and a striped purple and red jumper. They looked right on her, her clothes, and I made a mental note to stop trying to blend in with the background so much, if I'm ever out clothes shopping again. I imagined what it might be like to go shopping with Nina, buy her some pretty clothes. I had a lot of random thoughts that day. If I ever cook a meal again it'll be a hearty vegetable stew, and if I ever go to Henry's grave again I'll tell him all about this, that sort of thing. I tried to think through what might happen, follow a logical line but prison or a shoot-out with all of us ending up dead were definite possibilities so I stopped that.

Just when I couldn't stand the sound of Des's emery board as he filed his nails for a moment longer, it was time to go and look at our meeting point again.

I was glad to be doing something useful. I've always had difficulty visualising locations even when I know them well. Where things are in relation to each other, that kind of thing. I was even more pleased when we got up there, and I realised the distance from the café to where the cars would park was greater than I had imagined. All possible, but good to be clear. I could hear Henry in my ear talking about how important good planning is if you want to achieve results, but I didn't share it with my friends. That's what we were now, friends, I was sure of it.

'He will park here,' Grace said, gesticulating towards the top of the road, 'and we'll be waiting here.'

She pointed to a tree on a slight incline, where we would be able to see all around us.

'He comes towards us like this,' she said, 'and we wait here.'

I could imagine her directing successful school plays. She was good at explaining. It all seemed so clear when she told us how things would be, I believed it might work. It was our best chance, and maybe the money would be enough without any further action. Wouldn't it feel good, I kept thinking, to know that we had rescued a whole person, made her world different, given her the life she should have had all along? And wouldn't it be the best thing in the world to see Nina's little face and know she was safe? I think I zoned out of what Grace and Daphne were saying for a moment. When I joined in again, and it can't have been more than a moment's lapse, Grace was miming dragging something heavy over to the bins. I felt shocked, and I must have looked it.

'We can't just leave him here,' Grace said. 'I'm hoping the Shoe people will clear up but if not, I'm thinking about the children on their way to school the next morning.'

It was a fair point. If we tucked him out of the way, no one would have to deal with the nastiness until we'd made an anonymous phone call and got the proper authorities out, with bio-hazard suits.

'Wouldn't the world be a great place,' Daphne said, 'if everyone was as responsible as us?'

I was about to agree but then she and Grace burst out laughing and I realised that they were making a joke. I wasn't sure if it was funny. Of course, we were planning a murder and that's not a very responsible thing to do, but I hoped we were on the side of the angels, so it was different. A mercy killing, that's how we needed to think of it.

I tried to keep thinking that way. All the way through. I tried to listen to the violin, just enough and not too much. Without getting carried away. If I'm honest, I've never been more aware of what was happening minute to minute and second to second than I was then. It was as if I was suddenly in a slow-motion film.

We were there early. Of course. We are probably never late, any one of us. Old people aren't late, usually. Des came too but he went and stood by a tree, behind the café. It was cold and dark and scary as hell, but we stood and waited, jiggling on the spot we'd marked out earlier to keep warm and trying to boost each other's spirits. I wished I could forget what we were waiting for. For a few moments it felt as though it was just us, the night and the trees. If I squinted hard I thought I could make out the shapes of the leaf buds on the branches. It seemed as though there was a special message for us hidden in there. Nice stuff is going to happen again, the leaf buds promised, if you bide your time and wait.

At about eleven forty-five, the Shoe people arrived and slipped away into the trees. They were very quiet, and I was pleased to see that the little dog had stayed at home out of the cold. I wanted to smile, wave, make some kind of gesture to show I appreciated them turning up but Grace and Daphne had been very specific about that.

'However much you want to speak to the Shoe people when they come,' Grace had said, 'remember that toad may be watching from somewhere nearby. Even if we can't see anything at all, we have to bear in mind that we could be overlooked at all times. Just imagine that there's a helicopter overhead with a person inside with a telescope. You won't go far wrong that way.'

I remembered a documentary I had seen about the war in Vietnam, and tried to imagine crawling on my stomach across the tennis courts.

I could hear the car crunching up the unpaved road towards us before I was ready to face it. For a moment I let the sound of wheels on gravel remind me of summer trips I hadn't made. It must be the sound you could hear late at night on a campsite, I thought, lying in a tent. Grace nudged me.

'You OK?' she whispered.

I nodded. Toad man got out of the car. He brushed himself down and made a good show of not having a care in the world. He looked over at the three of us as if he'd bumped into us at a small party.

'Ah,' he said, 'ladies, ladies, ladies.'

It struck me that I've never been called a lady as often as I have since this criminal business began, and I stored the thought to share with the others later.

Grace and Daphne were both craning their necks to see if Nina was in the car.

Toad man looked over his shoulder at the car as though he was checking too.

'Ah,' he said, 'you're very sensible, best to check. She's in there all right, aren't you, my dear?'

He raised his voice on the last part and I could definitely see a little movement inside the car. Not enough to be sure though, and I could see that Grace and Daphne agreed because they were both holding themselves very tensely. Something about the line of their shoulders. I touched Grace's arm and she stepped forward slightly.

'OK,' she said, 'let her out and we'll keep our agreement.'

Daphne touched her top pocket where the money was. I'm not sure if she realised she was doing it but I could see toad man was clocking everything.

'I don't think that's the way it goes,' he said. 'Do you?'

'We agreed,' said Grace.

Her voice was firm and scornful, with not a trace of a shake. I took my hat off to her, I really did. I knew if I said anything it would come out as a pathetic squeak. I concentrated instead on trying to see Nina in the back of the car, make sure she was OK. It was impossible to tell. My night vision has never been good, and worse since I had my cataracts fixed.

'Oh dear,' said toad man, 'I've changed my mind. Money first, please, if you'd be so kind. I don't want to play by your rules.'

We all kept looking ahead. We'd agreed this beforehand, whatever happens, keep looking at him, don't look at each other or behind or anywhere else. I stopped trying to make out the shape of Nina in the car. Grace took another step forward.

'Give us the girl,' she said.

She said it quietly but there was something in her voice that suggested steel. I imagined it must have worked a treat on the kind of boys who brought Stanley knives to school.

Toad man didn't say anything. He just stood there, hands by his sides as if he was waiting for something, which of course he was.

CHAPTER NINETEEN

Nina

Nina was aware that Romana had not eaten for nearly three weeks now. They had stayed in the same house all that time, and Nina had seen her nearly every day. Nina had stopped looking at the fish. She stopped looking on the day the toad man brought in a little plastic bridge for the fish to swim through, and a small castle for the bottom of the tank. 'Here you are,' he had said. 'I know you like that fish.'

Romana found ways to show Nina how long she had starved herself. It wasn't always safe to talk, so sometimes she stroked her cheek with the right number of fingers, and sometimes she was much more blatant, holding them out in front of her. The toad man and the woman who were in charge never seemed to see. Nina wondered briefly if Romana was a stooge, part of a plan aimed at demoralising the girls, but she didn't think they were that smart.

Nina couldn't see any difference in Romana at first. She wasn't even sure whether Romana was telling the truth. Today, though, things changed. Today she was sure. Romana was in the waiting room after Nina's first punter and she looked awful.

Nina didn't look at Romana at first. She was too hurt, too shaken herself after her latest client. She felt unable to comprehend what was happening to her. She wondered when it would become normal to be raped and then realised that she dreaded that most of all. If it became normal, if she stopped fighting it for even a moment, Nina knew that she would be lost. She would never get back to being herself.

She looked at the window. The heavy blind prevented most of the light from coming in, but there was an edge of grey sky showing through. Nina longed for it. Longed to smash the sickly overhead light and pull up the blinds so that she could see the clouds.

'Don't,' Romana said. She said it so quietly that Nina wasn't even sure whether she had really heard it or not. She looked over at Romana, who indicated with her head towards the little camera in the centre.

'They love to have a reason to get angry,' Romana said, 'don't play into their hands.' She coughed and Nina could hear that it sounded painful.

'I need to get out,' Nina said. 'This is driving me crazy.'

'OK, let me tell you what I know,' Romana said. 'I stopped eating seventeen days ago and they're not sure what to do with me, they're going to have to call a doctor soon or I'll die, but I honestly think they might finish me off first.'

Romana waited while the camera did another turn.

'Anyway, they've started treating me like I'm more or less invisible already,' she said, 'so I've been able to snoop a bit. We're moving tomorrow, that's one thing, so you'll be back in the world again. And you'll get your chance to run. I hope you make it.'

'Romana,' Nina said, 'why don't you come with me? Two is better than one, you know. And where? Where are we moving to?'

Romana smiled, but Nina could see that it was a sad smile.

'I chose what I chose,' she said, 'and I couldn't run anywhere now. I started off saying I didn't feel well when I actually did, and it seemed like an adventure. Now I feel absolutely terrible. You go, and if you can, get help for me. I'll wait it out. And I'm sorry, I don't know where we're going.'

Nina wondered how she could ever have dismissed Romana, thought she was a silly girl. She seemed marvellously brave now.

'Another thing,' Romana said, 'I hate my name, Romana. I thought it sounded glamorous at first, you know, when they first gave it to me, but that's stupid. I don't want to die as Romana, it's not me.'

Nina waited again while the camera spun.

'I'm Ronnie,' she said, 'that's my real, honest name.'

'Ronnie,' said Nina, 'suits you much better. Come on, Ronnie, change your mind, come with me. It'll be fun, I'll look after you.'

'I can't,' Ronnie said, 'you'd take twice as long if I dragged along. But what I can do is,' she stopped to cough again, 'I can talk it through with you now, make sure you've got a sensible plan and not a half-baked one. OK?'

Nina nodded. The two girls talked in whispers and snatches of time for longer than usual. Nina flinched at every sound, sure the next man would be coming to get her at any minute. It seemed like ages before Marianne came in. She was one of the other girls, and Nina had seen her often but never really to talk to. The girls were kept away from each other most of the time, Nina presumed in order to minimise the chances of any kind of organised rebellion. In addition, Nina had seen Marianne laughing with the toad man before, and that made Nina sure she couldn't be trusted.

'Hey,' Marianne said, 'guess what? It's snowing.'

Nina and Ronnie were both quiet. They had talked about this girl before, and neither of them felt comfortable around her.

'It's true,' she said. 'It will be difficult travelling around later so it's going to be quiet. Snow day.'

She picked up one of the pornographic magazines from the small coffee table in the middle of the room and started reading.

'"Sally has a master's degree in biology,"' Marianne read aloud, '"and a mistress's degree in human biology. She's a blue-stocking but her garters are as frilly as the next woman's."'

She threw the magazine across the room in disgust. 'Where do they get this shite from?'

Nina wasn't sure what to do. She had understood the rules for the last few weeks. Keep your head down, don't talk to the others, and above all keep resisting. That had been her mantra. It had seemed like not trusting anyone had been the only way, and suddenly there was a hope of companionship. Nina knew that she could be undone by a kindness. Most kids' home kids could.

'Listen,' Marianne said, 'I don't give a fuck whether you two want to speak to me or not. But I'm not a fucking snitch, whatever you think. I just know how to play the game better than you, that's all. And at the moment, I know that no one is watching that camera,' Marianne pointed to the blinking eye attached to the central light, 'and I know some stuff that you might need. I'm willing to share, but not if you think I'm a fucking snitch.'

Nina's need to know more about the situation far out-stripped her fear of Marianne. Even if she was a snitch.

'Where are we?' she said.

'It's not the question you should be asking,' Marianne said, 'but I'll answer it anyway. We're on the outskirts of Hastings, up the hill from the sea. What they do is, they hire a holiday place and set us up. I'm sure they've got other girls like us, other places. Brothels, that's the old-fashioned name for it in case you hadn't noticed where you are. And what you're wearing.'

All three of them were dressed only in bra and pants, despite the draught coming in from outside. Even poor sick Ronnie was huddled up in her underwear, trying to keep the heat in by holding on to her knees.

'So tomorrow we're moving on, going to London. Bright lights and all that. It's not good news, though, they'll be even more careful when we're there, because they'll be more para-noid about us running.'

Nina only heard 'London'. The one place where she might find safety, where she knew people.

'Sorry if I thought you were, you know, one of them,' Ronnie said.

Marianne shrugged. 'Whatever,' she said.

There was an awkward silence and then Ronnie said, 'What are their names?' There was an urgency in her voice that Nina recognised and worried about.

'I mean,' Ronnie continued, 'say if one of us did get away, I don't even know who they are, what to tell anyone. They're so bloody careful. I mean, I know she's Fee, but is that a name?'

'That one I do know,' Marianne said. 'He's Pat, Patrice

Home. He's Belgian. And she's Fiona. That's why he calls her Fee. They take the money while we do the graft.'

Nina committed the names to memory. She chanted them to herself, even after the snow cleared and the men came back to the house.

'You've got to work twice as hard now,' Fiona said, pinching Nina's arm. 'You've had a nice morning, sitting around chatting. You want to eat, you have to work. Lazy girl.'

Nina stared at her. Dyed blonde hair, not quite shoulder length. Blue eyes. Thin lips. Slight speech impediment when pronouncing words with s in them. Slight accent that seems to come and go, may not be real. Long fingernails she uses to pinch with. Cruel, cruel, cruel. I'd be able to describe you, Nina thought as she stared at Fiona. I could draw a picture that anyone could recognise. I could assemble you from a photofit or make you out of Lego. I'd know you anywhere. I'm not going to forget you.

The thought sustained her through the next few hours. That and the decision to run. Nina was going to run as soon as she could, she had decided. London was the place. It should be easy there.

As they travelled up to town Nina thought that London had never looked more beautiful. She stared out of the car window at the dingy streets and scuffed snow. If she could get clear, she thought, she would never leave London again. Tall buildings and empty trees springing out of pavements, people sleeping in doorways, people walking, people running, people talking to each other, people. People everywhere. Women everywhere. Someone would help her, Nina thought. There were enough people in the streets, going about their business, eating, drinking and laughing, enough to make sure that one or two of them were good, one or two of them would help her, and that was all she needed.

'What are you looking out of the window for?' toad man said. 'Don't you want to look at the back of my lovely head? Look at that, Fee, she's looking out of the window as if she belongs in my nice car.'

Nina flinched. Most of the other girls had gone in a minibus, Nina had seen them leave. Just her and Ronnie in the fancy black car with toad man and Fiona. She wasn't sure why. Ronnie was asleep. She looked terrible, and Nina hoped that they were going to take her to a hospital. In fact, Nina thought, it was her responsibility to make sure that they did.

'Excuse me,' Nina said, 'but Romana really isn't well. Could we take her to a hospital?'

Toad man didn't look round.

'Did you hear anything? I didn't. Just a kind of buzzing in my ear,' he said.

Fiona made a noise of exasperation, as if Nina had asked a hundred times instead of once.

Ronnie opened her eyes and smiled at Nina.

'It's OK,' she whispered.

Nina got her bottle of water from the bag at her feet and held it to Ronnie's mouth. Ronnie's eyes sparkled for a moment.

'Just a sip, Neens,' she said. 'Remember.'

Nina looked at the way Ronnie was slumped in her seat. Her wrists looked impossibly thin. Her hands were picking at the thin scarf trailing round her neck as if it was covered in burrs. Nina realised that Ronnie looked like a very old woman.

Like a woman Nina had seen being wheeled past on a trolley once when she had been at the hospital. Like someone who might die. Nina looked towards the toad man again, trying to pluck up the courage to speak. Ronnie grabbed Nina's wrist.

'Don't,' she whispered, 'it's not worth it. I'm OK. Honest.'

Ronnie leaned her head back against the car window as if the effort of saying those few words had worn her out. Nina settled back into her seat and looked out again. Buses, red ones, carrying people to work, to doctors' appointments, swimming lessons, college. All the ordinary things that seemed so impossible for her. And men, Nina realised, men everywhere, walking around as if they owned the place. Men who wouldn't think twice about hurting her, hurting poor Ronnie, doing anything they wanted if the price was right. Or doing it anyway if it wasn't. Nina knew that there were good men out there, she was sure of it. She thought back over her short life and could only think of Bilbo. Thinking about him made him suddenly real, and it was as though he was there in the car beside her. Nina wished that she could reach out and touch him.

'Nina is not,' he would have said. 'Nina is not, what is Neens not? What not?'

Nina is not sad, she would have answered, knowing that's what he would have meant. Nina is not sad, Bilbo. Nina said it to herself now, so quietly that even Ronnie, snuggled up against her, couldn't hear.

'Nina is not sad.'

Nina watched the road signs and saw that they were in south-east London, maybe New Cross or Forest Hill. They pulled up outside an ordinary-looking house in a cul de sac off the main road. They were newish houses, little and boxy with tiny, neat lawns. It seemed a most unlikely place for a brothel and for a moment, Nina had an irrational hope that things might have changed.

The car stopped outside one of the houses and toad man jumped out. He opened the rear door and snarled at the girls, 'You two bloody stay in here, right? No funny business. I'll get you back if you do.'

He said something in French that sounded vicious before reaching over and pinching Ronnie's leg, hard.

'Hi,' he said, turning to the woman who had just come out of the house next door. 'Hi, we're here to pick up the keys for number ten. The Airbnb.'

Nina was amazed that his voice sounded so different when he spoke to the woman. Smooth, like a continental romantic hero.

'I've got them here,' the woman said, looking into the back seat where the girls were.

'That's my daughters,' he said. 'Some of their friends might be dropping round later but I'll make sure they keep the noise down.'

The woman smiled in a reserved way. Nina could see that she wouldn't be any help at all. She thought about screaming at her to help, call the police, get them out, but she could tell from the woman's pursed lips and crossed arms that she wouldn't want to get involved. Toad noticed it too and grinned at Nina.

'Looks like a lovely place we're staying in,' he said.

Nina tried not to react. Faced with his arrogance, spite and entitlement, she knew she could only bear witness for the time being, nothing more. Remember all the facts that she could, and try to survive. Look for her chance, and survive long enough to bring him down. She remembered all the teachers who had said that it was good to have some ambition. Nina followed toad and Fiona inside as though she was walking in a dream.

I've got that, she thought. I've got ambition you wouldn't believe. Nina stared at the plain white walls in the front room of the Airbnb. For a moment she missed the fish, wished it was here with her. Such a tasteful room. Such an incongruous setting for a torture chamber. There was a painting on the wall of a chair in a sunlit room and Nina wished she was there, sitting on it, all of this forgotten.

Fiona went into action straight away on her computer, putting photos of the girls on the internet and making appointments for men to come round. Whatever else happened, Nina thought, she was determined to stay alive long enough to make sure that this didn't happen to anyone else.

'I don't think Romana is well enough to work,' she said. 'She's definitely running a temperature and she's very pale.'

'Look at that,' toad man said to Fiona, 'she's nicer than you. You didn't say anything about Romana, you couldn't care less, could you, sweetie?'

Fiona glared at Nina and made a gesture that Nina could only interpret as the intention to get her back later.

'That's OK, my sweetie,' toad man said. 'You can work twice as hard, how about that? We'll get them in and out really quickly, if you'll pardon the pun. In and out, you get it?'

Nina helped Romana into a chair. I'm going to run, she promised herself, I'm going to get out of here.

*

Nina's life did not improve in the days that followed. If anything, she was worse off than before, hardly allowed to have more than a few hours' sleep between clients and watched at all times. She saw Ronnie only for occasional snatched conversations in passing, so Nina was surprised one morning to see Ronnie dressed with a bag packed and waiting by her feet.

'It's worked, Nina, I'm getting out,' she said. 'They're going to take me to hospital.'

Ronnie held her hand up for a high five.

'That's wonderful,' Nina said.

Nina's head was teeming with questions. How could they let her leave? Surely it would be too dangerous for them, surely they would be frightened that she would say something to someone about what was going on?

'I know what you're thinking,' Ronnie said. Her voice was quiet, like a whisper. 'But they're moving on again. I heard them talking when they thought I was asleep. They're going to move to another Airbnb, I think, not far from here. That way they think they'll be safe if I talk. And also,' Ronnie stopped to cough, 'also they've threatened my sister. She's only twelve, and she's in a rubbish foster family, and I think they mean it. So I can't tell anyone about what's going on, Nina, I can't. I'm so sorry, I wanted to save you too.'

'Hey,' Nina said, 'you don't need to. I can save myself. You look after yourself and I'll see you again somewhere happy. Start eating again, right?'

Nina blew Ronnie a kiss. She felt scared for her. Would they really take Ronnie to a hospital? It didn't seem possible. Nina could feel danger everywhere, as if the world was made of danger, one big scary place with hundreds, thousands of nasty things waiting round every corner. She knew that her own body was on the verge of collapse. Fiona and toad man had kept their promise to increase Nina's daily numbers now that Ronnie wasn't working. There were a couple of new girls working alongside Nina but she kept her distance. She didn't have room for anyone else, that's how she felt. Closed off to everyone and everything. She was determined not to take the drugs that toad offered to all the girls, but it was getting more and more difficult to get through each day. Other people were weights she couldn't afford to carry.

Ronnie was right. Later that day the whole operation moved to a new location, an Airbnb a few minutes away by car. There were at least two carloads, and Nina had no idea whether Ronnie had come along in another car, or whether she really had gone to hospital.

Nina could hear Fiona talking to clients as soon as they got to the new place. Always the same wheedling tone. 'Hey, baby, we can help you, baby, thank you, sweetie.' She felt sick.

It took a little while before the first customer turned up, and in that time Nina was able to look around the house. She couldn't believe her luck. There was a glimmer of hope. A chance, a better chance than Nina had had before. The front door. It was the weak link Nina had been waiting for. It might be possible to escape, she thought. The front door was locked only by a Yale lock and the handle twisted easily and quietly. If Nina could only calm down, stop herself from jumping at every noise, she was sure she would be able to seize her opportunity and get the hell out.

Nina thought of Bilbo that night, and how terrible it would be if they threatened him, like they had Ronnie's sister. Bilbo was the nearest Nina had to family, and the thought of seeing his face again gave her strength. She guessed that toad and Fiona were probably not expecting her to run any more. They'd started to treat her a little better, and even to ask her opinion on things sometimes. Things like bed covers and positions of chairs, and every time it made Nina marvel. Did they really think she was one of them, that they were all in it together working for the same cause? Did they, could they, imagine that she cared a damn? It was extraordinary how they fooled themselves, Nina thought.

Nina's first chance came the day after they had moved to the new house. Fiona and toad were upstairs in their bedroom, Nina had seen them go up. The other girls were in the living room. Business was often slow in the mornings. Nina had been forced to see clients until four a.m., and every part of her felt sore. Even if I die, she thought, it will be better than staying here, and yet she was so battered, so scared, that it would be the simplest thing in the world to convince herself that she was safer staying where she was. Nina thought of the heroines from books she had admired – Offred, Maggie Tulliver, Elizabeth Bennet, Scout, what would they do? It was obvious. Of course they'd leave. They'd leave regardless of the danger.

Nina slipped downstairs and pulled the handle. The door opened without a creak and she was out so quickly she could barely process the information. She had expected to feel free, to experience a jolt of excitement, to feel different somehow, but she didn't. Nina felt scared, cold, sore, and she still felt like a prisoner. It's in your head, girl, she whispered to herself. She made herself keep on walking. At every point where there was a choice of direction, Nina moved towards wherever the most people were. If there was a crowd at a bus stop, she waited there for a moment or two to catch her breath, but other than that Nina kept choosing the most populated streets. She had no money for a bus or train, and cursed herself for not trying harder to get her hands on some, even if it was only the loose change from toad's pockets as he dumped it on the table.

It was cold, and the jacket Nina had been wearing the day she was kidnapped had long since disappeared. Nina knew she looked odd. She was wearing a short skirt and a small, frayed T-shirt with a towel she had managed to grab and put round her shoulders. On her feet were the standard house issue flip-flops that all the girls wore, and Nina's feet were freezing. It's London, Nina thought, no one cares about stuff like that, but still she felt as though there was a huge flashing light above her head, a neon sign saying 'runaway'. She looked into the faces of some of the passing strangers but they were closed off and unresponsive. There was a woman with a buggy waiting at one of the bus stops Nina passed, and she remembered what Bilbo had always been told.

'If you're lost, Bilbo, ask a woman with a baby. They're good at directions,' the staff used to say. It was supposed to keep him safe.

'Excuse me,' Nina said to the woman with the buggy. She had intended to ask for directions, but the woman looked scared and she held on to the handles of the buggy tightly, pulling it towards her.

Nina backed away, holding her hands out in front of her to show that she meant no harm.

'I haven't got any change,' the woman said. 'I don't carry money, go away.'

Nina wanted to tell her that she wasn't begging, just asking for directions, and that she would never, ever hurt the baby in the buggy but she suddenly had a picture of herself, as if she was watching from the top of a tree. Of course the woman was scared. A grubby girl, wearing flip-flops and a towel in February. She had become one of the scary people, the not quite human. I'm untouchable, she thought except for when someone wants to hurt me, to rape me. She almost decided to go back and she probably would have if it hadn't been for the baby. The baby in the buggy, a little boy of about a year wearing a padded jacket and a tiny pair of smart white trainers. He wasn't aware that his mother had backed away from Nina, he just wanted to make friends. He smiled at her, before hiding his face in his hands, pulling them away and shouting, peep-bo.

Nina smiled back and his mother relaxed a little, proud of her son's ability to charm strangers.

'I'm sorry,' Nina called over her shoulder, waving bye-bye to the baby as she backed off, 'I didn't mean any harm.'

Come on, girl, she whispered under her breath. Keep going, you can make it. The baby had given her a boost, as if he had been able to see the real Nina, and it helped.

The next busy street stirred an old, forgotten memory for Nina. She remembered another street, full of bustle and people. Nina had been with her mother. It was summer then, or at least spring because there were leaves on the trees. There was sunshine, she could remember that because the sun was in her eyes. Nina must have been very small, small enough to hold her mother's hand and be dragged along, even though she was complaining. Her mother was in a tearing rush, Nina was sure of that.

'Come on, Nina,' her mother had said, over and over again. 'Come on or we'll be late.'

I'm late, I'm late, for a very important date, Nina had kept thinking. She wanted to ask her mother where the line came from, and why they were late, but they were going too fast for her to catch her breath properly.

Nina's mother had been crying. Nina wasn't sure whether she had realised that at the time, but looking back she could clearly see that her mother was fighting tears. Where were they going? What could have been so important, so upsetting? Nina tried to place the memory in its correct chronological slot in her life, searching for clues like a detective or an archaeologist. The dress. Nina remembered the dress she had been wearing, a pink flowered one. She remembered trying to admire her reflection in shop windows as her mother tugged her along.

It must have been the day Nina became a looked-after child. She was sure of it. That was the dress she had been wearing when they took her away from her mother and sent her to the first foster family, the ones with the dog. The family where she cried all the time, and yes, it was coming back now, the place where she cut the dress into tiny pieces with a pair of nail scissors. A protest, Nina thought now, but at the time she hadn't had the words to name it. She simply knew that if she didn't have her mother, she didn't care about anything else, not even her beloved dress. Nina stood in the street in her towel and her flip-flops and tried to explain a little to her younger self. I'm sorry I let stuff happen, she thought. I'm not going to any more, ever again.

Nina stood at a busy crossroads in Lewisham, trying to decide which direction to take. One way led through a forest of high-rise buildings, and the others all seemed to circle the shopping precinct. She was trying to decide when she saw the car. The big black car. The car that might belong to toad man. It had a creepy air to it, as if the engine was growling in a low voice.

Nina headed down a back street. She didn't think the driver had seen her, and she wasn't even sure that it was him, but this was no time to be taking chances. She took the less busy roads now every time there was a choice, and she kept to the sides, close to the houses and shops. At one point she saw a woman with a shopping bag who looked exactly like her mother but, of course, her mother was more than ten years older now and she had never lived in Lewisham. It couldn't be her. Nina remembered tales she had read of people lost in the desert, how they thought they saw fountains, water, the very thing they hoped for most. The mind could play those kind of tricks, she knew that. It's not real, she told herself, nice try, brain, but I'm not buying it.

Nina had been walking for a couple of hours when she saw the coffee shop. She could see the three old women through the window, chatting and laughing as if there weren't any problems in the world. They looked as though they came from a different planet to the one Nina lived on. They probably had dogs and houses and grandchildren, she thought. Probably their grandchildren were successful and happy and went to university. Before she had thought about what she was doing or what she would say, Nina pushed the door of the café open.

Nina wasn't sure about older people any more, but she felt she was out of choices. It was the old men who had put her off. The old men she had met in the brothel, although 'met' was hardly the right word. One of them had seemed kindly, like the old grandfather in *Heidi*. He'd arrived with sweets, and a lollipop he wanted her to suck. Nina had thought that maybe he would be her helper, maybe he would be the person who would aid her escape.

'I'm not here by choice,' she had said to him. 'They're keeping me here against my will.'

Nina realised her mistake as soon as the words were out of her mouth. He had been excited by the thought. This kindly-looking old grandfather had loved the fact that she was helpless. In fact he asked her to say it again, and again. Nina didn't try the same thing with any of the other punters.

So old people were totally off the list of possible helpers for Nina until she met the three women, but she knew from the start that they were different. By the time she entered the café, Nina was sure she had seen the car, the big black one, out of the corner of her eye several times. She was freezing cold and she needed the toilet. It would be the easiest thing for him to stop the car, pull her in and then she would be back there again, inside her very own nightmare. Everyone knew that Londoners minded their own business. No one would say anything. Even if someone did notice, he would probably have an explanation ready. He'd say she was his daughter or his granddaughter or something, and no one would believe her. He had everything on his side and Nina had no choice but to trust the women in the café.

As soon as she stepped inside, Nina felt better. The women looked at her with kindness, as if they'd agreed between themselves that they would help her, as if they had been waiting for her. She felt as though she wasn't on her own for nearly the first time that she could remember. These women were on her side, she believed that before they spoke. They were different. They all seemed to take charge of the situation, although none of them was jostling for the lead.

'I totally want to be like you three, when I'm older,' Nina said to Meg later, when they were safely inside her house and making tea together.

Meg had laughed. 'Do you know,' she said, 'I think you could do better than that. Well, not better than Grace and Daphne, but better than me. Honestly.'

Nina could tell that Meg meant what she said, but she didn't take any notice. Meg and the others couldn't do anything wrong in her eyes.

'You three are like my grandmas,' Nina said to them. 'I never had grandparents, but if I did, I'd want ones like you.'

She blushed as she said it, and hoped that it wasn't a stupid thing to say.

Daphne and Meg had fluttered a bit, and Nina thought she saw a tear in Daphne's eye. Grace didn't flutter, though, that wasn't her style. She stood straight and tall and smiled a smile that made Nina pleased that she had said how she felt. She felt safe with these women, and it was a great feeling. So safe that she lost her step, stopped looking for danger round every corner. Even when they got into the car to go to Margate that night, even though Nina could feel the fear coming off them in waves, she still felt secure. She was with the grown-ups, that's how Nina felt. With the grown-ups, who could keep her safe. Who wouldn't let anything happen. Even as she recognised That Car, even as she realised that Meg was crying and muttering something about a violin, Nina still felt that, on balance, things would turn out OK. She was totally unprepared for the violence of being dragged from the car. It seemed worse, somehow, than the first time she had been taken by toad. That time she hadn't known what was waiting, this time she knew only too well. And this time she had Meg, Grace and Daphne to worry about too. They would think it was their fault, she knew they would. And she was so, so scared.

'Do you realise,' toad said, as soon as Nina had been bundled into the car, 'how much trouble you've put me through?'

'And me,' Fiona said, turning round in the passenger seat to grab a handful of Nina's hair. 'I could have been at home, taking care of business. We've lost money tonight.'

'That's OK, Fee,' toad said. 'Nina's very sorry and she knows we almost had to move to a new place because of her. We've spent every minute looking for the right place but it's OK because now she's back and she's going to work very hard and pay us for all the trouble we've gone to on her account. Isn't that right, Nina?'

Nina didn't say anything. There was no point. Whatever she said, they'd get the better of her. They had all the advantages on their side.

'All the advantages,' said a voice in Nina's head that sounded like Grace. 'All the advantages except brains. That's what you've got, girl, now use them.'

Nina had no time to dwell on how awful things were. Toad and Fiona were true to their word, and she was booked every half hour as soon as she got back. Some of the punters turned up more than once in that time and Nina realised that they were being offered freebies to keep her in line.

She didn't see Ronnie until later that day, when Ronnie was brought out to sit with them in the waiting room. Nina was shocked at how awful she looked.

'Ronnie,' she said.

Fiona slapped her.

'New rule,' Fiona said. 'No talking between girls. If you're pissed off with that, blame Nina here. She's the reason for it.'

A couple of the girls looked daggers at Nina but she didn't notice. She couldn't stop looking at Ronnie. Ronnie who now looked even thinner, who was visibly shaking, who looked cold in spite of the temperature in the room.

'And in case anyone thought they might be clever and do what Ronnie has done,' Fiona said, 'I think she'd be the first to tell you not to bother. Or he'd be the first, I'm never sure which one is correct for a freak.'

Ronnie hung her head.

'She's right,' she said, so quietly that Nina had to strain to hear her. 'It's not worth it.'

Ronnie was taken away after that, and Nina wasn't sure where they had put her. It wasn't a huge house but big enough for there to be several closed doors. It was a prison. Nina was never left alone.

When toad came to get her later, Nina realised that something else was happening, something that might give her another chance if she played her cards right.

'Get dressed,' toad said, pulling her off the sofa where she had been trying to rest for a few minutes between clients. 'Put some clothes on, for God's sake. You're coming with me. If you're lucky, you might get a glimpse of your beloved old ladies.'

'I haven't got any clothes,' Nina said. 'You took them away.'

'Fucking mouthy bitch,' Fiona said. She fumbled in a box by her bed and threw Nina some jeans and a T-shirt.

'That'll be enough,' she said.

Nina was shaking so much she could hardly get her feet into the jeans. The ladies, trying to help her in some way. Maybe it would work. Or they could get hurt, and that would be the worst thing.

Toad didn't speak to her on the short drive. He was furious, Nina could tell that. She thought she recognised some of the streets but she wasn't sure. One street looked much like another in the dark. Something was happening, though, and that had to be better than nothing. There's something more, that's what she kept repeating in her head, there's something more and I'm not going to give up.

The car stopped in the park. It looked like the countryside, but Nina knew they hadn't travelled far enough to leave London. She wondered if they were going to kill her here and bury the body.

'Don't try and get out, the car's locked. Stay there nice and quiet like a good girl, so that your friends can see you,' toad said.

Nina looked out of the window as he left the car, and sure enough, she could see them. Her heart leapt and she waved frantically but they were looking at him, and only at him. She saw Daphne step towards him and hold something out, and she saw him step forward to take it. A ransom, Nina realised, a ransom just like in the fairy tales. They were going to pay it to him, she was sure, and she felt proud, excited, full of hope and terrified that he would hurt them.

'Thank you,' she said quietly. 'Thank you, thank you. I will repay you one day, I promise I will.'

Nina couldn't hear what was happening, so she didn't hear the noise that made toad jump. She only knew things had changed when toad came running back towards the car, with Daphne and the other women and someone else at the back, she wasn't sure who, in pursuit and shouting. Nina banged on the window, tried the locked door and waved her hands but toad was back behind the wheel in seconds and they were screeching round and leaving the women behind.

'There was someone there,' toad said. 'Your fucking stupid friends brought someone with them, I could hear them. They can't fool me.'

'I couldn't see anyone,' Nina said, 'are you sure?'

Toad slammed the brakes on and pulled in to the side of the road. It was a residential street but there were no lights on in the houses, no one to help Nina.

'You can shut the fuck up,' toad said, 'or God help me, I'll do the job for you. You have caused me more trouble than the rest of my girls put together, do you realise that?'

Thanks, ladies, Nina thought. I know it didn't work but thank you. Please try again.

The excitement Nina felt at seeing them disappeared as soon as she was back at the house. Toad made sure that her life was unbearable. It was the lack of hope that was the hardest to deal with, living a life without a plan B. There wasn't even a way to commit suicide that she could think of. No belts, no rope, no pills, no razors. No matches, even. Nina wondered what her ladies would do. She imagined Grace kicking toad to the floor, and the others joining in to beat him to a pulp.

Nina was so preoccupied the next day that she almost missed the fact that toad was going out. He usually stayed, him and Fiona, in order to keep an eye on everything, like jailers. For one of them to go out was a big deal. Nina thought it was the best chance she might have of finding Ronnie. That's what Grace, Daphne and Meg would do in her position, Nina was sure. Her ladies would find Ronnie and help her in some way, regardless of the consequences.

'Don't go thinking you can try anything funny,' Fiona said, 'because believe me, I have got your number. You stay right here close to me until your next Mr Right comes along.'

'Of course,' Nina said.

She waited until the next client was through with her, then instead of going to the bathroom, Nina tiptoed downstairs to the closed room she had noticed next to the front door. She didn't know why she thought that was the one, it was just a feeling. Nina felt sure that they would want to keep Ronnie as far away from everyone else as possible. Nina turned the handle as slowly and quietly as she could. It was locked. Of course it was locked. Nina decided to give up and go back upstairs but as she turned to leave, she noticed the bolt. A big, heavy bolt at the top of the door. Nina pulled it back and tried again. The door opened and Nina stepped into a darkened room.

'Nina, go away, I'm OK, if they catch you here…'

'Ronnie. Ronnie, I've been so worried about you. Are you OK? No, that's a stupid question, I want to help you, that's all.' Nina took her cue from Ronnie and spoke as quietly as she could.

'Bless you, love,' Ronnie said. 'Away with you now. I'm OK. I'm sorry you didn't get away. Try again, don't give up.'

Nina held Ronnie's hand for a moment.

'I can't leave you here,' she said. 'Come with me. Let's try and run again.'

'Maybe soon,' Ronnie said. 'Shoo, go on. It'll be worse if they find you here.'

Nina left, remembering to bolt the door behind her. She went back upstairs before she was missed. For the rest of the day, Nina thought about Ronnie. About how she might be able to rescue her, get her away from this place before it was too late.

CHAPTER TWENTY

Grace

Thursday, 28 February

My lovely Daphne is a hero. No other word for it. There's something about her, especially at night, she's like superwoman. She's amazing, there's no other word for it. That toad man was standing there in the dark park, and he wasn't worried about us at all. He looked as though he was laughing. I've seen that look on kids who know they're trouble. The ones who know straight away that there's nothing you can do that will bother them. Dean, I thought. I could smell the trouble so strongly I could almost touch it and I was thinking, if I had a little gun right now I would shoot that toad man right between the eyes. I'd forgotten the code word, the gosh that we were supposed to say to activate the Shoe people, I'd forgotten everything except for how much I hated him. And Eleanor, I thought of her, and I thought, I won't let you down again, child, which was insane because my Ellie had been dead for more than fifty years. Way more. She'd be almost an old lady like me if she was here now, we'd be growing old together. That's one of the odd things about having a child when you're still a child yourself. They nearly catch you up. I don't know how I had time to think all of that while he stood there, waiting for what we were going to do next. I really don't, but I swear all those thoughts went through my head, one after the other as if they'd been queuing up.

'Open the car door now, and give me the girl,' Daphne said. Her voice was clear as if she was on stage, and if she had been, you could have heard her in the rear stalls. She held the money up so that he could see it without actually holding it out towards him.

I could see he was wavering. He took one step towards her and there was a noise, a scuffling noise from behind the café. The Shoe people said afterwards that it wasn't them, it must have been a fox or something, but I'm not sure. There's lots of things that make noises in the dark. Eleanor used to be scared of the noise the tree frogs made in Jamaica and we made up stories about them to make them less frightening. It wasn't a tree frog I could hear in that night-time park in Brockley but I thought I heard a cough from behind the café. A human cough, not a fox. Whatever it was, the toad man was well and truly spooked. He lost his composure in the blink of an eye. He leapt back towards the car and at the same time Nina tried to open the door from the inside but of course he'd locked it so we could see her scared little face as she banged on the window while he jumped in and revved up.

'Open it, Nina,' Daphne shouted, 'try again.'

I guess she thought that when he got in the lock on the back door might have been taken off but it wasn't, Nina was still locked in, and he swung the car round so hard she fell back against the seat. Meg rushed at the car, moving her hands through the air as though she was pulling at the door handle. For one moment I thought he might knock her down but Daphne pulled her out of the way at the very last moment and he drove off down the hill and out of the park. Much too fast.

'Shit,' Daphne said. 'Shit, shit, shit, we nearly had him, did you see that? We could have got her.'

Daphne was beside herself. I could see she thought the whole thing was her fault.

'You were great,' I said. 'Come on, we're so close, he had the upper hand that time but we can try again, it's OK.'

Nonsense words really, but I didn't want Daphne to blame herself, and I didn't want to give up. We still had a job to do.

'I'm sorry about that, ladies,' Des said, coming out from behind the café. 'It may have been me who coughed, I think it was nerves.'

He was trying to take the blame, but I didn't believe him.

'You're supposed to be good at this sort of thing,' Meg said.

Daphne and I both stepped forward, ready to remonstrate with her, but Des held his hand up.

'Fair enough, fair enough,' he said. 'I have to admit that I have never been cut out for a life of crime. I'm sorry.'

'I believe that Des is right,' said the male half of the small hired killing duo. I hadn't noticed that he was there until he started speaking. 'He's not cut out for it, most people aren't. It's a circumstantial thing. Being in the wrong place at the wrong time. And if anything,' he went on, 'I'd like to say that you ladies are actually better suited to it in many ways. I was impressed there. By the way, the name's Greg. Like the pie shop. Vegan sausage rolls.'

He held his hand out to shake first Daphne's, then mine, then Meg's. I could tell he was unsure of what to do next, and I wondered if he was going to cry. He looked very emotional.

'Cut that out, Greg,' Clara said. 'We screwed up good and proper and I think what my brother means is that he's sorry about that.'

The situation was getting out of control. Everyone, including me, was trying to take the blame for the non-death of the toad man, and somebody needed to pull things together. I stepped forward. It's a teacher thing. I missed my chance once with Dean, and I'll live with that for ever.

'Come on, everyone,' I said. 'Let's go back. Meg, can we come to yours for a debrief?'

'Phone me,' said Clara. 'This unit is still in play. Phones still active.'

The Shoe people went silently back the way they had come. Greg looked back once and waved.

By the time we are all settled into Meg's sitting room with a cup of tea and a biscuit it's one o'clock in the morning.

'Does anyone want to stop?' Daphne said. 'Because I'm for going on.'

I feel as though I'm in one of those medical dramas where the emergency staff have to agree to continue or stop CPR.

'We can't leave her,' Meg said.

It's the first thing she has said for a while. Bravo, I think, well done, Meg.

'Meg is one hundred per cent correct,' I say. 'We can't and we won't.'

'We've learned one very important fact from today,' Des says. 'It's not entirely wasted time. We've learned, ladies and gentlemen, that we are right, he is very, very greedy. He came out for that money, and our best chance is to try that again.'

'Don't forget,' says Daphne, 'we still have the money. Nothing has been handed over yet. We need to keep trying.'

That's my girl, I think.

We all agree to go on, but everyone's mood is low. I'm glad when Meg goes to bed and Des to have a shower. Daphne and I are on our own and I feel I can relax, let go of some of the stress.

'Excuse me asking,' Daphne says, 'but back there, in the park, I heard you saying "Dean". I remembered that thing you said earlier about extraordinary circumstances bringing up echoes of other extraordinary times and I thought, it would be good to know more. I mean, only if...' she looks shy as she speaks, 'only if you want to.'

My heart goes out to her. I imagine what she must have been like as a young woman, gawky and unsure of herself. We could have been friends then, I think; we might have helped each other as long as I didn't frighten her away.

'I was an angry young woman when I was twenty-five,' I say now. 'Would we have been friends?'

'Oh gosh yes,' Daphne says without skipping a beat. 'I never learned to be angry. I could have done with someone to show me how.'

'Step right up,' I say. 'I have been angry all my life. Angry that I didn't manage to protect my lovely little daughter. Angry that when I had another chance to redeem myself, another moment when I could have made a difference for somebody, hang on, no, when I could have actually saved someone's life, I missed it.'

'I can see why you want this to work now,' Daphne says.

She's right. We sit in silence for a moment. I almost don't need to say any more, but I know I've sat on it too long. I stopped teaching after Dean, and I never spoke to anyone from Overcroft School again. Never. Not even my close friends who worked there. They guessed most of it, of course they did, but they never knew the whole thing.

Daphne sits opposite me, waiting. It's a companionable silence. I don't feel pushed into speaking but I'd like to put the burden down for a few minutes. It's different with Eleanor. That's a burden I'll never put down, because she's mine and mine alone to carry. It's all I can do for her.

Dean Smith is something else. Dean Smith has always been too heavy for me to carry.

'Has anyone ever come to you for help that you can't give?' I ask Daphne.

I can see that she's thinking hard, and that she wants the answer to be yes, to make me feel better. Honestly, I think, if the answer is yes you wouldn't have to think about it. It would be there at the top of your head and you wouldn't be able to push it away.

'I think,' Daphne says after a moment or two, 'I think that the answer is no, certainly not directly. But indirectly, that's something else. I believe I may have managed not to hear things I should have heard. I believe I may have been so wrapped up in my own troubles that I've missed important things that people may have been trying to say to me. Which is just as bad, really. The stuff I told you about Andrew and my past, I know I've let it consume me for a great deal of my life. In fact I thought about nothing else for many years. Think of all the requests for help I might have missed. And I'm not just trying to make you feel better.'

I can see that she means it, she really does. I reach for her hand and I hold it tight while I talk.

'Dean Smith,' I say, 'year eleven, fifteen years old. Not a boy a teacher would notice apart from when he's playing up. Which was quite often, not as often as some but more often than most. Am I OK to go on?'

I can still hear the shower running so I know we haven't been talking for long but I'm tired, tired as a dog, and I'm hoping that Daphne will say, let's stop now. She doesn't. So I tell her all of it. How Dean had said, 'I can't,' and how the echo of that phrase, I can't, has followed me down the years. How I might have been able to stop him, how he might have wanted me to stop him, how I had been too busy thinking about myself to pick up the signals anyone else would have seen.

'I'm not sure about that,' says Daphne. 'Perhaps he didn't really want to be stopped.'

I've thought of that over the years, of course I have. It doesn't help. I was still the one he chose and I let him down. I don't say that to Daphne. I can see that she's trying hard.

'So what happened?' Daphne asks. 'What did he do that you think was your fault?'

I can't believe she hasn't put two and two together yet. That she doesn't remember his name from the news, such a plain name but such a ring to it now, a byword for horror like Charles Manson or Myra Hindley.

'Maybe you read about it,' I say, 'the boy who took two small children from the shopping precinct. They were cousins, out shopping with a woman who was mum to one and aunt to the other. In Stratford centre, before the fancy Westfield one was built.'

I can see the realisation dawn on Daphne as I speak. She does remember, I can see she does. The whole country knew at the time, it was all anyone talked about for weeks. It was caught on video, you see, what Dean did – an early version of a CCTV camera. Everyone was familiar with the image of him walking down the street, each little girl holding one of his hands. For a while I was the most unpopular person in the country, after I gave evidence in court. No one knew exactly what he did, the details were too grim to release, but anyone with an imagination could see that I should have helped him.

'I might have stopped him,' I say to Daphne. 'I think he wanted to be stopped.'

'Yes,' she says, 'you might. There's no getting away from that. And if someone had gone round killing Austrian newborn babies in 1889 they would probably have got Hitler. But life isn't like that, is it? Life isn't a clever novel plotted backwards. We do what we can with what we've got, that's all. That's the long and short of it. Of course you wished you'd stopped him. I wish you had, too. But I'm not sure that we can always police each other. Isn't it hard enough to police ourselves? Isn't that exactly what you're saying? And who's to say that he wouldn't have done exactly the same whatever you had said to him? It's not as if you had reason to carry out a citizen's arrest or anything. You didn't know what he was going to do, how could you?'

I know what Daphne is saying makes sense. I've always known somewhere that it wasn't really my fault.

'Lost opportunities,' I say, 'that's the thing. That's why I'm in it now.'

'You and me both,' Daphne says, 'you and me both, Grace. Lost opportunities. I've got money, I guess you've gathered that. My dad invested for me in a little start-up company and then he disappeared. The start-up company was Apple. Imagine that, I've got money and I've never been able to use it properly, give it away. As fast as I give it to charities it comes back.'

Daphne looks at me so earnestly, wanting me to under-stand. I want to comfort her but it's such an odd guilt.

'Hang on a moment,' I say. 'You feel guilty because you can't give your money away fast enough?'

She blushes. I love that.

'I've seen the other side of life, that's the thing,' she says. 'I was in prison, long ago and far away, for soliciting. Before I got the money. I hadn't got any then, and I was trapped into earning it, but I got caught. I lived with women in a prison for a couple of years, and I know how hard their lives are. I do what I can but...'

Daphne shrugs. It feels odd, having given each other our stories to carry. Maybe that's how women bear the load, I think – we share the weight of each other's stories.

'We'll get it right this time,' I say. 'We're going to win.'

CHAPTER TWENTY-ONE

Meg

After midnight, Thursday, 28 February

I could hear them talking after I'd gone to bed. Daphne and Grace, Grace and Daphne. Chatting away about everything that had happened and more, but I didn't feel left out, even though I was expecting to. When it came down to it I was so miserable about Nina that I was comforted by the buzz of their chatter as I drifted off to sleep. Companionship amidst the horror, that's what it was. Almost like a family. There was the sound of Des in the shower and my two friends chatting and all we were missing was Nina. I wondered where she was, and whether she had been able to go to sleep. I couldn't bear to think about what might be happening to her, so I designed an imaginary bedroom for her instead. The sort of room a teenage girl might like. A big room with a sofa near to the bed, and a desk in the window with a chair that wouldn't be bad for her back. It was my room, I realised, as I imagined a pretty yellow colour for the paintwork, the master bedroom as Henry always called it.

'I guess we can't call it mistress bedroom,' he used to say.

'That might sound like something naughty was going on there.' That's how he thought of any kind of intimacy, something naughty.

I remember once early on in our marriage, when I still thought I might have another child, one I'd be allowed to keep. I decided to seduce Henry, kickstart the whole thing. I'd read an old marriage manual that suggested that reluctance to perform in the marriage bed was an indicator of a true gentleman, and that in these cases, wives were duty bound to step in. I did my best, see-through nightie and everything, but it just made him laugh. I don't know what made me think of that then.

My room was the biggest of the three bedrooms, so I decided right then and there that I would move out, go into the smaller back room and give this one to Nina. If she got away. If we managed to do the thing we had decided to do, if we were successful. It was too difficult to think of, so instead I tried to go to sleep, but I kept reliving that moment when I hadn't managed to lock the car door to keep her in. And tonight, when I hadn't managed to get her out. None of us had. My hands twitched, longing for another chance to rescue her. My Nina. I tried to stop thinking about her, even for a moment, but it was no good. The only thing that took my mind off her was picturing Henry. Henry as he was the last time I saw him, tucked up neatly in his coffin. It was the best place for him, I was sure of that.

I was up before the others that morning. See, Henry, I thought, I'm an early riser. I could hear the violin as I got washed and dressed. Lilting, echoey, sweet. I could imagine my mother with her head on one side and her eyes shut as if she was channelling the music from somewhere behind her eyes to her fingertips, which I suppose she was. She had a special violin face, that's what I used to call it when I was little. I didn't like it then. I used to cry, and say stop it, stop it, and my mother would put the violin down and laugh. I didn't want to share the attention, I suppose. I thought about that while I fussed around downstairs, getting croissants out of the freezer and making real coffee. How much each person needs to be special, I mean, and how each person has a past and a story to tell. That toad man, for example, did he have a mum who loved him? The kind who sat by his bed when he had a high temperature? The kind who looked at him and didn't see a toad at all, just a dear little boy with the world at his feet? I shuddered. That poor woman, I thought, giving up her time and her love and her energy for a toad.

'Are you OK, missus?' Des said.

I jumped a little. I'm not used to anyone being in the kitchen except me. Even when Henry was alive, it's not a place he often came to. He'd put his head round the door and sniff, as if he'd been forbidden to come in any further. There wasn't usually much to smell.

'Do you worry at all,' I said, 'about what we're doing? Should we be trying again? What else can we do? Do you think killing someone makes us bad people, even if we're doing it for a good reason? Even if we have no choice?'

I kept my voice low. I hadn't known I was going to say all that until it came bursting out but it felt good. I wasn't completely happy with what we were doing, that was the long and the short of it. Even though I worried about that sweet girl with all my heart, there was something about killing a person that made me uneasy.

'That's a lot of questions,' Des said, 'and I might not be the right person to ask, ma'am. I mean I haven't always made good choices and there's quite a few people would say I'm a terrible person. But the way I see it is, the world has changed. There isn't a society that's going to look after everyone any more. That was a dream, really, wasn't it? It wasn't real at all. The dream is over. So we're left with everyone looking out for themselves, and some people can't do it. So other people have to help them, and sometimes that means doing unpleasant things.'

I realised that Des had spent a lot of time thinking about this. He seemed to guess what I was thinking.

'When I was in prison,' he said, 'I had a lot of time to think. And excuse me, ma'am, for saying this, but I think us people of colour, we read the writing on the wall more quickly, if you don't mind me saying so. The writing was more obvious to us, because it was addressed to us first. I did what I did to protect my sister, nothing else, and I'd do the same again.'

He took the wind right out of my sails. I think from the way he spoke he had killed somebody before, but he seemed such a good man that I was sure the person had deserved it. We are both the same, I thought, siblings under the skin. Guardians of public morals. I wondered if it would be best for me not to think about toad man's mum. I hoped for her sake she had died early herself, perhaps of something painless in her sleep.

We had a council of war when everyone was up. Grace took charge. She was good at making sure everyone had a say, that we were all on the same page, I think that's the correct expression. I told them how worried I was and they listened to me, they really did, but we all agreed that there was no choice, no other way of stopping him. Henry floated through my head followed by toad's mum but I pushed them out. I voted to go on, and agreed that it would be wrong to back down and walk away, leave Nina where she was. Yes, I had niggling doubts, but Nina was the main thing. Nina mattered more.

'It's even more important now,' Daphne said. 'We absolutely have to finish what we started, we can't leave her there with him. I reckon the plan is worth a rerun. I think he might be keen to get his hands on that money now he's seen that we really were offering it.'

We all agreed. There were probably a million reasons not to try again, but it didn't matter. The stakes were high. That lovely girl. 'Meggie,' she called me. That picture I couldn't shake of her looking at me through the car window, waving like a much younger child. Waving as if she was trying to say, don't worry, I'll be OK, even though she knew that we all knew she wouldn't be. Maybe it helped her just to know that we were all rooting for her, I thought. I knew that it was important that we kept on trying, that we didn't give up now. She was brave enough to wave to us, we needed to be brave enough to keep on trying.

'How's that violin, Meg?' Grace said.

I was surprised. I never expect anyone to remember anything I've said. I mean, I presume they'd have more important things on their minds. I think I might have blushed.

'The violin is quiet right now,' I said.

They asked me to tell them the whole story then. I think they might have asked so that I wasn't brooding on the whole murder thing. They're thoughtful like that. I didn't really want to talk about it but I didn't want to seem standoffish, or disapproving. And we had time to kill.

I had never told the violin story before, even though it had always been with me.

'My mother was playing her violin in the shelter,' I said. 'I think it was October 1940. Like I said before, she used to play for the people stranded down there for the night. Only till nine or so, because the children were supposed to go to sleep then, although it must have been very difficult for them. It was the Northern line. This night, her violin wouldn't stay in tune. She couldn't understand why, and she kept stopping to tune it. "I fiddled with my fiddle," she used to say, "but it wouldn't fiddle with me."

'At two minutes past eight, she said, and I always remember the exact time because she was so precise. She said the station clock stopped then. At two minutes past eight a German bomb hit a water main. The water rolled into the shelter and it was chaos. A bus drove into the crater the bomb had made, I've seen photos. Loads of people were trapped underground, where they had been bedded down. They couldn't get to the stairs. Imagine it, trapped underground with water rising, some of it sewage water. There were woman with babies, little kids, all screaming. Trapped like rats in a bucket. My mum got out, but she ditched the violin. She said it took her a full minute to decide that she had to leave it, and during that minute the water rose from her knees to her waist.'

I didn't tell them the other part. The part about how when I was little, my mother used to say she swam to the next station, as if it was the easiest and most normal thing in the world. I believed it, of course I did. I still think of swimming along the tunnel whenever I'm on the Underground. It wasn't until she was dying and having a hard time of it that she cried, and told me about the people she had ignored, the babies that had been held out to her that she hadn't been able to take.

'Survival comes at a high price sometimes,' said Grace. I don't know how, but she seemed to have heard the parts of the story I had chosen to leave out.

'OK,' said Daphne, 'from now on we will totally listen to what you say about the violin. We'll try again, and this time we'll include the violin in all our plans.'

We all laughed at that but I think they meant it as well. Only Des didn't join in. He was shaking his head and clasping his hands together.

'Gosh,' he said. 'Imagine that, trapped, water rising. Shit, man, I mean, that would be the absolute worst.'

I realised that he had become very pale, sort of washed-out-looking.

'It's OK,' I said, 'it was a really long time ago.'

'Yes but,' he said, 'you never know, do you? I mean, you wake up in the morning and you never know whether you're going to make it through the day.'

'Oh, Des,' said Daphne, 'I'd forgotten about your claustro-phobia. That must be the worst story ever for you.'

'It's all right,' he said. 'I'll be back to what passes for normal in a minute. Most people who've been inside at Her Majesty's pleasure feel a little odd about closed spaces. I'm going to go into the garden for a moment. Quick smoke.'

'Oh dear,' I said after he had left. 'Do you think I should have kept that to myself? He looks quite green.'

They were reassuring, the others, and I realised that I was

starting to lose the sense of always saying the wrong thing that had been so much a part of me when Henry was alive. I had never made any good friends, I kept myself closed off from people during my marriage. I can't blame everything on Henry, I know that, but it does seem a shame to find out so late in life that I love being with people. That there's more to me than meets the eye. Henry used to hate that expression.

'Ninety-nine times out of a hundred,' he used to say, 'what meets the eye is what's there. Especially to a trained observer like me.'

I should have asked him why he thought he was a trained observer. There's a lot of things I should have asked him.

I was so busy worrying that I missed the next part of the conversation. By the time I tuned back in again, Daphne and Grace were both looking at me and I could see that they expected me to answer something.

'Sorry,' I said, 'I was miles away.'

They looked at each other as though they had been expecting that and were just confirming it with each other, but there was no malice in the look. In fact they both smiled.

I was just going to say something when Grace's phone rang.

'It's him,' she said. 'Keep quiet.'

She answered on loud speaker. 'Hello,' she said.

He cut in immediately. 'No need for that crap, dear,' he said. 'I'd like the money. We made a deal, didn't we?'

'We did,' Grace said, 'and it wasn't us who got spooked.'

I couldn't believe how calm she sounded, scornful even. I noticed that Daphne was covering Grace's other hand, the one not holding the phone, and for the first time I felt a little left out. It wasn't their fault, I knew that, but I still couldn't help wondering what it would be like to have that kind of special physical contact.

'Let's try again, shall we?' toad man said. 'Only this time I think we'd better change the rules a little. This time I'd like to see just one of you. The other two can stay home and drink their cocoa.'

Grace started to say something.

'I said cut the crap, can you?' toad said. 'I'm talking. Shut up and listen to me. I'll meet with one of you, just one. I'll meet with the fat white one with the straggly grey hair. I'll send the details later.'

And he was gone, call ended. They both looked at me and I realised that it was me. Me he had said he would meet with. Me on my own. It was a cruel description but a fair one.

'You don't have to, you know,' Daphne said. 'We don't have to dance to his tune.'

Grace didn't say anything. I could tell that she was thinking the same as me.

'We do have to,' I said. 'If we want to help her, we do have to. And he knows it.' Daphne started to protest but Grace stopped her.

'I think Meg is right,' she said. 'I think we have no choice but to go along with him. If you want to, Meg.'

I've never been brave. Never been the kind to volunteer, or to stick my neck out in any way. It's why I've had the life I've had, I suppose, why things have been so quiet. It might have been different if I had kept my little daughter. I think I would have stuck my neck out for her, if I'd had the chance.

'I'm fine,' I said, 'of course I'll do it. Of course.'

I was thinking of the stories I'd read about people doing

extraordinary things for other people. Swapping places in the queue for the gas chamber to give a perfect stranger a chance, for example, or blocking the entrance to a classroom when a mad gunman walks in. Putting everyone first in a lifeboat when the ship is sinking, covering a child's body with your own during a massacre. People have done all those things and more. People are remarkable. I needed to step up too.

'What could possibly go wrong?' I said.

It was an attempt at humour and it went down well. Both the other women burst out laughing and that was how we were when Des came back in. Laughing fit to burst.

'That's what I like to see,' he said, 'ladies happy in their lives. What's the joke?'

'The joke is,' I said, 'I'm going to meet him on my own.'

There was a silence.

'That's not funny,' Des said. 'Meg, I don't think you realise how bad this man is.'

The others looked concerned. I could see that Des had reminded them how dangerous it was and they were ashamed that they had treated it so lightly. I knew that they were about to tell me again that I didn't have to do it, so I jumped in.

'I know it's dangerous,' I said, 'I'm not daft. I know he might try and hurt me in some way, and I even know that I might not come out of it alive. That sounds dramatic but I think it's possible. Despite all of that, you need to look at it from a different perspective, that's the thing Henry could never do. I hope you don't mind me mentioning Henry now and then, it's a habit, I think.'

They all shook their heads to show that they didn't mind, and in a way that brought home to me more clearly than anything else what trouble I was in. I was sure they only didn't mind because they thought I might die.

'Only I've got a debt to pay,' I said. 'I had a chance once, a long time ago, to look after someone. Someone special. I was young and silly and most of all, I listened to what people said, and I didn't step up, I didn't do it. Doing this won't make up for that, I know that. The world isn't a big score sheet and there's no one keeping tabs, but in my mind I'm keeping count and this will help, believe me, whatever happens. I couldn't live with myself if I didn't do it. And do you know what? Living with Henry all those years, I'm tougher than you realise. I'll be just fine.'

It was a long speech and I could see that I had taken them by surprise. I'd taken myself by surprise as well. So much I'd left out, but I think I told them enough to be going on with. I'd never said anything to anyone except Henry about my little baby. And I didn't want to say any more. I knew that if I started talking about her I'd be undone. An old-fashioned word, but it described exactly how I would feel. It's an ordinary story, teenager has baby and gives it up for adoption. It doesn't sound like anything amazing. People lose their entire family in house fires, their children are murdered in front of their eyes, all of those things happen. All that happened to me was that I had a baby when I was seventeen, a dear little baby with blue eyes. I signed the papers, I watched her go, I had no idea that what I was doing would stay with me every day of my life. I thought I was turning the clock back to the time before she was born, and no one explained to me that that can't happen. No time travel. So I never knew whether she was alive, or happy, or ill, or whether she had children. I didn't know if she was in prison or cold or dyslexic, and I didn't know whether she ever forgave me. Those are terrible things to live with.

'We need to eat,' Daphne said, 'keep our strength up. Maybe we'd all feel better if we did something normal, like get a meal ready.'

I was grateful that she had changed the subject. She was so thoughtful, they both were. Real friends. Friends who tried to make things OK, who didn't argue with me, who just got on with things. It was by far the most comfortable thing she could have done. The others took their cue from her, and although I could see they were worried for me, they didn't say another word to try to dissuade me. I almost wished they would.

It was well into the afternoon by the time the toad man rang again. He wanted to meet that night, before we had time to come to our senses, I suppose. He asked for more money in order to hand Nina over, which Daphne said she'd been expecting.

'We have absolutely no reason to think he will stick to his word,' Daphne said, 'so we're going to have the Shoe people right behind you. It's our best chance.'

I argued that I'd be better going it alone, trusting to luck and determination, but I knew that was mad. We'd made a decision, and we were going to stick to it. It would be comforting to have the Shoe people waiting round the corner out of sight.

The meeting point was at the back of the shopping precinct. Toad would drive past in a car, take the money and open the back door so that Nina could get out. Any funny business, he said, and he'd speed up and wouldn't try again.

'What we need to think of,' Grace said, 'is whether we just want to get Nina safely, give him the money and close the chapter, move on and have happy lives, or whether we want to do what we agreed to? Whether we want to save future Ninas that he might get his nasty little hands on?'

'You're never going to stop it happening altogether,' Des said. 'There will always be people like him, men who exploit young women.'

'There don't have to be,' Daphne said. She had been quiet for a long time, chopping vegetables and looking thoughtful. 'I mean, if enough people sent messages to people like him, saying that it's not OK, what they're doing, then maybe they would think twice?'

We all looked at each other and at our feet and tried to think of what to say.

'OK,' Daphne said after a minute or two, 'that's ridiculous, I know it is. Let's just get Nina, that's the important thing. We'll ask the Shoe people to go, for back-up rather than anything else.'

'You can't change the world for everyone, sweetie, but you can change it for one person,' Grace said.

I pretended I agreed but as I nodded I got a sudden flash, a picture of Henry, dead. I remembered how great it had been to wake up the morning after he had died and remember that he wasn't there. That he would never be there again, that I was free. It was the best feeling ever. Whatever happened afterwards, it would be so good to remove that toad before he did any more harm. There could be hundreds of Ninas, young women who were right now playing with dolls or doing their homework or running in the park, unaware that their future was going to contain something as horrible as Nina had described. I gave my spare keys to Grace and Daphne, in case.

My chance to be a real hero, I thought as the violins soared. If only I was forty years younger.

CHAPTER TWENTY-TWO

Daphne

Thursday, 28 February

Daphne felt personally responsible for everything that was happening. It was her money, her friend who had helped them, and now Meg was going to be in terrible danger. Daphne knew it would be on her conscience if anything went wrong. This was why people chose not to get involved in helping other people, Daphne thought. They wanted to avoid the ghastliness of being responsible when things didn't turn out the way they had hoped.

'If you could go back a few days,' she said to Grace when Meg was out of earshot, 'see Nina coming and turn away, stay out of it, would you?'

Grace looked as though she was thinking hard about it, but Daphne could see that she had worked out the answer already. 'I know that one,' she said, putting her head to one side. 'The answer is no. We chose this, Daphne, all of us. And for the right reasons.'

Grace looked over at Meg, who was listening as Des explained to her about learning to cook in prison, and the how he had got such a reputation that even the prison officers used to ask for his recipes.

'Meg as well,' Grace said. 'We could have chosen to leave if we had wanted to, any of us. You know what I think, Daff? We're all responsible for ourselves. We have to follow our instincts, like animals. It's all we can do. None of this is your fault.'

Daphne felt a flash of happiness and, just for a moment, she was back in Australia in the 1970s. The place she had gone to where nobody would know her. Where no one would know she had been in prison. Or on the streets, selling sex. Where she would be able to rest, and recover, and never, ever have to have sex with anyone again. Unless it was her choice, and she didn't think that would happen.

Daphne had found a job in a bookshop in Sydney, near the sea. The sea was restful, calming, and Daphne never took for granted the fact that it was around every corner, at the end of every street. She walked a lot, and kept herself remote from everyone, resisting all offers of friendship. She was sure that anyone who became close to her would guess straight away that she was not like them, not normal. That she had done terrible things with men, for money, and that even if she had not kept any of the money herself, she had been complicit in the obtaining of it. She was dirty. So she had lived alone in Sydney, where everything was different, where no one knew her, and it had gone to plan until Beth came to work with Daphne in the bookstore. Beth, who gave her the same kind of happiness just by being with her, in the same room, as Daphne was feeling now from Grace. Beth and Grace even looked slightly alike,

Daphne thought now, tall and elegant and smiley, despite the forty-year difference in their ages.

'OK,' Daphne said, 'you're right as always, my friend. Onward and upwards. And Meg is doing well, isn't she? She's coping with this as well as any of us, I reckon.'

'Imagine,' Grace said. 'Imagine what Henry would say.'

Both women laughed.

They were sitting down to dinner when Des made his announcement.

'I've got to say it,' he said. 'I'm thinking you ladies need some protection. Especially Meg, if she's going to meet that man. So I've got something that might help you, make you feel more safe.'

Des put his knife and fork down and reached into his pocket. He got out a small gun and put it on the table. Daphne thought it looked like a toy.

'Des,' she said, 'that isn't… I mean… we wouldn't, honestly. It's not a thing. I can speak for everyone, I think.'

She looked at Grace and Meg. Grace nodded back, but Meg seemed not to have heard. Daphne realised that they had all stopped eating except Meg, who seemed to be cramming more and more food into her mouth without remembering to swallow. Daphne wondered whether she should say anything.

'Meg,' Grace said, 'I'm worried you're going to choke.'

Meg blinked and tried to get her food down her throat without spitting anything out.

'Sorry,' she gasped as Daphne held her water glass out to help.

'I've been to a shooting range,' Meg said when she had

recovered herself and more or less stopped coughing. 'I was actually quite good. But if I ever had a killer instinct, it's long gone, honestly. It's been gone for ages. I don't want the gun. Honestly, I'll be fine.'

'Meg,' said Des, 'I'm no fan of firearms, believe me. But I think there might be a case for it this time, just to carry it. It might make you feel safer, I'm not sure.'

'I think carrying a weapon is a dangerous thing,' Meg said. 'It won't make me feel safer at all.'

All three women murmured agreement and looked at Des. Daphne hoped he wasn't offended.

'You meant well,' she said, 'and thank you for looking out for us.'

Des shook his head. 'You lot certainly know your own minds,' he said.

Daphne smiled. 'Women do, mostly,' she said.

'One last thing,' Des said. 'Please, Meg, please, would you take it if I remove all the bullets and show you how to load it, in case? You can leave it at the bottom of your bag if you want to, but at least if you need that little bit of something extra, it'll be there.'

Meg shrugged. 'I suppose it can't hurt to take it,' she said, 'just to humour you, mind.'

Daphne was worried. Meg was being sweet to humour Des, she thought, but she didn't seem like a person who could cope with even carrying a weapon. Daphne couldn't imagine her hurting anyone. She hoped that having it in her bag might make her feel more confident, and resolved to talk to Grace about it later.

'Don't worry about me,' Meg said. 'I know I might agree

with people too easily. I know I'm anxious to please. But I'll do this right, I promise you. I won't screw up.'

Daphne put a hand on Meg's arm.

'We care about you, that's all,' Daphne said. 'It's a really brave thing you're doing here. You're doing it for Nina, and for all of us.'

Grace nodded. 'Are you absolutely sure you're happy to do it?' she said.

'Stop worrying,' Meg said. 'I know I'm a bit stupid. But I'm happy to have the gun, even if I never use it. Maybe it will be a lucky charm. I know I'd be better off if I stopped talking about Henry, and I'm going to, but it's a nervous habit so you'll have to indulge me just a little. And one of the things Henry used to say, quite often, was that after a nuclear holocaust there'd be nothing left but cockroaches and Meg. It sounds horrible, doesn't it, as if I'm some kind of creepy-crawly beast, but I think he meant it well. I think what he meant was, Meg's a survivor. I'm going to take it that way, anyway. May as well see the sunny side.'

'Here's to Meg,' Des said and he held up his cup of tea. 'I can tell you now, I've been so worried about this. I feel much happier now that you've got some protection, even if it's not loaded.'

He put his fork down and mopped himself with one of Meg's serviettes. 'I remember when my sister was seventeen,' he said.

After they had eaten the time went very slowly. Twice Daphne shook her wrist, thinking that her watch must have stopped. She felt tired to her bones, and when she looked at the other two women it was obvious that they felt the same way, but she was anxious to keep their spirits up.

'You can change your mind any time,' Daphne said to Meg.

'Sometimes things have to get done,' Meg said. 'I've found that, before.'

Daphne thought about what would happen if Meg changed her mind and decided against going through with the plan. At least then Daphne would be able to step in, maybe do the thing herself, not have to risk anyone else's safety. It wasn't likely. Meg looked extraordinarily calm for a woman who would be meeting a very bad man in a few hours, alone and armed only with an unloaded gun that she didn't want. Almost jaunty, Daphne would have said. She knew that Meg had her reasons. They all had their reasons. All of them with their private battle scars, their hard-wired reasons for wanting to help Nina.

'Is there anything I can do, anything at all,' Daphne asked Meg, 'to make things go more easily tonight?'

'Bless you,' Meg said. 'I'll be fine, don't you worry.'

The three women talked a little while Des sat on the floor at their feet. They talked about what they would do next if toad man didn't turn up, about what would happen if he tried to grab the money and run, and about what they could do if Nina was hurt. They agreed that they would only give half the money, and that they would tell him where the other half was once they had Nina. That Daphne would be standing by with her car in case Nina needed to go straight to hospital. Daphne thought they had everything covered.

'Let me summarise this for you, if it helps,' Des said. 'Meg sticks to the script. That's important. She offers him half the money but asks for Nina before she tells him where the other half is. If she feels threatened at any time, more threatened than is bearable, that is, she coughs three times and the Shoe people come from round the corner and it's curtains for the toad.'

'Oh hang on,' Meg said. 'Can you say that part again please?'

Des looked baffled. 'Which part?' he said.

'The curtains part, of course,' Meg said. 'I used to love that expression, when I first read it. I thought it was wonderful, I never thought I would get to hear anyone say it in real life. Especially not with the word "toad".'

Grace looked at Daphne. It was a look full of concern, and maybe some fear, too. Meg was starting to sound unstable, and certainly not up to the challenge ahead of her, that's what Grace's look said, and Daphne almost agreed with her. It was too late to back out, but Meg was starting to sound more and more as though she didn't understand how serious things were.

'It's OK,' said Meg, catching the look that passed between the other two women. 'I'm not losing my marbles or anything like that. It's just easier, for me, I mean, if I don't get all dramatic. You know, keep things light.'

She took a breath as if she was going to say something else, but didn't. Daphne guessed it was another Henry reference that Meg had decided against, and her heart went out to her.

'How did Henry, I mean... Would you like to talk about what happened to him, and all that? We've still got an hour or so before we need to get ready.' Daphne wasn't sure that it was the right thing to bring up past difficulties for Meg, but she obviously liked talking about Henry and it might take her mind off the ordeal ahead.

'Oh,' said Meg, 'oh no, let's leave sleeping dogs where they are and let them have a rest. I'll tell you all about it another time.'

Daphne was sorry that she had brought it up. She could feel herself blushing and she was overwhelmed by a sense of her own awkwardness. Daphne knew that she was terrible in social situations, that she was different from everyone else and that every word she said reinforced that. When she used to go to work parties she had ended up going from group to group, trying to join in with the conversations. When it was really bad, each group seemed to turn their backs on her and exclude her as if it was a choreographed event. She often escaped to the toilets and wept. Eventually Daphne had gone only briefly to any gathering where she might have to talk to people in that way, always making sure that she had a cast-iron excuse ready so that she could leave early. Daphne knew that her colleagues had talked about her, that they had found it funny that she was so reluctant to go to anything.

She couldn't help it, that was all. It was part of her, this feeling of being wrong. As far back as she could remember. Being different, not having a natural group, a tribe. One of Daphne's first memories was of slipping her hand out of her mother's when shopping in the northern city where she had grown up. Slipping her hand out so that she could follow a man she saw in the street, a man with brown skin like Daphne and her mother, and white and grey like everyone else she knew. Daphne couldn't remember actually thinking that he might be related to her, nothing as clear as that. She wanted to be with him, that was all, be with someone else who looked like her. No wonder her mother had been out of her mind with fear.

'Daphne,' Meg said, 'I'm sorry, I didn't mean to upset you. It's just...' She tailed off.

We should have a hug, Daphne thought. I should reach out for her. She busied herself with clearing away some teacups.

All the women were subdued as they waited. They went over the script one more time and talked through all the things that could happen.

'Remember,' said Grace, 'you're no good to Nina if you're hurt. You have to run, just run, if anything happens that you're not comfortable with. He won't follow you, he won't move away from the car. That's his safety blanket. So don't stay still if he starts anything, just get away.'

'It's also the last thing he will expect,' Daphne said. 'No one thinks that old women can run.'

'I was the fastest runner in the upper fourth in nineteen sixty-four,' Meg said.

'The upper fourth?' Des said. 'What on earth is that? Is it some kind of club?'

The women laughed until they found it difficult to catch their breath.

'It's year nine,' Grace said. 'Year nine in old-fashioned speak.'

Des threw his hands up in mock despair and pulled a face.

'I'm going to wash up,' he said. 'Why don't you three go and get ready?'

The women stopped laughing, sobered up as suddenly as if Des had thrown cold water at them.

'I can't believe it's that time already,' Meg said.

Grace took both of Meg's hands in hers. 'I guess no one would ever be ready for something as big as this,' she said, 'and if you want to back out now, no one would blame you. There will be another way to help Nina, there's always another way somehow. It's important that you don't do more than you feel OK with. You hear?'

Daphne thought that she would have said exactly that to Meg if she had been able to think quickly enough. It was just right, the right tone, the caring way she had said it, everything. Meg squared her shoulders.

'I'm fine,' she said. 'First night nerves, that's all. Henry used to say that I could have been on the stage, if only I had been a bit taller. And thinner, I guess he meant. But it was these stupid nerves that held me back, not my height. Among other things. I'm going to have a quick slurp of the cooking sherry, that'll help, and everything will be fine. What could possibly go wrong?'

The joke didn't work so well the second time around.

Everything, Daphne thought. Every damn thing.

CHAPTER TWENTY-THREE

Meg

Thursday, 28 February

Des showed me how to load the gun in case I needed it and I watched and listened. It was good having something to do and I've always been practical. Sitting around made me nervous and I didn't want the others to realise that I was absolutely terrified. There was no point in sharing and making everyone more jittery. For exactly point nought five of a second, I wished Henry was there so that I could tell him. I tried to picture how the conversation would go. Henry, I'd say, I've got myself into a bit of a predicament. I always spoke like that to him, played things down, made myself look stupid. It seemed to be what he liked and I thought it was no skin off my nose.

That's what husbands are for, he might have said, to sort out things like that for the girlies. To step in whenever there's a little something they can do to make life easier. I used to hate the way he spoke to me but at that moment I couldn't help wishing I could hear him speak again. Just the odd sentence. I listened hard.

Don't mess with our Meg, I could hear Henry say. She'll give you what for if you're not careful. I stopped dead between the kitchen and the living room and waited for him to say something else. Go, Meg, go, Meg, he said. I was astonished. I wished there was someone I could tell. The thing is, he utterly never would have said that. It was a landmark, a very important milestone. It was the first time in nearly fifty years that I was happy with what he had said, and the first time I had written his lines for him. I wanted to clap. The very first time I had chosen for him, told him what to say. It was more than important. I felt a current of excitement despite the anxiety and the heat of the moment. I didn't know why it had never happened before. Henry could say whatever I wanted him to now, I realised, no need to stick to the script. No need at all. He would never argue back. Puppet Henry, this was going to be the new way. Come on, Meg, the Henry in my head said, I know you can do it. You've got this.

I loved him more in that moment than I ever had before. I stood up straight, pulled my shoulders back and breathed deep. I felt less terrified and less alone, a more substantial person, a person not to mess with.

Daphne and Grace were sitting at the kitchen table trying to look nonchalant, but I knew that they were terrified for me. They didn't believe that I could do it, I could see it in their eyes. I needed to let them know that I was fine, that I wouldn't let them down. I thought of Nina. She could be my daughter, I thought, forgetting for a moment that my daughter would be heading for sixty, probably with grandchildren of her own.

'Am I ever ready for this,' I said. I even smiled as I said it, and that took them by surprise. I hoped they were starting to change their minds. I buttoned up my best cardigan and girded my loins, whatever that means. I really was as ready as I would ever be.

I felt strange going out so late, as if the natural order of things had been overturned. I caught the 484 bus to the shopping precinct as we had agreed. It was a journey I was totally familiar with from a thousand trips to the shops but it seemed different at night, like a bus in someone else's city. I couldn't see out of the steamed-up windows but I tried to remember where we were at every point in the journey. Park, bowling green, hill down into Ladywell, left down Lewisham High Street. I was glad Grace and Daphne weren't there. They had wanted to come with me, but I was very firm. There was no point annoying him by not doing what he said. We might only have this one chance. It wasn't the same for Des. He was on my bus, sitting towards the back. We all thought that he hadn't been seen by the toad at all, so it was safe for him to be there as long as he took care not to look suspicious. I wasn't sure that would be a thing he could carry off, but when I got to the precinct I realised that everyone hanging around outside it late at night looked suspicious, and that he would fit right in. It was a suspicious place, full of deeply suspicious people. It was me who looked totally out of place. The people gathered round the doors had blankets or sleeping bags, bits of cardboard to lie on and overflowing carrier bags. I was dressed for a shopping expedition, with a basket over my arm and my good winter coat.

I didn't know where Des went to at this point, I couldn't see him. I was busy trying to look as though I had every right to be there.

'What do you want, lady?' said a man. He was suddenly so close to me that it made my neck tingle. 'Did no one tell you that the shops are closed now?'

Several people laughed. I had to think quickly. They didn't seem dangerous, these people, but I imagined how I would feel if I was homeless and an old woman in a good coat turned up clutching a shopping bag which might be full of cash. It actually was full of cash, that was the thing, and although I'd rather give it to these people who had nowhere to go than to the toad, I had to think of Nina. And it wasn't, strictly speaking, my cash to give away anyway, nice as these folk might be.

The thing about our Meg is, my internal Henry said, she's good in a crisis. Always knows what to do. One thing I'd say for sure is, you can depend on Meg.

I gave my new Henry a virtual high five for being so supportive and tried to forget that the real Henry would have been furious that I was there at all.

'I hope you don't mind,' I said to the man by my ear, hoping that the others would realise that I was including them all, 'but I've come here to meet someone. I'd really like to come back another day and talk to you all. But tonight there's stuff I have to do, I'm sorry.'

I meant it, I really did. They looked so nice, helping each other and sharing their drinks and cigarettes. Especially when I thought of toad. I hoped they didn't mind me standing there, crashing their gathering.

'Have you got sandwiches in there?' one of the girls said.

She looked young and terribly thin, and I couldn't believe I'd been so stupid. Of course I should have brought sandwiches. And flasks of tea and small cakes. I thought of all the nights when I had sat at home, thinking of myself and Henry and our problems and not realising that there were people out there who would have liked a sandwich. How easy it would have been to have made some and brought them down. Henry would have hated it, of course. He would have tried to convince me that it was their own fault, and that everyone would be all right if they just worked hard like he did, stayed away from drink and drugs and sex and minded their own business.

I remembered that as well as carrying the envelope of cash for the toad, I also had my own private emergency fund in my top pocket. I'd started it in the early days of my relationship with Henry, keeping a small stash of cash on me in case. In case of what, I wasn't sure. I suppose I imagined leaving, escaping and starting a happy life. It made me feel secure to know that it was there. I decided I'd give it away when the main business of the evening was done. I looked at my watch. Ten minutes to go. Keep a cool head, I told myself, no sudden moves.

I turned away slightly, so that only the man breathing down my neck and the very thin girl could hear me. The others seemed happy enough to go on with their plans for the night.

'I'm in a spot of trouble,' I said quietly, 'and I really would like to help you out when it's over. I'd be happy to come back. I'm a person who keeps her word, I can assure you. But right now, I'm meeting someone here, and handing something over, and I need to be left alone, just for as long as it takes. I'm sorry if that sounds vague.'

'I'm sorry for your troubles, ma'am,' the man said, 'and I'm grateful, but not embarrassingly so, that you've taken the time to address me as a fellow human being. I'm sorry if my initial response was to scare you somewhat, that was never my intention.'

He bowed, a proper bow like dances and actors do, swooping his hands out and hanging his head almost to the floor. It was not what I had expected. The very thin girl laughed.

'He's always doing that,' she said. 'He used to be on the stage, innit, Gordon?'

Gordon shuddered. 'I presume you mean,' he said, 'is that not correct, Gordon, and to that I will answer in the affirmative. Although strictly speaking, the stage was not actually my workplace. It was more the big top where I earned an honest crust.'

I looked at him more closely. I'd picked up the American accent and now I saw that he was black with very short grey hair, and about my age. He didn't seem to be drunk, or off his head, or any of the things Henry would have thought synonymous with a life on the streets. The girl seemed to be more typical, although I was aware that I had no idea what was normal for street life. She was white, very white, almost transparent, and her blonde hair was scraped back in a ponytail.

'I'm Susannah,' she said, 'and this is my dad, Gordon.'

I did a double take on account of the huge difference in colour between the two of them and they both laughed.

'Family is what you make it, ma'am,' Gordon said. 'Please don't think we are mocking you. I've been looking out for Susannah for a while now. It helps, to make links, when the world is against you. A person on their own can get lost so easily.'

I tried to keep a tight rein on my emotions. Of all the things to happen, I thought, this is not what I expected. I looked at my watch. Five minutes. Five minutes till handover and I didn't want to jeopardise anything by getting caught up with Gordon and Susannah. I must have shown my agitation on my face. I've always been easy to read, Henry said, although I now believe that isn't true. He never even guessed how unhappy I was. He didn't know a thing.

'I suspect from your demeanour that although you'd prefer to be on your own right now,' Gordon said, 'it might help you to know that Susannah and I will be close by, watching out for you. We'd be honoured.'

'Thank you,' I said. I didn't mean to say it, I should have sent them away, but it burst out of me before I'd had a chance to think it through.

They melted away, the two of them, becoming part of the small bunch of people who were settling down for the night by the doors of the shopping centre. There was a small overhang by the doorway, so that most of them would be dry if it rained. I moved away from them and towards the road. I couldn't see Des, but I knew he'd be there somewhere. I was scared. It would have been crazy not to be scared, but I wasn't sorry that I was involved. I felt supported, on the side of the angels for at least once in my life. I moved along the road a few steps so that I was properly tucked away from the view of the doorway people. I felt in my pocket for the small gun, and wondered for the thousandth time whether it would be helpful to get it out. I don't remember hearing the violin.

He was on time. Bang on time. I must have been cold, it was a cold night, but I didn't feel it as I stood there. I was primed, like a tightrope walker just before she steps out, like a tennis player on a tie-break. I was as ready as anyone has ever been for anything. I had my hand inside my bag and I was hanging on like crazy to the envelope with the cash. Come on, Nina, I said under my breath. Come on, sweetheart, I'm here, I'm waiting, you're nearly safe.

He was driving a different car. I'm not sure why, although afterwards the others thought that it may have been to confuse me, put me on the back foot. It didn't. I remembered what Nina had said about him driving different cars, and somehow I was prepared for it. I expected him to come in a different hat, as it were. It was a pale car, nondescript, looked like all the other cars on the road. A Skoda, I think Des said afterwards.

I could see him smiling as he drove towards me. I've thought about that and I'm not sure how on earth I could have seen him smiling, because it was dark and badly lit round the back of the precinct. That's probably why he chose it. So I'm not sure really, whether I made the memory up to fit the facts, but it feels very definite. He raised his hand from the wheel in a little gesture of hello, slowed right down until he was practically next to me, and then stopped. I scanned up and down the road. No one in sight. I tried to look in the back of the car, but it wasn't such a plain car as I had thought, because the back windows were blacked out. I couldn't see anything except his smiling, horrible, toadlike face.

'Have you got something for me?' he said, leaning out of the window.

'First things first,' I said, marvelling at myself even as I said the words. I sounded in control, like someone from a TV drama. We had decided it would be best to keep it simple. 'Where's Nina?'

He looked angry for one second then he rearranged his features into his customary bland expression.

'Nina,' he said, as if he wasn't quite sure why I had mentioned her. As if she was an acquaintance we had in common that we hadn't chatted about for ages.

I resisted the impulse to say, yes, Nina, the girl you stole. I just stared, and kept my face clear. So clear, in fact, I wondered whether I looked slightly deranged. Two sandwiches short of a picnic, as Henry would have called it. I certainly felt rather unbalanced but clear and focused at the same time. Only one thought going through me, one aim in mind, everything else forgotten. Just give me Nina, I thought, and then I said it, quietly and firmly. Like you might speak to a man balancing on the edge of a bridge railing if you were trying to talk him down. Don't do it, you might say, but without any urgency in your voice.

'I've got half the money here, but I need to have Nina first. It's what we agreed.'

'Count it,' he said.

I started to say something about trust and honour or some nonsense like that but he cut right across me.

'I said count it, and I meant now, here, in front of me so I can see, you stupid bitch,' he said.

I got the envelope out of my bag but my hands were shaking so badly I couldn't get the money out straight away.

'Just a moment,' I said, 'I've always been a butterfingers.'

I can't believe I said something so stupid. I don't think I've ever used that expression before, and I'm sure I never will again. Toad man gave a kind of dismissive snort and I thought, right, that's good, he's not seeing me as any kind of threat.

Safer for me. I made myself slow my breathing and tried to concentrate on getting the notes out of the envelope without dropping any. I ignored the violins playing frantically and out of tune. I counted it out, fifty, one hundred, playing for time and holding the notes up so that he could see.

I'd moved the gun so that it was tucked up my arm. My winter coat has Velcro at the cuffs, to keep the heat in, so it was easy to pop it into my sleeve. I liked the feel of it. I wasn't planning on using it but it was company and I moved my arm as I counted so that I could feel it against my side through my coat. It calmed me down.

I'd got to nine thousand when toad man said, 'Oh stop it, for goodness' sake. I'm getting bored. Just hand it over.'

I stood my ground.

'Nine fifty,' I said, 'nine one hundred, nine one fifty.'

I couldn't stop. I could see that he was angry, really angry, but I had been trusted to do a good job and if that included counting it out then I would count. I would count until it was time to stop. Stubborn, that's me. I think there was something soothing about the repetition as well.

Toad man opened the door and jumped out of the car. He slapped me round the face, a resounding slap, a slap like in the movies. My head jerked to one side as if it might fly off my neck, and even through the shock I thought, same side as Tuesday's punch, that's going to be sore in the morning. Henry had been a slapper, so I knew.

I stood straight, didn't lose my footing.

'Nine two fifty,' I said although I wasn't sure that the number was consecutive. There was a ringing in my ears.

'If you'd like to send Nina out now,' I said, even as he

was gearing up to hit me again. I think it's the training I had from Henry, standing my ground and keeping on. It kind of symbolised our time together, me trying to stand firm while he chipped away at me, and I'd got rather good at it.

I think it might all have gone smoothly if it hadn't been for the dog. I don't know what dog it was or where it was but I could hear a dog barking somewhere nearby. It didn't sound like a happy dog. You can tell a lot from a bark, and this dog sounded lost and alone and scared. The bark turned into a kind of whimper at the end and then tailed off. I lost count of the money altogether and looked around to see if I could spot the dog, help it in some way. It sounded so much like Bingley, that was the thing. People who don't know about dogs say that they all sound the same, but it isn't true at all. There are as many different barks as there are human voices, and an owner will be able to pick her dog out of hundreds or thousands, I'm not sure which. I would have been able to pick Bingley out of millions, I know that.

I'd never thought of owning a dog before Bingley turned up. I thought they were unpredictable, terrifying, liable to turn into wild beasts at any time, that's how I'd been brought up. My mum would cross the street to avoid walking past a dog. She used to grip my hand so tightly I could feel the fear radiating down her arm. So when I opened the front door that day and saw him there, a little bundle of matted fur, my first instinct was to scream. Like women are supposed to scream when they see a mouse, that sort of scream. If there'd been a table to jump on to I think I would have jumped. There wasn't, so I had a closer look. I wasn't even sure if he was alive but then he opened his eyes and looked at me and that was it. I was smitten. I picked him up, holding him at arm's length in case he flew at me like a deranged wolf, and I took him into the living room. Henry was at work that day, so I had all day to look after him. I intended to take him to the police in the evening, see if could find him a home, but he deserved at least a good wash and a feed before he went. I'd never washed a dog before. I'd never washed anyone except myself, and I had no idea how joyous it would be.

I didn't have any dog shampoo, but I used human grade instead and an old hairbrush to fluff him out afterwards. He looked gorgeous by the time I'd finished, and the name Bingley flashed into my head like a neon sign from another planet.

Bingley, I said and he looked at me as though he was relieved I'd guessed the right name. He ate a chicken breast I cooked for him and some plain boiled rice. When Henry came home Bingley looked as if he'd always been there, sitting nicely on a cushion in front of the fire. I knew that I wanted that little dog to stay, but I also knew that Henry didn't like anything that wasn't his idea. I was ready.

'Henry,' I said as I opened the front door, 'Henry, I've got the most wonderful surprise for you.'

He looked indulgent and ruffled my hair. It must have been a good day at work.

'Liver and bacon casserole?' Henry said. 'Orange polenta cake, poached salmon?'

I shook my head. I wished that I had cooked something he liked to jolly him along but I'd actually been far too busy giving Bingley a makeover.

'Even better than that,' I said. 'I thought you needed a dog. So I've got you one. Tadaa!'

I opened the living-room door and thrust my arm out to indicate the fluffy, shiny-eyed Bingley, still warming himself in front of the fire.

'I'm sorry,' Henry said. There was a warning note in his voice. 'I'm sorry but did we discuss this? Have I forgotten something important?'

I knew I had to think quickly. I'd been so blinded by puppy love all day that I hadn't thought it through properly.

'I was reading a book,' I said, 'you know, that one I've been reading recently.'

I knew he wouldn't have taken one bit of notice of what I was reading so I felt safe.

'Anyway,' I said, 'the main character in that, the main man, he has this dog, and he says, every thinking man needs a dog for a companion. So I thought of you, and how much you would like taking a dog for walks, that kind of thing. So I got Bingley.'

It was feeble, I knew that even at the time, but I was desperate.

'Bingley?' Henry said. 'What kind of name is that for a dog? If he's going to be my dog I think we'll come up with something much more fitting.'

He came up with Prince, the most obvious name in the world, but I didn't make a fuss. Better to be called Prince than thrown out on the street, I thought. I still called him Bingley when we were alone, of course, and I took pleasure in undermining Henry's training of him whenever I could.

That was my undoing. Bingley's undoing, really. Henry had a special chair, a mustard-coloured velvet chair that had been in his family for generations. That's what he said, anyway. I thought it was perfectly ordinary, but I went along with his requests to be careful with it, never let the dog sit in it, that kind of thing. In fact, I never even sat in it myself. It wasn't very comfortable. One day, when Henry was at work, Bingley decided to try it out. I should have noticed, of course I should. I should have helped him off, explained to him, whatever would have worked. I didn't though, I was reading a book and I was feeling lazy. I also had no idea that Henry would be home early. I didn't even hear his key in the lock, that's how engrossed I was. So the first I knew of Henry being home was when he burst into the room shouting.

'What's that filthy animal doing on my chair,' and worse. Bingley jumped off, of course, and the worst thing is, when I look back, that at first he was wagging his little tail and acting pleased to see Henry, but that didn't last long. Henry scooped him up, held him by the scruff of his neck and shouted right into his face. He was a good dog, Bingley, a very good dog, but he was a rescue dog nonetheless and he'd probably had people shouting and being mean before, so he knew what to do. He bit Henry. On the nose, and it was a hard bite so Henry dropped him and I rushed to pick him up and Henry stood in front so that I couldn't. I was crying and carrying on and I think Bingley thought that he would protect me because Henry was still shouting about legacies and antiques and picking invisible pieces of Bingley fluff off the chair. So he bit Henry again, on the ankle this time. I knew as soon as it happened that I wouldn't be able to help him but looking back now, I can't understand myself. I can't understand why I didn't just grab that dog, walk out of the door and leave.

I started keeping money with me after that. Always a couple

of notes in a pocket or even in my bra in the summer. That day I didn't have any, couldn't think what I should do, dithered around like a silly old lady. Henry stormed out holding poor old Bingley as if he might explode any minute and I fluttered after him, apologising and promising I'd make sure Bingley behaved himself but he slammed the door in my face and didn't come back for three hours. He came back without Bingley, of course. I never did find out what he'd done with him. It was almost the worst time of my life. I cried, I tried to make bargains with whatever higher power there might be, but there weren't any available in Lewisham that day. All the time, right through the three hours and for many nights afterwards, I thought I could hear Bingley barking. Yelping, really, it was a noise of pure terror.

I'd never heard anything like it before or since. Until tonight. Until I was standing there, counting money and waiting for the next slap, waiting for Nina. The dog sounded like Bingley, but it was more than that. The dog sounded scared and alone, that was the bottom line, and I forgot any worries I might have had for myself and thought instead of Nina, scarcely older than a pup, and about trying to locate the yelping animal and help it.

'Come on, Nina,' I shouted, 'let's go and find the dog.'

It wasn't in the script, it wasn't what I'd planned but it seemed right, that's all I can say. And I could tell that it was because of the noise of the back door of the car opening. Maybe he didn't have a child lock on this car because it wasn't his best car, or maybe he had forgotten to use it, I'm not sure. But Nina opened the door and was out of the car before I could think it through and I shouted, 'Nina,' at the top of my voice and the homeless man from the circus was suddenly right behind me and he grabbed my hand and I grabbed Nina's and we moved towards the huddle of people over by the doorway but he had a gun, the toad, I recognised the shape of it in his hand and he grabbed me back and held it against my head.

'Go on,' I said to Nina, 'run.'

I meant it, too. I'm not a hero or a victim, I don't mean that, but the thing is, if he was going to take anyone, it might as well be me. He certainly wouldn't get much for me on the open market, he couldn't really pimp me out at my age and I'm used to bullies. I've been used to them all my life. So if that no-neck ugly toad man wanted to take someone away with him it might as well be the person he wants least. I stared at the circus man, it must have only been for a fraction of a second but I put everything into that stare to try to make him understand and I think he did. He held onto Nina more securely and made a tiny saluting gesture towards me.

Toad man was still hanging onto me and I wondered about getting out my sleeve gun but I thought it might be amazingly stupid to start a gunfight even if I could have slid it out easily. His hand pinched into my arm and I stumbled as he pulled me back towards the car.

'Get in, get in,' he said but it wasn't like in the movies.

In films and on TV, people being forced into cars slip in easily, and if it's the police pushing them in then they place a protective hand over their heads, to stop them from making complaints later, I suppose. In real life, it was much more complicated. First, he pulled me towards the car. Nina was screaming by this time and reaching out towards me as the man from the circus, helped now by Des, pulled her away. Then the toad flung the door open and pushed me towards it but I'd been standing around in the cold for quite a long time and my right knee had gone stiff so I couldn't bend quickly. I needed to rub it to get myself moving but that wasn't possible so I had to make a kind of lunge towards the car, which meant that I dropped quite a number of the bank notes I had been holding on to. There was a wind that night and it picked up a few of them so that they flew to first one side, then the other. Toad man was torn between hanging on to me, running after Nina and scrabbling for the fifty pound notes.

He went for the easiest option. He chose me, bundled me into the car and slammed the door.

CHAPTER TWENTY-FOUR

Grace

Thursday, 28 February

That seaweed tang is so strong that I sneeze. This is bad trouble, right in front of us. That man has got Meg. I feel like I could tear him apart with my teeth, break his arms just by looking at him, but I have to be careful because of Nina. I look at Daphne and I can see she's as distraught as I am. Not Meg, I think. Oh, not Meg, how will she cope? Her life is so tidy. Her cushions match her curtains. I want to shout, 'Leave her alone!' I keep quiet, though, and Daphne does too. We're biding our time, trying to think what we can do that will have the best possible chance of helping. I'm breathing deep so I don't gag on that smell. That smell of trouble.

We didn't tell Meg we'd be following her quite so soon. She was terrified as it was, and very keen to play by toad man's rules. I could understand why, but it wasn't possible for me or Daphne to stay at home a minute longer and leave her to face all the danger on her own. I've spent my whole life feeling responsible, being responsible for terrible things happening to people who didn't deserve them. I can't add to the list now. There are enough ghosts queuing up to shout at me in the night.

We jumped into the car soon after Meg left and parked as near to the precinct as we could. We hovered at the back of a little crowd by the doors where no one would notice us. It seemed that most of the people there were homeless, and coming together at night for company and a bit of warmth from the shops inside. Meg was standing off to one side, then she moved and I couldn't see her any more. I wished I could go and help her, stand with her in solidarity or something, anything that might help. I looked around to take my mind off my inaction. I've never been good at standing back. I recognised the Shoe people. They looked uncomfortable, standing apart from the others and facing in different directions, as though they'd had a row.

'Hi,' I said. I kept my voice down.

'Hello,' said Greg. 'Des told us what's going on. We're ready.'

I hadn't seen Des yet. I had thought that the Shoe people would be more hidden, although I could see the advantage of hiding in plain sight, mingling with the little crowd. Everything was worrying, nothing seemed right.

Daphne and I caught sight of Meg again and we moved further back into the shadows. The Shoe people followed. The chatter around us sank to a murmur.

'Don't forget,' Daphne said into my ear, 'it's really important that he doesn't know any of us are here, not while he has the girl. Best to keep back unless we absolutely have to jump in. Leave it to the experts.'

I wasn't reassured.

'Don't worry,' Clara said, 'we know what we're doing.'

She touched her head. I guess she wanted to indicate that there was a lot going on in there. I looked at Greg and I could see that he was embarrassed. I looked at Daphne and I could tell she was thinking the same as I was: how did we manage to find such an unlikely pair of assassins? And did they really understand the situation? Did any of us? I decided then and there that I needed to step up, take more of the responsibility on my own shoulders.

'You two,' I said to the Shoe people, 'stand at the back please. If we need you we'll give a clear signal. A whistle. Daphne, let's move over to the side.'

Some of the homeless people had been chatting together in a huddle next to Meg, and as Daphne and I stood watching, one of them pulled away and came over to us. He was tall and black and old and handsome and for a moment I thought I might know him. From a school I had taught in, or maybe back home. The others watched him.

'I'm Gordon,' he said, 'homeless at the moment, but not stupid. The lady over there seems very scared, but she's asked us to keep away and we'll do that. Now it seems to me that although she hasn't seen you yet, you may be connected to her. And we don't want to upset her by asking her but my friends and I, we can see that something is going on. So it seems that my friends and I might need to be aware of that something? Might we, perhaps, be in danger from that something? In short, ladies and gentleman, would anyone mind not mugging us off, as I believe the popular expression goes?'

'I'm sorry,' I said. 'I'm sorry if we have brought trouble with us. I guess you were here first, and you deserve an explanation. Everything is happening rather quickly and I don't know who to trust, who to tell. I feel I don't know anything at all at the moment.'

'That I can understand,' Gordon said, 'only it would be more than useful if we could at least know whether we should find somewhere else to be this evening. A few of us are quite vulnerable and may like to avoid any unpleasantness. Most of us, I suppose, apart from me. I'd be very happy if I could be of some kind of help, if that's possible. I'm strong and I'm smart and I haven't been in a fight for, oh, for ages.'

I lost my words temporarily and I was grateful when Daphne answered for me. I could see that the Shoe people were impressed too. They stared at Gordon as if he had landed from another planet, which, to be fair, he almost had. Lewisham is not on the tourist route and American accents are not common. Nothing about Gordon was ordinary. He was gentle and calm and I trusted him straight away, no reservations. I could see that Daphne felt the same.

'Thank you so much for your support,' she said. 'I'm not sure exactly what's going to happen, and I'm not sure if we should move people away, what do you think, Grace?'

I didn't want to put anyone out, but I was very sure that I didn't want one more thing on my conscience. It was full. I knew how dangerous toad might be. People who live on the streets had surely got enough bad stuff happening already. They didn't need our crap too.

'I hate to turn up here and ask you all to move,' I said.

Gordon looked thoughtful and I tried to work out how to explain.

'The thing is,' Daphne said, 'there's a man—'

She was going to say more, but Clara suddenly popped up, as if she had been switched on.

'I thank you for your kind offer,' she said, 'but we are able to deal with this ourselves. In house,' she added for emphasis.

Daphne looked at me and gave a tiny shrug. I think Gordon noticed.

'Let's do what I believe the young ones call, chill. Let's chill,' Gordon said.

He looked at Clara and then at me and Daphne and I realised that he was trying to tell us something. Clara is a loose cannon, I'm sure that's what he wanted to say.

'Maybe we should have come alone,' Daphne said quietly, so that only I could hear. 'We might have been better off without them.'

'It'll be OK,' I said. I wasn't sure, but when she was next to me I really did think it might be.

Meg had moved away from the group and I could no longer see her from where I was standing. There was a slight bend in the road that hid us from each other. Gordon drifted back to the edge of the small group of people and Daphne and I sat on the floor. It was cold, but I knew we both felt that we didn't want to stand out, to make ourselves look like gracious ladies. I hadn't realised there were so many local rough sleepers. I knew it was bad, I knew the numbers had increased, but there were so many. People from every walk of life and every age from teenagers to a man who might have been a hundred years old.

The pretty but very thin, pale young woman sitting nearest to me grinned.

'Oh,' she said, 'look at us if you like. We're just like everyone else, aren't we?'

'Susannah,' Gordon said, 'don't you start any of that nonsense. I don't know much about these ladies, but I can follow my nose. And my nose tells me that these ladies are on the side of goodness and light, you hear me? So don't torment them.'

I would have said something, told him that it was fine, but Daphne grabbed my arm and pointed.

'Look,' she said, 'it's him.'

I looked towards the road and I could see nothing, no big black car, no toad man. Maybe a car had stopped just out of sight, I wasn't sure. The little crowd went quiet as if something had happened and I thought I heard a car engine. I strained to listen. I could hear some kind of scuffle and I thought I could hear a man shouting 'Get in'. Clara had her hand in her pocket and I guessed that was where her gun was. I put my hand on her arm and I could feel her jump.

There was a scream from the road, I don't know whose, and we both scrambled to our feet. Daphne ran off before I could say don't. It all happened so quickly that I'm not sure of the order of things but Daphne was gone for a moment and came back with Nina. Nina. Daphne was holding Nina's arm and talking to her but Nina was distraught. She was sobbing and saying something over and over again and as they came nearer to me I realised what it was that she was saying.

'Meggie, Meg, he's got Meggie.'

'He's got Meg?' I said, unable to believe it until Daphne nodded.

Des was out of hiding and running towards the road, with Clara and Gordon right behind. Clara fished something out of her pocket and I might have heard a shot although it didn't sound like I thought a shot would but there was so much shouting and slamming of car doors that I could have been mistaken. Greg stayed back and tied his shoelaces, I know that because I nearly tripped over him. I heard the sound of a car revving and roaring off and I hoped with all my heart that Meg was OK but Daphne and I had to concentrate on Nina.

This is the moment when I feel I can tear him apart with my bare hands. Nina is sobbing. 'It's my fault,' she says over and over. 'It's my fault.'

Nina flails and tries to run but Daphne holds her.

'It's not your fault,' Daphne says to Nina. 'Meg will be OK, don't worry.'

She says it all in the same soothing tone, holding Nina tight and stroking her hair. Daphne looks over at me across the top of Nina's head and I can tell she's not feeling so positive. Of course she's not. This is Meg, Meg whose jumpers are arranged by colour. I'm sure she won't cope but there's no point in me saying that. If you can't say something nice, my grandmother used to say, then don't say anything at all.

I put my arm round the two of them. 'Come on,' I say, 'we're talking about Meg here. Meg is good in a crisis, she's focused, she'll be just fine. We're going to be laughing about this with her another day.'

Daphne gives me a sceptical look and I shrug. Nina's sobs quieten a little. Sometimes lies are right, I think. Sometimes the truth has to be bent.

'Excuse me, ladies,' says Gordon.

I've forgotten he's there. Nina flinches at the sound of his voice and Daphne murmurs into her ear.

'Excuse me, but I'm sure you're very concerned about your friend,' Gordon says. 'I am too. I got a glimpse of the gentleman involved, and I'm sure you're right to be as worried as you are. He looks like a nasty piece of work. It's just, I wondered, well, the thing is, I'd like to put myself at your disposal. You may have some small task that I could help with, or maybe you'd like a minder. I'm at your service, ma'ams.'

Gordon sweeps to the floor in a dramatic bow. Nina even stops crying for a minute while she watches.

'Yes please,' she says. 'Oh yes, will you help us, will you help us get Meggie back?'

Daphne looks at me for a moment and I'm tired. I don't know what to say. I think how nice it would be if someone else was the leader. If I could step down for a moment. All my life people have expected me to be the one who knows.

'What about the police?' I say. I was going to say more, explain why I think we might need their help now, now that he has Meg, but Nina's reaction stopped me.

'No,' she says, and it's more like a scream. 'No, please no, don't do that, he'll kill her and he'll kill Ronnie and he'll get away with it.' She is shaking, trembling so hard we can all see.

'It's OK,' I say, 'no police.' We can't, I think, we've got to keep trying on our own, she's right, she knows him. I just wish I could feel more sure.

Daphne sees that, I think. She smiles at me, and it's a smile that says, take five, friend, I've got this covered. She's amazing.

'I think Nina is right, we'll leave the police out of it for now. And I think it would be great to have you on board,' she says to Gordon. 'We're going to need some help.'

Clara tuts and paws the ground with her Doc Marten boot like a pony raring to go.

'No offence, Clara,' I say, and I was going to say something trite like, many hands make light work but she glares at me so I tail off. I probably shouldn't have used her name, even though she said it wasn't her real one. I just keep thinking, Meg, Meg, what are we going to do about Meg?

'Sorry,' I mouth at her.

'Shall we all go back to Meg's?' Daphne says. 'You need a rest, Nina. Meg will be home soon, we'll think of something, and in the meantime I know she'd want us to look after you properly while we talk about what to do next.'

I don't have another idea. It seems like the best thing to do.

'Also,' Daphne says, sounding a lot calmer than I feel, 'if she manages to escape by herself, she won't know where we are, if we move around. Best to go there, and wait while we make a plan.'

We decide to leave the car so that we can stick together, and we are an odd little bunch going back on the 484 bus. Daphne and I sit either side of Nina like prison guards, so pleased to have her back but so worried about Meg. It's great that Nina has got away, but she's shaking and shivering and talking to herself and I wonder whether she will ever get over this. Nobody says much. I think we're all thinking the same thing: Meg, how can we get her back, what's happening to her? Daphne has her arm round Nina and it seems the most natural thing in the world for me to reach up and hold the hand that's resting on Nina's shoulder.

'Meg,' Nina says, 'he's got Meg and it's all my fault. I should have stayed there. I can't believe I've done this to her.'

Daphne and I look at each other.

'Maybe if I go back, and I ask him to let her go.'

'No,' we say together.

'That's the worst idea,' Daphne says. 'Honestly, Meg would be furious. She wants you to be safe more than anything else.'

'Don't underestimate her,' I say. 'Old women can be very fierce.'

I look at Daphne and I'm sure we're both thinking the same thing. This is Meg we're talking about, Meg. Meg who is still worrying what her husband would think, even though he's dead. But Meg who loves Nina with a passion, I think. Meg who is stronger than she looks.

'Do you really think so?' Nina says.

'Yes,' Daphne and I say together. 'Yes, she'll be fine,' I add.

'About you, though,' Daphne says. 'Do you need to go to hospital? I think it would be best for you to see a doctor, make sure you're OK.'

'I'm fine,' Nina says. 'No doctors, not yet, they'd ask questions, wouldn't they? I'll go when Meg comes back. I'll go with Meg.'

Why didn't I think of hospital? My brain is working very slowly, as though the gears are grinding down.

Even when we pile into Meg's house I can't think straight. I keep thinking about the police, and about what Nina said about offering herself instead, and I wonder whether it would work if it was someone else who offered, me, for example.

Daphne seems to know what to do. She gives Nina a job making tea, and I can see that's the best idea. Nina says she will think about medical help again in the morning. She's stubborn, that girl, our girl, reminds me again of Eleanor.

'I want to wave to the aeroplane,' Eleanor kept saying before I left for Britain, standing in the sunshine and pointing to the sky.

'You can't. They won't let children in to the airport,' I said.

It was me really, of course. I thought that if I knew my little girl was going to be waving from the terminal I wouldn't be able to get on. I'd sit there by the steps to the plane, refusing to get on like sheep refuse to get on the lorry to the slaughterhouse. It was hard enough to leave without that.

Of course, she didn't let it drop. My mum wrote to me and told me that Eleanor would stand in the garden for hours, waiting until a plane flew over, then she would jump up and down and shout to it until she was hoarse, waving her teddy bear and calling my name. It nearly killed me. Those first weeks when I was at the teacher training college and it was cold all the time with a chill that went through to my bones as if my skin wasn't even there any more. All I could think of was her standing there in the sunshine, calling my name. I couldn't give up, not when she was so resolute.

I think of her as I watch Nina, four and a half thousand miles and a lifetime away but with the same courage. She's found a piece of paper on the table and a pencil and she takes the drinks orders of the eight people we now are. Six inside, and Clara and Greg in the garden at the back. They want to help, but they're keeping a low profile, that's what they said, and at any other time that might have struck me as funny but nothing is funny now. Green tea, that's what Gordon wants, and the rest are a mixture of ordinary tea and coffee. We could be at a family gathering somewhere. Somewhere where no one gets kidnapped and everyone is safe.

Daphne and I look at each other and nod. We leave Des in charge of making the drinks and motion to Nina to come with us upstairs. She lies on Meg's bed, touching the covers as though she might find something she has lost.

'You could stay here and rest,' Daphne says. 'We can take it from here. And I want to be sure, when no one else is around, that you aren't hurt anywhere. You can tell us.'

'I'm OK. I'm young, I'll mend. No doctors, and please, no police. All I want is to rescue Meg and Ronnie, then I'll think about myself.'

Daphne looks at me and there's worry in her eyes, an exact reflection of my thoughts. I don't think there's anything we can do except stumble on and I can see that she agrees.

'Try to have a rest, at least,' I say but Nina jumps up off the bed.

'Not yet,' she says. 'There will be time for that later.' She gives each of us a quick, hard hug and heads off down the stairs.

Everyone looks towards Daphne when we go down.

'OK,' she says. 'We have to pool our knowledge here. Let's go through what we know, point by point. Get the new people up to speed.'

She opens the door to the garden and beckons to Clara and Greg, who sidle in and stand next to the door as if they might leave at any moment.

'Thanks, ma'am,' says Gordon. 'I hope that myself and my daughter here, Susannah, can help out in some way with your problems. In fact I'd like your problems to be our problems too. We don't have money, that's not something either of us can offer, but between us we've got damn well everything else, especially brains and brawn.'

Clara tuts but Daphne ignores her and goes through all the details. I can see that she's trying to spare Nina any embarrassment, because she's very light on detail when it comes to the toad, and why we're after him, what he's done to Nina. I'm so proud when Nina speaks up.

'Daphne is trying to give me an easy ride,' she says, 'but I think it's important that everyone knows what he is, that man. If something isn't named, it's harder to rub it out. The truth of it is, he's a pimp and a trafficker. He sold me like I was a piece of meat; no, worse than that. I'm only young, but I'm old enough to realise that what he did to me, well, I'll be dealing with it for ever. My life is changed, maybe ruined. I think girls have died working for him, I'm sure of it. There's one right now, she's really ill, I don't know, and I'm terrified at what he might do to Meg.'

That girl is so brave, I think, so composed. There's bruises on her arms, and she's lost loads of weight but it's her eyes that show the damage most. Her eyes are haunted, and they look like the eyes of a very old woman. A woman who has seen too much.

Clara looks round the room carefully. 'I know men like this,' she says. 'There are always men like this in every country. And the thing is, what they want is money. It's the only thing. Money and power. And your friend, our friend, they can't make money from her. Not by selling her, anyway. They can only make money by getting at what she has already, or what she has access to. So I think they'll be in touch. I really do. And we need to be ready.'

Clara sits down on the floor as though speaking so much has tired her out. Greg leans over and gives her a pat. Des speaks then.

'We can't afford to sit around waiting,' he says. 'I've only met Meg recently but I know that this is not something any woman, or man, who has lived a normal life would be able to deal with. We need to go and find him, surprise him, smoke him out.'

'I've been trying to think where we were,' Nina says, 'going through it in my head, but I just don't know. I ran when I got the chance to escape, without taking any notice of where I was. I'm so sorry, I wish I'd looked, taken note, so that we knew where to go now. I just kept choosing the road that had the most people, and then the roads that had the least. I probably doubled back on myself loads of times before I found you guys in the café. When he kidnapped me back it was the same house. He hadn't been able to arrange a move, and that was one of the things that pissed him off the most. He's trying to move right now, I expect.'

'You are a smart, brave lady,' Gordon says, 'and I want you to think hard now. I've got to know this area pretty well over the last few years, and I'm wondering if there is anything, any feature of the street that you can remember. Numbers, buses, anything at all that might give us a clue.'

Nina closes her eyes and we can all see how hard she is trying. Come on, Nina, I think.

'There was a tree, I noticed it because it was flowering, and it's early for that, it was the only one in the street,' she says. 'It was outside the window of the house, and I looked at it when I was, when I was in the house.'

There's a shuffle of embarrassment amongst the group as the realisation dawns on us of when she might have noticed the tree, and what she would have been doing in the house at

284

that moment. I feel a surge of anger so intense I think again that I could kill the toad man with my own bare hands if he walked in, and I can see that reflected in the faces round me. Especially Clara.

'We need to calm down,' I say. 'Come on, guys, let's try to think. Tree already in flower, it's early for that, where is it? It has to be within walking distance of here – Nina, how long do you think you were walking before you came into the café?'

'It's so hard to tell,' Nina says. She looks as though she is going to cry. 'It seemed like hours, but I don't think it was.'

'OK, well, we know it was just after half past ten when you came in,' I say, 'because our class had just finished.'

'And it was definitely light when I left, I didn't leave in the dark,' Nina says, 'but I didn't walk in anything like a straight line. In fact I went past a big police station twice, I remember that because I thought about going in, but I couldn't, I just couldn't. I didn't think they'd believe me. He always said, that man, the toad man, he always said that no one would believe me.'

'OK,' says Gordon, 'this is good, well done, young lady.'

'If I could say something I have been thinking,' Des says. 'You are very calm in a crisis, Nina. You'd make a good copper if you ever decide to go in that direction. Not that I'm advocating it.'

Everyone nods and murmurs in agreement and Des blushes. Nina smiles, and it's like the sun coming out. She looks so young when she smiles.

Gordon says, 'Does anyone mind if I just speak for a minute?' He looks around and we all nod. Clara nods so vehemently that her head seems in danger of flying off.

'What we have is some coordinates, some places we can start looking straight away. Nina walked for about two hours, passing the police station in Lewisham twice. That means, I think, that we should start with a half-hour radius from the station. We're looking for a flowering plum blossom tree. Most London street trees are cherry, there's a difference, plum flowers earlier, we need to look for a tree that's flowering right now. We could go in three groups, reporting back to this point every hour, does that make sense?'

'Hang on,' Daphne says. 'We can do better than that. Nina, the phone Meg gave you, does it tell you where she is?'

'No,' Nina says, 'it tells her where I am, but she's got her location switched off.'

She gets her phone out again to check.

'Nah, still off,' she says.

Something is beginning to nibble at my brain. I know something, something that will help but I'm not sure what it is.

'Hang on,' I say, and they all look at me expectantly. Like a class of schoolchildren waiting for me to start the lesson. 'Hang on, I think there's a database.'

'A database of what?' Daphne says.

'They don't say the address on the website,' Nina says, 'only when someone makes a booking. And I'm not sure what they call it, they keep changing the name, that's what I heard.'

'No,' I say, 'they'll be expecting that, they've probably changed it already. No, there's a database of trees, that's what I'm thinking about. If you're sure about this plum thing, Gordon, there's a man who lives on my street and that's what he does. He plants street trees, and you can sponsor them and be a guardian, you know, water them and look out for

286

them. I planted one in memory of my daughter. Anyway, he's made this database of all the trees in Lewisham. Flowering plum aren't common, Gordon has told us, so I'd say that might mean it's pretty easy to spot where they are.'

Nina looks as if she might cry. 'Thank you,' she says, 'thank you. You lot are smart.'

I make a note to myself to tell her later about how smart and clever she has been. Daphne gets her iPad out of her shoulder bag and starts tapping away.

'Three possibilities,' she says, 'unless it's been planted since this was updated. Hawstead Road, that's Catford, Cliffview Road, that's really quite near here, and Manwood Road, that's Crofton Park. Any of those ring any bells?'

'No,' Nina says, 'but I wasn't expecting them to, I really didn't think to look at the road signs. I'm so sorry.'

Everyone starts speaking at the same time to tell her not to worry, that it's not her fault, that she shouldn't feel guilty.

'OK,' says Gordon and he splits us into three groups. I hope Des doesn't mind but there's no time for worrying about people's feelings. Gordon must have been a teacher at some point, no doubt about it. He's worse than I am for organising people. He looks towards me and Daphne.

'I think Nina should stay here, get her head down a bit and wait in case Meg comes back,' he says.

Nina bursts into tears. 'Please don't leave me here on my own. I can't face it, I don't want to be alone, I'm scared.'

'Sorry,' says Gordon, 'I wasn't thinking.'

Des jumps up. He's been uncharacteristically quiet since we got home, and now I can see that he is terribly upset.

'You come with me and the ladies,' he says. 'We will

be a group. I will guarantee that nothing will happen to you. I will watch you like a bodyguard, like the bodyguard in that TV series, I will never take my eyes off you.'

He sits down again as though he is embarrassed at what he has said.

'Or you can come with me and Greg,' Clara says. 'I've got this, I'll keep you safe as houses.' She pats her pocket. 'Don't worry,' she says, 'the safety catch is on.'

I catch Greg looking at Clara and I realise that he's very proud of her.

'Erm, me too,' Greg says. 'I'd look after you like you were my dog.'

The tension breaks a little then and everyone laughs.

'What?' Greg says. 'I love Shoe, I would never let anything happen to her.' He looks down to his feet, as if the dog might be standing there. 'She's at home,' he says quietly to no one in particular.

'Much as you would be welcome with Susannah and I,' Gordon says, 'I still think someone should stay home in case Meg comes back. And I think you need a rest.'

'Greg, you can step down from bodyguard duties,' Clara says. 'Sometimes men aren't the right choice for a job. Almost always, in my opinion. I'll stay here. You go. I'll brief you in the garden. I am the only woman for the job of bodyguard.'

Clara coughs, and I think it's to cover a display of emotion. Greg looks thrilled at his chance to step up.

Nina's face shines for a moment. 'Do you think Meg might come back on her own?' she says.

I can't look at Daphne.

'Deffo,' I say. 'I wouldn't be surprised at all.'

Greg makes a show of checking the window locks and lifting the receiver on the landline.

'OK,' Nina says, 'I'll hold the fort here, with Clara, in case Meg comes back. Go get her.'

I can see how tired she is. That girl is brave.

We agree on which street each group will go to and we're off. Out into the night.

CHAPTER TWENTY-FIVE

Meg

After midnight, Friday, 1 March

I didn't think anything at all for a while after I was bundled into the car. I didn't think, oh good, at least Nina has got away, and I didn't think about how I might be able to escape. I just was. I tried to breathe, in through the nose, out through the mouth, like in mindfulness training. I tried to keep myself together and if truth be told, I tried not to wet myself. After a few minutes I concentrated hard and tried to get hold of the new, supportive Henry I had invented but I couldn't find him for ages. The other Henry was there, of course, the Henry who wanted to point out to me how ridiculous I was, how stupid not to have seen it coming, how he had told me all along to stay out of other people's lives and concentrate on what I knew best: myself. I didn't want to listen to that Henry. I wanted the kind one, the one who believed in me. I couldn't find him until we drew up outside a house and that horrible man, the one who really does look like a toad, jumped out of the driving seat and opened my door.

'Out, bitch,' he said.

He tugged on my arm so that I couldn't get my balance. I could feel the anger pouring out of him, like Henry on the day he got rid of Bingley. Thinking of Bingley seemed to help, and I managed to swivel my bottom round in the seat so that I could get my feet on to the ground. I launched myself out with no dignity at all, but it seemed like a tiny victory to have been able to leave the car without falling flat on my face.

'This way, bitch,' he said.

He pulled me along behind him. I concentrated on staying upright and walking, but I still managed to have a quick look around. I've seen the cop shows. Henry and I used to love a good thriller, and I have never been able to get over how many crimes are solved by people taking a bit of notice and knowing where they are being held. There was a flowering tree to the left of the house. It looked ghostly in the moonlight and I noticed it specifically because I knew most of the trees weren't flowering yet. I couldn't see a street sign, but I thought it was one of the streets round the back of Hilly Fields.

Inside the house he shoved me into a dark side room off the hallway and slammed the door shut. I could hear a bolt being pulled across.

'What the fuck?' I heard a woman's voice say outside the door and then toad was all full of shh, and calm down, and they went down the corridor and into another room, I think. I couldn't hear them after that.

'Hello,' said a very small voice from the other side of the room. 'I'm Ronnie, nice to meet you.'

I was so surprised I almost shouted. I groped around to try to find the light switch.

'There's no bulb in it,' the person called Ronnie said, 'but your eyes will get used to the dark in a minute. You wait, you can see lots.'

I couldn't see anything so I moved cautiously towards the sound of her voice. She was lying on a sofa, and even in the dark I could make out that it was the kind with wooden arms where you can never get comfortable. She scooted up to one end when I reached her.

'Come on,' she said, 'take the weight off. Sit down.'

I sat, and as soon as my bottom reached the sofa I started to tremble as the shock of what had happened finally hit me.

'It's OK,' Ronnie said, 'it's OK.'

She patted my shoulder. I peered over at her and realised that she was very young, and possibly the thinnest person I had ever seen. Thinner even than Susannah, the young homeless girl. I think Ronnie heard my sharp intake of breath.

'I've been on a hunger strike,' she said. 'I'm thin, aren't I? Do you know what's the oddest thing? I don't even feel hungry any more. I'm not tempted in the slightest when they offer me food. Dead cow in a bun, no thank you. They said they'd take me to hospital but it was a bluff. I needn't have bothered.'

She sat very still and silent after she had spoken, as if the effort of speaking had worn her out.

'What about you?' Ronnie said after a few minutes. 'Who are you? And what on earth are you doing here? Sorry to mention it and all that, but I can see that you're a little older than most of the women here. Are they kidnapping old ladies now? Are you in care as well? Did they steal you from a nursing home? Blimey.'

She seemed so worn out, so very tired that I didn't want her to speak any more. It was an instinct, a sort of maternal thing. It seemed important for me to start talking. I thought that if I stopped, she might fade away. Plus I didn't know how long we had before the dreadful toad came back in, or what he was going to do next. So I told her what had happened. Henry One, the old-style, disapproving Henry, didn't approve. For goodness' sake, I could hear him say, don't go telling anyone anything. Don't you realise that you're in a bad situation? Don't you understand that it's talking to people and getting involved that got you to this place, you stupid woman? I pushed him away. No thanks, I told him in my head. I don't want to hear any of your rubbish right now.

Ronnie clapped when I got to the part about Nina.

'I know her, I knew she'd do it,' she said. 'She is so strong. I was terrified for her when I heard her come back, but I'm thrilled she's got away again. I only saw her once when she came back, they kept her away. She had a hard time, I think. She can cope though, not like me. She's clever as well, she likes to read books and everything, did you know that?'

I told her that I did, and that Nina and I had talked a lot during the short time we were together. We'd swapped suggestions for books and agreed on a couple of well-loved ones, too.

'Is Ronnie short for something?' I asked. I wanted to keep her engaged and alert.

'No,' she said. 'Do you know, I usually tell people that my mum wanted a boy, but I feel like telling you the truth. I don't know when...' Ronnie tailed off.

I waited. I've got a lot of patience in the right situation. People are like dogs, that's the thing. Worth waiting for if you just step back and let them come to you.

'My real name is Ronnie,' she said. 'I wasn't always a girl.

Well, I was, but no one knew. I was going to save up for the operation, before this all happened.' She gestured to indicate the room we were in. I guessed the rest but I could see she wanted to say more.

'It sells well,' Ronnie said. 'I'm popular, I think that's why they'll never let me go. He found me, that toad man, when I was sleeping in the doorway of a shop. My foster dad had caught me wearing my foster mum's dress, so he threw me out. It wasn't even a nice dress either. It was from Primark, for God's sake.'

She was so indignant that I smiled, and she must have realised how she sounded because she giggled. Ronnie went quiet after that, so I just held her hand for a while.

'My life is strange too,' I said after a while. 'I feel like I'm living the wrong one. I should be sitting knitting by a fire, stirring soup and waiting for my grandchildren to come round. Is that how it is for you? Minus the grandchildren obviously.'

Ronnie laughed. 'That's it exactly,' she said. 'I should be going on dates and doing my coursework. Fussing over pimples and begging my mum to let me go to a festival. I would have loved to go to a festival.'

'You can,' I said. 'There's no reason why not.'

Ronnie squeezed my hand in her bony little paw.

'Ssh,' she said, 'I can hear them coming back.'

I felt sick with fear. They weren't going to want to keep me, that was definite. They knew that I knew what they were doing. They knew now that I knew about Ronnie as well. That they had a very sick young person on their premises and they had not tried to get medical help for her. I felt for the gun in my sleeve to make sure it was there. The door from the hallway flew open and the sudden light made me screw up my eyes.

'Keep still,' toad said, 'both of you, and give me your phone.' The last part was addressed to me.

'I haven't got one,' I said.

'Of course you haven't, you lying bitch,' he said. 'Stand up.'

He ran his horrible hands up and down my body. I was worried about him finding the gun but he never got that far. It was the most cursory search ever. I think he literally couldn't bear to touch me.

'I'll send Fiona in in a minute, she can do another search,' he said, backing out of the room and wiping his hands on his trousers. 'I know you've got a phone.'

'Have you?' Ronnie whispered when he'd gone. 'Have you got one?'

'It's in my knickers,' I said. 'Safe place on an old lady.'

I don't know why this struck us both as funny but it did, and we both laughed until we couldn't get our breath.

Ronnie stopped laughing when I held her hand and took it to the gun in my sleeve. She felt it for a moment and then I heard a sharp intake of breath as she realised what it was.

'It's not loaded,' I said. 'It's OK, it won't hurt anyone.'

'That is so not what I'm worried about,' she said. 'Do you realise what kind of a temper that man has? He would be so mad if he knew you had this. He's dangerous. I suggest you load it.'

'He won't know I've got it,' I said, hoping I sounded more confident than I felt.

'No?' said Ronnie. 'Then what exactly is the point of it?'

I thought about that for a moment. It was a good question. And even more pertinent now that I had her to look after. I took the gun out of my sleeve and had a go at loading it. It was more difficult in the dark and I wasn't sure I'd done it right but I didn't tell her.

'There,' I said, 'that's done.'

We stayed quiet for a while after that. I was hoping she could get some sleep but I could tell from her sighs and wriggling that she was awake.

'Hey,' she whispered after a while, 'hey, can I see your phone? I want to check something.'

'I don't think we should,' I whispered back in the tiniest whisper I could manage. 'I think someone might be outside the door. I've been listening and I can hear the odd rustle. My guess is, they're waiting till I get my phone out and then they'll burst in. I saw that in a film once. Or something like it.'

'Oh,' she said. I could see she was still thinking.

'What kind of phone is it?' Ronnie said. She was speaking so quietly now it was almost like a voice inside my head. A breath in my ear.

'Good gracious, I've got no idea,' I said. 'Some kind of iPhone.'

There was a noise outside of footsteps as if someone was walking away, although I knew it could be a trap.

'Show me, quick,' she said. She sat up, moving without a sound.

Ridiculous to say, but I felt struck down with embarrassment. The idea of pulling up my skirt and reaching into my knickers in front of this young person, even in the dark, was very odd. Not to mention that whoever had been outside the door might be there still, listening for any sound. She sat there, though, with her hand out waiting for the phone and I didn't want to disappoint her. Enough things seemed to have gone wrong in her short life and I wanted to please her. Beside that, I was very aware that we were running out of options. If there was anything we could do that might increase our chances of getting out, then she was right, we should try it. I didn't even know what she had in mind but I trusted her. It was as though she had become the grown-up in the situation.

Ronnie turned away slightly whilst I groped in my knickers as silently as I could.

'Here you are,' I said, handing the phone over. 'I've wiped it with a tissue, I hope that's OK.'

I could see that Ronnie was fighting not to laugh.

'In this place,' she said, so close to my ear that I could feel the warmth again, 'with what I've seen and done, that's the least of my worries. But thanks.'

I turned the phone on for her and she started looking through the screens.

'Bingo,' she said after a moment, 'you've got location services. I was worried you wouldn't have it. Who's Henry? He's the person who's going to be able to see where you are – I've switched it on. Shall we try sending him a text as well? Will he be awake?'

I literally couldn't answer. I felt so stupid to have forgotten, and on top of that for a moment, just a moment, I imagined that Henry was awake, at home, and that I'd be able to ring him and ask him to come and get me.

I've got myself into a bit of a scrape, I'd say, and he'd say, well, I'm not surprised, you're such a silly girl.

Ronnie was waiting for me to answer.

'Even better,' I said, 'Nina has that phone. I don't know why I didn't think of it. I'm so sorry.'

Help, she texted, loc serv on.

She gave me back the phone and I slid it into my knickers with the gun just before the door opened. It was Fiona.

'Stand up,' she said. 'You, old lady, not the freak show.'

She was a lot more thorough than the toad. She dug into my armpits, shook out my pockets, everything. Nearly everything. She did not venture into my knickers. How strange, I thought then and still think now, that a person who earns their money literally by selling access to other people's private parts would not have realised that older women have private parts too. I was so affronted that I almost pointed it out to her. Instead I waited while she patted my bottom, looked in my boots and generally searched everywhere apart from the one place she should have been looking.

'Not so clever now, are you?' she said as she left.

I would have loved, at that moment, to contradict her. I was glad my self-control had had a lifetime of training. As Fiona shut the door, Ronnie held up her hand in a high five gesture. I was becoming very familiar with this and I hardly hesitated.

'We've just got to wait, and they'll come and get us,' Ronnie whispered. 'I'm so glad you're here. Thank you so much.'

She curled up on the sofa and put her head in my lap. I could not have been more surprised. I could tell from her breathing she was going to sleep this time. It was a lovely feeling having a person asleep on me. Henry, the real Henry, had not been keen on physical contact. I couldn't help thinking how nice it would be if I could curl up on someone's lap too. I tried to imagine what that might be like, but it was a difficult thing to think about.

The minutes went by very slowly. Of course I started thinking of Bingley, and imagining it was his head I was stroking, but after a while I was glad it was Ronnie. You can't live in the past, that's one of the only sensible things the old Henry said. Life moves on, and you have to move with it. So I wasn't exactly scared, sitting there in the dark. Not for myself, anyway. I was terrified for Ronnie. I could feel her breathing under my hand and it didn't feel right. Kind of jagged and uneven. Every few breaths there was a kind of catch in it, as though she had been running or crying. All I could do was hold her, and say very quiet nonsense into her ear in a calming sort of way.

It's common knowledge that when a person is dying, their whole life flits past in front of their eyes. I'm not sure about that, I suppose no one is, but that night I might have thought I was going to die, because I had an action replay of all sorts of things I didn't know I had remembered. Getting married, that was one that I'd filed away under mistakes not to be dwelt on, I think. It was good to have a flash of how bright the morning was, how pleased I was to be wearing something pretty. Pale grey, my dress was, with tiny pink and blue flowers. It was fitted to the waist and then it swung out to the floor. I thought I looked as good as I ever had but Henry called it my wedding nightdress. I don't know what happened to it but I didn't wear it again.

I remembered Henry's death on a loop, too. Another sunny day, autumn this time. I'd suggested going for a walk, it looked so nice out. I wanted to feel the sun on my face before winter, I remember saying that and I remember Henry laughing.

'The sun on your face indeed,' he said. 'Who's been reading women's magazines?'

I hated the way he said 'women's magazines', as if they were the worst thing in the world. Mostly they were quite cheering. And I hadn't got the idea from there anyway. It was as if Henry didn't, couldn't, think that I was ever able to think for myself.

'No,' I said in my mild voice, 'I just thought it would be good to get some vitamin D.'

Of course that made him laugh all the more.

'Now I've heard it all,' he said, as if I had suggested something totally outrageous. A tightrope walk, for example, or a bungee jump.

'After all,' he said, 'it's not as if we have a dog to take for a walk or anything, is it, Meg? No little doggy wagging its tail at the idea of going walkies?'

I don't know why that made me so mad. Maybe because I hadn't slept well the night before, listening to him snore through two walls. After all, it was no worse than the routine teasing on any day of the week. I just snapped, that was it, I think. I couldn't take any more. I had so wanted to go for a walk and of course most people would say, why didn't you just go? Those people haven't lived with someone like Henry, that's all I can say. It's not worth upsetting some people, not if you have to live with the consequences, which I did. The last straw, people say, or the straw that broke the camel's back. We say it without even thinking about it but it's a real thing, and that's what happened that day. He had such a jeering tone as he said it, it broke my heart.

I took my jacket off and draped it across Ronnie. The poor girl probably felt the cold much more than I did. She was so terribly thin, I could feel her bones poking into my lap as if she had no skin on her at all. I'd like to cook for her, the same sort of food I made for Bingley when he first arrived, I thought.

Chicken, or lentils and beans if she's a vegetarian. Rice, easy food to chew and food that stays down. Milk in small quantities and some potatoes. I planned an entire shopping list while we sat there. It's amazing how similar humans are to dogs.

I'm going to do it right this time, I thought. I've been given a second chance to save a life, to save two lives, actually, maybe even more. Nothing is going to get away from me this time. It doesn't matter about the gun. I remembered a women's self-defence course I'd gone to once, in the seventies. I had been looking for the pottery class but I'd found self-defence instead and I liked it much more. I never told Henry. He wouldn't have liked the idea. I think he thought that he was all the protection I needed, which is a funny thought. Go for the eyes if you're cornered, that's what the instructor said. Index finger and middle finger, make a V and jab. You can't be hesitant. Jab and twist. Don't go all ladylike on me now, she used to say, own your actions. I took my hands off Ronnie for a moment and flexed them. They're knobbly with arthritis now but apart from that I reckon they're as good as ever.

CHAPTER TWENTY-SIX

Daphne

Friday, 1 March

Daphne decided against taking everyone back to her house. Meg's house seemed like the right place to be. Most of them were familiar with it, and it was a way of keeping Meg involved and part of the gang even though she wasn't there. Above all, it was a place where Nina felt comfortable. Grace gave a little nod and squeezed Daphne's hand when she suggested it.

'After all,' Grace said, 'she might be home soon and she'll be pleased that we used her house as a base.'

It seemed unbelievable to Daphne that Meg had been kidnapped, that she was in danger. Almost, but not quite unimaginable.

It was after midnight when Daphne, Grace, Nina, Des, Gordon, Susannah and the Shoe killers got back to Meg's house, and the street was silent. Daphne hesitated as she was about to put Meg's key in the lock, and she was grateful when Grace understood and took the key from her. Daphne couldn't stop going over things again and again in her mind to see what she could have done differently, how she might have kept Meg safe. It was hard not to let Nina see how worried she was.

It was a relief when they split up into groups and left to do the search, even though Daphne was worried about Nina.

'She'll be safe in there with Clara,' Grace said as Daphne looked back to the house. 'Windows and doors locked, she's got our numbers, and Clara is a force to be reckoned with.'

Daphne, Grace and Des set off for Cliffview Road. It was the nearest of the addresses to Meg's house, and Daphne was keen to stay close to Nina. She was sure they were on a wild goose chase, but it was right to check. Daphne knew how much Nina wanted to come but she was relieved that she was safe at home.

'If he gets hold of me or Grace,' Daphne had said to Nina, 'he's not going to know what to do with us. He's probably got enough on his hands with Meg right now. I bet she's driving him mad.'

They were all quiet for a moment. Daphne had been hoping to lighten the atmosphere, make them laugh a little bit, but as soon as Meg was mentioned, everyone started to think about her. It was terrifying to think of what she might be going through.

'She's steely, isn't she?' Nina had said in a quiet voice.

Steely, Daphne had thought, that didn't sound like Meg at all. Grace was nodding, though, so Daphne nodded too, and they left Nina and Clara tidying the kitchen.

'Honestly, Daff,' Grace said as they walked down the road, 'Meg does know how to look after herself. I know that's not the impression she gives at first, but there's something else, you must have seen it too.'

'I haven't,' Daphne said, 'but I trust you, and your opinions. I'm rubbish at initial impressions.'

Grace sniffed and reached for Daphne's hand.

Des coughed and both women laughed.

Daphne had an uneasy feeling that there was something she had forgotten, something she should have done. Des might have felt the same too, because he kept looking back over his shoulder. At the end of the second street he spoke.

'I was thinking that maybe we shouldn't have left Nina. What if Clara goes to sleep? She looked tired. She must be scared. I could go back and check on her if you like. I can run, I'm a fast runner, and no offence, but I'd be back with you by the time you get to Cliffview Road. It's just I'm not sure I trust her not to give Clara the slip. She's smart, our Nina. I want to make sure she's actually in the house, not running around trying to help.'

Daphne thought that Des had a good point. It would put their minds at rest if he checked that everything was OK. Grace agreed.

'Right,' Des said, 'see you at Cliffview, don't start without me.' He ran off back towards Meg's house.

'Are you OK, my lovely Daphne?' Grace asked, as soon as Des was out of sight. 'I mean, as OK as anyone could be under such crazy circumstances?'

'There's something we've forgotten,' Daphne said, 'I'm sure of it. Something important. You know that feeling you get, when there's something you know underneath the surface but you can't quite touch it? Like trying to remember a dream.'

'Let's talk it through,' Grace said, 'because it seems to me that how you're feeling is the logical way to feel right now.

In fact it would be crazy of you to feel any other way. It's difficult to process what's actually happened. Daphne, don't you sometimes think we should tell the police now? I don't like the police any more than the next woman but surely now?'

Daphne tried to think straight but her thoughts were whirling.

'OK,' she said, 'for and against. Two old black women, two homeless people and an ex con. The ex con, by the way, our lovely Des, he's got history. I can't go into it now but he had a high profile. In jail on a murder charge but released after years of campaigning, he's the guy from Greenwich, remember? When the world still cared a little bit about racism?'

Grace did a sharp intake of breath and Daphne thought that she should have told her earlier.

'I remember,' Grace said. 'I thought I knew him but it wasn't the right name. I campaigned for him.'

'Don't tell him,' Daphne said, 'he hates a fuss. He changed his name. Anyway, he's not well loved by the boys in blue, you can imagine. Even without him though, and without the homeless people or the Shoe killers, even just you and me. Say we go to the police with a story about a girl. The police go to the house and they find him there, the toad, and I guess he's got a contingency plan like letting all the working girls out of the back door, something like that. He's told us he's got papers that prove Nina is his daughter. On top of that, wherever he's got Meg stashed away, he's going to be so mad if the police come that he might just decide she's, she's…' Daphne tailed off.

'He might just decide she's easier to move around when she's dead,' Grace said, 'not to mention that it's the women who get prosecuted if there is any proof of prostitution. So if he chooses to say "my daughter is off the rails", I think the guys in blue might listen to him.'

'But I can't stop thinking about how scared Meg must be. And what if they actually hurt her?'

Both women stood still, trying to work out what to do for the best. Daphne remembered how alone she had felt when she was with Andrew. She had gone to the police station once and had no help at all. Daphne shuddered as she remembered how terrible it had been not to be believed. It had taken every last shred of strength to walk into the police station in York and try to explain what was happening to her. The policeman had laughed. He'd looked her up and down and decided, just like that, that she wasn't pretty enough or tiny enough or white enough to be telling the truth.

'Listen to this,' he had called to a couple of fellow police officers. 'This lady here says she's being forced on the game by her boyfriend. What do you think?'

They had looked her up and down as if she was standing there naked. Daphne could still remember the shame she had felt.

One of the police officers said, 'I think this young lady had a row with her boyfriend, and decided to pay him back. Am I right, miss?'

The policeman came so close to Daphne that she could smell the coffee on his breath. She made a snap decision to stand her ground, not to move away from him. Surely then, Daphne had thought, he would believe her.

The coffee-smelling policeman laughed. He seemed to be some kind of senior.

'First lesson in interviewing a woman,' he said, 'if she's not intimidated, she's a wrong 'un. Mark my words, I just got so close to this young lady that anyone with a clear conscience would have stepped back. She stood her ground, this one. I don't think anyone would be able to make her do anything she didn't want to do, if you catch my drift.'

The others all murmured agreement.

'We see lots of young girlies like you,' the policeman said, 'gone a bit too far with their fellas in the heat of the moment and then wish they hadn't. If we followed up all of them, we'd never be able to catch the real criminals.'

He had sent her away, Daphne remembered, and then patted her bottom as she turned to go. She had no choice but to go back to Andrew. She hoped things had changed, that today's police understood more, couldn't act in the same way, but still she couldn't trust them.

'No police,' Daphne said now, more than fifty years later. 'No police yet, anyway. I think we were right. Let's see if we can do this ourselves. Just one day of trying, then we need to work out a story that doesn't include Nina and get the police, the army, anyone we can who can help Meg.'

'Agreed,' Grace said.

The two women walked in silence for a while, checking their route on Grace's phone. Neither of them knew exactly what they were going to do when they got there, but they both trusted the other, and they both knew they'd get it right. They would do what needed to be done. They didn't need to speak to know that they were in tune.

They were almost at the house when Grace's phone buzzed.

'It's Nina,' Grace said, looking at the number. 'Hello?'

She listened for a moment and then said, 'OK, we've got it, thank you, stay where you are and don't worry.'

Grace turned to Daphne. They both looked towards the flowering tree, ghostly and ostentatious on the dark street.

'It's here,' Grace said. 'Remember Nina has got Henry's old phone? It's linked to Meg's. Apparently Meg has switched on location services. She texted Nina just now, right after we left. Nina can see Meg's location on her phone. Cliffview Road, it says, about halfway down.'

Daphne looked up and down the road. They were almost exactly halfway down. She wished that she had some kind of faith so that she could send up a quick prayer. Grace seemed to read her thoughts.

'Hey,' Grace said, 'we can always send a quick prayer up anyway, maybe to the tree spirit or something.'

Daphne knew she was blushing. She felt that she had been caught out being stupid. And being scared, that was the worst thing. Grace must know that she was scared. Grace held Daphne's shoulders and turned her slightly, so that they were facing each other.

'Hey,' she said, 'I feel scared too. But we're OK. Are we going to wait for Des? Or shall we go get her?'

'OK,' Daphne said, 'we've got this.'

The house was dark, no lights on and nothing moving. Daphne led Grace into the front garden and round the side of the house. There was a little path from the front to the back garden, and about halfway down was a door. There was no curtain on the window next to the door and Daphne peered in.

'Kitchen,' she whispered, 'no one there.'

Daphne tried the handle of the door. She moved it slowly and quietly but it was locked.

The two women moved further around the back of the house. There were French windows, but Daphne was sure they'd be locked. No one in London leaves doors unlocked unless they're really stupid and Daphne knew toad wasn't that. They'd have to look for a different way in, get to toad when he wasn't expecting it. For the first time in years, Daphne wished she was younger. More agile, able to shin her way up a drainpipe or climb a tree to get on to the roof.

'If you're thinking what I'm thinking,' Grace said into Daphne's ear, 'I'd just like to say that I was never any good at breaking and entering, even when I was young. And I'm not going to take it up now.'

'Good thing I'm here, ladies,' said Des.

He had crept up behind them without either of them noticing.

'Sorry if I made you jump,' Des whispered. 'All fine at Meg's. I didn't want to make a noise. I've spotted a good way in, you two wait here.'

He pointed to a shed leaning against the back wall of the house.

'Easy,' he said, 'no problem at all.'

Daphne could think of several very good reasons why Des's suggestion was a terrible one. It didn't look strong enough to hold his weight, for a start, and the noise he would make, for another. It would wake the whole house. Des seemed to pick up what Daphne was thinking.

'Nah,' he said, 'you ain't seen me in action. I bet you, and sorry, Daff, I know I said I wouldn't bet, but I bet you I can get in there without anyone hearing.'

Des blew a kiss towards Daphne and leapt onto the roof of the shed in two easy and quiet movements. He slid the window up and hopped over the sill.

'Jesus,' said Grace, 'did you see that? What on earth do we do now?'

Daphne didn't know. She really didn't know and she was tired, cold and scared. For just one moment Daphne wished she had never met Meg or Nina, never got involved, never tried to help. She could have spent her retirement planting trees or writing poems.

'It's OK,' Grace whispered, 'it's for Nina and Meg, remember?'

Daphne thought of Nina's sweet face. So trusting even after all the bad things that had happened to her. And Meg, poor Meg with her lack of self-esteem. Grace was right. Whatever happened, they had to try. Daphne knew she wouldn't be able to live with herself if she walked away.

CHAPTER TWENTY-SEVEN

Meg

Friday, 1 March

It was the longest night ever. Even worse than when Henry died. I guess that's what happens when a seventy-year-old person is kidnapped. It's the opposite of time zipping by fast when you're having fun. I wasn't sure whether I was more scared of that toad man coming back in or poor Ronnie dying on my lap but neither of them was a pleasant prospect. I tried to keep our spirits up.

'Come on, Ronnie,' I kept saying, as if it might jolly her along, keep her going a bit longer. 'Come on, I need some help with that toad, you know. I can't do it all by myself.'

She smiled sometimes, so I knew she was listening. I think she was saving her strength. I could see that she liked it when I talked so I made up some stories for her. The kind of stories I might have told a child if they couldn't sleep. There were tales of Bingley and his great courage, and tales of babies who could lift cars off crushed parents and speak every language in the world.

'You should write some of this down,' Ronnie said.

I had thought of that before, but I knew that Henry would have poked fun at me, and not in a friendly way. He didn't like that sort of thing. Making up stories, showing off. I pushed him away and got out the new improved Henry instead.

'My husband used to say that,' I whispered to Ronnie, crossing my fingers where she couldn't see. 'He used to say, Meg, you should write those stories down. Draw little pictures too, lots of people would love them.'

Ronnie nodded in agreement with the fictional Henry. She looked pleased, and for a silly moment I wished I could meet the not-real Henry, my not-real husband. I'd thank him for everything he's done for me. And for Ronnie. I could introduce him to all the new people in my life.

'I feel sick,' Ronnie whispered. I had to strain to hear her.

'Hold on,' I said, 'this is the worst part. Things are going to get better soon.'

I had no idea whether I was right, of course. I think I was saying it to myself as much as anything, although to be honest once I took stock I couldn't see that things could be much worse. Not when you looked at it plainly, without the rose-tinted glasses. I was being held prisoner by a vicious pimp and pinning all my hopes on a couple of women I had only known for a few days, a man with a gambling addiction and a pair of small hired killers with a dog named Shoe. I wasn't sure where my optimism was coming from.

'I've come through worse,' I whispered.

Ronnie seemed to rally. 'Have you?' she said. 'Tell me about it.'

She snuggled down into my lap for all the world like a small child waiting for another bedtime story.

'Once there was a very grumpy man named Henry,' I said. 'He was so grumpy that the leaves on the trees turned brown when he walked past, even in spring. Small children ran away and clutched their mothers' hands, and teenagers decided they'd rather go to their rooms and do their homework than stick around. The people who disliked him the most, though, were dogs. All dogs, any dogs. Dogs absolutely hated him. The nicest, fluffiest, quietest dogs were the worst. They barked, they yapped, they even tried to bite him if they could. They knew, you see, they knew what he was really like.'

I wondered where the story was going, even as I said the words. I didn't want to give Ronnie nightmares.

'You can't fool a dog,' Ronnie whispered. 'I bet if there was a dog here he would hate Pat.'

'Pat?' I said. I couldn't think for a moment who she was talking about.

Ronnie laughed. I could see from this close that her teeth were in a terrible state. Orthodontist, I thought, if we get out of here. Ronnie and Nina both need proper dental care.

'Oh, the man,' she said, 'the one that looks exactly like a toad.'

It was strange to think of toad having a name. Especially a name as innocuous as Pat. I wasn't sure what would suit him better, but Pat seemed like a name for a gentle old person. Short for Patrick or Patricia, lilting names.

'Imagine his poor mother,' I said, 'trying to think of a nice name for him, not knowing he would turn out so badly.'

I could feel Ronnie giggle.

'If I ever have a baby,' she said, 'I'll call her after you. Meg. Or maybe Greg, if it's a boy.'

'I've known some very nice Gregs,' I said. 'In fact it may be a Greg who helps to rescue us.'

I told her a little bit about all of us. All of my gang. She loved that. She was nearly asleep by the time I'd got to Shoe. I could feel her breathing become more regular and there was longer in between each breath.

I sat there in that cold little room and I knew that I needed a plan more than I ever had done. Even after Henry, even that night, I still only had myself to worry about. This was different. I tried to think clearly. Locked room, what was that riddle about people escaping from a locked room and leaving nothing behind? I thought dry ice was involved, and I had no idea what that even was so that wasn't going to help. Window, I thought, go for the most obvious thing. I've seen lots of films where someone casually escapes out of a window as if it's the easiest thing in the world. My eyes were accustomed to the dark, and I looked at the window. It was a Victorian sash and although I couldn't move in case I woke Ronnie, I could see that it was painted shut, just like ours had been. We did it because otherwise they would have been too difficult to lock, but I remember being sorry because I would have liked to open them sometimes in the summer. Henry said it was best to make sure they stayed shut.

I can't imagine, now, why I accepted that. Looking back, I can see that I had absolutely no backbone. Henry said things were one way, and I said, 'Yes, sir.' I wondered, there in the locked room with the locked window and the sleeping girl, whether that made him worse? Whether he hadn't wanted to be like that at all? I stopped thinking about escape for a moment as an awful thought struck me. What if, inside, he had been more like my new improved Henry? What if I had brought out the absolute worst in him and then not allowed him to stop being as bad as he was? There was a violin screeching so hard and out of tune in my head that I couldn't think properly. I tried to think about Bingley but there was something else, some other reason why I knew Henry was bad, why I knew it wasn't my fault. I could not put my finger on it, that was all. It was like having a tune stuck in my head but not being able to remember what it was, that's how I felt. I knew there was something else.

'Thing is, Meg,' I said to myself, 'it doesn't much matter now, about Henry and all of that stuff. You're just being dim if you think it matters. You've got to stop living in the past. This is what matters – you're in a locked room in a house with a very bad man and a sick young woman. You're waiting for help from a bunch of oddballs and the time might have come to call the police.'

I tried to convince myself that Nina would be OK if the police came. That they'd take Ronnie to hospital and put Nina back in school where she belonged but I couldn't make myself believe it. All those years of making myself believe whatever Henry said must have used up my ability to trick myself. That and the fools in government around the world who are looking the other way as the world splutters to an end. I wasn't gullible any more. I knew, beyond any doubt whatsoever, that toad would be good with the police. He knew how to speak to them, they could see him. All they would see when they looked at us was old women, stupid old women. We didn't have a claim or a plan. Some of us dressed strangely, we associated with alleged criminals, some of us were women of colour, and I was sure that we were all invisible. Beyond the pale, that's what my mum used to say for things that were unacceptable. That was us.

I looked towards the window again. Moonlight poured in as though it had been switched on, and with the increased light I felt an unexpected surge of optimism. They will come, I thought, they will be here soon. They are my people.

Ronnie woke up.

'What is it?' she whispered. 'I can feel you've gone all tense. Is something happening?'

'I don't know,' I said, 'but I do know that they're coming, my friends, I know they won't leave us here.'

Ronnie looked at me the way a person might look at someone who had declared that they still believed in fairies. She wanted to believe too.

'Let's have a look at where they are, on the phone,' she said.

I wasn't sure. There seemed lots of reasons why that wasn't a good idea. Firstly, if they weren't where I hoped they were I thought I might give up hope, and Ronnie might be disappointed too. Secondly, and most important, if toad came in suddenly, if he crept in on us, then we would lose whatever advantage we had by having a phone.

'That's ridiculous,' Ronnie said. 'It's like saying, I won't take my umbrella because it's raining. The umbrella might get wet.'

I could see that she had a point, and I couldn't help being pleased that she had the strength to argue. I weighed it up for a few seconds but her hopeful little face made me reach under my skirt and into my knickers again to get out the phone. I should have known better. Stupid Meg, moon-faced Meg, that's what he used to say, and he wasn't always wrong. Still, I powered my phone up and I was just starting to explain that we would only have the phone out for a few seconds, when I noticed a wavering light outside the window. Not a strong light, more like the beam of a small torch or the light from a mobile phone.

'Ssh,' I said and I pointed towards the window. I wasn't even sure of what I was seeing, whether I had wished it into being, but I realised that Ronnie could see it too. She went very quiet.

'Is that your friends?' she asked. 'Is it Nina?'

Ronnie was sitting close enough to me that I could feel the excitement fizz through her.

'I think it is,' I said. 'I might be wrong, but I think it is.'

We could hear little noises outside now. Nothing much, but we listened hard and we could make out light footsteps and some shuffling leafy sounds. Suddenly Ronnie jumped and I looked to see what she had heard. I squinted at the dark glass and there she was. Grace. I was sure it was Grace and she held her thumbs up to me. I waved like crazy. I waved as if I had been alone on a desert island for weeks, months even. Ronnie laughed and joined in too and I think we forgot where we were. Just for the smallest of moments but enough that we didn't hear the door open. We didn't know he had come into the room until he switched his torch on and shouted, 'What the fuck are you doing?'

He was across the room in absolutely no time and he yanked the phone out of my hand. I realised what was happening just as he got to me so I clung on to it but he was stronger and he had the advantage.

'I'll take this,' he said.

He lunged at me with his fist out, trying to punch me in

317

the face, but Ronnie pushed herself up and in front of me. She blocked the punch. I could hear the thud of fist against bone as he hit Ronnie on the side of her head. She stumbled back on to the sofa holding her face. I could see there was blood. I felt furious. I remembered that old TV series, the one where the man gets so mad that he bursts out of his clothes and turns into the Incredible Hulk, and I felt as though it was happening to me. I pulled my skirt up and reached into my knickers for the gun. The weight in my hands was comforting. I didn't want to shoot him, but I thought I might be a good enough shot to hit the wall behind his head or the window, if I needed to. Give him a scare.

I had an underskirt on, a petticoat we used to call them, plus tights, and my skirt was long and full so I had a bit of a job locating the gun at first. It felt like ages anyway, although it was probably only a second or two. I stuck the gun up my sleeve. Toad was quiet while I fussed around and I wasn't sure what he was doing. Gawping at me in my underwear, I thought, but when I looked up properly I realised that he was looking on my phone, scrolling through it.

'Hey,' I said, 'that's private.'

'I don't think you've realised quite where you are,' he said, 'or who you're talking to.' He punched me then and although I was becoming familiar with his blows to my head, this time I understood the cartoons. You know, the ones like Tom and Jerry where someone would get a blow to the head and then they'd lie there with their eyes crossed and stars floating above their heads or the symbols from a fruit machine. That's exactly how it was. I couldn't get up but instead of oranges and lemons lining up I had Henrys, loads of Henrys in lines of three. Over the top of the Henrys I could hear Ronnie crying.

'Who's Henry?' toad said.

I couldn't understand him for a moment. It seemed very much like the wrong question to be asking.

He stared at the phone and then asked again.

'Who's Henry?' he said.

I was still reeling from the punch and I couldn't understand why he was asking me such a stupid question. He slapped me this time, a full open-hand slap to the side of the head with all the force he could muster behind it.

'My husband,' I said. 'He's dead.'

I don't know and I'll never know, I suppose, why I gave toad more information than he asked for. I could have just said, Henry is my husband, or I could have told him any one of a vast number of lies which might have made things easier. No, not me, I had to tell him the truth, the whole truth and nothing but the truth and it was just enough information to allow him to understand what was really happening.

'Bingo,' he shouted. 'Thanks for that, old lady.'

He turned to leave the room and Ronnie mouthed at me, 'Nina, Meg, Nina.'

I wasn't as quick as she was. I didn't realise until he'd left the room and Ronnie explained to me properly.

'There's only one person on your location thingy, right?'

I nodded. My ears were still ringing.

'Then he knows,' Ronnie said. 'He knows that it's Nina, he knows where she is.'

I was still struggling to put two and two together when Grace smashed the window and climbed through.

'Mind the glass,' I shouted but she seemed to have turned into some kind of superhero. I think she's had a lot of training from Extinction Rebellion. She pushed the glass out from round the frame and on to the floor of the room and climbed through like someone from a film. Daphne was right behind her and at the same moment, Des came through the door and into the room, holding Fiona by the shoulder and pushing her in front of him.

'Oi,' Fiona shouted, 'come here, Pat, Pat, where are you?'

I rushed to the broken window just in time to see toad hare off down the street in his car, the big black scary one.

Des produced some string from his pocket, tied Fiona's hands together and pushed her to a sitting position on the sofa. I rang Henry's old phone from Des's phone while Grace rang Clara.

'Nina,' I said, 'I want you to stay calm and listen to me. Leave the house now, you and Clara, go out of the back door, out of the gate, turn left and run. It's OK, we're coming, you'll be fine, but do it now.'

I turned to the others. 'We need to go, right away, now. Can either of you run?'

They had taken off out of the door and down the street before I had finished speaking. I ran after them, hitching my skirt up as I ran.

'Des,' I called over my shoulder, 'call an ambulance for Ronnie.'

'I'm OK,' Ronnie said.

I realised she was running right next to me.

'No,' I said. I had great difficulty speaking. 'Stay back, get checked, we've got this.'

'Sorry, Meg,' Ronnie said. I realised that even though she was as thin as a stick, she was able to talk and run at the same time with less effort than me. 'I want to help, it's good for me. And besides,' she said, taking my hand, 'you need a pace setter, like in the Olympics.'

CHAPTER TWENTY-EIGHT

Nina

Friday, 1 March

Nina wished she could have gone with Daphne and Grace to rescue Meg but she had used up all of her bravery over the last few days and months. Her whole body was rebelling now and she could feel herself shake as if she was very cold. She knew she would be a hindrance, something to drag them down and no help at all. Clara was trying her best, Nina could see that, but she really was one of the last people Nina would have chosen for any kind of emotional support.

'Would you like to play cards?' Clara asked. 'I know several games.' Nina couldn't think of anything worse.

'No thanks,' she said.

'Ah,' said Clara, as if Nina had said something deep and meaningful, 'I totally get you. Still, it's not good to be left alone. Maybe you'd like to talk about your favourite colour, or the best toy you had when you were a kid, or something like that.'

Nina saw that Clara had exhausted the possibilities of her small talk.

'I'm quite tired,' she said, 'maybe I could…' Nina indicated the sofa and although the idea had started as a way to get Clara off her back, as soon as Nina looked at the sofa she realised that she would like very much to lie down.

'No problemo,' Clara said. She continued to stand to one side of the window, looking out every few seconds and fingering her gun. It was very unrelaxing, Nina thought as she lay down, but it did feel rather safe.

Nina had almost dropped off to sleep when Clara cleared her throat.

'Nothing amiss,' Clara said, 'but I need to walk the perimeter. Check the outside of the house. I've got the key, and I'll lock you in every time I go out, so you'll be quite safe.'

'I'll come too,' Nina said, but Clara explained in no uncertain terms what a bad idea that was.

Nina didn't like to tell her how scared she was without her. 'Fine, OK, no problem,' she said. She forced her voice to sound normal and not to wobble, even though she was terrified. She was sure that toad would get her again and she knew she would die this time. Even if her body stayed alive, Nina knew that the essential part of her would not survive another minute of being forced to do terrible things. The ladies, though, she had to help them. It was right that Clara needed to go and check. She went, and Nina was left alone. Instantly the house became filled with creaks and groans.

'I'm sorry, Meg,' Nina whispered to a photo of a young Meg on her wedding day, 'I should have gone with the others to look for you but I'll wait for you here, instead.'

It helped a little, having someone to talk to. Nina looked closely at the photograph. It was the only picture on display, as if after their marriage there was nothing else that needed recording. Meg looked like the saddest bride Nina had ever seen. Her eyes were puffy and her smile looked fake. Nina put the photo down and wandered from room to room putting all the lights on. It was strange, being alone in Meg's house. Like accidentally looking at someone's diary.

Nina looked out of the window instead. Clara seemed to have got into a routine, checking the outside of the house and then all the rooms and windows. She may not have been good company, Nina thought, but it was good to see her marching around. Des came back at one point, and Nina saw him speak quickly to Clara. He mimed at her, holding his thumb up and then shrugging his shoulders in a questioning way. Nina nodded and held her own thumb up to show that she was fine. Des held his hand over his heart and blew her a kiss, and Nina noticed that Clara blew him a kiss too, as he left. It seemed uncharacteristic. Clara went back to her patrolling and Nina wondered whether Clara, too, was moving around out of fear. She certainly seemed preoccupied.

The time went slowly. Nina went over the possible things that could be happening to her ladies. It was all her fault, the women were only in danger because they had helped her. Nina hoped that their new friends would be able to help. At the very least there would be safety in numbers.

Nina put the kettle on to make tea. Clara had gone back outside after refusing a cup, saying that she never drank on duty. All the ordinary noises seemed amplified in the night-time kitchen, especially the electric kettle, which roared like a monster. Nina panicked and turned it off. She poured the hot water on to the tea bag even though it wasn't boiling. Nina felt as though someone was watching her and she wished that Clara

324

would come back in. The house was full of noises and Nina felt her old anxiety and fear of new places. First night with new foster parents, first night in a children's home. Getting used to everything. Some children panicked but Nina had tried to stay very still and listen. She tried that now. All houses had noises, creaks and sighs, Nina knew that but the noises in this house seemed louder somehow. She looked outside to check that Clara was still there. She switched the lights off and sat in the dark. It seemed more companionable and Nina was suddenly aware that she was so tired. So terribly tired. She curled up in the corner of the sofa and closed her eyes.

Nina woke to the sound of the phone that Meg had given her. She sat up and tried to orientate herself, knocking the cold tea to the carpet.

Nina listened while Meg explained that Nina had to go, get out, leave immediately. Apparently they were also telling Clara, who Meg thought was outside. Nina promised that she would, but as she finished the phone call Nina noticed the mess the tea had made on Meg's pale grey carpet. There was a huge puddle of ginger tea. Nina hadn't managed to drink any of it before she fell asleep. There was no way she could leave it there for Meg to find. Clara was outside, Nina would have to trust that things would be OK for a moment or two. Meg was house-proud, Nina thought, and she respected that. She would be the same if she ever got her own home. Looking back later, Nina realised that she had not been functioning at all well, but at the time it seemed so rational.

'Two minutes,' Nina said aloud as if Meg was in the room. 'I'll just get the worst of it up.'

She blotted and scrubbed but the stain was a stubborn one,

and Nina felt more and more terrified. She had just decided to give up and get the hell out when she heard the noise. A tiny scrabbling. As if a few mice were trying to get in the door with a mouse-sized key. It stopped, and then started again. It wasn't the noise of a creaky house. It wasn't the noise of the wind. There was nothing ordinary or simple about the noise. It reminded Nina of something but she wasn't sure what. And there was someone there, she was sure of that. Someone outside the front door, where the mouse sounds were coming from. It was probably Clara, Nina thought.

'Clara,' she called, 'Clara, are you there?'

There was no answer, but Nina thought that she might have heard a little sound. Something like a groan, but that couldn't be possible. Clara was as solid as a mountain, Nina thought.

She ran into the kitchen, drying her soapy hands on her jeans as she went. 'Shit, shit, shit,' she said quietly, realising how much time she had spent on getting rid of the tea stain. The mouse noise was still there and Nina suddenly knew why it was familiar. Why her legs had known to run at the sound of it before her brain had even worked out what it was. Jason. The boy in the children's home, with Bilbo. Jason who had wanted to be her boyfriend. Jason was always boasting about his skills as a house burglar, saying that he could get into any house, any time, regardless of what locks or security systems people put in.

'Most times people just use a standard spring lock,' Nina remembered him saying. 'Anyone can get in with one of those, just look.'

Nina had gone outside with Jason and watched as he flexed his school lunch card for a moment before inserting it at the side of the lock, wiggling it about and throwing the door open with a triumphant tadaa.

That was the noise Nina could hear now. A credit card of some kind moving around in the front door lock, up and down, trying to catch on so that it could be sprung open. She needed to get out, and quickly.

I'm sorry, Meg, Nina thought, sorry I didn't listen to you and run straight away. But I'm glad your carpet is OK.

Nina took the back door key from its hook by the door. She was about to turn it in the lock when she saw a shape in the garden. On the floor in a heap but a shape that could only be a person. Nina knew that it was Clara. She wanted to go and help her, but she was sure it was a trap, and that toad would be out there waiting for her. It would be dangerous to run. Fiona or one or more of the other men, toad's cronies, were probably waiting just out of sight now for her to run. There was no chance of escape that way. Nina moved away from the door and fled upstairs. Her heart was banging so hard in her ears as she ran that she almost missed the sound of the front door being opened.

He was in the house, she knew it. Nina ran into the bathroom and locked the door.

CHAPTER TWENTY-NINE

Meg

Friday, 1 March

I couldn't believe I was running. I hadn't run since I left school, not even for a bus. I could feel every one of my extra pounds. I listened as I ran and I could hear the violin playing along with Bruce Springsteen singing 'Born to Run' on the speaker inside my head. It helped me to go faster. For one or two seconds only I felt something that might have been a rush of adrenalin as I rounded the last corner before home, and I understood why running can be addictive. Maybe there's a senior citizens' running club I could join, when this is all over, I thought.

I pointed my house out to Ronnie. She had kept up well despite her frailty but she looked very unwell now. She staggered the last few yards and then sank to her knees outside the house.

'One minute,' she gasped.

I had been so busy running that I didn't notice that the door to my house was standing open until I was at the gate. Toad's big black car was outside, the engine still running.

'He's there,' Ronnie said. 'Go, go and find her, I'm OK, just go.'

I didn't think she was OK but I left her anyway. I wasn't happy about leaving her there but I didn't see that I had any choice if I was going to help Nina. Besides, Ronnie was a fighter and she really wanted me to go on. She made a little movement with her hands to shoo me away inside and I ran. I thought about all the cop shows I'd watched. I knew that a person couldn't just walk into a house and look around, it had to be much stealthier than that. I had to be thinking, where would he hide? Is he in this room somewhere waiting to jump out on me? I tried to think like he would and get into his head. I moved slowly along the hall, staying close to the left-hand wall. When I got to the living room I threw open the door like I had seen the good guys do on TV. No one there. Just a big, wet, coppery-coloured stain on the carpet, partially covered by tea towels. Blood. I was sure it was blood. It had to be. What else would be spilt there, and hastily cleaned up? Nothing. I was absolutely sure it must be Nina's blood, and everything went grey for a moment. It was all for nothing. Nina hadn't managed to escape, in fact she must have gone from being trafficked to being dead, and now there was no hope at all. She had come to us, to me, for help and we had let her down in the worst way possible. We hadn't just done nothing, we had made things worse. It was unforgivable. I had to find him, toad, the man who had done this. It wasn't fair, that was the worst thing. It wasn't fair on Nina and it wasn't fair on us. We had tried so hard.

I stopped for a moment in order to get my thoughts straight. I had to do this, and I had to push away the memory of that other time I was on my own in a tricky situation. I closed my ears to the snoring, and to the violin. It wouldn't help

329

right now. I knew that the others must be around somewhere, but I had no idea where they were or how long it would take them to get here. Every second counted in case Nina was still alive. I couldn't wait. There was no point wishing the others were there. They weren't, and I was going to have to manage on my own. It's difficult, killing a person, and I knew that better than anyone. I had the biggest case of cold feet ever and I thought, surely toad behind bars would be safe enough, although I knew that wasn't true. This was not a game and part of me wanted him dead, especially now that I was sure that dear girl had been murdered or at least badly hurt. I was glad I had the gun, and gladder still that I'd loaded it. I got it out of my sleeve. I was ready to shoot him, but if by any chance Nina was still alive, I might try to frighten him instead. I had to think that, or I don't think I could have gone on. I would frighten the living daylights out of him and grab Nina, get her to hospital. If she was dead, that would be a game changer. I'd probably be able to kill him with my own bare hands. Even if I died trying, it would be worth it. Maybe he'd think twice before he did that to any other young women. I thought of poor Ronnie and it didn't seem to matter much, me dying. Not if I'd done something useful on the way. I was old and expendable, and it felt like the right plan.

I could hear both Henrys applauding as soon as I'd made a plan. I'd never heard them agree with each other before so I knew I was on the right track, doing the right thing. The only problem was the violin. It was still sawing away gently, still terribly out of tune. First-night nerves, I thought.

I was sure toad was upstairs. I could feel him up there. It was my house, and I knew its ways. I remembered that other night when it had felt like this, as though upstairs was full somehow, as though the whole house wouldn't be safe until I had done what I had to do. I should have looked out of the window but I didn't, I was completely focused on the inside of the house, listening with every part of me. I moved towards the stairs as quietly as I could. Creeping. The third stair from the bottom always creaked, so I avoided it, like I had done that other time. I couldn't believe how calm I was. I was focused, that was the thing. I had a job to do. I kept thinking the same thing, over and over. Just a little scare, I thought, maybe that's what he needs. No hesitation, just a little scare. I have always been able to fool myself. I took a couple of deep breaths at the top of the stairs. I stood up straight, grabbed the gun in both hands and held it out like I'd seen on TV.

The upstairs of my house is quite straightforward. There's the bathroom and toilet at the top of the stairs with two bedrooms on one side and one on the other. Three bedrooms altogether.

'I don't know why we've got so many bedrooms,' Henry used to say, 'no one's going to come and stay.'

They might, I used to think. I might make a friend who needs somewhere to stay, or maybe I could offer one of the bedrooms to a homeless person or a refugee. Or a cousin might turn up who's traced me on the internet and wants to stay in London for a few days, to meet me. Or I might adopt a child who needs a home. Like someone kindly adopted my little baby, my dear little girl with the bright blue eyes.

Stop it, Meg, I thought, pull yourself together. You've got a job to do. I couldn't hear either of the Henrys at all. I was just starting to think that I might be wrong, and that maybe it wasn't toad's car outside after all, when I heard a laugh. A soft laugh, just a small sound. More like a snigger. It was me he was laughing at and that's a thing I hate. It isn't kind, and it isn't fair. I listened again, and I could tell the noise was coming from the far bedroom, the one to my left. That was my bedroom. I'd changed rooms after Henry died. I didn't want anything to be the same. I should have sold the house, I guess, moved to somewhere new without memories.

You didn't though, did you, Meg? I could hear the old Henry saying. You're too scared of everything even to do the obvious thing. Anyone else would have moved straight away.

The laughing stopped for a moment, and I held the gun more tightly. I needed to act. I walked along the hallway as quietly as I could.

'You're like a big elephant,' Henry used to say, 'I can hear you coming from a mile away. No, make that two miles.'

I was very quiet this time. I kept to the edge where the floorboards didn't creak so much, and I moved slowly. Very slowly. As slowly and quietly as I would have moved if I had a baby and I was trying not to wake her up. I liked thinking of that, and it carried me down the hall until I was standing outside the room the noise had come from. The door was slightly open. I planned to throw it open like a cop, burst in and catch him at a disadvantage. Scare him to death and then... I wasn't quite sure what else. Maybe things would develop organically, like they had before. It'll work itself out, I thought, you can't plan everything. Some things are best left to chance.

I got to the door, ready to go, but toad must have watched the same cop shows that I had. Just as I got to the door he pulled it open so that it crashed against the wall and he jumped out. I thought he had a mask on at first but then I realised that his face was horribly contorted. He roared at me, roared like in a horror film and it made me jump. I have never coped well with being startled. I seem to jump out of my skin much more often than other people and I really, really don't like it. I was hyper-aware of everything round me. I could hear someone running up the stairs and Des's voice shouted, 'I'm here, don't shoot,' but I didn't process the words.

It was a reflex, shooting the gun. I don't think it would have made any difference if I had heard Des properly, because at that moment I was sure Nina was at least terribly harmed, and at worst, and most likely, dead. The man who had done it was in front of my face and I was pointing a gun at him which didn't seem to scare him at all. What else would a person do?

My ears shut down from the noise. Much louder than on TV. Everything started to move in slow motion. As though someone had pressed a switch. Toad was practically on top of me so I saw everything. I saw the way he paused, looking puzzled, and then put his hand to his chest where the bullet had gone in. I saw him look at the hand and see the blood on it, and I saw that he knew how badly he was hurt. He looked at his hand, and then at me, and then at his hand again and I wanted to look away but I owed him that much at least, I needed to look him in the eye. It seemed only right.

'Meg,' Des shouted, 'be careful,' and I heard that but I was on an absolute roll now. I shot toad again and as I did I heard the bathroom door open and Nina came out.

'Be careful,' she shouted, 'Fiona is in the garden.'

Des ran to the window and looked out.

'It's not,' he called, 'she's sorted. It's OK, it's Clara, she's hurt but she's OK. The others are coming now, let's keep them all away for a moment.' Des motioned out of the window that they should stay away.

I was ecstatic at the sight of Nina.

'I thought you were dead,' I said, and she said, 'I thought you were,' and we both cried.

'I'm sorry about...' I said and I motioned to toad, lying on the floor. She shrugged and I thought that maybe we could all pay for her to have therapy, when it was all over. She was going to need it.

'Go downstairs,' I said, 'this isn't something you should see.'

'I've seen so much worse, Meggie,' she said.

I believed her and for a moment I felt pleased with myself for putting a stop to his nastiness. Toad didn't move again, and although I tried to think about his mother, I couldn't. I didn't even think about people hearing the gunshot and coming running until afterwards, but they didn't anyway. That's south-east London for you. People turn over in their beds, pretend they think it's a car backfiring and thank whoever it is they thank that they're safe and sound. No one came, and I hugged my Nina until she could hardly breathe.

'Now go on,' I said. 'Go and see Ronnie.' She flew down the stairs and then there was just Des, me and the body of toad.

'Best if we sort this out ourselves,' I said and he agreed. I wouldn't want anyone else to have the kind of nightmares I had, and I suspected Des had them too.

'We'd better check,' I said. 'Make sure he's, you know.' I could see that Des wasn't going to do it so I knelt down and felt for a pulse. There wasn't one, and I was sure that the person who had been toad no longer existed.

'We've got to clean it all up quickly,' I said. I wanted every trace of him gone as quickly as possible. 'Maybe if we use the rug, to roll it in.' I couldn't bring myself to call toad 'he' or 'him'.

'Good idea,' Des said. He didn't move and I thought he looked green. One thing I was sure of, if he had really committed a terrible crime, the one he was convicted for, either he had a very good reason for it or there was a miscarriage of justice. That man was not a real criminal. We stared together at the body and while we were standing there, the woman who hung out with toad popped into my head. His sidekick.

'Des,' I said, 'what about the woman? His partner? Where is she?' I could feel the fear flooding through me as I imagined her going to the police and giving a full description of me.

'I left her tied up in the house they were using as a brothel,' he said. I could hear more than a hint of pride in his voice. 'She'll be fine, I left her some water. I freed all the girls from their rooms and sent them off. I reckon it won't take her too long to get free, and she's not going to cause any trouble. I think I can promise you that.'

Des looked positively smug for a moment and I decided not to ask any more questions. She could hardly report toad missing, after all. Sometimes you have to trust people, I thought.

I could hear talking downstairs as the others came in. It sounded as though they were all together, such a comforting sound. Des wilted as soon as he'd finished speaking and it was clear that he wasn't going to be good for much so although I was sorry they had to see the body, I was glad when Grace and Daphne came up and sent him away.

'I should never have given you the gun,' Des kept saying. 'I should have kept it myself.'

He had his head in his hands and as he went off down the stairs Daphne tried to comfort him.

'It's OK, Des,' she said. 'Meg did a good thing today, we'll work it out.'

I did? I thought. Really? I started to feel a little bit, just a tiny smudge of pride. So different from when Henry died and I was all alone, so nice to have all these people helping and saying the right things.

'It's OK,' I said, 'I'm not going to make a habit of it. Just this once.' I crossed my fingers behind my back.

The three of us were alone again, to clear up. Just us, pact honoured, job done, Nina safe. It was a very special moment. We rolled him in the rug and as we did it our hands touched. We looked up and caught each other's eyes.

'Well done, Meg,' Grace said. Daphne nodded and squeezed my hand. 'So good to have you two in my life,' she said.

We're really friends, I thought. It made everything bearable.

By the time we'd got him decently covered up they were all standing at the bottom of the stairs. Gordon, Susannah, Des, Nina, Ronnie, Greg and even Clara, with a bump on her head but otherwise OK. Everyone tried to offer advice on what to do next and the best way to clean up. I couldn't take it all in. Nina was talking nineteen to the dozen about the spilt cup of tea that wasn't blood and Greg went to get salt to sprinkle on the real bloodstains, upstairs. I would have liked to be alone with my special friends for a little bit longer but there was lots to do. I wanted to try to get Ronnie to eat and I knew the cleaning up would be difficult. I was pleased when Clara spoke up.

'I'm sorry we missed the engagement,' she said, as if they had been late for a tea party. 'We'd like to compensate for this in some way by assisting now.'

By the time we all went to bed the sun had risen but Nina and Ronnie were still up, lying on my bed together and looking at universities online. They had decided to phone their social workers in the morning, say they had run away for a while. I hoped I could offer them a home once they were eighteen. It wouldn't be long to wait. Ronnie had already managed to eat a bit of porridge and Nina had eaten everything she could find. Gordon and Susannah had gone with Des to stay in Daphne's house. I thought they might be there for quite a while. She had loads of room, she said. Daphne and Grace stayed with me. We sat together, drinking tea. The Shoe people had done a tremendous job of clearing up, and had taken the remains of toad away with them. I never asked what they were going to do with it, with him, but I sent some chicken for Shoe.

It was Grace who said it. 'Any regrets, ladies?' she asked.

'Of course,' Daphne said, 'there's a part of me that wishes we hadn't met Nina, hadn't known. It will never be over for us, not really.'

I looked at my hand, the hand that had pulled the trigger, like an assassin in a film. I wanted to tell the truth.

'I'm glad,' I said. 'I would do it all again. They're safe, Nina and Ronnie, and that's what matters.'

I think they were surprised by that, but the thing about real friends is, they stick by you. They nodded and told me I was right, and that I was brave.

I tried to say the same kind of things when we all went to see Nina to say goodnight. Ronnie had fallen asleep so we spoke quietly.

'I'll never be able to repay you,' Nina said. 'I can't believe a person would help another person like you've helped me.'

'I'm so glad I could help,' I said. 'I'll always be pleased, no matter what happens.' I looked over at Grace and Daphne and I could see that they knew as well as I did that there would be long-term repercussions from this day, for the rest of all our lives.

'Some things are worth doing,' Grace said. Daphne nodded. 'I hope you can put this behind you. Don't dwell on any part of it, it doesn't define you. Don't let the fear and the knowledge overwhelm you.'

What she said, I thought. She smiled, my Nina, as if she had no idea what we were talking about. I hoped as hard as I've ever hoped anything that she never found out.

In the days that followed, Des felt the stress and the strain, I could tell he did. He felt guilty for everything. The whole world on his shoulders. He wanted some closure, which is a fashionable thing these days but it doesn't always happen. If we had tipped off the police about Fiona, to stop her setting up shop again, it would have opened a whole new can of worms. A full can.

The only person I could talk to about everything was Henry. I talked to him a lot. I think he already knew what had happened the night he died, the sleeping pills in the soup, I think he'd always known that.

'This tastes bitter,' he'd said at the time. It felt right to explain it to him, how I had only meant to send him to sleep for a while, stop him from mocking me about Bingley and the little baby. It was the snoring later, that's what did it. I had to stop the snoring. He had sleep apnoea, so no one ever questioned it. I hope he understood, my Henry. The old Henry, that is, I'm done with the new one. All that positivity and new-age stuff, it didn't suit me. I like a man who tells it like it is. So I told him all of it, and asked what he thought. He didn't answer. Didn't say anything at all, but I could hear the violin if I strained. A lovely tune, it was playing, sad and lilting.

ACKNOWLEDGEMENTS

I am indebted to my publisher, Manpreet, and my agent, Julia, for their hard work and support in difficult times.

Thank you also to my large and lovely family, you are all fabulous.

Lastly, I wrote this book thinking of, and being thankful for, all the women I have ever known who I would be glad to have by my side if I was planning a murder. You know who you are.

Turn the page to
read an exclusive extract from
The Stranger She Knew, the tense
and gripping debut from
Rosalind Stopps

Available to buy now!

CHAPTER ONE

September 2017
Lewisham

I could hear the words in my head but they wouldn't come out.

I'm fine, I wanted to say, you can leave me here, I'll be OK. It was the blood, that was all, I could smell blood, and I've always hated that. I wanted to explain to them. It makes me feel funny, but not funny ha ha, I would have said but they've got no sense of humour, young people. I didn't like the way the man was looking at me. I'm not just a stupid old woman, I tried to say. I may not have been speaking very clearly but there was no need for him to look at me like that. I tried to tell him, don't look at me like that, young man. I wanted to say it in quite a stern way but my mouth was doing that thing again of not working properly, as though I was drunk or I'd had something nasty done at the dentist. All that came out was a slur of s's and some spit. I noticed he didn't like the spit much, ambulance man or no ambulance man, he didn't like that at all. I'd say he flinched, leaned back a bit, but he couldn't go far because he was kneeling next to me on the floor.

It made me laugh that, him kneeling, it's not a thing you see much. Reminds me of going to church when I was a kid, I tried to say, but the spitty thing was still going on. Try to relax, he said to me, try and calm down, deep breaths, we'll get you sorted. I gave up on talking, tried to roll my eyes instead but of course that made him call his colleague over, the young woman with the thick ankles. She was wearing a skirt and I was surprised at that. I'm sure they're allowed to wear trousers these days and if I was her I would have done. Cover up those ankles. I might have rolled my eyes again. They probably thought I was dying or something, because it was all rushing around after the eye rolling, no more of the calm down stuff, just lobbing me onto a stretcher like I was already gone and couldn't feel anything. At least I was wearing trousers, I thought, and it made me laugh. It felt like a laugh inside. I don't know what it looked like on the outside.

I might have gone to sleep for a moment or two after that. I'm surprised I was tired because I'd been doing nothing but lie around on the floor resting since I fell. I didn't know how long I had been there but it must have been quite a while. Someone told me later I'd been there for two whole days and two nights. I'm not sure if that's right or if it's just another one of the things they say to old people to keep them in order. I'm still thinking about that one. I certainly remember watching the clock on the wall and thinking that it was going slowly, and that I might need to wind it up or put a new battery in it. I couldn't remember which. And I can remember hearing someone push something through the letterbox. It was probably only a flyer for some kind of pizza place or a nail parlour but I tried to shout. I thought it was just a fall, you see, I've got big feet, clown feet I've been told, plus I've always been rather clumsy so I thought I had just fallen over the coffee table. I was wedged in between the coffee table and the sofa and the smell of blood was horrible. Turned out I'd only bashed my head a bit, no stitches needed, but at the time it smelt like an abattoir and that's what I mainly remember.

Two days. I nodded like I agreed with them but two days, honest. I'm not sure about that. I'm going to ask some of the others when I can, I'm going to ask them how long they lay on the floor for if they had a stroke, and if just one of them says, two days, it will be obvious that it's something they say to everyone, the two days thing, a big old lie. I've caught them telling lies a couple of times so I won't be at all surprised.

I don't remember much about the ambulance journey. There's the smell, I remember that, the blood from the cut on my head, and another smell, a dirty smell that showed up in the ambulance. Maybe it was a smell from the person who had used the ambulance before me. They needed to work on that, clean it up a bit better. I'm sure the smell couldn't have been coming from me. Who smelt it, dealt it, that's what they used to say in the shop I worked in when I was a student. It reminded me of the day one of the boys in packing brought a stink bomb in during stocktaking. It brought tears to our eyes, but none of us girls said a word, in case we got teased.

I didn't say anything in the ambulance. I just went to sleep and the next thing I knew, the young man who had been kneeling by me and the well-meaning woman with the thick ankles, they'd gone. It would have been nice if they had said goodbye or cheerio or something so that I'd known they were going. I'd got used to them being there and I felt lonely without them. They should have said something but they didn't, or they didn't do it loudly enough, so when I woke up there was a different woman. She had a badge on that said, 'hello, my name is Agnita'.

Hello yourself, can you not speak then, I wanted to say, have you got badges for other things you want to say? I imagined a person covered in badges, all of them saying useful things like, would you like a cup of tea, or, mine's a pint. Count me out, I thought, I'm not wearing any badges, they can't make me. And they didn't, but get this, what they did was even worse. They wrote it, on the wall above my bed. 'Hello,' it said, 'my name is May. Please talk to me.'

I couldn't believe it. Please talk to me, indeed. As if. I don't need anyone to talk to me, thank you very much and if I could just untwist my mouth enough I'd tell them so in no uncertain terms. I haven't had anyone to talk to for a long time, no one except for my daughter, Jenny, and she's so quiet I can hardly hear her. Speak up, I always say, speak up or I'm going to read my book and ignore you. That makes her nervous, and I'm sorry about that but there's no point mollycoddling a grown child. No point at all.

I fantasised for a while about scrubbing the words off my wall. If I could just stand up for a moment I'd make sure there wasn't a trace of writing left. There wouldn't be any 'please talk to me' then, I can assure you.

They tell me I've got the sequence of events all wrong. They say that I went to the hospital first, had scans and saw doctors and that sort of malarkey, and that I only came to the nursing home later. I don't know why they say that. I've got no idea at all, so I don't argue, I just keep quiet and watch them all. It's not something I'd forget, is it, a whole trip to hospital and everything that goes with it?

Honestly dear, you've been unwell for longer than you think, said the one with the purple streak. (Hello, my name is Abi.)

I hate being called 'dear' and I don't trust any of them. It'll be a cost cutting thing. It's my guess that they just cut out the middle person and bring the old people straight to the nursing home, save money on hospital beds. They tell the poor old dears they've had some treatment but they don't remember and everyone is happy. That's the thing with me, you see, I'm quite clever underneath this old lady exterior. That's what it feels like, an outfit I'm wearing.

As if I woke up wearing a fancy dress costume complete with wrinkles and grey hair, and I can't take it off. Inside it's different. Inside me I'm about thirty, with occasional forays backward and forwards. I don't think the other old people are like that. I've watched them. It's real for them.

I didn't see any of the other old codgers that first day. As far as I remember I was on the floor in my front room, in the ambulance, and then this room. I'm not complaining. It's all very nice and everything, this room, clean and bright, but it smells of gravy at all times. It's like living in a gravy boat I wanted to say, one big gravy boat sailing away into the night, full of old people on their last trip. I'd like to be able to say that to Agnita, she's the one I'm supposed to go to if I have any 'issues'. She's not a nurse. Mentor friend, they call it but she hasn't got a badge that says that.

So that first day, she sat with me for a while, telling me this and that about St Barbara's, that's the name of this gravy boat. St Barbara is the patron saint of miners, firemen and prisoners, she said, so that's appropriate. I didn't listen to everything she said, but I liked the sound of her voice, all soft and lilty like a bedtime story. She told me that she came from a part of the West Indies that used to be Dutch, and that was why her accent was unusual, I remember that. I remember it mainly for the frustration I felt, wanting to let her know that I was a true Londoner, not racist like the other old people. They weren't proper Londoners, I could tell at a glance. They seemed more like the sort of people who'd moved to London from Hull. A sea of bad perms, crimplene and right-wing nonsense. The most important people in my life have been people of colour, I wanted to say but all that came out was spit.

Come on now May, there's no need to be alarmed, she said, I'm a trained carer. Something like that anyway, but it wasn't fair, I wasn't alarmed. Well I was, but not by her, I don't know why people always think it's about them. Trained carer, I wanted to say, trained carer? An untrained toddler would have been able to see that I was actually alarmed by the fact that I couldn't talk. I couldn't join in with the conversation I hadn't asked for in the first place, and I didn't want to be having it anyway. I must have got a little upset after that. She looked offended, and that's bonkers. How could anyone be offended by an old woman who spits instead of talks?

She left me alone for a while, but she left the door open. I could see two rooms across the corridor. One had the door shut, and the other was open. I couldn't see who was in it but I could hear the television blaring so I knew it was occupied. And I could see people moving up and down the corridor with trolleys. Pill trolleys, cup of tea trolleys, book trolleys. This was clearly going to be a place where they didn't leave a person alone for five minutes. I wasn't sure what to think about that. I've been lonely in my life, I'll admit it, but I've learned to like my own company too.

I slept again then, and when I woke up I realised exactly

7

what was going on. I didn't have a voice, that was the long and the short of it, I was trapped until I could make myself understood. That was a difficult thing to come to terms with. No one could understand me and while there was a kind of freedom in that, it was not a freedom I wanted. I was set apart from the rest of the world, a separate kingdom with my own self as ruler and subject. I was going to have to make my own rules; work hard.

I'd heard a radio programme about someone famous who had had a stroke and then practised and practised and got themselves better and climbed Everest for charity or something. I should be able to get better a lot more quickly, I thought, because I didn't want to climb any mountains at all. I just wanted to go to the toilet unaided. I wanted to manage the whole process without swinging through the air on a hoist, or being helped by two carers while I lurched along with a three legged stick. I wanted my dignity, that's what I wanted the most.

I never thought that going to the loo would be such a big deal in my life, but in between toilet visits not a lot happens in here. There's TV, and meal times, and therapy of various sorts, but the other people are very dull. Mostly of the common or garden vegetable variety; no conversation to speak of. I need to practise my talking, that's what the speech and language therapist says, but it's hard to do that when I'm surrounded by people who are either busy working or busy dying.

There's one, I've never seen her, I guess she keeps to

8

her own room, but every night at about seven o'clock she starts shouting for her mother. If it was me in charge, I'd get someone to dress up as her mother and give her and the rest of us a bit of peace, but I don't think they've thought of that. I'm thinking about doing it myself, when I can get around a little better. I could just put my head round her door and say, there there, it's all OK dear, Mother's here. She might stop calling out, she might sleep better and then we'd all be happy.

There was a shouter on the ward where I had my Jenny. It wasn't her mum she was calling for, more like she was asking for divine intervention as far as I remember. God, please help me she kept calling. I'd had my baby by then, but I could still hear her, we all could, the new mums. There was one across from me, she kept muttering, God help her, whenever the shouting woman went quiet, and for some reason that made us all laugh. It was good to have a laugh together, made me feel like one of the gang. A conspiracy of women, that's what we were, that's what Helen called it and I didn't mind at all that Alain often missed visiting hours. He wasn't the only one, having babies was women's work back then. I'd read the books of course, I wanted it to be different for us but I knew how hard it was for him.

It will be different, Alain used to say, we won't be like all the others. I've got to make things right for all of us, we're a family now. He had interviews for jobs as far as I remember, it wasn't that he didn't want to come. The visiting hour was short, literally an hour, I think.

I understood. When he did come though, oh, all the other mothers took to him. He'd go along the ward saying hello to them, commenting on how pretty their babies were, that sort of thing. He always brought flowers, every day that he managed to come in, and he usually cried at the sight of little Jenny.

She's so perfect, he said, I'm sorry I just can't help it.

He loved to sit and look at her while she was sleeping. It worried him when she cried. I got into the habit of telling Jenny to be quiet, and if I'm honest, I never really stopped until she was grown up. I've had a lot of time to think about that in here, and as soon as I can get the words out properly I'm going to tell her. I'm sorry, I'm going to say, I don't know whether it's my fault that you're so quiet now, but if it is, I'm sorry, and I think you should spend the rest of your life shouting, just to make up for it.

She's been to see me quite a few times in here. It's nice to see her but the last thing she needs is me getting all sloppy over her, so I've tried to keep myself to myself. It's the spit. Any attempt at talking and it's there, splishing and splashing out of my mouth like one of those water slide things they have in outdoor swimming pools. I thought of that when Jenny was here the other day. She used to love going down the water slide on holiday and I wanted to remind her of that and explain why I was spitting at the same time but of course it all came out in a wet jumble and she had no idea what I was trying to say.

Do you want a drink, she said, or the toilet, it's OK Mum, I'll call the nurse.

They're bloody not nurses I wanted to say but it came out as a growl and then she pressed the buzzer and I was being swung through the air to the toilet like I was a sack of old bones, which I suppose I am. The swimming pool, I wanted to say, remember the water slide and how many times you went down it? You were so tired you'd often fall asleep eating your dinner on that holiday. Mush mush mush spit dribble slobber, that's what comes out. All anyone can guess is drink or toilet, that's the only things that I'm supposed to care about now. Like one of those dolls Jenny used to have, where you poured the water in the mouth and put a nappy on the other end so it could come out. That doll always creeped me out and now I know why, it was my fate, waiting for me.

Don't try to talk Mum, it's OK, Jenny says and I try so hard not to cry that I knock the water out of her hand as she offers me a drink.

Now now, May, one of the carers says, there's no need for that, your daughter has come to visit you, let's be nice. It's not fair, I think, it's not fair and if at that moment I could have blown the place up I would have, daughter or no daughter. I've never liked things that aren't fair.

When I was at school there was a fashion for biros with more than one colour, and you clicked a button to change the colour of your writing. I didn't have one, so when Carol Eliot's got lost, it was me everyone thought had taken it.

I didn't, I didn't, I said, but the teacher still insisted on searching my bag based on 'information received'. It wasn't there of course, but some of the girls believed it anyway, and for months they held their pens to their chests when I walked past.

I stopped trying to remind Jenny of the water slide, I stopped trying to tell her I was sorry, I turned my face to the wall and waited for her to go home. I was very sad when she had gone.

I've got to get out of here. September is usually my favourite month. There's a feeling of new year, new possibilities, but no fireworks. Sunshine. I think I was reading in the garden only last week or the week before, when I was still at home and everything was different. I think I was, only I've got into a muddle over dates. I'm sure I was at home with all my body parts working when the children went back to school, I heard them walk past my window and then there's a blank part and now they tell me it's the twenty-second of September. The thing is, as you get older, you don't look at the date every day like you do when you are at work. You take things a bit more slowly, you wind down a little. It doesn't mean I've been ill for nearly three weeks just because I wasn't noticing the date, and I'd tell them that in no uncertain terms if I could.

Something a little different this evening. Just after the tea trolley and before the pill trolley, they came round shutting all the room doors. I thought it was just mine at first, and that maybe I was in trouble, or Jenny had complained about me or something, and they were teaching me a lesson. But I listened hard, I've always had good hearing, and I heard them shutting all the doors, up and down the corridor. We were banged up. A lockdown. I knew the words because I've always liked the prison shows on TV. I listened, and I could hear them roll a trolley down, I could hear those trolley wheels. I'm quick, and I realised what it was. It was creepy. The death stretcher, that's what it was, the last journey, the only way out of here. Poor old bugger whoever you are, I thought. I wondered for a moment whether I should show respect by bowing my head or something.

They opened the doors a few minutes later. I think it was only a few minutes. I tried to make my eyes as questioning as possible but same old, same old, Kelly just asked me if I'd like a drink or a wee. I jumped (figuratively) at the chance of a bit of a hoist and a nose, so I made a particularly enthusiastic sound in the appropriate place. It sounded a little like, yeeeeuuugggsshshshsh.

They always use the hoist when they're busy. It's quicker. It can take me half the day to get across the room otherwise, even with two carers helping me.

Come along now, May, Kelly says.

She has that voice on that means, I'm busy and you're a nuisance. If I had a way of having a tantrum I'd have one. I'd sweep all the tissues and the polo mints and the orange squash right off that tray, and lob the sticky toffee pudding left over from dinner right at Kelly's hair. She's got this complicated hairstyle, all winding plaits and Princess Leia and it would look just the thing with a handful of custard and sponge on the top. It's the assumption, that's what I don't like, the assumption that whatever I do, I'm doing it as part of a plan to disrupt their lives as much as possible, ruin their busyness. I know it's only a short time since I went to the toilet last, and that when I got there I couldn't make much impact anyway, hardly a trickle. But it's my right to go to the toilet whenever I want to, I know that much.

So Kelly and Lee-An strap me into the hoist and lift me up, swing swing, into the air and across the room. Talking all the way about hair extensions. I've got used to carers talking to each other as if I wasn't there. It's restful sometimes, listening to chatter about wallpaper and children, dinners waiting to be eaten and holidays planned. I don't mind, most of the time, but I'm sad this time what with death rolling past my door so recently. I'm lonely, I'm not sure what hair extensions even are, and I miss Jenny. She might be nearly forty and as quiet as a mouse, but she's my only family and I can't help thinking that it would have been nice if she could have stayed a little longer. I'm on my own, after all. She has a long journey to get home and she doesn't drive, that's true and I should remember that but I'm upset.

I can't have a proper tantrum but I manage a side swipe to the left that knocks the half-drunk mug of tea to the floor as they swing me round. You'd think it was some kind of chemical, the way they carry on, something from a Batman film that could burn through floors, walls and bones. She looks at me, Kelly, not a look that anyone would want to receive, especially from the person who is operating the hoist that gets you to the toilet. I look away, settle down a bit into the sling, so that she can see there isn't going to be any more drama.

Something catches my eye. The room across the corridor, not the one with the open door and the booming television, but the other one. The one that's usually closed and silent. There's someone in there, a man I think. It's difficult to tell once you get old. The person is tall, because I can see the back of his head over the top of the chair he is sitting in. There's something familiar about the tilt of his head as he faces the TV. As if he's breathing it in, listening hard. I can hear a man's voice and the hollow sound of questions being asked. I'm not sure until I hear the music, dum diddy dum, all threatening and serious, but I'm right, it's *Mastermind*.

Alain used to love that show. He was good, too, he often got more right than the contestants. *Mastermind*. I haven't thought about that show in ages.

ONE PLACE. MANY STORIES

Bold, innovative and
empowering publishing.

FOLLOW US ON:

@HQStories